Dream Comes True

Ofem Ajah, M.D.

VANTAGE PRESS
New York

FIRST EDITION

Copyright © 1997 by Ofem Ajah

Published by Vantage Press, Inc.
516 West 34th Street, New York, New York 10001

Manufactured in the United States of America
ISBN: 0-533-12078-0

Library of Congress Catalog Card No.: 96-90506

0 9 8 7 6 5 4 3 2

To my wife, Francine, for her understanding and support while this work was being completed, and to my children, Anijah, Tuniche and Achayen. Finally, to my mother, Obaya, who almost single-handedly made me what I am.

Contents

Acknowledgments

I would like to thank Mrs. Beverly Falconer of the Endoscopy Unit, InterFaith Medical Center, 555 Prospect Place, Brooklyn NY 11238, for urging me to complete this work.

I would also like to thank Mr. Jolly Ekpe for his help.

A Good Friday

Unlike nearly all of his friends and colleagues at InnerFaith Hospital, Dr. Stephen Latham disliked Fridays, especially the last Friday of the month. Many of his patients received their pay or stipends on the preceding Thursday. A good number of them had nothing better to do than to buy drugs with their money. An even smaller number of them practiced "speedballing," which, as one of the practitioners explained to Dr. Latham, was the consumption of a potent concoction consisting, at its core, of opiates, cocaine and alcohol. Speedballers had a tendency to imbibe or inject until they dropped. Unfailingly, one of them, at least, would land in the emergency department at the end of a binge. Sometime during the afternoon, Dr. Stephen Latham would get the call.

Friday, too, of all the days of the week, was packed with clinical activities, including endoscopy procedures, ward rounds, outpatient clinics, and an X-ray conference. The gastroenterology division had been organized that way for as long as anyone could remember. Change would not come easy, as the entire departmental staff had organized their weekly activities around the Friday schedule. On Fridays, he often wished he had the power of bilocation.

This particular Friday, however, started uneventfully. The day had started with the usual morning rendezvous in the endoscopy unit where he saw and complimented Ms. Hayes on her new hairstyle. Even at sixty-eight years of age, her hair looked flamboyant and exquisite. When men—and women—said beautiful things about her hair, they meant them because there was no way to overstate the glamour. She would smile appropriately when complimented, perhaps in realization of the fact that the hours she spent in her salon every Thursday afternoon were worth it.

Other staff members had also been present and Stephen had appropriately exchanged greetings and pleasantries with them. Usually, he would acknowledge Ms. Juliette Painter last and in an uninterested manner. The latter was the most gorgeous and the youngest of the nurses. She was single, desirable and waiting for "Mr.— or preferably,

1

Dr.—Right." Stephen did not want to reveal any soft spot for her. Everywhere Ms. Painter went in the hospital, especially when she walked past groups of young men, she caused quite a stir. Inside the Endoscopy Unit, Stephen, the chief, had to behave responsibly because the other nurses were watching closely.

The scheduled endoscopic procedures had been completed before noon due to cancellations. All his inpatients had been seen by the interns and residents. Fortunately, none of them was acutely or severely ill so he planned to see them later. The X-ray conference and the afternoon clinic had been uneventful.

Everything in the breakneck schedule was going as well as planned or was ahead of schedule. Stephen was happy that he had only several hours to go.

Once again, he was thinking about the Friday schedule. Specifically, he was wondering about ways to lighten it. Ideally, he thought, Mondays should be spent recovering from the weekend and Fridays, preparing for one. That would leave him with a three-day week.

It was already three-thirty in the afternoon. Stephen was making his floor rounds with his Residents and Interns when he received an urgent beep from the emergency department. That was a very inauspicious time to be paged from the emergency room or from any other patient floor for that matter. The nurses were changing shifts. The only other worse time was when the Interns were changing shifts, a clumsy and time-consuming exercise in passing the buck.

Stephen rushed to the emergency room and was lucky enough to get the patient's chart without effort or queuing. At that time of the day, everyone who had anything to do with the patient wanted to document it before leaving for the day. No doctor or nurse slept well without documenting an encounter with a patient. There was no guarantee that, by the next day, the patient would not leave against medical advice, be discharged or die. There was an adage that if it was not documented, it did not happen. The chart was usually a hot commodity at that time of the day with representatives of various hospital departments and divisions queuing or scrambling for it. Stephen grabbed the patient's chart.

First he had to call his wife Juliana. "Hi J., there's a problem and I might be late. I have an emergency procedure to perform." She had told him before he left home in the morning that she would do the laundry in the afternoon. The implication was that he would babysit little Christopher, their son, while she went down to the basement. Caring for the tempestuous and hyperactive Christopher was, in his wife Juliana's opinion, a full-time job.

Whenever anyone asked Stephen what his wife did, his standard answer was "a full-time job." For the most part, the answer was non-specific and unsatisfactory and people usually said so with their body language. He would then add, "taking care of our son Christopher."

"When do you hope to come home? Do you remember I got the laundry this afternoon?" she asked him.

"Soon as possible. Got to go. Bye."

Just before he hung up the phone, his beeper went off due to an incoming outside call. Certainly, the caller was not his wife calling to ask for "a little something," her euphemism for money. He had earlier missed an outside caller. It has got to be important for the guy to call back, he told himself. The operator connected him with the caller. It was his friend Bright calling to inform him that he had booked a tennis court for seven to nine P.M. that evening at Marine Park. He thought for a moment about his plans for the evening. Something would have to give. He could not postpone the endoscopy if the patient was bleeding. He would have to stop the bleeding.

He juggled his plans for the evening. Juliana would have done the laundry the previous day but he had to attend the lecture on sexually transmitted diseases. If he had known that the speaker would be so drab, he would not have gone. He had learned nothing new. The only part of the evening he had enjoyed was the dinner. He would have to press his wife Juliana one more time to postpone the laundry. It would be tough because he had just confirmed that he'd be available to watch Christopher. She would be nonplussed but would not stand in the way.

Throughout the week he had been attending one party or activity each evening over the protest of his wife who had asked him to stay home at least one evening so she could do the laundry and some other chores. When he was departing for the lecture on sexually transmitted diseases the previous day, he had vowed to stay home today. Once again, he was going to disappoint her. He could solve the problem once and for all by asserting the right of a husband to go and come when he had to, as long as his conscious was clear, his mind was clean and his intentions noble. But the situation called for tact rather than diktat.

He had a long way to go before the tennis court. The endoscopic nurse on call, he hoped, was not Ms. Painter who had not given up on trying to seduce him. So far, Stephen had succeeded in fending her off and he would not like to be left in the endoscopy suite alone with her. There was no telling what the rage of a woman spurned could accomplish.

He figured he would finish with the patient by five-thirty, reach home by six, assuage his wife and dress for the game by six-fifteen.

3

He would then drive for the next forty-five minutes, arriving at Marine Park just in time for the game.

He told Bright he would be there and hung up to see his patient.

The patient's medical chart was still in Stephen's hands. He reviewed it, taking note of how much blood the patient had vomited, when the vomiting started, what drugs he had ingested, allergy history, previous bleeding episodes and the physical examination conducted by the emergency room physician. All the information he desired had been meticulously collated by the emergency room physician, one of the best in the hospital.

At the bedside, Stephen introduced himself to the patient and proceeded to interview him. The patient, Eric Williams, was in no mood to talk. "You are the fifth doctor to come here asking questions. I already told them doctors and nurses everything. I ain't got nothing for my stomach pain since I came except this damned tube in my nose. I ain't talking no more. I don't know why I came to this damned hospital. I told the ambulance to take me to St. Mary's hospital."

Doctors always approach their patients the way detectives do their clients, the suspects. When a doctor is called in to contribute his opinion or expertise, everything the patient may have told his colleagues is considered suspect. He would not necessarily trust it to be the complete or whole truth. He would want to hear the history of the illness from patient all over, whenever possible. It did not matter how many times the patient may have already recounted the history. The subspecialists, who know a lot about their narrow chosen fields but very little about other fields in medicine, suffer from the highest doses of this kind of healthy skepticism.

There are many reasons why a physician may not completely rely on the history obtained by his colleagues, no matter how many of them may already have interviewed the patient. The medical interview is an important art that not all doctors can perfect. It is so important that it may lead to the correct diagnosis in more than 70 percent of cases. Patients place a lot of faith in blood, urine and X-ray tests because they do not know this fact. Depending on what the patient's symptoms were, certain questions may be key. Unfortunately, they may be left out by the impatient, intimidated or incompetent physician. It is in patients' interest that the next physician they encounter cross-checks information that is already official.

In addition to uncovering new, clinically significant pieces of information, the recap is necessary because some patients give conflicting information that needs to be reconciled. It is natural for patients to withhold material information from one doctor but not from another because of their level of comfort with the particular physician. On the other hand, some physicians feel embarrassed or discomfited to ask certain questions due to their own upbringing or social inclination. It would not be easy, for example, for a young female doctor who has been raised in the most pristine social climate, to ask a male patient in priestly regalia who comes into the emergency department with a sore throat, "Do you engage in cunnilingus?" Yet such question, though sleazy and obscene, would be absolutely necessary. Her older male boss, lacking such qualms, could talk to the patient man to man and clinch the diagnosis.

By simply addressing Mr. Eric Williams by his full name, Stephen may not only have established rapport, but he may also have subconsciously prevented the wrong patient from undergoing stomach surgery. Astute physicians have recognized the value of a complete and careful history and the advantage of recapitulation. If and when patients catch up and develop respect for the diagnostic yield of their symptomatologies, they would quit complaining about tautology and just keep on talking. Talk, after all, is cheap.

Eric Williams had within the short period of arrival in the emergency room told his pathetic story over and over to the triage nurse, treatment nurse, medical student, the Intern, the Resident and finally the emergency department's attending physician.

When Stephen introduced himself as the gastroenterologist, Mr. Williams riposted, "I ain't got gas, I got blood in my stomach." Ignoring the unintended pun and by removing the irritating stomach tube from the patient's nostril, Stephen was able to cajole him into cooperating. He told Stephen of his severe headache that started the previous day. Actually, his ordeal started three days earlier when he became so angry with his girlfriend that he spent two days drinking alcohol and snorting cocaine. In the process, he spent some four hundred dollars of his SSI check. He had hardly eaten any food in those two days. A throbbing headache had ensued in response to which he had taken a total of ten tablets of Advil within twelve hours. Soon after, he started having severe stomach pain and vomiting.

While evaluating Mr. Williams, the latter's girlfriend came in from the waiting area to help with the interview and, possibly, the diagnosis. Stephen could tell from a distance that she too was a drug addict. Her skin was coarse and dry, and her hair, sparse, was crumbling at the temples and falling off. She was wearing a baseball hat backwards. It was obvious that she had been wearing the same set of clothes for the last three days.

5

"Doc," she addressed Stephen, "Eric worry too much. He got bad nerves. Is this blood not caused by worriation (sic)?"

Stephen, who was temporarily taken aback by the neology, recovered fast enough to respond. "Right now, we are taking him upstairs for a test on the third floor. I can't answer your questions now," he told her. He and the transporter wheeled Mr. Williams to the endoscopy unit upstairs.

"Mr. Williams, please calm down. Everything's gonna be fine," said Ms. Painter, the nurse. She had been told that the patient was coming up from the emergency room and had set up the instruments for the procedure. "It will be over in a short while," Ms. Painter assured Mr. Williams. The patient ogled the pretty nurse forgetting about the pain in his stomach. Beauty is a placebo. The specter of a beautiful nurse may be all that some men in distress need for temporary relief and Mr. Williams seemed to have improved clinically with Ms. Painter's soft talk and touch.

Many former male patients had called Stephen in the past to tell him how great a nurse Ms. Painter was. A few were audacious enough to slip their complimentary cards into her side pocket. Stephen knew that such adulation had little to do with her professional skill. She was not even involved directly in the care of some of those patients. None of the patients tended to remember the other nurses: Ms. Ranoche, Ms. Nosborrow and Ms. Hayes. They were all very hard working and diligent. The only thing that set Ms. Juliette Painter apart was her youthful beauty. The aspect that surprised Stephen was that even the female patients tended to remember only Ms. Painter's name when they called back to express their gratitude or ask questions.

Stephen had anecdotal evidence that male patients tended to tolerate painful procedures better in the presence of the beautiful Ms. Painter. He had quietly compiled the data on how well men behaved when Ms. Painter was the nurse and compared it to how they scored with the other nurses. Fearing what publication of such a report might do to the unit cohesion, he decided against it. The other nurses may come to believe he had a secret love for, or even an affair with Ms. Painter. His wife, Juliana, the head nurse on the fourteenth floor, would almost certainly have read the report. She, too, might suspect or, worse still, accuse him of having a crush on Ms. Painter, their next-door neighbor.

"This is the tube we're gonna pass through your mouth into your stomach," Stephen said to Mr. Williams with the endoscopy tube in his hand. "Your stomach will be displayed on this TV screen for you and us to see. If we find an actively bleeding ulcer, we're gonna stop

6

the bleeding by burning it but you will not feel any pain from the burn. Before we start, we're gonna give you some medicine to sedate you. The worst part is when the tube is passing through your throat and that lasts one to two seconds. We may also have to take some tissue for analysis. This procedure is very safe but, for the record, there's a very small risk that we will cause bleeding or tear your intestine. If any of these occur, we will take care of it."

Mr. Williams surveyed the room and remarked, "A whole surgical team?" referring to the team of residents and interns, some of whom were wearing scrubs.

"Mr. Williams, there is no cutting involved and you should not feel any pain," Stephen tried to reassure him.

"I don't wanna feel nothing. I wanna be knocked out," Williams demanded.

This procedure could have been done without sedation or anesthesia in some other places. Stephen's patients did not want to feel any pain or discomfort. Indeed, Stephen never used to sedate his patients until several years ago when he discovered he was losing them to his competition. He still felt uncomfortable with market forces dictating how he practiced medicine especially because sedation was not without risk. But he had to survive. Nowadays, he was hitting his patients hard with heavy doses of Somnazolam and Demerol. Most patients liked it, but the addicts like Mr. Williams craved it.

"I'm gonna give you enough medication to make you drunk," Stephen promised the patient.

"How long will it last?" Williams asked for the last time.

"Do you mean the effect of the medication or the procedure itself?"
"The medication."

"It all depends on what we find. Sign this consent form here. Relax and stop talking." Stephen ordered one of the trainee doctors to give the patient "fifty and two," referring, in the endoscopy unit jargon, to the respective doses of the sedative medications used—Demerol and Somnazolam.

"What is that?" the patient asked, obviously confused by the term "fifty and two."

"You must keep quiet and stop talking," Stephen said firmly. Patients have many rights, including the right to ask questions. But there comes a time when a doctor must draw the line for the patient's best interest.

Mr. Williams was sedated. The lights were switched off to make the room more somniferous. Then, Stephen inserted the tube through

Mr. William's mouth into his food pipe while watching the television monitor.

"That's your food pipe," Stephen told the baffled Mr. Williams who was not drowsy despite the large amounts of the sedative medications. Alcoholics are a tough bunch to deal with when it comes to sedation.

Mr. Williams began to retch as the endoscopy tube irritated his throat. He was given, at Stephen's behest, more sedation by one of the Residents. Retching made the procedure more difficult to perform. Sedation, with Somnazolam and Demerol, was titrated carefully until the retching was eliminated. Sedating a patient for a procedure was a tricky business. The danger of oversedation, from which it would be difficult to bring the patient back, lurked throughout the procedure.

"It looks clean," Stephen told the patient about the food pipe being free of blood. The tube was advanced further into the stomach. "This is your stomach. See that white area? It is the ulcer you must have bled from. You see what Advil can do to your stomach? Motrin, Ibuprofen, Aspirin and Alka-Seltzer could have done exactly the same thing. Next time you have a headache, take Tylenol. It would be more gentle on your stomach."

Stephen usually did not talk to the patients before the test was over. He was having trouble making Mr. Williams drowsy with medications but his words seemed to be having the desired effect. Alcoholics and hardened drug addicts often achieve a paradoxical high rather than sobriety and Mr. Williams may have just reached his peak.

Stephen passed the tube into the small intestine and inspected it well. He came back to the stomach thoroughly inspecting all the areas. Mr. Williams was still watching the inside of his stomach on the monitor with awe and keen interest. He began to retch again. On the whole, he had been a good patient.

Stephen asked, "Are you satisfied?" turning first in the direction of Ms. Painter and then to that of the junior doctors. They all nodded, indicating that they were satisfied that they had not missed a lesion.

"Okay, Eric, it's over. We are coming out now. Bear with us." Stephen tried to reassure the patient. Gradually, he withdrew the tube while inspecting the intestines. Mr. Williams was now breathing comfortably. He must have been very grateful that the procedure had ended successfully as it did with all patients Stephen had treated. Patients were usually grateful that they had been given the opportunity to peep inside their bodies more than they appreciated the fact that a diagnosis had been made and the prognosis estimated. Given the preoccupation that many patients had with their viscera, it was not unexpected that they appreciated the chance to end the speculation and imagination.

Mr. Williams was disconnected from all the monitoring equipment and was being taken to the recovery room when he asked, "When are you going to do the test?" The doctors and nurse turned to each other and grinned. None of them uttered a word but they all understood that his amnesia was caused by Somnazolam. The latter, made by Blaxo Pharmaceuticals, was a very interesting drug. Given in the right dosage, which varied from one patient to another, it could fully sedate a patient and, yet, paradoxically keep him or her fully awake. It acted just long enough for the procedure to be completed, assuring the patient forgot the bodily invasion. Its activity could be turned off like tap water with the available antidote, leaving the patient with no residua.

The trick in using the drug was to give it slowly while monitoring the patient's vital signs and mental status. Elderly and very sick, emaciated patients tended to tolerate it poorly. Stephen never forgot the ninety-eight-year-old woman who died on the table when Dr. Rousam gave her just a little bit of the drug too fast. He had tried to cover it up but because of his abrasive personality, rumors and innuendos had led to an official investigation. In the end, he had been censored and restrictions placed on his license. That experience caused Stephen to develop respect for Somnazolam. Even when the patient was retching and the trainee doctors were pleading for more sedation, he usually held them in a short leash.

Nobody fully knew its side effect profile. One untoward effect that stood out well was amnesia for a short period following its injection. When it first became available for endoscopic procedures, many patients used to call Stephen asking him when he would schedule them for the procedure when, in fact, he had already done it several days earlier. The problem was solved later when he started explaining to the patients well in advance that they were unlikely to remember the procedure and going back to discuss the findings well after the effect must have worn off.

Somnazolam was available in Europe as a sleeping pill. After several reports that it had been used in date rape in Europe, Blaxo Pharmaceuticals had refused to make oral formulations available in the U.S. The risk of lawsuits and adverse publicity under-weighed the commercial value especially as the sleep-inducing drug market was so competitive.

"Mr. Williams, it is over. You are not bleeding. Somebody will come and talk with you later," Stephen promised him.

Eric Williams was still under the influence and any explanation given at that time would be wasted effort. He was taken out of the room but not before he turned his neck sharply to say "Thank you, Nurse," to Ms. Painter. It was deja vu all over for Stephen.

Actually, Ms. Painter had done very little for the patient. Just like with so many other patients before him, Mr. Williams was acknowledging Ms. Painter's exquisite beauty. He would not be surprised if Mr. Williams called within the next few days to thank Juliette Painter for being so wonderful to him. But Stephen did not mind the arrangement in which Ms. Painter got all the plaudits, the patient his satisfaction, while Dr. Stephen, smiled his way to the bank with the check.

Mr. Williams was no different from Stephen's friends. Men had the same emotions when it came to women, no matter their status in society. They just managed to disguise or reveal them in different ways. Dr. Godswill, for instance, always called the endoscopy unit at about four in the afternoon ostensibly to speak with Stephen when he knew fully well that Stephen was most unlikely to be there and that the best way to reach Stephen was to page him. Dr. Godswill's ulterior motive was always to talk to Juliette Painter.

Stephen himself was not above the hide-and-seek games. He had called the fifteenth floor several times to ask about the status of his patient. He always hoped that the pretty Ms. Chapman might be the one to answer the call. On his way into the hospital this morning he had branched into the Neuro-Surgery clinic to ask his friend Dr. Edward Bryer a question. Not only did he know that Edward had not yet arrived but he could also have asked the damned question over the phone. He had just wanted to see Nurse Liz Bonomey.

The encounter had gone very badly. Liz had been sitting opposite one of her male coworkers. Not realizing they were in the middle of a conversation, Stephen had asked her, "Liz, please, is Ed here?"

Before she could answer the question, her coworker had howled in a heavy Caribbean accent, "I am talking to her, man." It had then dawned on Stephen, as if he did not know before, that men could do silly things to each other to impress an innocent and lovely face.

Everyone was gone from the endoscopy unit but Stephen and Nurse Juliette Painter who was cleaning and disinfecting the instruments. Stephen's mind was at his home where he still had to settle his itinerary for the evening with his wife and at the tennis court where his three buddies would be waiting. He surveyed the room to ensure that, in his haste, he was not forgetting anything. Satisfied, he bade Ms. Painter good-bye and made for the door.

"Good night, Ms. Painter, see you tomorrow."

"Come back here, Dr. Hasty," Ms. Painter ordered him. They had become so familiar that such an order did not necessarily signify contempt. On the other hand, *he* always took care to treat her respectfully.

Turning back Stephen asked, "What can I do for you, Ms. Painter? My tennis buddies are waiting for me. I am running late."

"Even if you cannot say good-bye to this ugly and stupid nurse, please sign the endoscopy report so that the hospital will be paid," she said. "I know this place has become too hot for you just because there is no one to protect you from this ugly and bellicose nurse. I know you don't care whether I am attacked here when you're gone or whether anything happens to me. Please close the door behind you as you step out. Next time you are leaving me, please do me the favor of talking to me like a human being. Don't just turn away as if my face is too ugly to behold" she emphasized, ending her diatribe.

She then produced the report from under the pile of loose sheets of paper on her desk. He perused the report written by one of the trainee doctors, found it factually correct and then signed it.

Stephen knew that Ms. Painter did not feel any animosity toward him. She had been sending feelers out to him but he was absolutely determined to stand firm. She craved one-on-one encounters with Stephen and engaged in little tricks to create them. Every encounter could, in her opinion, be contributory. On this occasion, she had hidden the endoscopy report so that Stephen would not sign it in the presence of all the staffs and leave. She had known that Stephen wouldn't leave because his instinct was telling him he still had something to do. Stephen tried to avoid such encounters for fear of what they might lead to. She was beautiful, single and free to mingle. He had the intuition to recognize all the feelers she was putting out but he always had a way out.

He turned to Ms. Painter and said, "You know and I know that Julie Painter is gorgeous and that was why I said, 'Good night, Ms. Painter.' I think you did not hear me because of the noise from the tap water. I've got to go. I am running late to my tennis game. You have a pleasant night." He rushed out of the room.

When Stephen got home, he was met at the door by his wife Juliana who had been waiting patiently for him to come so that she could go to the launderette in the basement. "Oh, I am happy you have come in time. I better rush before the laundry becomes too crowded. I need at least ten machines," she said while slicing the air horizontally with her hand in the direction of the bags of dirty laundry strewn about the doorway.

Stephen took a deep breath before revealing his plans for the evening. "J, I think we may have to postpone the laundry tonight. Did Bright call here?" Bright often left messages with Juliana whenever he wanted them to play tennis. By asking the critical question, he sought to inform her that he was going to play and that it was not his fault but Bright's. "Soon after we spoke, he called me that he had already made arrangements for the quartet to play and as you know without me or one of the others, the team becomes asymmetrical. You know how the game of tennis is. It is a game in which one player is useless on his own, two players tend to exhaust themselves quickly, three players destroy the fun and a quartet can have a good time."

"But couldn't you arrange it for another day? You know, I got an appointment with my dentist tomorrow and I have to take Christopher to the Neurology Clinic on Wednesday. I still got to do the shopping. We have run out of baby food and Pampers, I mean almost." Their supply of those items would last another two weeks. She added the rider to give her statement some credibility. She knew her husband to be a skinflint who would part with money only in situations like this when he had his back to the wall, looking for a way out to go and play tennis. He always gave her, in his estimation, enough money for shopping. Somehow she usually got him to buy the big ticket items, especially Pampers and baby food. Although he recognized her ploy, there was no time to scrutinize it. He figured it would be easier to buy his way out. He fumbled in his tennis bag for a pacifier and found it—forty dollars. Promising to buy some baby food and Pampers on his way back, he rushed out without further hindrance.

He got into his car and looked at the dashboard clock. It was 6:18 P.M. There was time to reach Marine Park before seven. It would all depend on his route and traffic conditions. He got to Bedford Avenue in no time. With at least ten consecutive green lights ahead of him, he revved his engine to full functioning. He made more progress than he had anticipated until he hit Flatbush Avenue. Traffic was slower than snail-speed as the avenue had been converted, at certain points, to a single lane by illegally parked cars. There were enough illegally parked cars on Flatbush Avenue for all Brooklyn cops to fulfill their daily summons quotas.

"They may well have named you Flat Traffic Avenue," Stephen began to curse in his frustration with Flatbush Avenue. He hated to drive on that stretch of Flatbush Avenue. There were always more people and cars than the available room could accommodate. Stephen thought of the alternate route he could have followed. It was too late. He just had to go with the flow.

12

With cars standing bumper to bumper and side mirror to side mirror, drivers did not yield easily to one another. They grudgingly yielded to authorized vehicles for two reasons. The first was to comply with their civic duties. The second, equally important, was to join the high speed coat-tail of the authorized vehicle. Entry into the coattail was tricky and risky. Stephen remembered what had happened a few weeks previously. He had been in the middle of crawling traffic on Brooklyn Bridge on his way to a lecture in Manhattan when a volunteer ambulance came roaring from behind. He had cleared the extreme left lane and prepared himself to tailgate the ambulance. As soon as the ambulance passed, he re-entered the lane positioning his car immediately behind the ambulance but ahead of the fast-moving caravan. The car behind him just barely avoided crashing into his rear as it came to a sudden, squealing halt.

He analyzed the situation and concluded that such a daring maneuver was not worth it. On a street like Flatbush, some damned red light up front would likely put the authorized vehicle and its ad hoc retinue asunder and make any distance gained, short. If only he could maintain his place on the fast lane, avoid risky maneuvers and go with the flow, he would arrive a bit late, he thought. For once, at least, he believed it would be better late than never.

To his right, a young man in clean, discrete dreadlocks tried to pass. He was driving the latest-model Lexus with a cute teenage girl by his side and very loud reggae and calypso music blasting from his car radio. The young man had his windows down for full effect of the music and the young woman. He was also in a hurry, probing disrespectfully to the left and right of Stephen's dilapidated Toyota Camry for an opening. Stephen was unyielding as he was making all deliberate and cautious haste to be on time. The next time they were side by side, the young man saw Stephen nodding and bobbing his head from side to side, to the music. He too, joined in the head dance, his grimace giving way to a sustained grin. The young woman appeared to be wiggling her waist, for Stephen could see the upward transmissions. Competition had given way to carnival. The parties drove pari passu until they reached Avenue S. They waved and smiled at each other and Stephen turned right to Marine Park.

Mrs. Juliana Latham looked at the dirty laundry scattered around the doorway and wondered why her husband thought a hastily arranged tennis game was more important than housekeeping. She thought his behavior was absolutely unfair and the manner in which he did it, utterly disrespectful. Perhaps, it had to do with men's priorities. Hobnobbing with their colleagues was more genteel than singing a lullaby to a naughty child who suffered from Attention Deficit Disorder. When he returned from the game, he would only add to the laundry burden.

The manner in which he rushed out of the house, she feared, indicated that there may have been more to it than he'd told her. The only other thing that would make her husband rush out so fast was if he was going to discuss business with his friends. He liked money and was making lots of it, that much she knew. The only problem was that she wasn't getting her fair share of it. The one thousand-odd dollars he gave her each month for incidentals, she thought, was not the appropriate fraction of his income that should fall under her control. It was true that she did not have to worry about housing, insurance for the dilapidated Camry he drove, the late model Acura Legend she drove, or Uncle Sam's taxes. She wondered if her husband behaved the way he did because he was providing those perks. The possibility of such association made her really angry.

"On Monday afternoon, he was in his office till very late," Juliana began to ruminate. "He came back and slumped in the bed, completely exhausted. Tuesday evening was devoted entirely to the hospital staff meeting. Again nobody saw him until eleven that night. The Brooklyn Medical Society took his whole Wednesday afternoon and evening. Yesterday, he went to the lecture on sexually transmitted diseases. Finally, he goes to play tennis today. Week after week is like that. Where is the life?"

She could feel her heart racing and her hands trembling. There was a soiled, wrapped diaper on the floor. She picked it up and slammed it into the empty trash can, asking herself aloud, "What is this doing here?"

With her temper tantrum over perks and her soliloquy continuing, she walked up to the refrigerator and grabbed her pack of Newport cigarettes she must have left there several days ago. She had trouble quitting smoking—the only bad habit she wished she had not learnt in high school. That was not to say she had not made progress in the right direction. Before she got married to Stephen, she used to smoke two packs per day. One of the bright spots of this, her second marriage, was Stephen's insistence that she give up smoking. Now, a pack would last her a good two weeks. She no longer smoked in public and InnerFaith Hospital had prohibited smoking within the hospital premises. If she wanted to, however, she could smoke in the bathroom like some other employees did.

It was just that she wanted to quit, in order to make her husband happy. If he would stop aggravating her, she thought, quitting would have been much easier. But her nerves were so bad that she nearly always returned to cigarettes to calm them.

She reached into the pack and fetched a cigarette. It fell to the floor and rolled about a foot away. She picked it up and tapped the butt against the dorsum of her left hand repeatedly in an attempt to shake it free of visible dirt. "I am not going to throw you away," she muttered as she shook the product—the benign name by which the manufacturers liked to call it—and then lit it.

It would be her first cigarette in days. No smoker ever threw away a cigarette simply because it had fallen on the floor. Reasons for such tenacity were numerous. The product is so injurious to the body that a few grains of sand or strands of fiber would probably not confer additional toxicity. Also, its effects on the body do not appear to be diluted by contaminating particulate matter. It is neither food nor medicine and cannot be treated as either. Thus, it is issued without dosing or serving size, side effects and an expiratory date. Of immediate comfort to Juliana Latham were the absence of any do-not-use-if-contaminated instructions on the cigarette pack.

Again, Juliana thought, if there was no aggravation or disappointment in her life, she would have given up the despicable habit. It was ironic that she had to turn to cigarettes as a panacea when she knew it to be a poison. She became more conscious of the fine tremors in her fingers when she bent down to pick the fallen cigarette. She realized her nerves had not acted up like this in years.

Walking over to the wine cellar, she surveyed the collection. Stephen was opposed to her drinking also, although not to the same degree as he hated smoking. The stock of wines was meant for company. The first bottle of wine she grabbed was Purple Mountain Chardonnay which she had taken with Southwestern turkey the last time she had gone to a reception with Stephen. It was a good blend for that occasion. Perhaps a red wine would be better right now, she thought, because her mind was already red as fire. Not only would they blend better, but the wine could protect her heart somewhat. There was a bottle of 1993 Bocage Merlot. She poured herself a glass.

With Christopher asleep and the room dead silent, it was time to get herself, her thoughts and nerves together. Hopefully, she thought, the alcohol and tobacco would give her thought processes the necessary uplift. Even as she poured herself another glass, she regretted that she was doing so much harm to her body when her mind was already so tormented.

With a few sips, she began to calm down, though she remained pensive. Presently, she helped herself to another glass. She looked around the house. The dirty laundry bags were still in place while the carpet was begging for vacuuming. She exclaimed aloud, "Juliana has seen better days," while lifting the glass of wine to her mouth for yet another gulp. But it appeared to her as if that statement was contestable. She began to examine the different epochs of her life in search of those happy days.

Could the better days have been the nine months or so that she spent in her mother's womb? she asked herself. She began to ruminate audibly about intra-uterine life. "First, I don't know when I became *me*. Second, I lived in absolute, solitary confinement in an egg-shaped room, less than the capacity of a kindergarten lunch box. One person, my mother, had unlimited power and control over me. I lived, and could have died, at her whim. Who knows if my present troubles are the result of congenital abuse or neglect or exposure to some noxious agents? If those were the happy days, do I want to return to that kind of caged, lonely and overly dependent life?" she asked herself rhetorically. The answer, with no doubt in her mind, was an absolute no. She wrote off her intra-uterine existence and began to focus on her infancy and early childhood.

Juliana stretched her left hand across her neck to palpate the keloid on her right shoulder blade. All thoughts of her early childhood inevitably led to the lesion. Her mother had never fully explained the circumstances that led to the original cut. She did remember that her mother had taken her to the hospital for a mild attack of cold. When the nurse placed her on the examination coach, a carelessly placed scalpel had lacerated her back over the right shoulder blade. The cut had healed with a disfiguring scar. She thanked God that that area of her back was of almost no esthetic value. She usually dressed conservatively. Her mother had sued the hospital on her behalf, won a handsome settlement and squandered it. Every time she thought about or felt the scar, an image of traumatic and lacerated childhood was conjured up. Her mother was always reluctant to disclose all the details of the incident for fear of raising questions about the financial settlement. Unanswered questions about that accident, her convalescence and nursing eliminated her infancy and early childhood as the better days of her life.

Perhaps her tenure at Rivers Day Care Center came closest to those happy days. She fondly remembered the joyous "Old McDonald" song they used to sing in groups while swinging gently from side to side. She remembered also the toys her grandmother used to buy her

for "show and tell." Those were the fond days, the first year of kindergarten, before Rivers Day Care was closed down amidst accusations of sexual molestation against the proprietress and her cousins.

All together, nine kids had made very damaging accusations against Mrs. Greely and her two cousins after grueling interrogations by psychologists. On the basis of those accusations and the zeal of the District Attorney, Mrs. Greely and her cousins were found guilty and sentenced to twenty-five years each. The trial had lasted more than one full year and had brought the school and its pupils unsolicited publicity. It had taken its emotional toll on the kids and weaned them of their innocence.

After languishing in jail for three years, the Greely family had been set free on account of new evidence the judge found to be "inconsistent with the purest tenets of the law." That was the way to sanitize the behavior of the district attorney, who had illegally hidden from the defense some of the children's recantation. Although Juliana Latham was already in elementary school at the time of the Greelys' release, she and the other alumni of Rivers Day Care never full overcame the confusion and trauma the case had caused them. Certainly, she thought, that period could not qualify as the better days of her life.

Just as Juliana began to think of her grade school days, the phone rang. She looked at the wall clock. It was ten already, but Stephen had still not returned. It was very unusual for him to stay out that long and even more so for him not to call. Night-marauding in Brooklyn was a dangerous pastime and Juliana was obviously concerned. As an emergency room triage nurse, she had seen countless men rushed in—usually at night when honest men should be in bed with or without their loved ones—writhing in pain with blood oozing from grotesque cuts and swollen orifices. The question she had always wanted to ask them, but which she never did for fear of introducing prejudice, was "What were you doing out there?"

With her husband she would be able to ask that question without compunction. She hoped he was the one calling and not someone else calling about him. "I hope he is all right," she prayed.

"Hello" she blew into the receiver. It was her friend Martina. They had not spoken for a long time. Their conversations were usually long but far between. The interludes were impulsively created to let issues accumulate. Juliana and Martina could talk for hours, digesting relationships, and the latest fashion including hairstyles and food. It always suited Juliana better when Stephen was on call in the hospital. There were women's issues, she thought, a husband should not be privy to.

"Girl, what's up? I hope there is no fire out there," Juliana said before she and Martina, on the other end, broke into delirious laughter. The joke about fire dated back to their days in grade school. Their mathematics teacher, Mr. Murray, had been a man the children, especially the girls, loved to hate. He was so stringent and strict in marking examination papers that, on occasions, all but his chosen few students would fail. Mr. Murray was always quick to write off students who did not show early promise in mathematics and he appeared to derive some kind of wry joy in seeing them fail one examination after another.

On the other hand, he paid close attention to his few select students. At his spare time, he taught them not only mathematics but also examination tricks. His favorite strategy was for a group of smart kids to sit together and set up a mock examination paper. With further editing and permutation, he theorized, the students should be able to come up with a final paper that closely approximated the real thing since great or mathematical minds thought alike.

Prior to the final eleventh grade examination, Mr. Murray's four, as his proteges were called, met several times and made up a mock examination paper. When the kids saw their mathematics question paper three days later, one of them could not control his sense of déjà vu. He hollered, "Fire!" before starting to answer the questions. Mr. Murray, who had been supervising, thinking the room was on fire, was the first and only person to jump through the window, landing one flight below and breaking his leg. Most of the kids thought he had gotten his just desserts.

Juliana and Martina had never forgotten the incident. They had been particularly delighted that Mr. Murray had gotten his nature's due. He had been quick to condemn them to mathematical failure mainly because of their gender and he made no bones about it. The exclamation, "fire," had come to have different connotations and contexts.

"J., I got very hot news for you. Are you ready for it?" Martina asked from the other end.

"Fire," Juliana replied, and both of them giggled.

"Is Stephen home or on call?" Martina always sought to clear that out of the way. She trusted that there were secrets her friend Julie did not share with her husband.

"Stephen went to play tennis and has not been back since and I am concerned because he usually returns earlier than this."

"Are you ready for the top secret?" Martina asked again.

She must have an earthshaking secret, Juliana thought. "Fire, girl," she screamed at Martina.

Martina cleared her throat, as if to ensure that the secret she was about to reveal was not muffled. "Do you know that Bryant is expecting a baby by another woman?" There was only one Bryant they both knew closely—Bryant Jamieson, their friend Pamela's husband—but Juliana was about to ask which Bryant, for the avoidance of doubt, when Martina interrupted. "Bryant Jamieson, Pamela's husband, is expecting a baby by his secretary. She is seven months pregnant. Pamela told me several hours ago." Juliana shook her in disbelief.

"Completely unbelievable," she told Martina.

Juliana, Martina Hurston and Pamela Daylon-Jamieson were the best and closest of friends. They grew up together in the Projects and high schools of south Bronx in the days before the blight. When the area began to crumble, they, along with their parents, fled to other neighborhoods in New York City. They kept in contact with one another, meeting about three or four times a year. At least once a year they made it to the beach at Far Rockaway. For Juliana, the yearly pilgrimage to Rockaway Beach was always sentimental because that was where she met her two husbands. Eight years ago she had gone there at the peak of summer with Pamela and Martina. There, the three of them had met the budding basketball star Eugene Pulliam and his friend Abel.

The five of them had strolled along the beach front, eaten and swum together. While they played together, Juliana and perhaps the other girls felt there was something awkward with the group. Juliana wished there had been three men to match. She and her friends were free and searching but the status of the two men was not immediately known. Pamela had met Eugene at a wedding two weeks previously. The occasion then, as now, had not been conducive to intimate inquiry.

If Eugene and his friend were interested in them, who among the three would they choose and whom would they leave out? These were unavoidable questions because the women did not want to ruin their friendships with a childish scramble for men. On the other hand good men were hard to find and it had not been clear that the impasse would be resolved with civility.

Nature has a way of answering natural questions. The problem is man is usually too impatient to wait for the answer. Juliana and her friends handled themselves maturely. One did not put another down in jostling for position and superiority. Juliana had been content to wait for another occasion to meet Eugene. In the two hours they had been together, she had come to the conclusions that she was probably more compatible with Eugene than her other two friends and that she would have to get back to him before they did.

There were one hundred thousand-odd people on the beach that day with, perhaps, as many still on the way. Juliana and her friends came upon another group of friends from Queens. Eugene knew one of the girls in the group. Together, they were now five girls and three boys. The equation was getting more unbalanced, and the scramble likely to be more intense for the girls, Juliana feared. They decided to play volleyball having located a net close to a crowd watching a Peruvian band. While the Peruvian music was good, Juliana's mind, and perhaps those of the other girls, was fixed on the end game in the scramble for the young men.

"Pop . . . pop . . . pop." Shots had rung out from the middle of the crowd, all of a sudden. Hell had broken loose and a big stampede ensued. When quiet returned, Juliana, after a focused and brief search, located her two friends and Eugene. Pamela was lying prostrate on the ground having been injured in the melee. Presently, the ambulance arrived to take her to the hospital. Martina was already in the ambulance beside Pamela when Juliana wanted to board. The ambulance driver put his outstretched hand across the door, blocking Juliana's path. "I can only take one passenger," he had stated flatly.

With Pamela and Martina gone, there was no fun left on the beach. Eugene offered to drop Juliana home. "Where do you live?"

"Fort Greene," Juliana had answered. Fort Greene was well out of his way, Eugene had said, but he would drop her anyway. As they drove back through Flatbush Avenue, they initially did not say much to each other. They discussed the fire cracker prank at the beach and the ensuing melee which resulted in injuries to so many people, including Pamela.

Juliana clearly liked Eugene. He was tall and smooth talking. He appeared destined for basketball stardom, a seven- or eight-figure salary and abode in a millionaires' exclusive neighborhood. Most young men who stumble upon millions of dollars lose the desire for further education. Eugene was different in that he took his education seriously and Juliana was very impressed. He talked about his life after basketball and how he was planning for it. The main problem was that she was not sure he also liked her. The fact that he was going the proverbial and literal extra mile to drop her home was an indication, even if a small one, that he did. The big question was how many other women there were in his life. If there were none at that time, there surely would come later because of his inevitable celebrity status. Juliana did not think there was a basketball star without mistresses. Her bottom line: she was not prepared to share her man.

She decided to go for the kill, realizing that opportunity knocks but once. "I hope the fact that you have helped me will not put you out or in trouble. I don't like to mess up other people's lives," she said without looking at him.

"I am unattached; totally unattached," he replied without looking at her either. It was music in her ears.

The ride from Far Rockaway on Flatbush Avenue was bumpy because the damage done to the street by the previous year's severe winter had not been fully repaired. But Eugene's Jeep was the perfect vehicle for the road. With the interaction going well between them in the car, the jolts beneath were just barely felt.

"Julie, please tell me where to turn, I am at your service," Eugene had said as they made the turn at Grand Army Plaza. Julie had shown him the way until they reached South Oxford Street. When he pulled up in front of her apartment, she thanked him profusely. "Anytime, anytime, Julie," was his response as he jabbed the air with his clenched fist. They had exchanged phone numbers. As he drove away, he looked back for a final glimpse, a final look and a final smile.

Over the next eighteen months, the affair would become consummated, culminating in marriage. Eugene had secured a basketball scholarship to play for the University of Connecticut. There, he had excelled and his profile on and off the court soared. Juliana lived and worked in Brooklyn. Whenever she visited him in Connecticut or he came home to Brooklyn, the phone would be ringing off the hook because of women who had nothing better to do. The strains became unbearable and within two years, the marriage had collapsed.

She and her friends continued to visit Far Rockaway Beach every year until six years ago, or so, when she met Stephen. There had been a two-mile stretch of cars to the beach with all three lanes virtually crawling. Martina had been driving on the extreme left lane, with Juliana sitting beside her. The car in front of them had suddenly broken down. Martina had stretched out her hand and pled for permission from drivers on the right lane to let them in. At least thirty drivers had passed without heeding the plea. When Stephen reached that point he stopped and beckoned to them to enter in front of him. Juliana had noted his MD plate. "Only a doctor would be this considerate," she had said to Martina.

Later, on the beach, a fifteen-year-old surfer had been pulled from the water and required resuscitation. Stephen had been on hand. Juliana, also certified in CPR, had identified herself and participated in the effort. When the ambulance came to pick the victim to the hospital, the rescuers had given their names and phone numbers. Juliana had been pleasantly surprised to receive a call from Stephen later that evening. She had clearly hoped that he would call and for once her prayers were answered.

In the next several months they'd gone out several times. They clearly liked, and were ready for, each other. Stephen wanted children very badly but not out of wedlock. He was already in his late thirties and feared time was running out for him. One sunny evening when they were sitting across each other in the Evergreen Restaurant, Stephen had popped the question.

One secret Juliana did not divulge to Stephen was the fact that she had two episodes of Pelvic Inflammatory Disease (PID) during her first marriage. She had been warned that her tubes had become blocked making it almost impossible for her to conceive naturally. Her first husband, Eugene, had not been ready for children. The fact that Juliana had not been pregnant throughout the duration of that marriage in the absence of contraception, however, told her that the doctors had been right. A problem with fecundity existed.

When Stephen made the offer to marry her and start a family, she could not resist the temptation to accept it. It was a vexing decision for her, one she made while fighting back tears of regret. She knew that he would be disappointed. Her hope was that perhaps, working together, they would be able to overcome any hurdles in her tubes. If necessary, they would go for test tube conception or any other exotic, emerging technology.

Since their marriage, they had tried all kinds of technologies but Juliana had failed to conceive. The adoption of Christopher did not diminish Stephen's desire to have a biologic child of his own. While some other men would have broken their vow and turned to out-of-wedlock fatherhood, Stephen had remained faithful and supportive. She had no reason to suspect him of foul play. Now, with the fast breaking shocker about Bryant Jamieson's other woman and baby, nothing would be the same again.

First, she had to get the details from Martina. The devil, they say, is in the details and until the details were in, somebody could be playing a prank.

Since Stephen was still not in, she could afford to speak in audible and even loud tones. "How did Pamela get to know?" she asked Martina on the other end of the line.

"Bryant," Martina responded, "had been in a state of denial while the pregnancy was inconspicuous, although Jennifer, the camera woman, had made no secret of the fact that he was responsible. She must have felt there was nothing shameful about being pregnant for a prominent television personality," Martina observed.

"She had traveled with Bryant to various places on official assignments," Martina continued. "He was the producer and she, the camera women. Officially, they usually stayed in different rooms in the same hotel. In the loneliness of the night, she would usually creep into his room. Always, he would complain about the difficulties he was having with his wife Pamela and his mother-in-law. Although he never made any solid commitment to her, his complaints about his wife had grown so consistent that Jennifer had begun to think of the inevitable.

"Five months ago, Jennifer had told Bryant that she had not seen her period for the last five months. The latter had attempted to dismiss what he thought was a temptation. 'Find it,' he had told her. It was not long before he became convinced that she was serious. She started spreading the word that he was responsible. Everybody who should not have heard, heard while the only person who should have heard, Pamela, didn't. The next time Bryant traveled out for official duties, Jennifer called and spoke to Pamela. She stated that she was six months pregnant for Bryant and was soliciting Pamela's help to obtain financial help from him. If Pamela would not be helpful, she warned cryptically, further steps would be taken.

"When Pamela confronted Bryant with the message, his reply was that it must have been a wrong number. Who didn't know that Bryant was a very common name? he had asked his wife. Since the caller had not identified his last name, Pamela had been naive enough to believe her husband. Earlier today, Pamela and Bryant returned from an outing to find a family court summons posted on their front door and heavily secured with Devil's tape. It was then that Bryant not only admitted to his fling but asked Pamela for forgiveness and moral support."

As Martina splattered the details to Juliana, the latter could only shake her head in utter disbelief and disgust. They discussed the options open to Pamela, their other usual menu and set a date to meet soon. Then, they hung up.

There had been a shared belief among Pamela, Martina and Juliana that Pamela had the most solid marriage. That belief rested not only on the longevity of the marriage, twelve years, but also on the background and behavior of Bryant Jamieson. He and his parents were strict Jehovah's Witnesses. When he was not producing television programs, he was standing at street corners in desperate neighborhoods distributing *Watchtower* and *Awake!*

By comparison, Juliana and Martina had unsavory romantic epics. Eight years ago, with Juliana and Pamela married, Martina had been desperate for a nuptial flight of her own. There was a cooperative effort to find Mr. Right for her. When one day, at the Brooklyn Law School Library, Wayne Wright asked her a question about her Walkman, she and her friends said, "Finally." She had met a handsome, tall, well-groomed man and she was ready to settle down. He appeared to have been Godsent. Dates and timetables were set and kept and everything was on course. One morning, after the most pleasant night they had shared together, he had flown to Boston for his wedding to his high school sweetheart. Initially, Martina felt like going to drown herself over the treatment she had received at the hands of the clown.

Now that Bryant Jamieson had also betrayed the trust they had in him, there was no man Juliana and her friends could trust completely. Juliana looked at the wall clock. It was eleven but there was still no sign of Stephen. Not even a phone call that he was on his way. It was unusual of him. She worried about his safety. It was unlikely that he had been involved in an accident. Bad news always traveled fast and no news, Juliana felt, was good news. She thought of paging him but decided against it as retribution for his untoward behavior earlier that evening. The more she thought of the various scenarios, especially in light of Pamela's predicament, the more she thought there was some-thing wrong going on. Even if there was none at that time, she thought, the long exposures to women of lesser morality would ensure that something happened.

Juliana remembered the woman who whispered something into Stephen's ear at their wedding reception. The woman, Mel Borble, had walked up to Stephen's right ear, with Juliana sitting on his left side, and murmured, "If it doesn't work, see me. I got somebody you would love." The message had left a bitter taste in Stephen's mouth. With the audience looking on, he had managed to offer a sardonic smile. Later, he would tell Juliana what the woman had said. Her twenty-two-year-old daughter, Elsie, was in her last year in law school. Her mother Mel was acting stupid in playing Cupid for her.

How could she surmise that Stephen's marriage to Juliana might not work except, perhaps, she was planning to wreck it? Stephen could not understand such unrestrained and reckless desperation. He had never met her prior to the encounter. The fact that she was there at all meant that somebody in the bride's or groom's family thought well of her. When the woman was advancing toward his ear, he had thought she was coming to wish them good luck. With so many people wanting to speak and with some others too shy to do so in public, Stephen would have understood the reason for the good-wish whisper.

Ms. Mel had known Juliana's mother since they were teenagers. Possibly, she was trying to get back at her for some distant infraction. Juliana's mother's multiple failed marriages may have led her to conclude that Juliana had inherited the legacy and was positioning her own daughter for the right moment. It was also possible that she had heard a rumor in the audience that Juliana was in this arrangement for the doctor's deep pockets. It was not hard to imagine that such a rumor could have started in the crowd and acquired a life of its own. Every woman Stephen knew in the hospital had declared at one time or another, in jest, her willingness to marry a wealthy man even for one day so as to earn a heavy wallet.

"Let me see if that prostitute or her daughter made contact with him," Juliana said reaching for Stephen's phone book on the table. The listings were in two categories, one being "friends and family" while the other was "patients." She checked the names under "friends and family" carefully, running her right index finger swiftly underneath each name and address as she read them aloud. Most were names of professional colleagues and acquaintances that were well known to Juliana. The few strange names in the listing were not followed by any explanations or footnotes. There was no indication he ever called most of those people back, anyway. There was no entry under Borble, Mel or Elsie.

Still curious and not completely satisfied, she continued onto the "patients" category. Scanning the names with her eyes and finger from left to right, she was jolted by another entry—the name Oscar. It was not exactly the name she had memorized for about three years but it came close to it. She took a second look at it. The name in the book was Pedro Oscar. Juliana, however, was looking for Merry Oscar.

About three years previously, Juliana had been riding in a hospital elevator with two student nurses. When the elevator door opened on the fourth floor, no one alighted from, or boarded, the car but Stephen was standing there in the bay talking to a seventeen-year-old patient and his mother. It appeared the patient had gone down to the X-ray department for some test and his mother was there for moral support. Stephen had been facing the CAT scan area and had turned in the direction of the elevator as the door was closing. He had not seen his wife who was obscured by the closing door. The student nurses, on the other hand, had seen a full-body snapshot of him.

One of the nursing students had turned to the other one and asked, "Did you see that hunk?"

"Who is he?" her friend had asked in return.

"I don't know, but doesn't he look great. Tall, handsome, well built and, as you know, with a good wallet. I'm gonna have to check him out," she had vowed, gesticulating for full emphasis.

"He probably has a girlfriend or even a wife" her friend had cautioned.

"Then that's her problem, too bad." Both girls smiled looking at Juliana's direction, not realizing that they were conspiring against her.

The elevator had picked up some more passengers on the way. Though Juliana had been going back to her floor, she stayed on to learn more about those loose nursing students. Unfortunately, they had stopped talking because the elevator had become too crowded. It is one thing to talk loose in the presence of one stranger but idle talk in a crowded elevator could generate far reaching reverberations. Juliana had known they were going to the tenth floor. There, she had stepped out of, and was facing, the elevator as if to make egress easier for the students. Her real purpose had been to read their names on their ID cards. She was able to read and memorize the name of Merry Oscar, the one who had seen the hunk.

Now, having taken a second look at the name and the accompanying information, she concluded that Mr. Oscar Pedro was not related to Merry Oscar. It still amazed her that those young girls could have been so brash in the elevator. The fact that some women out there not only saw Stephen as a hunk but also craved him made her feel somewhat privileged. They could look at, but she would make sure they did not touch him. She scanned the phonebook all over again looking for any entry with Merry or Oscar but there were no surprises.

She became more frustrated that Stephen had not called or returned home yet. Her feelings were oscillating between concern that he may have been hurt and anger at his irresponsible outings. She was not going to take it anymore, she told herself. If he was out there with a woman, tonight would be their last together. She began to pace the house up and down talking to herself. "I am ready to conk somebody on the head," she declared.

She settled down and began to plot a strategy for making him stay home. She considered the feasibility, pros and cons of various options. Her first strategy was to physically block the way the next time he tried to hasten out like that. The problem with that strategy was that it would introduce a whole new dimension to their relationship. Apart from the fact that he never seemed to stay home, their marriage was as solid as a rock. He treated her with respect and grudgingly provided enough money for the running of the house. He had never raised his voice or fist against her. Why should she, she asked herself, be the first to introduce violence into the relationship? If obstruction led to shove, she would be no match for him, she concluded.

Juliana considered putting up persuasive resistance the next time she would want Stephen to stay home. The problem with that strategy as she saw it was that no line of resistance would hold up against a legitimate reason to leave home. If he were to say he had a dying patient to see, she would have to give way. And smooth-talking Stephen would always have a solid reason to offer.

She thought it would be a great idea to douse his dinner with a small amount of alcohol. Since he did not drink, he would not require much to make him drowsy. Then she decided against it because she did not want to embarrass him with alcohol on his breath while talking to his patients. Alcoholics are not held in the highest esteem. She imagined some patient or impatient nurse telling Stephen to cut down his wine intake while Stephen vehemently proclaimed his teetotalism. She did not want to do anything to ruin him. She just wanted him to spend more time at home with the family, not out there with the Borbles and the Oscars. On the other hand if he must go out, she would prefer the whole family to go together. The family that moved together, stayed together.

Having failed to come up with, or devise, a leash free of side effects, Juliana decided to go to bed for it was getting late and Christopher would be up soon. He had spent the whole day playing hard and the last three hours sleeping. She wanted to catch some sleep before he awoke because she would not and could not sleep when he was up even if she wanted to. She went into the drug cabinet to find a sleeping pill. She examined the boxes one by one, both tablets and injectables.

The drug that caught her attention and fascination was Somnazolam. She was quite familiar with the drugs Stephen used to administer to his patients prior to endoscopy. Not only did she and Stephen discuss the virtues of the agent but she herself had used it to calm truculent patients. It worked fast and for a brief period and the patients tended to forget what had happened to them afterward. In the dose she had administered to patients on the floor, she had known that it was devoid of any long-term sequelae. As she examined the drug more closely, it donned on her that the agent she needed to hold down her wayward husband was at hand.

First, she would have to check out its side effect profile. If it was going to affect him in any deleterious way, then she would not touch it. She pulled out the accompanying literature. She already knew how it worked and that it was made by Blaxo Pharmaceuticals of Orange

Court, New Jersey. She remembered the day the company representative left the consignment off for Stephen. As usual, she had been home alone and he had gone to play tennis.

Her interest was largely in the section that dealt with "side effects and toxicity." She began to read it aloud. "Somnazolam has been compared with a placebo in a double-blind trial among a large group of volunteers. The most common side effects were amnesia, headaches, yawning, lethargy, inertia and an evanescent rash. Almost all of the side effects were more common in the placebo group which had been treated with sterile water. There have also been single case reports in the literature of dark discoloration of urine, itching, body aches and pains, and impotence. All these effects have been self-limited and attribution to Somnazolam is controversial."

The reference to impotence caught Juliana by surprise. She did not want him impotent. Not only did she enjoy the sex, but she did not know how he would take it. When Dr. Cortez suddenly closed his lucrative practice about seven months ago and moved down to Puerto Rico, conventional wisdom was that he was just crazy. While the official reason was that he wanted to relocate to the Caribbean to enjoy the rest of his life, Stephen had confided in her that the man could no longer perform in the bedroom. Juliana read that reference to impotence one more time and concluded that the risk was minuscule. She would use it, after all. The first time he complained of being too tired or begged to be left alone, she would stop.

For the sake of completeness, she decided to glance over the rest of the drug information. She just wanted to take her time and make no mistakes. She discovered that Somnazolam was only available in the injectable form. That was a problem. Practically, there was no way she was going to give him injections. Calling the manufacturers in New Jersey to make tablets of the drug for her would have been unnecessary because of reports of it having been used in date-rapes in Europe. She began to read further and soon found the answer to the questions raised. When given by mouth, absorption and efficacy were unpredictable. The fact that some absorption took place from the stomach at all satisfied her. Besides, she did not necessarily desire a rapid onset of action.

The next obstacle she had to overcome was how she would administer the drug so that he alone would ingest it. Could she break an ampule and mix the contents with salad dressing, soup or juice? There was a substantial risk that it would be given to unintended consumers. The spectacle of guests feeling languid soon after drinking some juice in their home alarmed her. For an answer, Juliana went to the refrigerator to examine the stock of cooked and uncooked food. She found the vehicle for delivering the inebriating drug. It turned out Stephen was the only occupant of the household who drank soy milk. She decided to mix the drug with soy milk.

She poured a small amount of soy milk in each of two glasses for an experiment. She then took one vial of Somnazolam from the bottom of the rack so as not to raise any suspicions. Like every nurse knew, breaking a vial with the bare hand could be dangerous. To protect her fingers, she placed a pledget of bouffant cottonwool over the constricted neck of the ampule, grabbed it between her right thumb and index finger and tried to break it. She had underestimated it as it failed to break with the initial assault.

"What is this?" she complained aloud in the silent room as she repositioned her fingers. On the second attempt she broke it and emptied the ampule into one of the glasses of soy milk. She swabbed the unsullied milk with her index finger, and tasted it. She then rinsed her mouth and repeated the tasting with the spiked soy milk. To her satisfaction, the taste did not change.

She went back to the literature to assure that she had not missed any important warning. There was no mention of the drug's interaction with milk. The makers, however, did warn that the drug had been approved by the Federal Drug Administration only for short term sedation during uncomfortable procedures like endoscopy. There had been no approval for, or experience with, long-term use of the drug. In deciding to sprinkle the drug on his soy milk and expose him to long-term use of the medication she realized that she was veering into unknown territory.

Juliana brought out a container of soy milk from the refrigerator and squeezed the top open. She then went to the bottom of the medicine cabinet and fetched another ampule of Somnazolam. As before, she broke the neck off, avoiding injury with the help of the pledget of cottonwool. She looked right and left to see if it was real. She hesitated, almost changing her mind. Holding aloft the ampule in her left hand, she made an audible, animated and poetic appeal to the drug:

Odorless, tasteless, colorless, vial
The staid substance of my queer trial,
Would you make his nimble feet wobble
To the chagrin of Mel and Elsie Borble?
Please, no physical or mental scars,
Just assure he wins no Merry Oscars.

She then emptied the vial of Somnazolam into the soy milk and shook the container violently to mix the two liquids. Almost immediately, Christopher began to whine in his room. She put the spiked soy milk back into the fridge, cleared the area of all debris and went to lure Christopher back to sleep.

Stephen had stayed on the tennis court until nine that night. He had teamed up with Bright to defeat their doubles opponents, Sam and Innocent, two sets to one. It was a reversal of fortune for him and Bright as their opponents usually had the upper hand. Tonight, he and Bright played a neat and well-coordinated game and almost won even the third set, after a tie-breaker. He had made some unforced errors but was focusing on the larger, winning picture. As he drove back home to InnerFaith Hospital, he was still excited by his improvement and the final score.

Just when he was pulling into the parking lot, he received a beep. His heart skipped a beat as he feared Mr. Eric Williams had resumed bleeding. It was common for a patient he had successfully treated at endoscopy to worsen, usually at night, and resume vomiting blood. Usually, he would rush back to the hospital and perform the procedure all over again. On this occasion, he decided, if the patient started vomiting blood again, he would conveniently pass the buck by referring the patient to surgery. He was too exhausted after the game to perform another procedure that night if he could avoid it. He dared not document that in the chart or the fact that the patient had no health insurance. There was no doubt that he would have summoned the energy to go back and scope the patient if the latter had solid insurance. He decided to answer the call on his car phone so as not to disturb his sleeping wife and son—that is if she was not awake and waiting for him.

He checked his beeper and saw that the call was coming from Long Island. None of his regular patients lived there. Although a handful of his colleagues did, they were not that intimate to have a pressing need to call him close to midnight. He hoped the call was not coming from one of those Long Island-based telemarketers. Somehow those calls always came at the most inopportune time, disrupting his rhythm and concentration. He always cursed himself for having picked up the phone.

"Hello, this is Dr. Latham," he said anxiously into the receiver.

"This is Juliette. I am stranded at Long Island. Please come and pick me up. I am waiting at the entrance into the Roosevelt Field Mall parking lot. I have nothing left on me, and not even a quarter to make another call. Please come now."

Stephen kept wondering, while Juliette Painter made her desperate plea, why she had gone to Roosevelt Field in the first place.

"I am coming," he responded just as Juliette implored him again. "Please come now." Both of them hung up at the same time. As he drove eastward to Long Island, he was troubled by what may have taken his nurse there and kept her there so late.

It must be, he thought, that she had gone there to meet a man. Most likely the encounter had gone awry. If she ran into another woman in the man's company, he hoped she was physically all right. Less than a month previously, the woman in charge of security in the hospital had committed suicide after losing a scramble for a young man to a younger woman. He hoped that he was wrong in his speculation. It was also possible, he reasoned, that the man had come and picked her from Brooklyn but had refused to take her back for reneging on an agreement to stay the night.

There seemed to be something wrong with new lovers going from the city to Long Island to consummate their relationship. Stephen and Dr. Godswill called it the Long Island jinx. Four weeks earlier, Stephen's friend Dr. Emmet Godswill had gone to the exclusive Long Island night club, Ground Zero, with his hot new date. She had arrived at the hospital about two months earlier as the chief MRI technologist and had immediately caused considerable consternation among the men. Although many of the aggressive young men were passing notes to her in the cafeteria and in her office, it was Dr. Emmet Godswill's luck that shone. Their first outing, to Ground Zero, Emmet had hoped, would be a night to remember. On the contrary, things went so bad that he had to rush her back home prematurely. They never said a word to each other afterward. But Emmet had difficulty pinpointing what it was exactly that had gone wrong.

When Dr. Marcel Kim took his new love Ida to the famous Glen Cove flea market in Long Island six months ago, she started fussing about all kinds of minutiae. She started an argument about his "Caller ID." They had met at the Sugarhill Restaurant in the Bedford-Stuyvesant section of Brooklyn while attending a lecture on the management of depression. He had gone there with open arms, ears and mind. When the speaker said during the talk that for a whole lot of patients, depression often resolved when they fell in love, it was as if he had been speaking to Ida. Over the dinner, which was well prepared and delicious, they got to know each other very well, or so they thought.

When Ida visited Kim two days later, she had asked him, three times within one hour, "Are you sure you are not seeing anybody?"

"That's exactly what I am saying," Dr. Kim had responded. With that flattery, the affair had taken off like a perfect flight. They were going places together and their friends had only words of approval for them. There had been no sense of anything being amiss until they undertook the trip to the Glen Cove flea market. Ida began to berate him.

"I ask you again, Marcel, why do you have the caller ID? If you are totally honest with me, and you have nothing to hide, you would not need that device or service. It is an expensive service cherished by those who have something to hide. Criminals desire it because it can keep them one step ahead of aggressive investigators. But I know that you are not one of them."

"Well, those are the only sweet words you have uttered today," Kim had chirped in. Ida had continued her tirade so that by the time they got back home they hardly spoke a word to each other. For the first time in their relationship, they had ended their night separately.

Traffic on Interborough and Grand Central Highways was light as expected by that time of the night. Most Long Islanders were already home, tired and in bed. It would be several hours before they would start streaming back to the city to continue from where they had left off the previous day. The highways belonged to mostly marauders and the sidelines to radar-wielding cops. Stephen prayed and hoped to avoid either evil. He drove carefully, slowing down at bends to avoid a speeding ticket. With the road so free, he had a constant urge to accelerate.

He pulled down the visor with the aim of giving himself the cloak of invisibility rather than to protect himself from incident beams of light. Even when driving directly against the sun rays, he hardly ever used his visor because it tended to minimize his visual field. He could always deceive the sun by reducing his eye aperture with his lids, slanting his eyes, and constricting his pupils. Over all, the maneuvers would alter the angle of incidence of the sun rays. There were occasions when he thought the visor was just another redundant adjunct that added to the cost of the automobile. On this Friday night it possessed the desired potential to make him incognito.

Soon, he was at Exit 31. He began to wonder how he would find his hapless nurse in the complex mall system. As he pulled into the parking lot, he could see her silhouette at the gate. She appeared to be much shaken but not visibly hurt. He made a U-turn in the nearly empty parking lot and was now facing the exit. Juliette swung the door open and slumped inside the front passenger seat. Without asking any questions, he throttled the engine and they were on their way back to Brooklyn.

For the next twenty minutes, or so, as they raced westward to the city, there was dead silence between them. He wanted her to take as long as she wanted to make up her mind and collect herself together after what must have been a rather traumatic experience. Besides, Stephen's mind had shifted to other concerns. A collision, a break down or a moving violation, each would be the worst thing to happen to them. If any of those evils occurred, how would he explain it to his friends and family?

"I am sorry to put you through this Dr. Latham." She broke the silence. "I am sincerely sorry. I am very grateful that you came to pick me up. I hope that this will not put you out of your home, knowing how we women think and act." She went on to narrate how she had gone with her girlfriend to shop at the Roosevelt Field malls. The emphasis was on the word *girl,* so that Stephen might not develop any funny ideas. Their car had been snatched at gun point near the EAB bank, soon after they had withdrawn money from the machine. In the following minute they had spotted some cops in a patrol car and had reported the matter to them. It had taken nearly two hours for the cops to complete their report and a preliminary, but futile investigation. When the cops offered to give them a ride home, her friend readily and gladly jumped into the car. She had demurred, perhaps because of temporary insanity. Presently, she had found herself alone, but she still had serious misgivings about the police offer. What, she had wondered, would she have said to her neighbors who would surely have seen her being returned to the city from the suburbs like a criminal sandwiched between two heavily armed officers in the backseat of their patrol car?

As she narrated her ordeal between sobs, Stephen sped cautiously watching out for cops, broken down vehicles and drunken drivers. The road was more desolate than he had ever seen it. He tried to show empathy, brushing aside Juliette's concern for his marital stability. For a long time, she had been making overtures to him and he did not want to offer her any opening with what he had to say. "This sort of thing should not have happened, especially in a place like this. It could have been worse. We have to thank God that you escaped injury. It could have been worse," he repeated. "This kind of a thing happens all the time in Brooklyn," he added.

Juliette was still frightened and tremulous. "I had gone to shop there to avoid precisely this kind of danger. It looks now that I would have been safer in the city than in the suburbs. Perhaps one would have been more vigilant within the city. I don't think I can ever come to this mall anymore. I will live, shop and die in the city," she continued to lament.

They were silent again for upward of fifteen minutes. Now that they were beyond the tortuous Interborough and on Atlantic Avenue, Stephen's concern shifted from his nurse's safety to what he would tell his wife. There was no good explanation for his long absence from, and his failure to call, home. He would have to lie to her.

The way he rationalized it, lying is a mind game everyone played; a tool influential people had discovered to be often kinder than the truth. Lovers, including couples, he thought, were the greatest offenders. He asked himself how many times his friends Kim, Godswill and especially Kurman must have said to their women "I love you" knowing fully well that they were telling blatant lies? Uncountable, he concluded. Usually, the women would respond with broad smiles or some other appreciative gesticulation. In most cases the women also knew, or should have known, that the men were lying. In playing along instead of demanding proof or clarification, Stephen reasoned, they also lied. He hoped that his wife Juliana would play along with whatever lies he would tell her in order to avoid a row.

Stephen was convinced he had been lied to more often than he could count or remember. Earlier in the day he had called Chemical bank to transfer his outstanding credit card balance to Newfield MasterCard because of the more favorable interest rate. The Chemical manager had tried all tricks in the trade to stave off the transaction. Stephen could discern a tinge of frustration and irritation in his tone, traits that bankers should neither possess nor display. When Stephen insisted on going forward with the deal, the bank manager had given up, telling him "thanks for calling Chemical and have a great day."

"That was a lie," Stephen almost caught himself saying aloud. The manager, he thought, could have cared less if he collapsed with a severe heart attack right after hanging up the phone.

He turned in the direction of Juliette to see if she had heard him. She was fast asleep or pretending to be. "Long Island jinx," Stephen teased her in his mind. After the ordeal she was understandably fatigued and probably needed the nap. On the other hand, she could have been faking the nap to extract more sympathy from him. He wanted to arouse her but decided it was better to concentrate on driving and watching for any marauders. Having come this far it was imperative to avoid an accident that might make him the topic of yellow journalism. He imagined the morning headline might read like this: PROMINENT BROOKLYN MD, MISTRESS, HURT IN CRASH. To make the story even more sleazy and helpful to the bottom line, they may even quote eyewitnesses who had seen the couple making love in the car.

Presently, they turned on to Franklin Avenue for the final lap of the trip to the hospital residence. Juliette was fully awake now. She began to thank Stephen copiously for the help. "I'll pay you back anyhow, anywhere, anytime, Stephen," she vowed. The fact that she called him by his first name for the first time ever was not lost on him. But Stephen was concentrating on what lie he would tell his wife. It would be ideal if she was already in bed. If he could slip into bed, unnoticed, he might be able to narrow his time line in the morning. He regretted that he had not called throughout the evening.

Halfway down the block, Juliette asked Stephen to drop her so that she could stretch her legs. Stephen was all too eager to oblige her but he knew better than to believe her reason for wanting to alight far from the frontage. She had been standing upright for hours at the parking lot. If anything, her legs needed rest rather than stretching. Her real reason for alighting from the car down the block was to avoid walking into the residence with Dr. Stephen Latham at her side. No one could have seen them in that setting and failed to arrive at the obvious conclusion. Stephen himself had been very concerned about that scenario but he was too embarrassed to make the suggestion. He was all too relieved that she did.

The doorman and his friends never slept. Although they almost never said anything to Stephen, he still felt it would be inauspicious for him to walk past them with Ms. Painter at his side so late at night while his wife was already in bed upstairs. He could never underestimate their capacity to spread the word. Once they gave birth to the gossip, there was no telling where it would end. In a worst case situation, his wife Juliana might be greeted with it in the morning.

He circled the block twice in order to allow Ms. Painter to fade from the doorman's memory before he would emerge. Again his mind shifted to the story he was going to tell his wife. He was not good at telling lies. Maybe the reputation he had built for telling the truth would carry him through this difficult moment. He had never stayed out so late except when he was on call. His most inexcusable fault of the evening was his failure to call her. For that, there could be no explanation. Only a quick admission of guilt on that front would suffice.

He toyed with, then quickly rejected, the idea of telling his wife he had been in the hospital all along. Never before had he rushed to see a patient in his tennis attire, drenched in perspiration and foul-smelling. He believed in proper dressing and the right aroma for all the good impressions they tended to create in patients. Juliana also knew that because she made daily contributions to his dressing, shoes and perfume, ensuring that they not only stood out but also that there was agreement and blend among them. To claim that he had been in the hospital throughout the night, Stephen thought, would be asinine.

What if somebody had seen him in Long Island, he asked himself. When one goes and comes, one never knows who is watching. This point was never lost on Stephen. He remembered the case of the public prosecutor who drove his car the other day into a desolate part of North Philadelphia and fired several shots at his empty car and then blamed it on a black man and even positively identified the alleged assailant in a fog photo line up. His story unraveled when a homeless man swore that the prosecutor himself had fired the shots. Stephen resolved that whatever lie he was going to tell must incorporate his trip to Long Island.

On rare occasions, Stephen reasoned, a lie may not only be kinder than the truth, it could be virtuous. He saw it as a tool many of his heroes including United States presidents and other highly respected officials had found handy in times of crises. It all depended on the setting in which the lie was told. If it was told in the context of extricating society from an extreme situation, then it would be honorable, he concluded. Stephen had a lot of respect for the U.S. military and counted highly decorated officers among some of his greatest heroes. When Colonel Hackworth, one of the army's most decorated officers was faced with an extreme situation, he chose to lie. The Second World War had been raging in Europe with the Nazis sweeping through the continent as does a hot knife through butter. Mr. Hackworth had lied about his age—he was only seventeen—to enlist in the army. Society and the military never held it against him. Stephen still considered him one of his greatest heroes.

He remembered that President Eisenhower, his other hallowed hero, had also lied. Eisenhower had a personal reputation for telling the truth. But when Gary Powers and his U-2 spy plane were shot down over the former Soviet Union in May of 1960, the president lied by authorizing the space agency to issue a false cover story that a U.S. research plane investigating weather conditions in the North Atlantic had been reported missing. It had taken the president five days to figure out the lie.

Stephen also thought about the former Pres. Jimmy Carter, perhaps the president most akin to piety. Carter had come in to clean up the mess after Watergate. He was not supposed to lie to the American public. Toward the end of his single term, with American diplomats held hostage in Teheran, the military began preparations for a spectacular rescue operation. Yet Mr. Carter vehemently foreswore any such plans, in public, so as to deceive the hostage-holding mullahs. Unfortunately for Mr. Carter the attempt failed and he lost the election to Ronald Reagan. That, Stephen rationalized, was a noble lie designed to salvage civil society from the menace of terrorism.

In his opinion when a lie was told to conceal one's own foible, it became immediately objectionable and repercussions must surely follow. When former President Nixon told the nation, at the height of the Watergate scandal, "I am not a crook," he was lying. It turned out he was much more than a crook. He harbored a criminal fiber. He paid a heavy price for the lie.

The Los Angeles Police detective Mark Furhman also lied during the trial of the century. When he was asked, under oath, whether he had ever called any black person or referred to African Americans as "niggers," he claimed he had not. He could have said he had done so in jest or taunt, like many black people themselves do. Instead, he chose to lie. Subsequently exposed as a pathologic liar on tape, he and the prosecution lost the case.

The lie Stephen would tell his wife was not of that genre, he assured himself. It was designed to save two unpredictable women, his wife Juliana and their neighbor Juliette, from each other. Society stood to gain nothing if the two women locked horns on the fourth floor. Therefore, he concluded, his lie would not only be kind to the two women but it would also be a free service to society.

He parked his car in his underground parking slot. When he emerged from underneath, he was unprepared for the cold blast. He was still clad in his tennis attire. Since he left the court, the thermometer had plummeted but he had been basking in the warmth of his car. He rushed pronto to the frontage from where he could see the hallway and the elevator ahead of him. Surprisingly, the doorman and his friend were standing akimbo on either side of the aisle, beneath the canopy. They both wore dark Aviator glasses that made it impossible for one to establish eye contact with them. Both of them also donned baseball hats. The hats were directed foward indicating that they had been left behind by the current vogue in which young men turn their hats backward. From the sides of the hats, wimples shielded their temples from the wind's chilling effects. Stephen had seen them make passes at young women during the day. He had no doubt about their mission for the night.

Far behind them, by the elevator, stood Juliette Painter. For the first time during the night, Stephen saw her black-striped, white pique jacket with shoulder epaulets and front zip which she was wearing over a straight black pique skirt. She had a glittering choker necklace while gold-plated earrings dangled from her ears. To complete the attire, she had the famous Cole-Haan's woven leather sandals, the clearest indication yet she had been out on a hot date. No woman ran around crowded shopping malls dressed like that. She had retrieved, and pretended to be reading, her junk mail while holding the elevator door with one foot. It was apparent that she was looking out for Stephen. While she would not like to put the latter in trouble, she couldn't go to bed in peace not knowing he had emerged from the treacherous night. As soon as she saw him, she boarded the elevator for the uninterrupted flight to the fourth floor.

Stephen was concerned that the doorman and his company would deduce that Ms. Painter had been waiting for him but he couldn't even be sure they had seen her. He put up a good front walking with the swagger and poise of a successful tennis regular. The doorman had often seen him come and go with his tennis jersey and was unlikely to think that he would dress like that for an important date.

"How are you doing, guys?" he greeted them as he passed.

"Okay, and you?" they replied.

"Fine, and you have a good night." He moved on.

He stalled at his mail box and fetched his letters. Usually, he threw away all his junk mail without opening the envelopes. On this occasion, he perused each piece with faked interest and in detail in order to let Ms. Painter settle down. Since they lived in adjacent apartments he wanted to avoid having to enter his apartment as Ms. Painter was entering hers. That way, his wife would not suspect anything if she was still up.

Again, he began to revise the lie he was going to tell his wife. He considered various options and settled on blaming it on Dr. Lee Thanm for reasons that he considered justified. "It's payback time, pal," he chuckled as he boarded the elevator. Standing before his front door with his bunch of keys in hand, he took a look at Ms. Painter's door. It looked as if she had narrowly cracked it open. It would be too risky for him to draw her attention to it. After all, the apartment block was as safe as any other building in the city.

He inserted his keys into the hole and very gingerly twisted it open. The sitting room was still strewn with dirty laundry. He was surprised to find Juliana sitting on the sofa with Christopher lying prone on her lap. She was gently patting his back and singing a lullaby to him. She must have had a full day with her full-time job of tending Christopher if he was just falling asleep. Stephen felt sorry for her.

There was a thick cloud of smoke in the leaving room making it difficult for Stephen to breathe. He held his breath for as long as he could. Then he inhaled deeply taking in a heavy dose of smoke. Apnea is no panacea for filthy air, for sooner or later breathing becomes inevitable. It may help if the body of pungent-smelling air is rapidly swept away and replaced by odorless or freshened air. That does not happen when the air is trapped in the living room. For so long he had been trying to get his wife to kick the smoking habit. She had made a lot of progress and he was hoping that she would overcome in the immediate future. The smoke ball was so thick that she must have spent the night smoking to calm her bad nerves down as she often claimed. He would not have refrained from protesting her recidivism if his own conscience had been squeaky clean and his actions that night not so reprehensible.

He started to say something about his whereabouts. "J, I am sorry . . . " But she stopped him in his track by placing her extended left index finger over her pursed lips, while still humming and tapping on Christopher's back with her right palm. To parents raising children all over the world, that sign stood for "absolute silence, let the kid sleep." It was a motion that all men, no matter how anxiously they wanted to talk to their wives, obeyed for the sake of their kids.

With his hands cold after being exposed to the chilly wind outside, albeit briefly, he went into the kitchen to make himself a cup of hot coffee. He had an obsession with drinking a cup of coffee before retiring each night. On this occasion it was particularly indicated for his cold and clammy hands.

Inside the refrigerator, he found the last container of his favorite soy milk, shook it vigorously before adding it to the cup of coffee. He had planned to buy some soy milk on his way back from the tennis court but that plan had been superseded by events. The next day, barring an attack of amnesia, he would do that.

Stephen gulped his coffee and rushed into the bathroom for a badly needed shower. The bathtub was characteristically shiny. It appeared that Juliana had taken out her frustration that evening on the bathtub, scrubbing it until it glittered. She had the tendency to wash the bathtub when she was angry and frustrated. Stephen had always seen it as productive catharsis. He did not, however, take advantage of that tendency by deliberately making her angry. The air in the bathroom was fresh as she had closed the door while smoking in the living room. She deserved commendation for her bathroom environmental activism.

Stephen had friends and colleagues whose bathrooms were an eyesore. The last time he went to the Colemans' apartment for their son's birthday party, the shabby and rundown state of their bathroom had taken him aback. He had felt strongly nauseated and wondered how they kept their bathroom when company was not expected. Now, more than ever before, he thought Juliana deserved a hug for the effort.

While in the shower, he was seized by gradual but severe drowsiness and sluggishness. He understood why he had become so tired. He had been up all day and it had been a particularly long day. His legs were weak, his eyes heavy with sleep. He made it out of the bathroom fast to avoid falling asleep there.

Stephen would not succumb to sleep, no matter how severe the urge was, before delivering the explanation or apology he owed his wife. He came back to the living room for that purpose. Again, she puckered her lips, placed her left index finger over them and bade him to maintain silence. It was a critical moment in her effort to lull Christopher to sleep. The latter was still twirling on her lap and any conversation would have increased his consciousness.

Stephen went to bed, for it was already late. His conscience was clear; it was not his fault that he couldn't say anything. He did not immediately fall asleep as he had expected although he was still feeling as sluggish and sleepy as he did in the bathroom. He would have the chance to tell his wife his story in bed. He began to go over the account in his mind.

"Payback time pal," he chuckled again. Like before, he was referring to everything that had happened to him because of, or done to him by, Dr. Lee Thanm. Everywhere he went in the hospital, people mistook him for Dr. Thanm. Even people who should have known better—nurses and doctors who had worked closely with him—proved vulnerable to the error. Occasionally, when he moonlighted in the clinic or some unit certain employees would call him Dr. Lee Thanm repeatedly despite his attempts to correct them. He had given up on some other workers because they had proven to be incorrigible. While he took the mix-up in stride and showed no outward displeasure, the fact that the problem appeared so intractable still bothered him.

During last year's Christmas party, he had been introduced as Dr. Lee Thanm to the gathering, an error the master of ceremony had corrected quickly. Stephen had not been satisfied with the retraction because he did not want to be associated with Dr. Lee Thanm.

The latter had been accused of fondling several women during routine physical examinations. Asked at the disciplinary committee meeting why he had examined both nipples of the eighteen-year-old girl at the same time, for twenty minutes, contrary to training and practice, Dr. Thanm had claimed that he was only being thorough. As if that was not enough baggage already, a woman visiting her sick mother in the hospital with her husband only days ago lodged a formal complaint that Dr. Thanm had fondled her breasts in the elevator. In his unofficial defense, Thanm had been telling friends that the breasts were in the way as he was reaching for the elevator buttons.

Before he had left the Christmas party last year, Stephen had managed to take a full-size photograph of Dr. Thanm who was also at the party. After developing and printing it, Stephen had juxtaposed his own full-length photograph with that of Dr. Thanm's. He had sat alone in his bedroom with his wife and child away to the doctor's office, to examine the two pictures for symmetry and resemblance. He had come to the conclusion that Dr. Lee Thanm must have been dyeing his hair black to appear young. A few grey strands of hair at the temples had escaped unscathed to tell the truth. Although he was five years younger than Thanm, the latter appeared to be the same age as he. Stephen wondered about the concoction that made the old man look so youthful.

Contrasts were all over the pictures. Dr. Thanm had three eccentrically placed creases above his right eyebrow that apparently did not diminish his attractiveness to the woman. By contrast, Stephen's face had been as smooth as a baby's. "Where's the semblance?" Stephen had queried himself. There was Dr. Thanm's rich mustache, the gap between his upper central teeth and his puffed out chest. These were all features Stephen did not have or necessarily desire. Stephen had concluded that there was no resemblance between Dr. Lee Thanm and himself.

Still, he was puzzled that so many workers persisted in calling him Lee Thamn instead of Dr. Latham. "How could so many be so wrong so many times?" he had asked himself. It would not have mattered if Dr. Lee Thanm himself had not been perpetuating the impersonation. And Stephen was to discover the truth in a tense encounter.

With his wife doing research into travelers' diarrhea in the Carribean, Dr. Lee Thanm had been bringing his mistress, a hospital worker, into the apartment block. Typically, Dr. Thanm would call his wife in Kingston to assure that she was not en route to New York. Then he would call his mistress to come. Following Dr. Lee Thanm's instructions, she always told the doorman, and wrote in the visitors' book, that she was visiting Dr. Latham.

The scheme was devised to mislead Dr. Thanm's wife, who had a reputation for suspicion and wildness. Upon her return from the

Caribbean, she would try her utmost to find out whom he was seeing. She would go through the doorman's book, checking carefully for the names of her husband's guests while she was away. She would also call back all strange numbers listed in his phone bill. It was to stay one step of the game that Dr. Lee Thanm arranged for his mistress to pretend to be visiting Dr. Latham.

The scheme had come to a head one Friday morning. Stephen had been sitting in his office discussing the details of an upcoming conference with Dr. Kim when a seven-foot, broad-chested man in purposely-tattered denim overalls walked in and demanded to speak to Dr. Latham. When Stephen identified himself, the man approached, and began to threaten him. "I came to warn you to leave my girl alone. Me and her, we've been together for the last five years. Metty Taylor? Leave her alone." As he spoke, he was tapping Stephen's forehead with his left index finger while his right hand was tenaciously clutching an object in one of his numerous right pockets.

Stephen had not been prepared for the danger but he had to defuse it with eclat. "I know whom you are talking about but I am not the person. You got the wrong man. I know whom you want to talk to. If you give me a minute, I can find him for you. Please sit down," Stephen said, pointing to a vacant chair as his guest Dr. Kim looked on in amazement and fear. The intruder stepped back but refused to sit. "If you is the guy, leave her alone. She is my baby's mother. I ain't gonna warn you again," he said and stormed out of the office.

Every observant occupant of the residence must have been seeing Metty Taylor but none, including Stephen, may have known that she had been writing Dr. Latham's name as her host. Stephen had sent for Ms. Metty Taylor who was working on the eleventh floor. He had told her of the encounter and his intention to sue her and her boyfriend for harassment. She had told Stephen and Dr. Kim, amid sobs, that she did not want to have anything to do with her ex. Begging for forgiveness, she had exposed the scheme Dr. Lee Thanm had devised while denying any wrongdoing on her part.

Now as Stephen turned in bed, he felt justified to tell his wife that he had gone to Long Island to help Dr. Lee Thanm that evening. The lie was, in his opinion, a measured retaliation against Dr. Thanm. Juliana had a great dislike for Dr. Thanm not only because of his notoriety among the women in the hospital but also because of her personal experience with him.

The first time she ever met Dr. Lee Thanm—in the laundry—he had denounced her for adding too much detergent to her clothes. It had been none of his business but Juliana had not told him so out of respect for her husband's colleagues. The next time they met—in the underground parking lot—Dr. Thanm had complained that Juliana had parked her car too close to the wall. The third time—in the frontage of the building—he had asked Juliana to hold Christopher with a very short leash to avoid his being knocked down by a car. She had not needed Dr. Lee Thanm to teach her how to raise her child. Those negative encounters which led to her unmitigated antipathy toward him, would ensure that she would never seek the truth from Dr. Lee Thanm.

Presently, Juliana joined Stephen in bed. "So, what was it that kept you out so long," she demanded in whispers. There was no hostility in her voice. She was rather empahtic, speaking with the tone expected of lovers at that time of the night. "Dr. Lee Thanm," Stephen answered. "Dr. Lee Thanm went to shop at Roosevelt Field. By the time he had done all his shopping, somebody had stolen his car battery. He had no way to return to Brooklyn. Of all the people at InnerFaith, I wonder why he chose to call me. I went because he appeared to be in dire straits. It was inexcusable that I did not call you," he said as they wrapped themselves around each other's arms, lips and bodies.

A Shift in the Emergency Room

Stephen slept continuously throughout the night, a very unusual occurrence for him. When he awoke in the morning, however, he was still feeling groggy. He would have liked to stay in bed for some hours so as to shake off the lethargy. He could never lie idle in bed, however, because there were always chores pending and accumulating. Unfortunately, there were very few things he could accomplish in the recumbent position. Recumbency, obviously, was made for rest and for thinking about what to do in the erect position.

The wall clock summoned Stephen to rise. It was nine in the morning. In the last thirty minutes, as he lay in bed, he had been brooding over the day's tasks. He needed to visit the barber's shop. His hair was overgrown. He knew it because his nurses said so. He had reached the level of ease and familiarity with his nurses that allowed them to remind him of his grooming without necessarily being intrusive. "It is time for another hair cut," both Mrs. Nosborrow and Mrs. Ranoche would say and everybody would laugh over it.

Usually, he would show up the next Monday with a clean cut. The new look would inevitably set off controversy among his nurses. Mrs. Nosborrow liked him better when he was clean cut. She would efface him with a comment like "oh my God! Don't you look sexy?"

Ms. Hayes, who liked him hairy, would counter that she no longer loved him. To that he would say, with a grin, "Wait for the two or three weeks it takes my hair to regrow. You and I will be friends again. Every affair waxes and wanes."

The only nurse who would say almost nothing to him, except when no one else was around, was the one who desired him, Ms. Painter. Whenever Ms. Hayes cracked one of her amusing jokes, Ms. Painter might participate in the ensuing social laughter. Certainly, she was not antisocial because her interactions with the rest of the staff were appropriate and predictable. It was just that any outpouring of emotion toward Dr. Latham might have been misinterpreted by others. She was the youngest and the only single one among the women, the only one who had no child. Mrs. Ranoche and Nosborrow, by virtue of being

44

happily married with at least three children each, did not suffer from that liability.

Seldom, Ms. Painter would corner Stephen in the unit and ask him a personal question like "Why did you come back home so late last night?" She seemed to have been watching his every move at home and in the office. Once when Stephen walked into the unit in scrubs she turned left and right and, having seen nobody else, quipped "bare assets" while tugging gently on the partially exposed hair on his chest and smiling. Stephen was determined not to go for the kill as his friends Drs. Kim and Kurman had urged him.

On occasions, she had made bold moves but Stephen could never be sure if she was serious. When she was preparing for the New York State Nurses' Association meeting in Buffalo, she told Stephen she was looking for somebody to accompany her there. Would Stephen like to go? she had asked. She was, on that occasion, fit for the cover of any reputable magazine. Stephen had smiled and moved away but not before complimenting her on her wonderful hairstyle and overall elegance.

That was long ago. Now as he lay in bed, his thoughts were on the previous night's melodramatic drive to and from Roosevelt Field. He looked at the wall separating their bedroom from Ms. Painter's studio and wondered what she was doing on the other side of it. He glanced at the wall clock again. It was almost ten. His spirit was willing to get up but his body was weak. With each passing minute he remembered one more thing he had to do that day. First, he needed to go and jog in Prospect Park. His muscles needed the toning. He had not been there for a while and his plans to participate in the marathon were in jeopardy. But if he went to the park first, the barber's shop might be crowded by the time he would get there. After further adjustment in his plans, he decided to go the park first to take advantage of the clement weather.

On his way back from the park, he would take a detour to the hardware store on Franklin Avenue to purchase his own set of a barber's instruments. Concerned about the possibility of contracting the AIDS virus from the barber's instruments, he had been planning to procure his own set for a good while.

No one had ever arrived at the barber's shop and unfurled a parcel with a new set of instruments to be used exclusively for his own hair. The shop was always full of customers, young men discussing their exploits and sports, and neighborhood people just having a good time. The introduction of his own instruments would undoubtedly cause consternation. He would have to explain his bizarre behavior.

He would tell the barber and his customers that he was allergic to the dandruff in other people's hair. The lie would hurt no one. Rather, it might fetch him some sympathy. The truth, he feared, might dispense a notion of superiority and hubris to the, largely, low-income customers especially if it became known that he was a physician. On several occasions in the past, while rocking the chair at the barber's command, he'd heard somebody counsel the barber to give the doctor a great look.

His wife Juliana was also partially awake. She turned from left lateral to the prone before ending in the right lateral position. Stephen was also changing positions. This was the routine prelude to rising. He was now at the edge of the bed facing the wide bedroom. The floor was a mess with his medical journals and books. Whatever happened to his plan to buy a bookshelf, he did not remember. Among all things he planned to accomplish that day, he attached the highest priority to buying a book shelf, yet again expanding his day. That was the only way he was going to clean up the room.

The phone rang. He could no longer dillydally. He arose, as did Juliana and Christopher, in his bedroom. On the other end of the line was an overworked Intern calling to inform Stephen that the patient he had seen the previous day with bleeding appeared to have resumed bleeding.

"What is the color of his stool?" Stephen asked.

"Yellow and the test for occult blood is negative," said the intern.

"What did you get when you lavaged his stomach?"

"Clear fluid, free of blood."

"What are his vital signs?"

"Pulse is seventy-eight and blood pressure is one-twenty over eighty and—"

Stephen interrupted, "You still haven't told me why you think the patient is bleeding. How many units of blood did you transfuse him throughout the night?"

"None," answered the intern.

"Let me speak with the senior Resident."

"He is not in the unit right now."

"The patient is not bleeding. Tell your senior Resident to see him. Bye."

He hung up. "There goes my day," he exclaimed with resignation. In that exclamation, he was alluding to the fact that going to see the patient had to take precedence over all other plans. He could hardly accomplish anything, even when he thought he had leisure time.

He had to see the patient because he was not sure of what the intern had written. Most likely, the intern's note must have stated "Dr. Latham informed that patient is re-bleeding. Dr. Latham said the patient is not bleeding and that the case should be discussed with the senior resident." He probably omitted the rest of the conversation even though it was critical to Dr. Latham's conclusion.

There was a significant chance that the patient would re-bleed within the first two days. Trial lawyers knew that more than did interns. If the patient should re-bleed and the case went to court, the lawyer would have a field day with the intern's note. Much as he hated to be driven by legal imperatives, rather than his own good conscience and sound medical judgement in the care of his patients, he had to go in, reevaluate the patient and write a counter note just in case. He was convinced that the patient had not re-bled based on the fact that there was no blood in his stomach and rectum and the stability of his vital signs. That meant he did not have to hurry.

Juliana had been following the conversation between Stephen and the intern as she always did whenever he was called from the hospital. She knew that in his next move, he would have to go to the hospital. She could never predict how long he would stay. They had an appointment for a family photograph at Sears.

"Not so fast, Steve," Juliana said. "Before you rush out of the house so fast, don't forget that our appointment is at eleven-thirty this morning."

"Which appointment, J.?"

"Steve, have you forgotten that we have an appointment for a family photograph at Sears? We discussed it last night because I knew you'd have to go and see your patient this morning."

"I don't remember discussing it last night," Stephen said. He would not say they had not because he did not want a confrontation.

"The appointment is at eleven-thirty, just about an hour from now. The last time we were to go, you canceled. Remember? Let's get ready and go please. This is the best deal we can get."

"All right, get Christopher ready. Let's go. You know it takes me less than ten minutes to get ready." After the previous day's events, especially the way he had left for the tennis court, Stephen would let her win this round. He recalled that they had been talking about the family photograph for some days. Certainly, he needed an enlarged photograph of his family, something Christopher would be proud of in his later years. Who would say if and when the family's fortune might soar? The photograph might just possibly become a priceless piece of art. He would go to the hospital after the photographic session.

While they were getting dressed, Juliana asked him about the previous night's outing. She was standing before the mirror with make-up in her hand. Stephen looked at her contour in the mirror, their eyes met and they smiled in approval of the image.

"So Steve, what did you say happened to Dr. Lee Thanm yesterday?"

"I meant to tell you but I felt too sleepy in the shower and I just went to sleep."

"You were so sleepy, I could not arouse you. But that was after you had told me."

"No, I did not, J."

"Yes, you did. How would I have known?"

"Well, I don't remember anything about it." Still conciliatory and bent on avoiding conflict, he conceded his amnesia.

"Lee Thanm, it served him right. He is so full of himself," said Juliana.

The phone rang again. Everyone was fully dressed and set to go.

"Hello. Dr. Latham," announced Stephen.

"This is Ms. Camille Jenkins. Dr. Latham, could you please go and cover the emergency department? Dr. Kim has been working for the last eighteen hours and he is understandably exhausted. Dr. Lucas who was supposed to have relieved him three hours ago is unable to do so because of a death in his family in the Caribbean. We have been looking for a reliever, to no avail. If you are available, we could negotiate your remuneration now. I can assure you, we are very flexible at this point."

"Hold on a second, please." Stephen lowered the receiver down to his waist level, blocking any reception with his hand before turning to his wife. "J. I have to go and relieve Dr. Marcel Kim in the emergency room. The administrator, Ms. Jenkins is on the line. Dr. Kim has been working for the last twenty-four hours. You know what a mess that emergency room is. The guy must be more tired than you can imagine. I know this is going to be as hard for you as it will be for me but we probably have to postpone the picture session till another day even if it's going to cost us more. Let me go, for Dr. Kim's sake."

The humanitarian argument bore weight with her because she had a favorable opinion of Dr. Kim. Stephen had added six hours to the eighteen Dr. Kim had been working for to elicit more sympathy for Dr. Kim and more willingness on Juliana's part to let him go. She was also aware of the fact that on similar occasions in the past, Dr. Kim had rushed to Stephen's rescue. Like Stephen always stressed to her, one good turn deserves another. Juliana was also familiar with

48

the financial dynamics of such impromptu arrangements although Stephen deliberately suppressed that aspect of the arrangement so that she might not ask for her fair share.

Stephen bellowed into the receiver, "All right, Ms. Jenkins this is very hard for me to do because of the plans I had laid out for the day. Not only will this spoil my day, I would have a lot of apologies to make to the people I am going to have to disappoint. Some of the people will have to be settled materially and my ability to take up the offer would depend on how flexible you are willing to be."

"What do you want? Will two thousand do?" Ms. Jenkins asked.

"Make it twenty-five hundred," he said. Stephen turned around to see if Juliana was listening to the bargaining. Fortunately for him, she had drifted away.

"It's a deal. Dr. Kurman will relieve you at eight."

Stephen knew he could not refuse an offer to make twenty-five hundred dollars in eight hours. Such opportunities knocked very seldom in his practice. He wondered why he had not asked for more. After all, the hospital administration had their back to the wall. Dr. Kim had been threatening to abdicate his post. By law, the administration had to staff the emergency room with at least one physician at all times. Failure to do so would have brought the state in. No hospital administration in the city liked the State Department of Health breathing down their throat. The administrators' dislike for the state oversight was surpassed only by doctors aversion to administrative laymen telling them how to practice medicine. Stephen clenched his teeth, scratched his head in regret over not having extracted more from Ms. Jenkins. "Those Scrooges. They had their back against the wall. I could have gotten more from them," he lamented.

Presently, he changed into his scrubs, gathered his stethoscope and other gadgets. His phone rang one more time. His heart skipped a beat. Every time his phone rang, his plans were thrown into a new state of disarray. In twenty minutes, he must get to the floor to see his patient and then arrive at the emergency room to relieve Dr. Kim. After all, he was being paid twenty-five hundred dollars for eight hours. As he reached for the phone, he prayed the caller would not raise another issue that must receive emergent attention. Just as he grasped the handset, it stopped ringing. "Thank God," he prayed.

Juliana had said nothing to her husband's sudden and frequent change of plans and to his plea to let him go and relieve his friend, Dr. Kim. Her silence meant, to her and to Stephen, acquiescence. She understood the altruism inherent in the arrangement since the stranded and helpless Dr. Kim was badly in need of relief. And when it was time for him to go, she planted on him a reluctant kiss after wresting a good sum of money for shopping.

Stephen briefly saw his patient on the floor and still made it to the emergency room in good time. Dr. Kim was elated to see him. Stephen made it clear he had agreed to come mainly because he, Kim, was the one in need of relief. Implicit in the explanation was that Dr. Kim owed him a debt. The hand-over ceremony was brief because there were no patients waiting to be seen. All the emergency room physicians desired such clean slates. No one wanted to be saddled with patients badly managed by an exhausted, homebound physician.

Stephen signed the Physicians' Assignment book and marked the three asterisks after his name which was understood by the doctors and the administration that the shift was covered under a special financial arrangement. Then he exchanged greetings with his nurses, physician assistants, and other staff members. The first patient he saw was a thirty-year-old man who had called the Emergency Medical System to his fourth floor apartment because of a skin rash he had borne on his right shin for the last two years. The EMS technicians were very upset, justifiably so, because the patient had claimed he could not walk. He seemed to know his rights for he had insisted that the technicians carry him down the stairs as there was no elevator in the building. This was one of the worst abuses of the EMS system. Able-bodied young men (as far as Stephen could tell, women were not guilty of it) often pretended that they could not walk. These were men who lived in high-rise buildings often without functioning elevators. The EMS technicians were not allowed to abandon a patient even when the latter was obviously feigning paralysis. The bosses, apparently, did not care how the technicians got the patients into the ambulances. They just had to get them there. If the technicians found a three hundred pound caller pacing on the tenth floor of a dilapidated building and the gorilla suddenly feigned paralysis, the technicians had no choice but to carry him down the stairs. Low back pain was the wages of such heavy lifting.

This patient weighed two hundred and fifty pounds, not a light burden to bear. Luckily for the EMS team, he was their last assignment for the shift. Both technicians, a young man and a woman Stephen had come to know were very dedicated. They had seen a lot of abuse of the system but this particular episode, literally, broke the young woman's back. When she complained about her back, Stephen gave her a note to stay home and rest for the next three days, something he rarely did even when demanded by patients.

Then Stephen went into the room to see the patient.

"I am Dr. Latham. What is your name please?"

"Strong, Louis Strong," said the patient.

He may well have been Louis Weak as far as Stephen was concerned. His name was a misnomer. But he dared not tease the patient. Physicians know better than to express their personal feelings, even in jest, about aspects of patients' lives that had no bearing on the diagnosis or prognosis. Any indiscretion could jeopardize their relationship with their patients. Stephen was a strong believer in, and a practitioner of, that tenet.

"Mr. Strong, what can I do for you?" asked Stephen.

"I got a rash on my leg and my girl said it could be due to an ulcer from flesh-eating strep. She said I could lose my leg unless I got a needle and the red-and-black antibiotic; that strong one that turns your stomach when you take it. She said I must stop walking immediately. She is a nurse in this hospital; Ms. Joyce Stanwell. Do you know her?"

Stephen ignored the question and examined the rash which was an area of chronic change in the middle of the right leg. Eccentrically placed in the lower pole of the area were some excoriations from repeated scratching.

"You mean that you called the ambulance because your girlfriend said the rash on your leg may be an ulcer?" Stephen asked.

"She said I might lose my leg and I should not walk on it again," Mr. Strong said.

It turned out Ms. Stanwell was a messenger in the dietary department. Her main job was to transport food to the patients and the dishes back to the kitchen. She was not involved in any patient care whatsoever. Unfortunately, any woman who worked in the hospital, especially if she wore white apparel, was assumed by some patients, especially the uneducated, to be a nurse. No doubt, some hospital employees impersonated nurses and doctors in their communities. But their practices flourished not solely on the basis of their panache. Some physicians and nurses were too intimidating in their personality, too aloof in their body language and too esoteric in their choice of words. The rare physician who elected to tell his patient about "Streptococcus pyogenes-induced necrotizing fasciitis" risked losing his patient to the hospital-based quack who may have been mesmerized by a case of "flesh-eating strep" while transporting food to the patient's room. Unfortunately, any advice given by the "nurse" was likely to be incorporated by the patient into his overall insight and therapeutic regimen.

"An ulcer only means a break or gap in the skin. You got to take care of it. Keep it clean and dressed. The nurse will dress it now and

51

I will refer you to the clinic. This rash does not belong in the emergency department," said Stephen.

"Can you call the ambulance to take me home? I ain't got no car fare. And I ain't got no Medicaid card."

"I am sorry I can't help you with that. You gonna have to find a way to get home, unfortunately," Stephen said in a nonchalant manner as he headed to see his next patient.

He could hear Mr. Strong complaining bitterly that the doctor had not attended him properly. Specifically, he complained that the doctor had not placed the instrument on his chest as other doctors had done in the past. Though the discharging nurse tried to placate him, all her pleas seemed to be falling on deaf ears. Still pacing the aisle, he vowed to lodge a formal complaint with the administration. Stephen was prompted to take a second look at the patient's chart to make sure there was adequate documentation. He was satisfied with the cursory look he had cast at the chronic rash. Some patients expected the doctor to spend hours with them, examining them from head to toe. They did not understand that the physical examination was meant to be commensurate with the acuteness and seriousness of the problem. No matter what, some patients were bound to be dissatisfied. But the emergency room physician had to move on.

Mr. Joseph Troman, Stephen's next patient, was a seventy-year-old man who was brought to the emergency room after the home attendant complained that his hand had been jerking violently. The patient had a mental condition that left him with poor memory and mild confusion. Seizures had not been part of the picture. The home attendant had complained that the episode had lasted barely a minute.

Upon arrival in the emergency department, the patient insisted on being discharged home because there was nothing wrong with him. He said he had told the ambulance crew so but they had insisted on bringing him in for evaluation. By the time Stephen got to him, the home attendant had vanished. Stephen called the two phone numbers listed in the chart for the next-of-kin. One was not in service while calls to the other were not answered.

Stephen's first order of business was to examine the patient's mental status. His credibility would depend on his mental status. The history given to the ambulance crew by the home attendant could not be independently corroborated. Stephen was aware of several occasions in the past when home attendants had dumped their elderly clients in the emergency room in order to attend all-night parties. It usually happened on Friday or Saturday. The home attendant would bring her client during the day in order to have time to prepare for the party.

On at least one occasion that Stephen could remember, the party had taken place in the client's home.

The home attendant would complain, over the patient's vigorous objection, of the latter's bizarre behavior. In Stephen's experience if the elderly client had a clear sensorium he or she, not the home attendant, was likely to be telling the truth. Often, that was the only indication that the attendant was most likely abusing, or taking advantage of, the elderly or disabled client. Such a suspicion would prompt the astute physician to call the client's next of kin. Unfortunately, some of the patients' next of kins were no more responsible than the home attendants. They only emerged after the patients' demise to take stock of the heirloom. If Stephen could establish that the patient was aware of his surroundings and had appropriate response to simple questions he would let the patient go. He proceeded to question Mr. Troman. Standing behind him and slightly to his left were Willie Gibbs, the medical student and Nurse Jennifer Norville.

"Mr. Troman, what can I do for you?" asked Stephen.

Troman dipped his hands in his pocket and brought out three dollars and presented it to Stephen.

"What is this for, Sir?"

"This is the cab fare. You do look like the cab driver who brought me here. Are you not?"

"I am Dr. Latham and I am here to take care of you. You came here by the ambulance. You don't have to pay for the ride. Tax payers will pick up the tab. What can I do for you now?"

"I want to go home to my young wife and kids," said Mr. Troman.

"Do you know where you are?"

"Yes. D.C. General Hospital."

"Mr. Troman, you are in Brooklyn, New York. This is InnerFaith Hospital, Brooklyn."

"I want to go home."

"If you answer these questions correctly, I'm gonna let you go home now. First, what is today's date?" asked Stephen.

"Twenty-fifth of April."

"What year?"

"1910," answered Mr. Troman.

"Well, in 1910, you had not even been born yet. Who is the mayor of this city?"

"That bum out there who does not know what he is doing? We've got a contract out on him. Watch out. He is going to last only four years and we'll take him out."

"But what is his name?" Stephen insisted.

"Mike Tyson."

Although the patient deserved pity and not sacrifice, Stephen and his team permitted themselves brief laughter. They had seen Alzheimer's patients before with their inappropriate answers to questions. None, however, had ever been as amusing as Mr. Troman's.

"Mr. Troman, do you know who the president of this country is?"

"Don King. He too has got only four years to remain in office. We have a contract out on him too."

Stephen was now convinced that the patient needed further evaluation. There appeared to be some bizarre logic in his answers. Possibly his only interest had been boxing. For a man who lived in the world of boxing and whose brain had very limited capacity to retain facts, it was hardly surprising that the two most powerful men were Tyson and King. Stephen was eager to find out Mr. Troman's relationship to boxing. He would want to know if he was dealing with a former heavy weight punching bag whose brain had been messed up by repeated jabs to the head. Since the patient was not in immediate danger he ordered blood and urine tests and proceeded to see the next patient being rolled in by the ambulance crew.

The next patient was a thirty-six-year-old man who had called the ambulance to take him to the hospital because of severe pain in his rectum. He had been sitting in the barber's shop right across the street when he was stricken by the incapacitating pain. Somebody had called the ambulance for him. By the time the ambulance had arrived the pain had completely abated. He did not want to go to the hospital but the ambulance crew and the clientele in the shop had prodded him to go.

In the emergency, his papers were processed immediately as there were no other patients ahead of him. The triage nurse took him in right away. He was well known to her, having presented to the department about six months earlier with the same complaint. Actually their first encounter had occurred at Brookdale Hospital emergency department where the patient had presented with the same complaint. Although that was nine months earlier, memory of him was still vivid in her mind.

Ms. Brosier, the triage nurse, considered Mr. Bishop a filthy homosexual who would never learn from his negative experience. Many of the other regular staffers in the department also knew Mr. Bishop and had very high disapproval ratings of him. Ms. Brosier was expressing their collective feeling when she said, while handing the chart over to Stephen, "I have the homo in bed two. He came with his usual complaint—pain in the rectum. You don't have to hurry to see him because you did not advise him to insert anything in there. Once you finish with him, he will go back to the same practice. Take your time; he can afford to wait."

At that point two stern-looking policemen barged into the emergency room looking for a wounded felon. Nobody was surprised to see them. The emergency department was a familiar station in the investigation of every crime in which one party may have escaped with wounds. The countenance of the officers was such that a very serious crime had been committed. Even before they spoke, Stephen's gut feeling was that an officer may have been hurt.

Officer One asked, "Has any of you seen this man here in the last twelve hours?" while holding a hazy sketch of a man. One by one, the staff members, including Stephen, took turns to examine the sketch. They all shook their heads in disgust for failing to make the positive identification.

Officer Two explained why the man was wanted. "He was involved in a holdup in a bodega on Washington and Bergen," he said, pointing in the direction of that street crossing. The gesture was an unnecessary reflex as they all were familiar with the neighborhood. "The first officer that responded to the call exchanged fire with him. The officer was hit in the arm. Fortunately, he is expected to recover. We believe that the assailant was hit in the leg and is seeking care in some facility. There is a twenty-thousand dollar reward for information leading to his arrest. He is considered armed and extremely dangerous," the officer concluded.

The officer's carrot prompted the emergency room staff each to take a second, and in some cases a third and a fourth look at the picture. The fact that the criminal was armed and dangerous did not bother any of them. The harder each staffer looked at the picture, the more it appeared as if he or she knew someone like that. Stephen refused to take a second look though he also would have liked to receive the huge cash reward. He stood a slim chance of identifying the gun man. Among his coterie of friends were men and women from various walks of life, but, thankfully, none of them owned or knew how to operate a .45 Magnum. As he watched his staff scrutinize the hazy sketch and scratch their heads in disgust, he realized how twenty thousand dollars could almost create resemblance where there was none. He felt sorry for the mentally retarded who might be positively identified and made to confess under duress.

Once more, each of the staff members shook their heads and wrung their hands in utter disgust for letting the twenty thousand dollars slip by. As the officers walked away, the transporter, Mr. Climes, took a hard look at the phlebotomist, Jerome Seever, who was believed to be a drug addict but was fondly called "bloodsucker."

"Why are you looking at me like that?" Mr. Seever asked.

"I am still trying to make the positive identification, blood sucker. If only I did not have to testify in court . . . I would have sacrificed someone," said Mr. Climes.

Everyone burst out laughing.

Stephen was completing some paper work. The clerical work was often intimidating especially whenever he treated employees with job-related injuries. First he would complete the patient's medical record. Then he would fill out a stack of documents for the Federal agency in charge of occupational hazards, another set of forms for the Employee Union and the most annoying, a thick pile of documents for workers' compensation. It did not matter that the injured worker had no intention to seek compensation or that the injury was too minor to attract a sizeable award.

He needed to hurry because patients were now coming in a steady stream. The emergency department was unpredictable. Patients often came in a stampede and if that happened, Stephen and his two assistants and nurses would be easily overwhelmed. Unfortunately, the staffs were not expected to move at breakneck speed. Every patient wanted the doctor to dispatch the preceding patient but to spend quality time with him or her.

At the bedside, the patient was falling out with Ms. Brosier, the triage nurse. The exchange was intense and emotional. The patient, Mr. Bishop, had asked for the location of the men's bathroom in order to evacuate his full bladder. Ms. Brosier had told him to wait because she was busy. Mr. Bishop was justifiably upset because far from attending to any patient, Ms. Brosier had been busy browsing at the policeman's picture in the hope of winning the twenty thousand dollars. In the meantime, another nurse had shown Mr. Bishop the bathroom.

Having failed to win the policeman's reward, Ms. Brosier fetched a urinal for Mr. Bishop. She had forgotten exactly what the patient had asked for. Mr. Bishop was furious and Ms. Brosier could see the frown on his face. She launched a preemptive verbal blast.

"You have an attitude. I told you I would be with you. Didn't you see I was busy doing something?" She thrust the urinal to Mr. Bishop.

"What am I gonna do with this? This is not what I asked you for. If you don't like this job, you shouldn't be here. In fact, you don't belong here."

"It is not my fault you are here. Excuse my language but you are a pain in the you know where. You really are. I am only helping to clean up the mess but you've got an attitude and I'm not gonna take it." She turned in the direction of the other staff writing notes at the nurse's desk to see if they supported her dressing down the homosexual. She figured they shared her visceral disapproval of his sexual orientation.

"You need to be straightened out. Who is your boss here? I'm gonna have to write you up," threatened Mr. Bishop.

"Ain't no one else here but me. You can go to the administration on Monday. This is my name." She pointed to her badge over her left nipple.

Even as she put up the front, she was contemplating her defense should the patient make good his vow to lodge a complaint with the administration. Once they left the emergency room, most patients forgave and forgot what they considered negligent care especially when such care did not result in physical injury. But Ms. Brosier could not be sure that Mr. Bishop would follow the rule rather than the exception.

The exchange between Ms. Brosier and Mr. Bishop was so heated that the patient was likely to leave with lingering animosity except, perhaps, he was mollified by other staff members. Stephen sensed that Bishop had been hurt by the unfair insinuations about his sexuality. Unfortunately, should Mr. Bishop lodge a complaint, not much would come out of it. It would be hard for him to prove any wrongdoing when he was ignored by one nurse and attended by another almost immediately. The odds and witnesses were stacked in favor of the triage nurse. However, in the big picture, as Stephen saw it, such complaints were inimical to the finances and reputation of the institution. He approached Mr. Bishop with the latter's chart in hand.

"Are you the doctor?" asked Mr. Bishop.

"Yes, I am Dr. Latham. What can I do for you? Why did you come to the emergency room?"

"I was sitting in the barber's shop right across the street from here (pointing in the direction of the shop) when very severe rectal pain struck me."

"How long did it last?"

"About five minutes."

"So by the time you arrived here it had completely subsided?"

Bishop nodded in the affirmative.

"So why did you still come? Is this the first time you are experiencing it?" asked Stephen.

"I was advised by some customers in the shop that it might be the chair and that I might need the report."

"So, some smart guy said you could sue the makers of the chair if I attribute your pain to it and that's why you came?"

"And the barber's shop too. But I know the barber ain't got no money. Three years ago I had a similar attack and I went to Brookdale. The doctor ran all kinds of tests but he could not find anything wrong."

"So what did the doctor tell you was the cause of the pain?"

"After all the tests, they said I was suffering from proc—proc—I have forgotten the name."

"Proctalgia fugax?"

Mr. Bishop jabbed the air with his right index finger. "That is the name. That is what they said I got."

"Was the doctor who treated you Dr. James Salman?" inquired Stephen.

"Yes. Do you know him?" Mr. Bishop asked.

Stephen smiled but did not answer the question. He knew he was onto something. He had a few more questions to ask the patient. As long as the source of his uncanny knowledge of the patient's problem remained a mystery, the latter was likely to stay engaged and to accept his decisions and instructions with gospel faith. Two years previously, he had attended a conference on "Diseases of the Anus and Rectum" at the Downstate Medical Center where his colleague at Brookdale Hospital had presented the case of a young man he had seen several months previously. The patient, according to Dr. Salman, had been struck with the worse pain of his life while making love to his new girlfriend. The pain had lasted, fortunately for the patient, only several minutes and by the time the ambulance had taken him to the emergency room, he had become asymptomatic. Dr. Salman had detailed all the tests they had performed.

Stephen remembered it vividly because at the end of the conference, Dr. Salman had won the best presenter award, which entitled him to an all-expenses-paid trip for two to Niagara Falls. As was customary, Dr. Salman had neither mentioned the patient's name nor shown his photograph. Everything else Dr. Salman said about his patient matched Mr. Bishop. At the side bar over that evening's dinner, Dr. Salman had told Stephen that several misconceptions surrounded the case. First, the emergency room staff, especially one of the staff nurses, had presumed he was a homosexual and had treated him with spite. Secondly, the patient himself had thought his girlfriend, who was a mystic, had brought a spell upon him. He broke up with her immediately after that.

If he could establish that he was, in fact, dealing with the same patient, Stephen thought, he could dispose of him immediately for the pace was picking up. Several patients were waiting to be seen. Most of them were well known to the staffers. Most probably, the same select few patients were known to the emergency room staffers in other Brooklyn hospitals. They consumed care way out of proportion to their numbers. Some of them must have made the rounds from one nearby hospital to another within that week. One advantage for the system was that when proper history was taken by the doctor or given by the patient, unnecessary tests could be avoided. A few more questions for Mr. Bishop was all Stephen had to offer him.

Stephen, turning to Mr. Bishop said, "Let me ask a few more questions about the attack which was treated at Brookdale."

"Go ahead, Doc."

"Did it start while you were making love to your girlfriend?"

"Yes," nodding.

"Was she a mystic?"

"Yes. How did you know all that, doc?" asked Mr. Bishop. He couldn't believe that Stephen, whom he had never met before, had so much insight into his complaint. Maybe Dr. Salman had told Dr. Latham about him, he thought. Still, the fact that he still retained the minutest details of the case, was testimony to the kind of brain God had given doctors. He continued to wonder. "Did the Brookdale doctor tell you about me?"

"Not fully. Obviously, the state law prohibits him from mentioning your name when talking about your case. That way, your confidentiality is protected, although some people don't worry unnecessarily about it. The advantage to you is that your complaint will often precede you anonymously. If you meet a doctor who remembers your history, you could avoid phlebotomy and waste of time. Let me clear up a few issues before I discharge you.

"Given the circumstances under which you first became aware of this condition, you probably broke up with that your new lover. She had nothing to do with it. If you still love, and are still available for her, you can consider reconciliation. I have good and bad news regarding your condition. The bad news is that you may or may not suffer further attacks of pain in future. The good news, more importantly, is that it should not cost you a penny or your life. It will not degenerate into a more life-threatening condition like cancer. Finally, in every profession, including medicine, you will find some bad apples. I suggest that you forget and forgive your encounter with the nurse. She stands alone among all the nurses here as the bad apple. Let me handle her.

59

One other thing is that everytime a man presents with pain in the rectum or anus, he is presumed to be gay. Don't let it bother you as long as you are treated with customary respect and obscene comments are not made about you."

"She is so rude, she doesn't belong here. I had intended to lodge a written report but I will now make only a verbal one to the supervisor because of your intervention. Do you have an office outside the hospital?" Mr. Bishop asked.

"Yes. This is my card. You can call at any time for an appointment."

"I surely will."

Stephen completed Mr. Bishop's papers presently and went to see the next patient. His two Physician Assistants, Jamelon and Drammond, were working hard to clear the patients with rather mundane complaints. Mr. Drammond had just seen a sixty-five-year-old woman with severe pain in the left shoulder. He had thought it was a routine case of arthritis of the shoulder when he first saw the patient's chart and read the triage nurse's note. Drammond made an interesting discovery when he was about to examine the patient.

The patient had been seated on one of the chairs near the nurse's desk because of the simplicity of her complaint. She had placed her carry-on bag precariously at the edge of the chair, beside herself. Drammond tried to place the bag on the floor so as to create room for range of motion testing. He almost could not lift up the bag.

"Why is your bag so heavy, Ms. Brandson?" Drammond had asked her. She had replied that that was her change. Finding it kind of strange, Mr. Drammond called Stephen to the patient's side and presented the weirdo. Stephen peered into the bag and saw the large quantity of dimes, nickels and quarters. There were also three packs of cigarettes.

"Ms. Brandson," said Stephen, "why do you carry so much change on you? This is too much load on your shoulder. That is why you have shoulder pain."

"My grandson's got a drug problem. I can't leave the change at home. It will be gone," said Ms. Brandson.

"But why not put the money in the bank?"

"After paying all my bills, I can only afford nickel-and-dime transactions. My grandson would figure out a way to withdraw the money from the bank."

"What if you are mugged?"

Brandson stopped down and pulled from under her left sock a small black wallet. Inside it were well-arranged clean notes of various denominations. The total must have been more than five hundred dollars. "They gonna have to kill me," she said of the muggers, "before they can get this."

"Ms. Brandson, I need to also talk to you about the other content of your carry-on bag, the cigarette. You should give it up if you want to stay alive and well," explained Stephen.

"I got bad nerves. I could not relax without smoking all the cigarettes you are seeing in there."

"These would only make your nerves worse. It seems to me that you do not need medication. What you need to do is change your lifestyle. You're gonna have to find a way to save your money short of dragging it about. And you're gonna have to quit smoking two and a half packs per day. You will receive some Tylenol for your pain for a few days but I hope that you understand what we have told you."

Mr. Jamelon was also waiting to discuss his patient with Stephen. He did not know what to do with her. Steven turned to him and asked, "What do you have, Jame?"

"I got this twenty-eight-year-old woman who was seen here earlier in the morning with a deep glass cut in her right hand. Dr. Kim sutured it but she had refused injection of painkiller medications. Dr. Kim then gave her a prescription for Tylenol with codeine for the pain. She has filled the prescription and is here with the medicines. She says she doesn't like to take medications," said Mr. Jamelon.

"Does she want the injection now?"

"Absolutely not, she says."

Stephen was now boiling with fury and frustration. "Let's go and see her," he said.

"Ms. Jones, I am Dr. Latham. I understand Dr. Kim saw and treated you this morning."

"These are the medicines he prescribed for me. I just don't like taking medicines. But my hand is still hurting," complained Ms. Jones.

Stephen was now standing behind the patient washing his hands while Jamelon, his physician assistant, was standing in front of her. He dried his hands. He could not control his frustration and irritation at that point. With his teeth clenched, his hands clawed and tremulous, he moved and motioned as if he was going to place a choke hold on the young woman's neck. He inhaled deeply and restrained himself. That display was watched by Jamelon alone since Stephen was standing behind the patient but it was adequate reaction for him. It contrasted sharply with the niceties he had been showing his patients even when their actions were totally ridiculous. But what could he do for Ms. Jones?

Stephen moved through a semicircle and ended directly before his patient. "Ms. Jones," he began to address her, "you came here this morning with a cut you sustained from broken glass while washing dishes. You carried on for sometime before Dr. Kim could suture the laceration. You refused the tetanus and painkiller injections. He gave you a prescription for oral painkillers and antibiotics. You have now come back with severe pain and the medicines. You absolutely don't want the injections. I just want to tell you that if the wound becomes infected and you lose your hand or your life, nobody would, could or should blame the hospital, doctors and nurses. Perhaps whom you need now is the chaplain to say your Nunc Dimittis." He stormed out of the room, with Jamelon and the Nurse Eilen McCoy following suit.

He went to see Ms. Eugenia Brown who was already growing restless and fuming after waiting for two hours. "What can I do for you?" Stephen asked her.

"I have been waiting here for the last two hours while all the doctors are messing with the nurses at the desk. I don't need to come here and see the men touching and ogling the women. They should do that at home, not here while patients are waiting to be attended. I have been to many hospitals and this is not how to treat a patient. I was just about to sign out and go to Brookville," said Ms. Brown.

"First of all, none of the men at the desk is a doctor. You've got three medical students, a phlebotomist and an X-ray technician waiting for orders. If you would like to see one of them, I am sure they would not mind. Whether you would be satisfied with the service is another story. Secondly the average waiting time in emergency rooms in this state is eight hours. In Brookville Hospital where you intend to go, it is ten hours. I have worked there, too. I am aware, however, that the pasture on the other side of the fence is always greener. If you still want to sign out and leave, be my guest." Stephen felt the need to address the patient's complaints fairly and firmly.

Ms. Brown was a frequent visitor to the emergency room. She always created confusion during her visits to the emergency. During her last visit, she had claimed that her wallet with two hundred dollars had been stolen and had demanded repayment from the hospital. Still, in an earlier visit she had claimed that the X-ray technician had sexually molested her. Both cases were awaiting final determination. The staff had warned Stephen to be careful with the troublemaker. He took care to go into the room with two female nurse chaperones—Ms. McCoy and Ms. Norville.

"Let's get it over with please. I've got more important things to do," said Ms. Brown.

"What can we do for you now, Ms. Brown?"

"I got diarrhea. My bowels were not moving for four days so I gave myself an enema yesterday. I was running to the bathroom every five minutes throughout yesterday. It stopped this morning," said Ms. Brown.

"So you were perfectly normal until four days ago?" asked Stephen.

"I had diarrhea last week. It stopped after I took some medicine my sister had given me. I don't remember the name of the pill right now."

"So you had diarrhea last week?"

Ms. Brown nodded, with her voice mellow, admitting she did.

"Then the medicine you took caused your constipation?"

She nodded again.

"Then you took medication for the constipation which reproduced diarrhea?" asked Stephen.

"Unless I do that my bowels do not move," explained Ms. Brown.

"For how long has the vicious cycle been going on?"

"My bowels have been acting up for the last two years."

Stephen felt like telling Ms. Brown "Get out of here. Go and get a life and forget about your bowels." He could not afford to be so harsh. Physicians are one set of public officials who cannot always express their raw opinion to their clients though the self-inhibition is not always borne out of a sense of decorum. There is commonly the desire to accommodate, rather than alienate, the patient because it matters to the bottom line. The patient whose request is turned down here can get what he or she wants down the block from another physician. Some patients however, are so fastidious that every physician who encounters them is likely to throw his or her arms in the air in surrender. Stephen's method of dealing with such patients was to show firmness from the word go.

He turned to Ms. Brown and said, "My suggestion and advice to you are that you should not try to manipulate your bowels the way you have been doing. Since your diarrhea has stopped, I am discharging you without medication. I will give you two referrals, to the medical clinic and the Center for Mental Health."

"What, are you saying I am crazy? I am not crazy."

"No, that is not what I am saying. It is routine for us to refer patients with complaints like yours to the psychologist. Frequently, medications for depression are helpful."

Ms. Brown stood up. "I was given those before but I never took them because I'm not crazy and I'm not seeing any psychiatrist." She walked out of the emergency room. Stephen, too, moved on to the next patient.

Mr. Drammond was waiting to discuss his next patient. He had seen a thirty-two-year-old man from the Bedford homeless shelter who complained of severe cough, body aches and pains and weakness. His physical examination was normal as were his laboratory test results. Drammond had completed his discharge papers but Mr. Reuben Carlone, for that was his name, refused to go home. Drammond told Stephen that the patient was becoming very cantankerous. Stephen decided to talk to the patient alone. Too much bad blood had already flowed between Drammond and the patient and matters could only get worse if Drammond re-entered the room.

Stephen introduced himself to the patient. "I am Dr. Latham. My assistant has already seen you but it seems you are not satisfied with the care you've received."

"I'm gonna be straight with you because you are my man. Fact is, I cannot go back to the shelter. They will kill me at first sight," said Mr. Carlone.

"Who are they?"

"Like I said, I ain't gonna lie to you, my man. I sold some dope for some guys last night. Then I met one crackhead street worker. When I was finished with her, the money was gone. I ain't got the money, man. They must be looking for me right now. I got to be admitted until the matter is taken care of."

"My man, that is unfortunate, but I can't admit you because your examination and all labs are normal. If I admit you, my license could be taken away. Do you want something like that to happen to me?" asked Stephen.

"No, not at all. You are cool. You are cool. Hmmmmm. Can you call me an ambulance to take me to Kings County Hospital? I might have better luck there."

"That would not be justified either, unfortunately. What I could do is to call a cab for you."

"I ain't got no cab fare," said Mr. Carlone.

Stephen dipped his hands into his pocket and found three dollars, which he gave to Mr. Carlone. "Here, take. It is for your taxi fare. I will ask the clerk to call a cab for you. Take care."

By the time Mr. Carlone had dressed up, the cab was waiting on St. Marks Avenue. He shook hands with Stephen. "Take care, my man," he said and made for the door.

Good riddance, good relief, Stephen thought. It was not unusual for patients, especially unemployed shelter residents and the homeless to come into the emergency department demanding admission. That life was rough on the streets was obvious even to the most inept and indifferent observer. The sight of the homeless, diaphoretic men in a tug-of-war with their junk-filled wagons was not rare around the hospital. But no one needed to go into the streets to imagine the hardships the homeless faced. How they coped with the lack of proper toilet and bathroom facilities, the constant harassment and oversight of law enforcement, the scorn and spite of frightened motorists, not to talk of how they fulfilled the most desirable pleasures of life, food and love, was best left to imagination.

Yet, many patients who came to the emergency department would choose the streets over the shelter, especially the Bedford Avenue shelter. Patients had complained of the regimentation of life, the checking of identify cards before re-entry into the shelter once they stepped out to the street, lack of privacy, and the monotony of the diet. Drug use, though not officially condoned, was described by the residents to be pervasive in the shelter. Many of the inmates used to come to the hospital seeking admission for the stark contrasts.

In the hospital, the homeless received care just by asking. If he complained that his toe nails were too long, the podiatrist would be summoned to his bedside. If he desired the company of a beautiful young and innocent girl for twenty-four hours a day, he could feign suicidal ideation. The head-nurse on the floor would not rest until she found the girl for the one-to-one watch. If he did not like his bed, he only had to snap his fingers and it would be replaced, most likely, with one that could assume various positions. In addition, a physical therapist might be sent to straighten his stiff back. While he could not get any motorist in Brooklyn to let him ride in his car, he could, in the hospital, chose his own method of transportation from among walking, wheelchair and stretcher. In the street, the homeless subsisted on crumbs scavenged from decomposing garbage. In contrast, the hospital diet was well prepared, delicious and balanced.

There is no hotel, resort or inn anywhere in the world that would provide the package just outlined and more for absolutely free of charge. In the case of homeless Medicaid beneficiaries the services, fit for kings, cost them absolutely nothing. All the emergency room staff, including Stephen, had always assumed that those services, from manicure to medical cure and more, were the main inducements that brought homeless patients to the hospital, clamoring for admission. Now, he realized that the security provided by the hospital may have been a far more important part; the entree of the menu. When a man faces an immediate and mortal danger, hunger rapidly fades from consciousness only to resurface when he has taken adequate steps to assure his personal safety. While Stephen was grateful for Mr. Carlone's frankness, he could not help him. The best thing that can happen to a physician faced with a patient he could not help at all, or any further, is for the patient to drift and fade away in search of a second, a third and more opinions until he disappears. That, precisely, was what Stephen hoped for Mr. Carlone. He moved on to the next patient.

Eighty-year-old Mrs. Anthea Lewis was already well known to Stephen. She had been admitted to the hospital the previous week with pain in her upper abdomen. She, too, knew Stephen somewhat. At endoscopy, she had been found to have a benign stomach ulcer and had been adequately treated. Stephen liked to see such patients in the emergency room as he had a good insight into their problems. He usually did not have to ask them too many questions, the type of intervention many patients detested.

"Hi, Ms. Lewis, what brought you to the emergency room today?"

Ms. Lewis pointed to the central portion of her abdomen between the navel and the lower rib margin. "It hurts here, just like it did last week," she told Stephen.

"Did you take any medication for the pain?"

"Yes, my daughter gave me some Alka-Seltzer," said Ms. Lewis.

"Never, never, never again are you to take Alka-Seltzer for your stomach pain. It is not good for anyone with a stomach ulcer or any kind of stomach pain, gas, or indigestion. It could perforate your stomach or cause severe bleeding. Never again. I am going to discharge you home now as you are not bleeding. Take your Pepcid when you get home. Before you buy any medicine over the counter, call me and ask if it is good for you."

"Could you admit me for one day, at least? You know my husband passed twenty years ago. My three children are now living on their own. I have no one, but the wall, to talk to in my five-bedroom apartment. I came here by ambulance. They would not give me a home attendant because, they say, I got a little too much money in my account."

"Are your children in New York?" asked Stephen.

"One lives in Manhattan, one in Queens and my baby lives in Brooklyn, not too far from me. Here is a card with their phone numbers and addresses." Stephen took the card from her. The closest of the children to her mother and the hospital was her daughter, Sonia Lewis. Stephen placed a call to her. "This is Doctor Latham. I am calling about your mother. I am about to discharge her home," he told Sonia on the phone.

"Please don't discharge her. She lives alone with nobody to talk to. Keep her in the hospital. I can't come for her. I got business to take care of as do my brothers Willie and John," said Sonia.

"There is no justification for admitting your mother to the hospital. Let me call your brothers. Bye."

Stephen called Mrs. Lewis' sons John and Willie. Both said they were not available to help their mother or drive her home because they had businesses to take care of. They insisted that she needed admission as treatment for her loneliness. Stephen placed another call to Sonia. This time, the answering machine was on. He left a message for Sonia that he was discharging their mother home via the EMS and hung up. Ideally, he thought, he should have told them as it was, bluntly and viscerally; without holding back anything, even if they felt he was coarse. He should have told the Lewis siblings that like them, he had business to take care of. While it was not his business to propound, inculcate or enforce family values, the hospital was not built, and did not operate, to pick up the slack for dysfunctional and negligent families. Nor was the hospital a social club or a nursing home. Moralization, unlike empathy, is not a physician's liberty. He was happy to have shown the siblings restraint and politeness. If they were still not satisfied, that would not be his problem. He was not there to satisfy all comers. His empathy was for Mrs. Lewis, the matriarch. He went back to her to explain that he would have to send her home by the ambulance. He looked away in a moment of silence as she burst into tears. He would try by all means not to look at her again until the ambulance took her home.

His next patient was a twenty-seven-year-old man with fever. No sooner did Stephen enter the isolation room than he made the diagnosis. The young man appeared to have, involuntarily, lost a lot of weight recently. There were needle scars on his forearms, more on the left due to his right handedness, indicating past intravenous drug abuse. Most probably, he had never quit. His hair was sparse and thin while his face bore multiple raised pink spots and the corners of his mouth were cracked.

Stephen had seen scores of patients like him before and the deja vu always humbled him. The twenty-seven-year-old man before him had AIDS and would almost certainly die within the next several weeks to months. In his accumulated experience, no clearly effective therapy existed for the terminally advanced AIDS. The eventual futility of caring for patients like this was a situation physicians found very frustrating. For a moment, Stephen and the patient stared at each other. Then Stephen broke the silence. "What is your name please? I am Dr. Latham." He asked the question to avoid a clerical mishap, arguably, the most common cause of injury to many a patient. Simply checking the name could spare the patient a wrong procedure and the hospital, bad press.

The wrong foot amputated in a Florida hospital; surgery on the wrong side of the brain in Memorial Sloan-Kettering Hospital and the incompatible blood transfusion at Coney Island Hospital were still fresh in his mind. All these mix-ups, according to the media, could have been prevented by simple questions to the patients. When he was an intern at Union Hospital, a woman who had come from the Middle East to have a baby had been given the wrong blood only because the blood request form had been wrongly stamped with her name. She had gone on to develop severe complications which nearly cost her her life. In the end, she had made a complete recovery and traveled back with her healthy baby, an American citizen. Luckily for Union Hospital and the physicians involved, neither the state nor the media got wind of it. But her ordeal would forever stay with Stephen.

The patient's voice was feeble but clear. "Olton, James Olton," he responded. Satisfied that he had the right chart in his hand Stephen proceeded to take care of him.

"What can I do for you today?"

"I got cough and fever and chest pain," said Mr. Olton.

"Do you have tuberculosis?"

"Yes. I have been taking the medicines for the last six or nine months. Nine or ten different medications, enough to make you sick. I ran out of them medications six months ago. My memory is not so good. It comes with the disease . . . you know what I am say-ing . . . HIV positive."

"Does it hurt when you swallow food?"

"It does, right here (pointing to his mid-chest). Even when I swal-low saliva, it hurts."

"Do you sweat at night?"

"Yes, that was before when I almost never slept alone. I am still active but I use protection to protect my girl who is not infected."

"That is not what I mean. Patients with tuberculosis tend to sweat at night. Now, even when you don't do anything with your girl, do you sweat at night?"

"Yes, in between, I do. But I am very active at night. That is why my girl can't leave me."

"Is there anything else wrong with you?"

"They just told me last week that I have to go on dialysis because my kidneys are almost gone. I don't have any feelings in my legs. Right now without looking at them, I don't know where my legs are. Yesterday I tripped and fell twice at home while making my way to the bathroom. Nothing stays in my stomach. The little food I am able to eat comes out in stool soon after it gets in," said Mr. Olton.

"But if I may ask, how did you become HIV positive?"

"I got it from my former girl. She passed, though. Now it's my turn. She got it from her former boyfriend who was an intravenous drug abuser. He passed long ago."

Stephen, looking at the needle tracts on Mr. Olton's forearm asked, "Did you ever use intravenous drugs yourself?"

"I ain't gonna lie to you. I did. But I got HIV from my girl. She didn't know she'd been infected. I know your next question will be "Are you gay? Never have been; never will be."

Stephen did not want to argue about the source of the patient's HIV infection though there was a distinct possibility that he may have acquired it through injecting drug abuse. Although the distinction would be academic and arbitrary to Stephen, he realized that, to both patients and society at large, it carried enormous emotional consequences. He had seen nurses near tears and doctors in a solemn mood when AIDS patients who had acquired the infection in monogamous heterosexual relationships died on the floor. When gay and intravenous drug abusers died on the floor, the same staffers often shrugged their shoulders and went about their businesses as if to say the deceased asked for it.

With his hand on the patient's abdomen he noticed that the latter had an enlarged and rough liver. "It looks like you have enlarged liver, did you know that?" he asked.

"They said my liver is messed up too," said Mr. Olton.

"Were you ever a drinker?"

"I used to drink like a fish. I don't do that any more. In addition, the doctor said I got hepatitis C."

Stephen shook his head in disgust. Here was a young man who should have been in his bloom. Yet, at least in part, due to his personal indiscretion, he faced certain death in the not-so-distant future. His brain, the most important organ for normal functioning, was under attack by the HIV virus as were his food pipe, bowels and kidneys. Years of overindulgence in alcoholism and injecting drug abuse had laid waste to his liver, the chemical factory of his body. His lungs were being turned into redundant, foamy cicatrices.

His care would cost an awful lot of resources, time and energy. He would have to go on the kidney machine for the balance of his life. Sooner, rather than later, he would need to be on the breathing machine. All kinds of experts would be called upon to consult on him. Asked to explain his amnesia and leg anesthesia, the neurologist would almost certainly recommend a CAT scan of his head. For his diarrhea and difficulty with swallowing, the gastroenterologist would almost certainly recommend endoscopy. While on the breathing machine, multiple X-ray examinations and blood tests would be done.

The cost of this patient's care would run into hundreds of thousands of dollars if he didn't succumb to death quickly. The risk of transmission of hepatitis, HIV and tuberculosis to employees could not be calculated in dollar terms. Stephen began to write orders for the patient to be admitted to the tuberculosis floor where he would be secluded until the likelihood of transmission of infection to other patients and staff could be ascertained. If he had his way he could have ordered, "Watch the patient die. Don't do anything for him." After all, nothing would save him. But the idea was heretical.

Though it would be hard to fold one's arms and watch a twenty-seven-year-old man wither inexorably away, given the tight health care budget, he wondered if he would not be wiser to allocate the resources to patients with more favorable prognoses. Finally, he decided, not to arrogate to himself the right to decide which investment would be the most cost-wise for society. He wrote orders for the patient to be isolated, the kind of food the patient should be given and what laboratory tests should be done. He turned to Mr. Olton and told him, "I am admitting you to the floor." The patient himself had expected it and said nothing.

Stephen came to the nurse's desk to catch up on the paper work. He was sitting beside Christina, the emergency department clerk. A hospital police officer soon emerged to ask Stephen a question.

"Doc," he addressed Stephen, "have you finished with Ms. Vayner, please?"

Stephen, looking up said, "No. I haven't even started seeing her yet."

Five minutes later, the officer came back. "Doc, please have you seen her yet?" he asked again.

"Sorry, not yet." Stephen became curious about his relationship to her. Perhaps, she was his wife, he thought. "May I know how you are related to her? Is she your wife?" Stephen asked the police officer who became embarrassed and lost for words.

He could only reply "No . . . no," as he drifted away.

Christina had been watching the police officer. After the latter had drifted from the vicinity, Christina volunteered, "I hate him. I hate him with a passion. This is what he does every day. He refuses to stay at his post, the reason for which he has been cited at least three times in the past. He hangs out here and preys on these women at the time they are most vulnerable, offering to secure their cars parked outside and to drive them home when the doctor finished with them. You know how some of the patients we get here are. Some of them are very lonely and live on the edge of psychological stability and they come here just to talk to somebody. And when a hospital police officer stops to show them love and concern they just fall for it. The reason I hate him so much is that he has a dedicated wife and terrific children."

There was a ring of truth around all of what Christina Fisher said. She was a woman of high integrity and impeccable character. Her counsel was widely respected in the emergency department. The reason the police officer drifted away was because of her stern, disapproving look. Stephen always thought she should have been a doctor. Perhaps, while she was growing up in Puerto Rico, she lacked the opportunity. For her to hate the police officer with a passion meant she probably knew more than she had already volunteered. To find out, Stephen decided to play the devil's advocate.

"What if, Ms. Fisher, the officer is acting out of empathy?" Stephen asked. "He may be genuinely concerned about these patients, you know."

"Give me a break. Why is he never concerned about the male patients and the elderly? He has sympathy only for the very beautiful, young women. You have (looking at the wall clock) another four hours to go. You will understand what I am talking about. Watch and see how restless he will become when a beautiful woman, patient or visitor, walks in through the door," said Christina.

"I understand that you smell a rat. But is there evidence of wrongdoing on his part? Is there evidence that he has, indeed, had carnal knowledge of these women? Or even tried to? Don't get me wrong, I don't think he deserves the perks, if only because I am not entitled to them. I am just not ready to sacrifice him without hard evidence. I am only giving him benefit of the doubt."

"Doctor, I understand this male solidarity. Do you know that he clerks these women even before you get to talk to them and he often has more insight into their problems than you do? Do you know why some of these women's lab results come back faster than others? It is because he rushes upstairs to the lab to bring them. Some of the women think he is the assistant to the doctor, if not the doctor himself. You know patients are seen in the orders of arrival and severity of complaints. Two weeks ago he made Dr. Godswill see the least sick patient and the last to arrive, first. He led Dr. Godswill to believe she was his sister, whereas they had never met before."

"Do you know what the young woman's complaint was?" asked Stephen.

All other side conversations at the Nurse's desk had subsided and everybody was listening to Ms. Christina Fisher. Stephen was writing intermittently while listening. For the most part, the other staff members had no tasks at hand. That was the nature of the emergency department. At one moment it could be as busy as the stock market with patients yelling for pain medications, food, bathroom privileges or about empty intravenous fluid bags. Nurses, doctors, orderlies and other staffers would be running helter skelter to assess and satisfy their needs. Five minutes later, it could be completely quiet again. This was one such moment and all were listening to Ms. Fisher's testimony.

Cognizant of the attention being paid to her, Ms. Fisher swivelled in her chair to assume a position that would give her the maximum exposure. She continued her deposition. "The twenty-six-year-old woman's boyfriend had been in jail for about two years and he still faced another mandatory five. She had come to the emergency because of headaches, which she attributed to lack of sex. Dr. Godswill could not convince her that there was no linkage between abstinence and her headache. She told Dr. Godswill that she felt like knocking on the door of the young man who lived two apartments down the hall in her building. Doctor, I am telling you this man (referring to the hospital police officer) drove her home. Now, do you still want proof that there had been wrongdoing on his part?"

"Well, that comes close, but I am still not sure. . . ." said Stephen.

Mr. Seever, the phlebotomist, interjected, "Ms. Fisher, do you still remember her name? Just tell me her name and I'll go into the computer and obtain the rest of the information about her. She may still be in distress. I would not mind being her visiting doctor."

"Some women are sick," said Ms. Fisher.

"Just like some men. That is why we are here," said Stephen.

"What is her name please?" asked Mr. Steever.

At this point the nurse's supervisor walked in and leaned over the counter, across from Mr. Brosier. Everybody became silent. It was obvious that something was amiss. She almost never came down to the emergency department unless there was a problem to be investigated or solved.

"Ms. Brosier," she asked the triage nurse, "what happened with the patient, Bishop? He came and lodged a complaint that you were very rude to him and that you made certain unwelcome insinuations about him."

"Ms. Penneton," Ms. Brosier began her defense, "that patient has an attitude. He asked me for a urinal and I told him that I would fetch him one in just a minute. As I was approaching his bed with the container, he started carrying on and on. We are here to take care of patients and I don't think we should be abused like that. There was no threat he did not issue against me and other staff. Nobody called him a homosexual. In fact, I don't know his sexual orientation and, in any case, it doesn't even matter. We all know and deal with people who are gay. I just don't think it is fair for these patients to come here and abuse us like that. And I told him that I would not take it." Ms. Brosier surveyed her audience, as she offered her defense, for corroboration. She got it in the professional wall of silence that ensued. It was her word against Mr. Bishop's with neither side having witnesses.

Stephen stood up in time to see his next patient so as not to be an accessory to the lies Ms. Brosier was spewing. He thought the patient had been greatly offended. From his position at the bedside he could hear Ms. Brosier's spirited defense continuing, though he was trying hard not to listen. When he returned to the desk for the mandatory paper work, Ms. Brosier was still talking about the "homosexual with an attitude."

Stephen intervened. "That patient is not gay. Not that it matters to any of us here. He is suffering from the rare condition called *proctalgia fugax*." Everyone was paying attention because of the condition's exotic and romantic name. Mr. Seever asked him to repeat the name of the condition. "Proctalgia fugax is a condition characterized by sudden, severe but self-limited pain in the rectum. The pain usually lasts only a few minutes. It often happens during sex, like this patient's previous attack but other conditions can also bring it on. It's got nothing to do with homosexuality."

"What causes it, then?" asked Mr. Seever.

"The cause is unknown. The patient himself understands the disease. In fact, he would not have come to the emergency if somebody had not suggested that he might need the report for a lawsuit."

"Is there a cure for it?" Ms. Brosier asked.

"There's none. Really, there is no need for a cure because a typical attack lasts only several minutes. By the time patient reaches for his pills, the pain is gone," explained Stephen.

Ms. Brosier joined, "As you said, not that it matters. But are you sure that man is not a homosexual? Did you see how he was wiggling his waist from side to side as he made it to the bathroom? You should have seen his wrist drop and other mannerisms while talking to me during triage. The signs were unmistakable. With so many women

73

unmarried, it is unfortunate to see some men like that. But that is their choice and one cannot quarrel with that."

"He is not. The more important thing was that our presumptions did not interfere with the care we rendered," said Stephen.

Stephen's next patient was a thirty-nine-year-old female with generalized body aches and headaches that Physician Assistant Jamelon had just seen. Jamelon presented the case to Stephen. She was suffering from diabetes, hypertension and marked obesity. When they entered the room to see her, Stephen was struck by her morbid obesity.

"Good day, Ms. Dewey. I am Dr. Latham. Dr. Jamelon has already seen you. This is nurse Norville. I have already discussed your case with Dr. Jamelon. What is your height please?"

"Five-three."

"And your weight?"

"Two hundred and fifty pounds."

"I would like to tell you that your basic problem is your weight. You should be weighing about one hundred and twenty pounds. If you lose only fifty pounds, you may avoid taking all these Insulin injections for your sugar and you may not need blood pressure pills."

"They will say I got AIDS if I lose all that weight. I cannot do that."

"The choice is yours. You can live like this to satisfy your neighbors that you don't have AIDS and die soon of high blood pressure and your sugar problem. Or you can shed half of your body weight and live for a long, long time. Initially, your friends and neighbors might presume you have AIDS but after three or four years, they will change their perceptions. Think about it. Meanwhile, you will be given your refills."

They left Ms. Dewey, with the ball in her court, for the next patient.

Next came a sixty-seven-year-old man named Seb Bruwa. Stephen introduced himself and asked the patient why he came to the emergency department.

"I ran out of my blood pressure pills three days ago. I have exhausted the number of visits to my doctor's office," said Mr. Bruwa.

"Is there anything else wrong?"

"No."

"What medicines are you taking?"

"These are the medicines." He produced a blood pressure pill and a laxative.

"Do you suffer from constipation?"

"As long as I take this Dulcolax medication I am fine. I don't need a prescription for that. You know I can buy it over the counter."

"We see many patients with constipation here. Sometimes we have to take the complaint seriously and investigate it. What has your doctor ever done about the complaint?"

"Nothing. I really have not told him about it. I didn't consider it a problem. That is not why I came here today. I came for the blood pressure pills," said Mr. Bruwa.

"When did you first start having constipation?" asked Stephen.

"It started one month ago but like I said, that is not why I am here. Frankly, I don't think it is a big problem. As long as I take the laxatives I am fine. I have a high IQ and if it was a major problem, I would have known. I read medical journals. It started only a month ago. If it persists, I will take care of it. I really came to fill my prescription for the pressure pills."

"I am gonna give you the prescription. You have a high IQ and I am sure that in your reading you must have come across the fact that a sixty-seven-year-old man with a new onset of constipation must be investigated for cancer of the colon. Have you ever been screened for cancer of the colon which may cause constipation? The test is done by passing a tube through your rectum and looking inside. The cancer can be picked up early and removed. If you have cancer of the colon, that would be your best chance of a cure. The older you are the higher your chances of having colon cancer. In fact, next to lung cancer, a man of your age dying of cancer is most likely to have colon cancer. The reason I am saying all these is because you look so young and energetic at sixty-seven.

If I had to, I would bet all the money I have that you are in your late forties. It is recommended that at age fifty the screening test for cancer of the colon should be started. You are already seventeen years behind. I submit to you that it is better late than never. Discuss what I have told you with your doctor when next you see him."

"Close the door please. I want to tell you something sub rosa," Bruwa said to Stephen. Behind the closed door, Seb Bruwa made a confession, "I am really forty-nine years old. I did Uncle Sam a big favor but don't ask me when, what or where it was because I'm not allowed to tell you. Even if I had the permission to do so, I still would not tell you, not even for a million dollars. In return, the government gave me a new identity. New name, new social security, and a fantastic resume. When my new identity was being put together, I insisted that I be made eighteen years older than I really was and I guess they had no choice. The reason I made that demand was to be able to collect social security at least eighteen years earlier. I knew I would be able to get away with it. Like I have told you, I have a high IQ. I knew that one arm of the government doesn't know what the other is doing. I have been enjoying my social security for the last two years. My only regret is that I did not claim seven more years making myself twenty-five years older.

"I am not a stupid man. In the next few weeks I will turn fifty. Then I will start having the screening test for colon cancer. I want to live long. And you know what? Give me your card so I can be coming to your office."

"All right, Mr. Bruwa, wait here for me. I will complete your prescription in a minute. The nurse will call you and give you the discharge instructions including my card."

Physician Assistant Drammond's next case was a twenty-eight-year-old female with severe lower abdominal pain, fever, and painful urination. Drammond had already done the pelvic examination with Ms. McCoy as his chaperone. Clinically, it was obvious that the patient had a sexually transmitted disease. At the bedside, Stephen introduced himself and reintroduced Drammond and McCoy before asking the patient questions.

"Ms. Anderson, when did you start feeling so bad?" asked Stephen.

"I already told them it was three days ago. It is in the chart."

"I know. Please cooperate with us. I will be done in a just a few minutes. We think you have a sexually transmitted Pelvic Inflammatory Disease. I mean . . . are you . . . married?"

"I mess with one man only, my husband. I have been with him for the last three years. He doesn't mess with any other women. As a matter of fact, he is in the waiting area. His name is Moe. But could this infection be acquired by any other way?" asked Ms. Anderson.

"Very rarely. We only worry about that in the absence of possible human-to-human transmission," said Stephen.

"Can I go to the bathroom please? I am ready to produce the urine you guys wanted."

When she was gone to the bathroom, Stephen sent for her man who was watching TV in the waiting area. Moe Charmley was about five-eight in height and of medium build but he still had trouble holding his denim pant around his waist. It was so large that it looked like a sack with his waist line dropping almost to the floor. What was most remarkable about him was his hairstyle. It consisted of old, discrete braids with confetti at the tips. His affect was appropriately depressed.

"Moe," Stephen said to him, "your wife has got a very serious infection and we need your help to make the proper diagnosis. If she got it from you, she is likely to be reinfected even if we are successful in curing her now. The question I have for you is whether you have been sleeping with another woman."

Moe scratched his head, looked around the room as if to ensure that his wife was not hiding in a nook listening to his imminent confession. The nurse had stepped out of the room to help Ms. Anderson in the bathroom, leaving Moe with Stephen and Drammond in the room. Still, Moe was not comfortable with the question and Stephen sought to reassure him.

"Your wife has gone to the bathroom down the hall. We don't want her to be part of this men's talk now or afterward. But we must make the diagnosis to be able to treat her. So, is there another woman in your life?"

"Hmmmm. Not quite. But there is a couple of sisters down the block I talk to. They are clean, though."

"Moe, be straight with me. I am trying to help your wife and, in the process, help you. Have you had sex recently with those sisters in the last two weeks?"

"Yes, with only those two. But they are clean and they don't mess with nobody else."

"Did you use protection?" asked Drammond.

"Not with the cleanest one and that was about ten days ago. She doesn't mess with no other man. With the other one, yes."

"Here comes your wife. You need to be checked out and treated. No more sex until you, too, are fully treated. That is what your wife also will be told. You may go back to the waiting area. We will call you if need be," said Stephen.

Moe kissed his wife, who had just re-entered the room and resumed her recumbency in the couch, before shuffling his sack back to the waiting area.

"Ms. Anderson, as we were saying before you answered the call of nature, it is almost impossible that you got this infection from a nonhuman source. We just told your husband that he must be checked out. Insist on it before you make love to him again. Your prescription and discharge instructions will be written presently."

Stephen completed the paper work and went to see his next patient, a forty-one-year-old woman.

"Miss Derby Hulk, I am Dr. Latham. How can I help you?" he asked.

"I got stomach gas and pain. And constipation. The gas builds up over days during which I feel very bloated. In fact, when the gas builds up, I could go for days without bowel movement. Meanwhile, the pain would be very severe until I take an enema and move," said Ms. Hulk.

"For how long has this been going on?"

"For a while. For a good while."

"For weeks, months or years?"

"At least three years. At other times I have troublesome diarrhea."

"Have you lost weight during all these years?" asked Stephen.

"No. Rather, I have gained," she said.

"What investigations have been done since you started having these symptoms? I suspect that you have had multiple tests."

"You name it, I have had it. Colonoscopy, I have had it at least three times. Stomach endoscopy, at least three times. Sonograms, CAT scans, MRI's. I have had all of them and all have been normal. I have had gall bladder surgery but it did not help."

"Did they say you were having Irritable Bowel Syndrome?"

"Yes. That is what they said I got. But I don't eat anything that should irritate my bowels," said Ms. Hulk.

"We don't know what causes it. But it would not kill you. There is no need for us to perform any more tests. Just avoid junk food and increase your fiber intake. It may or may not help your symptoms." Before Stephen could complete the statement, he heard commotion at the nurses' desk and had to dash out of the room. One of the nurses was screaming loudly for him to come and see the young man who had staggered into the hall with a ghastly laceration to the neck. The mere fact that he was able to stand on his feet was a miracle. He slumped to the floor as the nurses and technicians initially recoiled from the grotesque cut. He was lifted onto a stretcher and placed in the trauma room. Suddenly, the emergency department came to life. Stephen was afraid the patient was going to stop breathing at any time. Every second that passed was crucial.

Stephen began to issue orders with rapid-fire. "Christina, call code three-three and I want Drs. Cagialini and Todd here, now. Tell them I don't care what they are doing at hand. They must come down stat. I want a respirator stat. Seever, Jamelon, start two lines. We must have two secure lines running." Another nurse was told what blood tests to send for. In between commands, Stephen was talking to the patient. Although, the patient had been hooked up to all kinds of monitors within the last three minutes, no adjunct could be as reassuring as the patient talking to the doctor.

It was important to establish the patient's identity early on. The worst case scenario would be for him to die a John Doe. Should he become unconscious, it would still be necessary to obtain informed consent from a responsible member of his family for nearly all interventions. Asked what his name was, he wouldn't answer. He wouldn't even say where he lived. He would only discuss the savage cut. When the nurse wanted to take a photograph of the gaping cut, he covered his face with his blood-soaked hands. When a frustrated Stephen threatened to abandon him unless he gave his name, the patient reluctantly replied, "Outridge."

Dr. Todd, head and neck surgeon, and Dr. Cagialini, vascular surgeon, had arrived. After a brief but focused examination of the laceration they, along with Stephen, decided to attach the patient to the breathing machine so as to have enough leeway to do their work. There was no time to force his first name out of him. Luckily, this being an emergency, they did not have to worry about informed consent. That meant they did not have to tell him the risks and benefits of, and alternatives to, inserting the breathing tube. He could have been alarmed to hear that the tube was capable of lacerating his throat or voice box and leaving him with hoarseness. If he was a musician, he might have objected to the intervention. More ominously, the chance that the tube could be inserted into the wrong place and suffocate him could have scared him to death.

They did not have to tell him about the various treatment options for his injury, the relative advantages and disadvantages of the various materials they would use to sew up his wound and the fact that he would likely live with a neck deformity for the rest of his life. There was no fear of a law suit alleging that the doctors had been negligent in making it impossible for him to turn back for a second look when a beautiful woman passed him by.

It also meant that Mr. Outridge had no chance to ask each of the doctors their track record with respect to the procedure. Since ethicists and trial lawyers raised the concept of informed consent to the prominent position it now occupied in health care, patients have been asking doctors, "How many of this procedure have you performed? How many were successful and how many, complicated?" The problem was no patient wanted to be the guinea pig. They all wanted the doctor who had performed hundreds, if not thousands, of the procedure in question, all successful with zero complication. The emergency room allowed doctors to accumulate the numbers for the necessary boastful advertisement.

The first trauma room in which Mr. Outridge was being treated was now a beehive of activity. The two surgeons and Stephen were taking care of his laceration with the able assistance of the emergency room nurses. Nerves were being rejoined to nerves, muscles to muscles, blood vessels to vessels. The key role belonged to Dr. Todd the head and neck surgeon who had extensive experience, though he would be the first to acknowledge and hail the cooperative effort of the team.

After three hours of suturing, interposing of tissue and reconstruction, the laceration was neatly closed. Anyone walking into the room at that point would have found it hard to imagine the bestiality that had gone into the cut. If all went well, the patient would regain full range of neck motion. Under less optional conditions he could end up with torticollis. That would almost certainly necessitate additional surgery. The surgeon would then have to worry about informed consent, insurance coverage, track record, hospital length of stay and more. For now, the team was involved in self-congratulation on having saved the patient. Emergency room staff liked the excitement and the challenge to save a life in danger.

Mr. Outridge remained in high spirits throughout surgery, possibly, because he had imbibed a lot of spirits earlier in the day. His breath was laden with alcohol. Also, his multiple bodily scars, bore out his prior experience with violent injury. Much to his relief, the doctors disconnected him from the respirator after surgery and he began to breathe on his own. Still he would not say what his name and address were. He must have had a strong reason to want to conceal his identity for he was loquacious when asked about other scars on his body.

He had a long midline scar on his abdomen. "What happened to your stomach?" Stephen asked him.

"I got shot six years ago," Outridge said in his deep alto as he parted his dreadlocks to the sides.

"How did you sustain this cut to your right chest?" asked Stephen.

"I got slashed when I was upstate in Ithaca. I nearly died then. I got a bullet here (pointing to his groin) where I got shot ten years ago in the Bronx. The doctors told me if I tried to take it out I'm gonna be impotent."

"And your potency is very important to you?"

"Are you kidding me? One last scar I want to show you is this one (pointing to his right palm). My own sister wanted to stab me. As we struggled for the knife, I got cut here."

"Were you in Vietnam?"

"No. I fought my war right here in New York City. As a matter of fact, it's still on," said Outridge.

"But how did you get this cut today?"

Mr. Outridge became inexplicably mum. Stephen was putting the final dressing on his neck. Gradually everybody, but Stephen and Outridge, left the trauma room. Then Mr. Outridge made his revelation to Stephen. "Close that door, doc," he begged Stephen. The door was already closed. "You would not tell anyone else, would you?" he asked Stephen.

80

Stephen, shaking his head, said "A man must keep his word."

"Doc, the man nearly killed me. I thank you for saving my life. I ain't got no papers, you know what I'm sayin'. I met this woman in the club the other day. She did not tell me she got a man. Me and her, we've been going out and having a good time. She promised to help me with my papers. These women are something else. She lives right at the corner of Franklin and St. Mark's. We were together this afternoon when this man walked in with a knife drawn. He wanted to cut my head into two like this (demonstrating with a stroke of his hand). Only God saved me. I was able to escape as he went after the woman."

"Were you drinking?"

"Just a glass, you know what I'm sayin'. When you are with a babe . . . "

"Any drugs involved?"

"Absolutely not. Once in a while, I might try pot, you know wha'm sayin', but I have not smoked in the last month or so. One more thing Doc, because I ain't got no papers, I don't give out my real name. My name is—again this is just for you—Anthony Forbes. Keep it in mind. I am going to make it in this country and I'm gonna come back and see you, man." They shook hands.

"Take care of yourself, man," said Stephen imitating Mr. Forbes' lingo. "Please wait here. I got to complete your papers so that you can go to the floor. I will right back."

Back at the nurse's station, Stephen sat down to document everything they had done for the patient. Most of the staff had reassembled at the nurses' desk to discuss and dissect the case. Although cases like this were not uncommon, they never ceased to excite the staffs. Usually they'd assemble to discuss the case. That kind of post-treatment analysis was an essential exercise in alleviating the distress that often ensued in the wake of such cases, though the discussants probably did not realize the therapeutic effect of their talk.

"It must be drug-related. That is why he doesn't want to divulge his name or talk about himself. There is no other reason why anyone would cut your neck like that. He looks like he was speed-balling," said Ms. Brosier.

"It must have been caused by a dispute over heroin. This is undoubtedly a heroin cut. Maybe he failed to submit the money. He should have known that the boss would not send the police to arrest him. I am sure they will still look for him to finish him off unless he pays up. Once you choose the business, you got to know the deal," argued Mr. Seever.

81

But Christina suggested, "He may have come to buy and gotten robbed. You know there are drug houses all over the city."

"Drugs are everywhere," said Nurse Norville. "Most of those coming here to buy these drugs take them to the suburbs."

"No. This is the hallmark of a financial dispute. Either he failed to submit the money he realized from selling, or he failed to return a borrowed amount. One other possibility is that he could have been found to be an infiltrator for the cops. In the underworld, you know, that is a crime punishable by death," said Mr. Climes.

"Which cops?" asked Mr. Seever. "This is a billion-dollar business. They are involved in the trade. The day Uncle Sam says stop it, they will stop the inflow of drugs like turning off tap water. There is no crack house or shooting gallery that's not paying protection money to cops. Why do you think they will all open for business the day after a major raid? Look out the window right now and you will see a police car. They are passing the drug houses by only to arrest the poor people for the most minor traffic violation.

"In fairness to the cops, not all of them are involved in the trade. The vast majority of them don't like drugs. They are just like the rest of us. Unfortunately, when the silent majority know the few bad eggs who are shaking down drug dealers and drug houses, they are just as likely to look the other way as most doctors and nurses who know of their colleagues who are stealing legal opiates from the patients. The men who are pushing, injecting, snorting and glamorizing the drugs must take the blame and responsibility," proclaimed Drammond.

"We got half of these men shooting and dealing drugs and another half are gay. Thank God I am not doing anything now. What is happening to men these days is really unfortunate," said Ms. Brosier.

Stephen wanted to enter the discussion but, first, he had a lot to write. Ideally, he should document every tiny bit of what had happened to the patient. With so many events having taken place almost simultaneously, that was a mission impossible. He would make his report as complete as possible. He had to write not only what had already happened to the patient but also orders for further management. He still had to find a bed on the floor and an Attending physician for the patient.

The patient had two names, one real and the other fake. Stephen was not sure if he should call him Outridge or Forbes. If he called him the former, he would be guilty of perpetuating a charade or, in fact, outright fraud. That could be misinterpreted by the patient as a character flaw he could further exploit. Perhaps the patient was out to recruit him into a fraudulent duo. He could come up with more egregious schemes that a committed Dr. Latham may find hard to turn down. Given the patient's pledge to come back in future, Stephen had to move with considerable introspection.

On the other hand, the patient confided and revealed his true identity. He was a lonely illegal immigrant, double crossed by perhaps the only person he had come to trust, a lascivious woman and living in awe of the Immigration Service. Calling him Forbes would certainly destroy a budding patient-doctor relationship. He would drive Mr. Forbes from the medical system and jeopardize further care of his wound. On a human level, he could not blow the patient's cover without breaking his promise to the patient that a man must keep his word.

If he reported Mr. Forbes to the authorities what would he do with the man with the high IQ, Mr. Bruwa, whose transgressions were costing society a fortune more. If he were to report both of them, what about the countless other fraudulent practices every physician encountered on a daily basis? It was not difficult for hospital employees to obtain prescriptions for their uninsured relatives under circumstances that could have cost the physicians involved their state licenses. Was he to take notes and turn them over to the state?

He was a doctor, not an FBI agent, he told himself. Indeed about several weeks earlier, a patient had called him an FBI agent. The young man had come into the emergency room with the diagnosis of peptic ulcer. In his possession, to boot, was a report of the X-ray study performed in a freestanding facility in Brooklyn that backed up the diagnosis. On close questioning, Stephen had suspected something wrong because the young man's symptoms did not fit the diagnosis. He had taken a closer look at the X-ray report and had become convinced that it had been doctored. He had called the X-ray facility for confirmation only to discover that the young man had never been there. The young man was engaged in illicit trade in licit drugs. Confronted with all the inconsistencies, the young man had stormed out of the emergency room saying, "I came to see a doctor, but I met the FBI."

Stephen had to determine whether his duty and loyalty lay with the patient or with society. He had taken a vow upon graduation from medical school to "first, do no harm." Was it harm to the patient or to society? And what happens when preventing harm to the patient was tantamount to harming society? It would have been too easy to decide one way or the other if the patient's offence had been more blatant, like posing a direct threat to a particular individual or group. In that case he would have made efforts to inform the authorities and the potential target without hesitation or regret. He was unable to end the vacillation partly because of the ongoing discussion of the role of drugs in the attack on the patient. So, he left the column for the patient's name blank in the meantime.

He wanted to tell his staff to quit the discussion on drugs and broaden their horizon, focussing on other possible factors. Because drugs were so ubiquitous, there was a tendency to explain every crime on their basis, even when the temporal or spatial relationship among the perpetrator, the victim and the drugs was tenuous or nonexistent. He wondered how many criminal investigations must have been botched by such arbitrary attribution. He waded into the discussion, telling his audience that before and despite the ascension of drugs, there were other passions that impelled men to commit crime.

He listed some of them starting with money. "Some wise guy said money is the root of all evil," he stated. "That includes, I suppose, all kinds of crime. I would modify it a bit and say money is the root of a lot of crimes. Both the absolute lack of it and the unbridled desire for more among those who have a lot of it, could induce a criminal to act. In fairness to money, however, I must also say it is the root of a lot of good. No one among us here can dispute the high feeling that plenty of money in one's pocket could engender. Conversely, when you have no money in your pocket you've got more than a mere inconvenience."

Jamelon added, "You look stupid when you've got no money. I know that when I got no money, no woman would talk to me. When I was in college, it was the guys with money that all the girls ran to. My friend Seever, I know, would have been in Atlantic City with a hot baby if he had money in his pocket."

"Absolutely," agreed Seever. "What would I be doing here if I won the lottery?"

"Sex is frequently the cause of crime," Stephen said without hinting that it played a role in this case. He was keeping his word to the patient that he would keep his word. "Like everything else in life, too much or too little of sex could be the basis of trouble. Too little of it when a housewife denies her husband sex, is often the cause of crime, and she often lands in the emergency with a bruised face in the middle of the night. Right here in this emergency, we have seen them, not once, not twice but many times. If I am wrong, you can contradict me. Men attacking their spouses over sex is unpardonable but we do see it.

"Women have also taken matters into their hands and committed crimes over sex. Who will ever forget the woman in Virginia . . . what was her name? . . . Bobbitt, who cut off her man's organ. Women in many other parts of the world followed her example. The media are replete with fatal-attraction stories in which one woman shoots another to inherit the latter's man. The Solos of Westchester and the Buttafuccos of Long Island come to mind. These were cases in which the women did not have enough."

"From what I understand that man who had his thing cut in Virginia became a better performer after it was re-attached. There were reports of long lines of disbelieving women going in to ask him if it was functioning again. They all came out very satisfied. I saw him on one of the shows. He was smiling very gleefully. I think those reports were true," said Seever.

Stephen confirmed, "Too much sex, like when a man covets another's spouse has been the cause of crime. We have seen that genre too, here. Who among you doesn't remember the man who came to the radiology dark room and caught his own wife with her coworker in a compromised position. He slapped his wife's coworker on the arm and left. If he had a gun, he probably would have shot them.

"Power and the willingness to exert it are a common source of crime. Who in this emergency department has not seen victims of rape or police brutality? Remember, police power play can be as simple as a choke hold on your neck."

Stephen moved to demonstrate it on Seever's neck, in order to lighten the room prompting all his listeners to giggle. Then he went on.

"Or it can lead to death in custody which we read about all the time. The biggest crimes in human history had absolutely nothing to do with drugs, money or sex. Think of slavery. Millions savagely captured by their brothers, sold to alien transporters who threw millions to the sharks in the Atlantic and sold the survivors to the masters for the worst forms of man's inhumanity to man. Think of the Jewish holocaust. Six million fed to gas chambers as if the chambers needed food. Think of genocides in the killing fields of Cambodia and the jungles of Rwanda. None of these had anything to do with drugs. We shouldn't let drugs cloud our horizon. Drugs are obviously important but other issues also pertain. Sometimes drugs are a red herring. The finding of a tiny amount of stale marijuana in the vicinity or possession of the victim or perpetrator does not establish a causal relationship. On occasion, it may even be planted by unscrupulous law enforcement."

Stephen's audience was nodding in agreement and appreciation for an impromptu lecture well delivered. Some in the audience may have been wondering why they had not thought of all the dimensions and differentials. They may have been thinking what a smart guy Stephen was. Little did they know that he was merely building upon privileged information from the patient.

Jamelon started to say something when Mr. Outridge emerged from the trauma room. As he walked toward the desk, all the staffs were quiet in anticipation of what the patient had to say. He leaned over the desk across from Stephen, his wryneck forcing him to stand back somewhat.

"Mr. Outridge, why don't you wait in your room? I am coming to meet you there. I have almost completed your admission papers," Stephen told him.

"I'm leaving. I want to thank you all for saving my life," said Outridge.

Stephen couldn't believe what he was hearing. "You can't. This is absolutely crazy. You know you almost died. You have undergone extensive emergency neck surgery. You need to be in the hospital for at least one day. You got one dose of intravenous antibiotics but you need more because of the emergency nature of the operation. You need painkillers because the local anesthetic will soon wear off and your pain is going to return with a vengeance. You need an injection to prevent tetanus. This is unbelievably asinine. It would be crazy for you to talk of going home."

"I'm gonna be all right, doc. Thank you for everything. I will be all right," insisted Outridge.

Incredulously, he made for the door as he assured Stephen he would be all right. He opened the door and disappeared into the oblivion of the street. He was just exercising his right to refuse treatment. He could not have been held against his wish and desire because he had a sound mind and was in a position to decide what should or shouldn't happen to his body.

Nobody in the emergency department had ever seen anything quite like that. Some of the staff members opined that he was going to exact his revenge. Some said he was going to use more drugs or was running from the police. Everything about him, including his identity, cause of injury and destination, was subject to wild speculation. Stephen called him the cat with nine lives. He remembered what his former eighty-year-old boss told him long ago that, in medicine, "if you live long enough, you see it all." This was stoicism, nonpareil and unprecedented.

It was five minute to eight; five precious minutes more and Stephen would earn his twenty-five hundred dollars for the momentous eight-hour shift. He looked in the chart rack. There was only one patient left to be seen. He would not have preferred to bequeath her to Dr. Kurman, his successor if he could dismiss her in five minutes. It all depended on what her complaint was. He grabbed the chart and saw that she had a simple complaint of having missed her period.

In her room, he introduced himself with the chaperone by his side though he was sure he did not need one to ensure propriety. He was not Dr. Lee Thamn. "What can I do for you, Ms. Vayner?"

"I missed my period, that is why I am here. I need a gynecologist. Are you one?" asked Ms. Vayner.

"No, I am a gastroenterologist. I could still see you. I might be able to help you."

"What did you say you are?"

"Gastroenterologist," repeated Stephen.

"I got that too, a lot of gas in my stomach. You can hear my gas from many feet away. But that is not what I am here for. Since you are not a gynecologist, I don't want you to see me. Please don't get me wrong. It is nothing personal. I just need a gynecologist. What kind of an emergency room is this that doesn't have a gynecologist? I am out of here to a real emergency room." She stood up and left. When she was at the door, Stephen wanted to yell, "Go and find your period and don't come back here!" but he held back for the sake of decorum. In refusing treatment, the patient had made his work light. All he had to document in her chart was "Patient refused treatment and walked out." He turned to Ms. Brosier, his chaperone, and shook his head.

"Some of these women are absolutely stupid," Ms. Brosier said.

The time was 8:00 P.M. to be exact. Dr. Kurman was ready to take over.

The emergency phone system was ringing off the hook. Ms. Brosier picked it up. The ambulance crew was calling to inform the emergency department that a forty-year-old woman in cardiac arrest was being rushed to the hospital.

Dr. Stephen Latham grabbed his bags and said to Dr. Kurman, "I have no checkout for you, have fun," before fleeing the vicinity.

Christopher's Mouth Injury

It was another Friday and Stephen was looking forward to his tight schedule with resignation like a soldier marching wearily into battle. He had retired early the previous Thursday as was habitual for him. The fact that he had a light schedule on Thursday and could return home in time was helpful. The previous Thursday was true to type. He had returned to his apartment at about four in the afternoon and announced to Juliana that he was going to play tennis with Bright, his friend.

Juliana had not raised any objection and Stephen was pleasantly surprised. Perhaps she was feeling guilty of having filled their living quarters with cigarette smoke, contrary to Stephen's instructions. In the last several weeks, it appeared, she had resigned herself to his unpredictable itinerary. She had made only two requests of Stephen neither of which the latter could refuse. First, she had reminded Stephen that the container of soy milk had been depleted to the last few ounces. Stephen had immediately thought that she wanted to milk him for more money ostensibly to buy more soy milk. His mind went straight to his wallet, thinking of how much he would spare. He was even more surprised when she announced that she had a little money left for milk. She just wanted, she had said, to dispose of the container and create more room in the refrigerator to store supplies for a neighbor's birthday party the next day. She did not want to waste the milk, she had told Stephen. One of the tenets she had learnt growing up poor was to be a dietary conservative.

If Stephen would be kind enough to drink a cup of coffee or tea, she could get one ready in minutes, she had said. While Stephen was dressing up for his game amorphous fumes arose from the hot cup of coffee, weaving and twisting into nothingness. As Stephen gingerly sipped the coffee to protect his tongue from burn, Juliana made her second request. Mrs. Daveney who lived on the seventh floor had just announced the passing away of her father after a protracted illness. Neighbors, friends and coworkers were making unsolicited donations to the Daveneys. Juliana felt obligated to go up to the Daveneys and make hers. Actually, it would be understood that the donation was being made on behalf of the Latham family. Could Stephen watch Christopher while she went up to hand in their donation? Juliana had pleaded. She would come back in five minutes, before Stephen finished his hot coffee, she had assured him.

Stephen had checked his watch. He would have more than enough time to reach Prospect Park for his game, provided Juliana came back in not more than a quarter of an hour. When she was gone, Stephen began to ponder the whole idea of raising money for the bereaved. Presently, he was seized by a gradual onset of drowsiness. He couldn't understand why he felt so, given that he had a light day and only thirty minutes earlier he had promised Bright a great singles game.

He had thought of the possible differentials of his drowsiness. The best he could come up with was apnea. Whenever he came in and found his apartment full of smoke, he would hold his breath to avoid inhaling all the carcinogens. He had become quite an expert in breath-holding. He did not want to raise the matter of smoking with Juliana on this occasion because she had been so receptive to his plans for tennis. Any misunderstanding with Juliana would derail his plans. He held his breath some more.

Juliana had come down from the Daveneys' to find Stephen sedate and calm as she had expected.

Over the last several weeks, Stephen had been living under the influence of the sedative drug, Somnazolam. Juliana ensured that the surreptitious ingestion was a regular fixture of his late night snack. The fact that Stephen alone drank soy, while she and Christopher preferred cow's milk made the experiment easy to perform. There was no chance of accidental poisoning of Christopher.

As the weeks had gone by, Stephen was developing tolerance to the drug, requiring more of the product to produce sedation. Juliana responded by adding two vials to the six-ounce soy milk container. She had also observed that the dregs of the milk tended to be more potent probably because the drug was precipitating at the bottom. So when she convinced Stephen to take the cup of coffee with the lees of the milk, she knew that there was no chance of his going to play tennis that Thursday afternoon. This would be one more evening he would be with the family and all those cheap women loitering around the tennis courts would be frustrated.

"Are you sleeping, Steve?" she had asked him. "You must have had a hectic day. I thought you were going to play tennis. Why don't you call Bright and let him know you are not able to make it?"

89

Without a word of protest, Stephen had picked up the phone and called Bright. The latter was in the bathroom answering a final call before leaving for the tennis court, his wife had said. Stephen had left a message for him. "Tell him," he had pleaded with Bright's wife, "that I am unable to make it to the court. I hate to disappoint him this way because I know he is all revved up. I'll talk to him tomorrow. Right now I am going to bed. Bye."

Stephen awoke this Friday morning feeling rather dazed. It was a bad way for him to start his busiest day of the week. He was still wondering why he had surrendered so sheepishly to sleep the previous day. Despite the long hours of sleep he had had that night, he did not feel revitalized. Maybe he had slept too much, he thought. Too much of everything, his mother had always told him, was bad. Maybe it had to do with his sleep being interrupted by Christopher who awoke several times during the night and by the blaring car alarms downstairs. He would have to move to the fifteenth floor to avoid the car alarms, which were increasingly becoming a nuisance, he told himself.

He arose, shaking off the lethargy at six that morning. The next ninety minutes were the most regimented period of his day. The first twenty minutes would be spent working out on the treadmill. He descended from the high-incline machine feeling happy and rejuvenated. Sweat sprang from his forehead and flowed down his body in obedience of gravity. Some of the sweat streams did not quite make it to his legs and feet. They evaporated on his trunk taking with them much of the heat his body had generated. The process lasted about fifteen minutes during which time he fixed himself a bowl of high-fiber cereal.

He used to prepare the cereal with a little of his soy milk. In the last several weeks, he had been excluding milk altogether after observing that addition of the milk made him inertial and lackadaisical. He now ate his cereal dissolved in plain water. It made a clear difference because he felt light and could move briskly through the floors. There was the additional advantage of helping him maintain his weight which he had always had some trouble with.

By 6:55 he must be out of the shower. Five minutes later he must be dressing up and listening to the early morning television news and weather forecast. On most days, he had no use for the weather forecast. He lived within the hospital premises and what was happening outside did not concern him. It was just that he had a fascination with weather forecasting, the way lay people, out of ignorance, marvel at the wonders of modern day medicine. Besides, he liked all the meteorologists on his favorite Channel Seven, Sam Champion, Bill Evans and Veronica Johnson.

By 7:12 he would be fully dressed. He was not a fanciful dresser and since he did not use makeup unlike some of his friends, ten minutes was enough time for him to go from stark naked to fully clad and ready to go. The next eight minutes, however, were for housekeeping issues.

Juliana was off that Friday. That meant she would outsleep Stephen's departure. Stephen aroused her. "J," he said while shaking her gently, "good morning. I am ready to go. It's 7:12 and I am fully dressed."

She stretched her muscles and limbs which protested with crepitation. "The Daveneys were very appreciative yesterday for the contribution," she told Stephen. "Both of them were there. Many other people were coming in with their contributions. The body will lie in State in the Frank Bell Funeral Home on Monday afternoon. Bright called back yesterday to find out if you were all right. I told him that you were not feeling fine."

Stephen interrupted her. "Oh, I should have called him back yesterday. It was absolutely irresponsible of me not to have told him that . . . "

"But you did, Steve. Remember you called to cancel the game?" reminded Juliana.

"No, I didn't. I would have remembered. I don't have Alzheimer's disease. At least, not yet. Be that as it may, I will talk to him today."

"You did leave a message with his wife that you couldn't make it to the court. He was in the bathroom at that time. You were tired and drowsy when you made the call. I was fully awake that is why I am telling you so. Believe me, you did."

"Well, that is why I don't remember," reasoned Stephen.

He looked at the wall clock. It was 7:20 and time for him to depart. He had ten minutes to be at his post. He kissed his wife good-bye. It was helpful that he did not have to drive for hours from his house in the suburbs. With all the variables that impacted on the morning commute, there was no certainty of arriving on time. Dr. Kim for one, spent an average of five hours on the road each day. On a bad day, when unnatural conditions prevailed, he could spend four hours to get here from New Jersey. Dr. Godswill's longest day on the road to date, Stephen remembered because the latter was to relieve him in the emergency, was caused by a woman-made disaster. The sleep-deprived young woman had been driving and applying makeup at the same time when she crashed her Dodge Caravan into the traffic inside the Holland Tunnel. It had taken the authorities five hours to clear the crash site.

91

The elevator Stephen boarded to the endoscopy unit that morning was very crowded. One of the interns on board asked him a question about a patient he had seen the previous day, mentioning the patient by name. "Call me later," Stephen told him curtly. In the past, the hospital had signs in elevators that advised staff "not to discuss patients in the elevator." The signs were not replaced, however, after all the elevators were given a face-lift. Inexperienced interns were generally not aware of the problems associated with such cavalier handling of patient information.

When Stephen was an Intern at Union Hospital, there was a day two physicians were discussing a patient in a crowded elevator. The first physician had told his colleague the patient "had a problem in the left eye but the surgery had been done on the right by mistake. The operation had not gone as planned and the patient would likely lose sight in both eyes," he had said. His colleague had asked, "Is it also true that they had not obtained an informed consent for the procedure?" Nodding, the first physician had replied, "Unfortunately, yes." Unbeknownst to the discussants, one of the passengers on board the elevator was the patient's wife. Just before the hospital had become extinct, the case had gone to court.

Stephen looked around the elevator but the warning signs were definitely gone. In their places were obituaries. He was looking at the one at his eye level. It said "We regret to announce the departure of Mr. Valerius Benning, father of Ms. Benning of the dialysis department. Mr. Benning slept in the Lord at his estate at the ripe age of ninety-six after a brief illness. He led a productive and successful life. May he rest in perfect peace."

One of the elevator occupants introduced herself as Brenda Treeham. "We are collecting money for this death," she announced pointing to the Benning obituary. "Anything you can offer would be helpful." She placed her cupped hand before each rider in turn. They contributed one or two dollars each. When she stretched her hand before Stephen he reluctantly offered a five-dollar note partly because that was the lowest denomination he had in his possession. To that, the collector demurred, "Doc . . . " She completed the rest of the sentence with body language. The riders understood that he was expected to do more because he was an august physician. He raised his contribution to ten dollars which immediately elicited a broad smile from the collector.

"Thank you for all your sympathy. The Bennings deserve it. She has worked here for twenty-eight years. Her husband owns the funeral home across the street. They are doing very well. The departed patriarch led an exemplary and successful life." Ms. Treeham continued to laud the quick and the dead in the Benning family without convincing Stephen that the fund raising was justified or, in fact even, authorized. She thanked the donors individually as they alighted from the car.

What bothered Stephen was that the Bennings may never see the money. They probably would not see all of it. Receipts were neither asked for by, nor issued to, the donors. Out of incompetence or intention to embezzle, Ms. Treeham had just lumped all the contributions into her side pocket where she probably had her own money. Stephen had been shamed into making the contribution. It bothered him that the old-fashioned way of expressing sympathy—with elegy and gesticulation—was no longer tenable. In the new order, sympathy and condolence are for the highest bidder and the indigent ran the risk of being called indifferent.

In this hospital community, this kind of fund raising is a thousand-dollar business, completely unregulated, unmonitored and liable to abuse. Stephen's thoughts went to the secretary in the department of doctors' bonuses, Mr. Bravecamp. Hardly had Stephen assumed duty than the first of Mr. Bravecamp's three sisters' deaths occurred. For the first time in his working life, Stephen's bonus pay slip arrived with an obituary. The audacious notice stated, "It is with the deepest sorrow that we announce the untimely death of Ms. Maria Bravecamp, sister of Mr. Lot Bravecamp of the department of doctors' bonuses in a ghastly motor vehicle accident, which sad event took place in Costa Rica last week. Ms. Bravecamp was yet another victim of drunken driving. Your kind and reasonable donation of, at least, twenty dollars (paid directly to Mr. Bravecamp, preferably in cash) would go a long way not only to assist this budding and industrious young man but to send a clear message to those who drink and drive."

A good percentage of the two-hundred-odd doctors in the hospital, including Stephen, for a variety of reasons, responded favorably to the young man's plea. Mr. Bravecamp gave them the impression that he had worked hard to secure their bonuses. He had called most of the doctors well in advance to inform them that the hospital was likely to renege on the payment and how hard he was working to see that they got paid. In fairness to Mr. Bravecamp, before he came to the department, bonuses were not being paid regularly though it had to do more with the precarious financial situation of the hospital in those days. By the time he arrived, there had been a financial turnaround. Most of the physicians had no trouble or qualms doling out twenty dollars to him.

Eight months later when time came again for the next bonus payment another sister of his died in a gas tank explosion in Mexico.

Stephen's slip came with another obituary. "It has happened again. An innocent young life has been nipped in the bud. Ms. Lucie Brave-camp was blown to pieces in the recent gas tank explosion in Guadala-jara, Mexico. She is survived by Mr. Bravecamp of the bonuses department. Contributions of twenty-five dollars or more in cash are being made by kindhearted, well wishers directly to the bereaved Mr. Bravecamp. Thank you for counting yourself among them. Signed, RSVP Bravecamp."

Stephen did not contribute this second time because he had suspicions and he considered the threshold, twenty-five dollars, preposterous. If Mr. Bravecamp had the misfortune of having sisters at the wrong place at the wrong time, then that was pathetic. He began to ask around for the truth of the matter. By the time Mr. Bravecamp posted his third and latest obituary, Stephen had known that it was all a scam. There was confidential information out of the personnel department that Mr. Bravecamp had no sister and both of his parents had died before he joined this hospital.

The information convinced Stephen that guidelines for obituary fund-raising notices within the hospital were urgently needed. In fact, it was surprising to him that there were none already in place. In New York State there were all kinds of guidelines, protocols, and algorithms for hospitals and physicians. They covered the whole gamut of issues from the complex like treatment of heart attack to the ridiculous like hand washing.

The guidelines on hand washing called for the use of soap, for rubbing the hands against each other for not less than one minute and for drying the hands with a dry but not necessarily sterile towel at the end. The guidelines also required physicians and nurses to attend a three-hour course devoted largely to hand washing. The penalty for failure to comply was the suspension of license.

Sometimes Stephen used to think the bureaucrats who formulated the guidelines had nothing to do. Who in the world did not know that he or she should be washing hands regularly? His own son, three-year-old Christopher, was already an expert at hand-washing. He had trouble getting Christopher to wash his hands for less than five minutes. For the state to mandate a three-hour hand washing course for health care providers was a sad commentary on the medical educational system.

The single biggest problem with the hand washing guidelines was the absence of clocks in almost any hand washing facility. Many doctors and nurses were probably washing their hands for fifty-nine instead of sixty seconds, a violation of the state requirement. The state and hospitals would be well advised to replace the mirrors in the bath-rooms and in front of faucets with timers. Frankly, who needed a mir-ror to wash his hands, a procedure performed under direct vision? Another problem with the guidelines was that supplies, especially soap and towel were not always available at the hand washing facilities. Stephen had his own ideas on how the sporadic shortage could be elimi-nated.

One idea that came to him was the regulation and taxation of obituary funds. If hand washing could be regulated, why not fund raising? The hospital could easily mandate that all funds raised must be properly accounted for. Nobody would quarrel with that. The hospi-tal could also demand a cut of whatever was raised. The amount real-ized could be used to purchase supplies for hand washing facilities thus guaranteeing full compliance with the state hand washing guide-lines. Part of the money raised could be appropriated for a raise for housekeeping personnel. That way hand washing paraphernalia would be more efficiently and enthusiastically distributed.

The hospital could also delineate which types of deaths should be celebrated with fund raising drives. All deaths should not necessarily call for fund raising. If the late Mr. Benning bequeathed an estate to his progeny, whose husband's funeral home was doing brisk business, why should poor folks be asked to contribute their widows' mite? Only those who believed in giving more to those who already had a lot and taking away even the little in the hands of the poor could defend raising money for the Bennings.

The hospital could decree that if the departed was a financial lia-bility on account of infirmity or profligacy, the survivor should be satis-fied with the good riddance and not look forward to any contributions. Contributions would be most helpful to those employers who had lost a bread winner. Care must be taken not to create a financial incentive that might impel some unscrupulous employees to commit murder, though.

It would also be important to define, a priori, how the funds raised should be spent. Stephen did not want his contribution interred with the dead as practiced in certain eccentric cultures and religions. He would want his contribution used to help the survivors. He was not in support of ostentatious burial ceremonies financed by charity. Those who made large contributions to the burial ceremonies should be given a say concerning the choice of the funeral home, the cost, height and orientation of the tombstone. Stephen was still ruminating when his beeper went off. He looked at it and saw it was his wife Juliana paging him from home. Whenever he got a beep from a known number, he would try to figure out who was at the other end and what the matter was. With his wife the spectrum of differentials was narrow and, the guess work, easy. Highest on the list, was to remind him not to forget to go to the bank as he had promised. He almost never remembered having made such a promise, though. It did not matter that she had just received her own paycheck. Second was her desire to ascertain when he would be coming home for the day. The immediate corollary would be to establish that he had not planned any outing for the night. Usually, the third most common reason for her to page him was to give him a list of urgently needed supplies with the understanding that he would visit the grocery store on his way home.

As he reached for the phone to call her back, Stephen was sure he had not promised to go to the bank. He prepared his answers. If she wanted to know when he would be returning, he would say it was too early to know which, in fact, was the honest truth. To the question of what his plans were for the evening, he would say, in a nutshell, they were still evolving. He just hoped she would not ask for money because he could never win that one.

"Hello, J. Did you beep me?" he asked her.

"Have you spoken with Bright this morning?" Juliana asked.

"Very briefly. I was in a hurry and he, too, appeared to be in haste on the other end of the line. He asked me how I was feeling and I said I was fine. I cut it short with a promise to get back to him later," said Stephen.

"Since you disappointed him so badly yesterday, I thought you should call him with an apology or an excuse. You know he and his wife were told yesterday that you were feeling drowsy after taking some headache medication. I think the explanation is cogent and he would understand. I still think you should call him as soon as you have time."

"Okay. I'll do so. I've got work to do now. Talk to you later," said Stephen.

Juliana was prompted by two concerns to beep Stephen that day. Since he started living under the influence of Somnazolam, he had become very forgetful of events happening in the next several hours following the ingestion of a dose. Juliana knew that Stephen must have forgotten his conversation with Bright's wife the previous day. The last thing Stephen remembered was his preparation for the tennis game. Juliana was extremely concerned that in his explanation to Bright he might confabulate. That would leave Bright with the impression that either he was outright dissembling or he was losing his mind. At the minimum, Bright would conclude that something was terribly wrong. It was not hard to imagine that rumors about Stephen's credibility or mental condition would soon start and spread. Nothing could undermine a physician like questions about his mental stability, short of a strong suspicion of AIDS.

Juliana was also concerned about the effects of the drug on his personality and performance at the hospital. One morning earlier in the week, Stephen had packaged breakfast consisting of scrambled eggs and pancakes. When she asked him whom it was for, he had responded the endoscopy unit nurses had asked him to bring it. When Juliana asked him to leave the packaged meal behind, Stephen had done so without much ado. Juliana had been greatly disturbed by his new onset of suggestibility. She knew that it was certainly due to the effect of Somnazolam. She had agonized over continuing the experiment and had come to the conclusion that the risks were predictable and, with the necessary savoir-faire, manageable. She also thought that the benefits outweighed the risks. She had weighed, and then dismissed, the chance that some other woman could seduce him in that vulnerable state.

With that single call, she and Stephen would now sing the same tune to Bright. In future, she planned, she would update Stephen about everything the drug would cause him to forget. As long as he stayed home when she wanted him to, he would stay out of trouble including the prying eyes of those desperate women. She remembered the hundreds of patients she had seen restrained in the hospital for their own safety. For the first time ever, she became aware of the hidden benefit that accrued to doctors and nurses when those bellicose patients were restrained. They could rest on their laurels and not worry about the condition of the patients for hours. Though the state law required release from the restraints and reassessment every two hours, she thought for some patients, longer periods of restraint were more beneficial.

She likened Somnazolam to the hospital restraints. It kept Stephen home, away from women like Mel and Elsie Borble and Merry Oscar and her mind at ease. It was better for him to be sedated and drowsy at home than for her to receive a shrill call that he had been hurt in one of those unnecessary outings. With so many drunken drivers, trigger-happy hoodlums and pro-active law-enforcement professionals out there, danger was ever so near. It was not too long previously that Dr. Graham had a brush with the undesirable elements. The encounter had left him much shaken but physically all right. Though he had lost his Rolex watch, all agreed that it could have been worse.

In recent weeks many other doctors and nurses had similarly been in harm's way but Stephen had managed to escape unscathed. As Juliana saw it, pure luck and circumspection on his part probably played minor roles. The main explanation for his escape from harm was Somnazolam, she concluded anecdotally. She wished there was a way for her to quantify how much danger he had already averted with the drug.

She looked at her schedule for the day. Top-most among her priorities was shopping, especially for soy milk, the delivery vehicle for Somnazolam. Second, she would have to play the weekly lotto. Then there were other chores like laundry, replying to letters and to recorded phone messages. She had previously promised to take Christopher to the pediatrician's and to the toy store. Every second she spent thinking produced another task that must be done. Her worst enemy was time.

It was already ten in the morning, the hour by which, Juliana believed, all serious-minded individuals must get out of bed even on their days off. She arose and went to the refrigerator to compile the shopping list. She could almost never wholly trust her memory when going shopping. Some item was bound to be forgotten often prompting her to go back to the store. This had led Stephen at one time to consider her addicted to spending his money. The fact that she often bought some of the items they already had in excess only helped to reinforce the notion.

These days she shopped smart with carefully compiled lists. Peeping into the fridge, she surveyed the grocery. Milk, ordinary cow's milk for herself and Christopher was also in short supply. She was not so sure if continuing to drink animal milk was a good idea. Dairy farmers were now treating the cows with genetically produced hormones against the caution of some of the most thoughtful scientists. Though the government had bowed to the milk lobby and issued assurances that the milk was safe for human consumption, no one would know for years, if not decades, with rock-solid certainty. She put an asterisk after the milk.

She thought of switching over to soy milk, taking Christopher with her. The clear advantage would have been buying only one brand of milk for the whole family. On the other hand, it would have messed things up for the experiment on Stephen. The fact that the latter alone drank soy milk made matters easy. There was no chance that she, Christopher or guests would inadvertently ingest the sedative. If all of them changed over to soy milk, young Christopher may come under the influence of Somnazolam. Really, it might not be too bad after all. His hyperactivity could be controlled. For a moment, as she appraised the idea, it rapidly went from exciting to exceptive. Drugging an innocent three-year-old with a medicine not licensed for use in children less than six years would be not only the worst form of child abuse, she thought, but it would also be inexpiable cruelty. For now, she decided, she and Christopher would continue to consume animal milk and Stephen, soy. She put another asterisk after the milk again, one for each brand.

There was still an abundant supply of juices but it was always a wise idea to buy more. She could never predict how long the juice would last. Almost everybody who walked into their apartment was addicted to some kind of juice, thought all the juices shared one quality of having poor nutritional value. More often than not, Stephen would walk in on his way back from work with a group of friends arguing intensely about an impending sporting or political contest. They would talk their tongues dry even before saying "Hi" to her. It was interesting to see the men swear, predict, and bet on who would win. The most passionate was obviously Dr. Kurman who lived on the fourteenth floor. He would never end the argument until everyone else agreed with his analysis.

She could never understand the fuss especially when the bone of contention was a boxing bout or the Super Bowl. What she knew was that they would exhaust their supply of juices before dispersing to their respective apartments. She never followed sports as enthusiastically as the men but she may have heard that the Bulls of Chicago, with their Michael Jordan, or the Lakers of L.A., Magic Johnson's team, was coming to New York. The contest was being billed as a do-or-die affair for New York. She would not be surprised if Stephen returned later that evening with his loquacious entourage. She wrote down "juice" and "ten dollars" next to it. The brand composition of the juices would have to wait until she reached the store. It would be determined to a large extent by what was on sale.

They needed meat and fish as their supply was almost exhausted. She wrote down meat, the third item on the list and set aside six dollars for it. The meat category actually subsumed fish also. The shopping list, she often told herself, was not an academic thesis but a personal reminder and she could afford to be loose with terminologies and categories. Thus, milk could be derived from animal or plant sources. Included in the "juices" category were all drinkable fluids except bottled water and milk. As for the meat, she would have to inspect it well before buying. Certainly, she would not buy meat from Hyman's because the chain had been cited by the department of health for selling outdated meat. The violation was probably not peculiar to Hyman's. Other meat vendors were most likely equally guilty. It was just that they had not been caught. The penalty for the violation was so paltry that even Hyman must have continued to sell outdated meat. The stores were in the business to make money, not necessarily to please official regulators. Discarding a whole consignment of meat or fish because it was a day too old was just not a way to make some money.

Juliana wondered why meat that was good one day would suddenly lose its fitness for human consumption the next day. The officials who worried about germs colonizing the meat did not realize that adequate cooking and sanitary handling could keep beef safe even if the cow had been mad. The best tests for determining whether meat was fit for consumption would have been to smell, cook, boil or fry before tasting. These were all procedures meat packers and housewives were expert in. But the health officials, with little culinary training or experience, only carried out visual inspection. For once she thought meat inspection should be left to veteran shoppers, chefs and housewives. Juliana prided herself as an embodiment of all three.

She looked at the empty bottles of salad dressing lining the door of the fridge. They were all nearly empty. The mustard, the French and Italian. She picked up the Ranch dressing and read the instruction on the neck of the bottle. It read, "To open, unscrew cap."

"Who needs that?" she asked rhetorically. The Italian and French manufacturers must have considered the American people morons, she thought, for the only other way to access the contents of the thick bottle was to break it and nobody wanted glass fragments in his or her salad. She would look for American dressing. Hopefully, there would be no such condescending instruction.

"What about condiments?" she asked herself silently. She pulled out the basement of the refrigerator and appraised the modest amounts of onions, peppers and tomatoes. She would have to get some more. The previous evening there had been a news report that onions could protect, against stomach cancer, those who consumed it in large amounts. She had seen the agony of stomach cancer patients. As she held the onions in her hand to feel their texture, she hoped they would protect her. The main problem was that most of such medical discoveries usually did not withstand the test of time. In the same news bulletin, it had been reported that eating plenty of carrots did not protect from disease. She struck carrots from the list.

Juliana revised her list one more time. There were certain missing items. She looked atop the fridge and saw only one plantain. Ever since she was introduced to eating ripe plantain in the hospital, she had remained hooked. She was happy that they were sold cheap at Dravo and Key Food. She added it to the list. She also added potato to the list. She remembered reading somewhere that the potato skin was high in fiber which was good for the bowels. On the other hand, she had read about the controversy surrounding the use of chemical fertilizers. Some of the chemicals had been detected in the skin of fruits and tubers. She paced the kitchen, opening consoles and cabinets. She also looked in the bathroom for needed supplies and discovered they were running out of bathing soap, dish-washing soap, tissue paper and hand towels. In a short time the list was as complete as it could have been.

The remaining items like the nighttime Pampers for Christopher were left out with good reason. One way or another, she would get Stephen to dig into his own budget for them. After all, he was the one with the deep pockets. She would call him later and tell him that part of the money he had given her had been paid to her manicurist while another portion of it had been given to the old woman for watching Christopher twice in the week. She knew Stephen never objected to her hiring the old woman because the alternative would be for he himself to stay home with Christopher.

It would help, she thought, if Stephen called first to inform her of his tennis or other outing for the evening. She would then suggest that he should pick up the big ticket items at Pathmark on his way from the game. Experience had taught her that there was no better time to ask Stephen for money that when he was ready to set out for his tennis game or a business meeting. He never liked anything to distract him as he planned his game strategies.

Juliana turned to Christopher who had been up for the last hour. The latter was more interested in watching his "Power Rangers" tape than in anything else his mother had to offer. He tried to load the VCR with the "Power Rangers" tape. He did not succeed despite the tips his mother shouted intermittently to him while busy preparing her shopping list. The time had passed when he used to feed junk into the cassette compartment of the VCR if he could not get it to play. Six to twelve months ago Stephen had to repair the VCR three times because of Christopher's tampering. Juliana was afraid that by the time he finished with the VCR it would land in the repair shop one more time. But she could not stop compiling her shopping list just to help him. After all, they were planning to buy another VCR. That would have to be on Stephen's list.

In recent times Christopher had become more organized in his hyperactivity. He no longer fed paper into the VCR. He had developed a predilection for Power Rangers' video tapes after being exposed to them at the day care center. Before he went to the day care, he was fond of the less violent and educational "Barney" tapes Juliana bought for him. He could sing all the "Barney" songs and recognize the alphabets from A to Z. All that changed with the introduction of the kid action video "Power Rangers." Soon after he had been registered at the day care center, Juliana and Stephen had taken him to Toys R Us, the largest toy store in Brooklyn. As soon as he had seen the Power Rangers paraphernalia, he had demanded them and had begun to cry uncontrollably.

His parents were forced to buy the whole set, consisting of tapes, toys and tabloid. He became a changed child. Upon arising each morning, he would destroy an invisible opponent(s) with karate chops, elbow smashes and wild kicks. He would throw a profusion of blows and jabs at the air with his clenched fists while screaming "Power Rangers! Power Rangers!" Juliana was very worried by the aggressiveness. Even Stephen, a man of competitive and macho instincts, was not amused by his son's imitation of the action video.

The flip side of the whole story was that his general hyperactivity and attention deficit were abating. In the past it had been impossible for Juliana to take her eyes off him. In those days he would jump from chair to chair or from the love seat to the floor in dangerous acrobatic displays. He would attempt to stand on the arm of the chair and gyrate as a gymnast in training. On several occasions, Juliana had caught him in a free fall that could have resulted in bodily damage.

With the introduction of "Power Rangers," Juliana could rest assured that he was not in imminent danger. He would take several minutes to load the tape in the VCR. Having repaired it three times, Stephen had condemned the VCR and planned to buy a new one, which would be kept out of Christopher's reach. The new VCR would be unveiled only if Stephen wanted to record important sporting or political events. Christopher would be allowed to fumble with the dysfunctional VCR. Out of perseverance and hard work, he would get it to work. As long as the tape was playing, he would be completely consumed and the environment, too, could rest in peace.

Juliana could usually accomplish some tasks while Christopher was watching "Power Rangers." As she was not interested in watching television, there was no conflict of interests. Before she started making up her shopping list, she made sure Christopher ate his pancake. Then he was ensconced in front of the television. She did look up several times to see if he had yet succeeded in getting the contraption to play.

With the list ready, she turned to Christopher. "Take off your clothes. Let us go to the bathroom, Chris. Then we go to the store."

"To Dravo?" asked Christopher.

"Yes."

"I don't wanna go to Dravo, Mummy. I am tired."

"Why are you so tired, Chris?"

"I wanna watch Power Rangers."

"When we come back from the store."

"I don't wanna go."

"I'm gonna buy you blue and green Power Rangers when we get to the store."

"And yellow too, Mummy?"

"Yes."

"And black too?"

"Yes," she said.

Despite his apparent lack of focus and his tender age of three, Christopher had already mastered the art of deal making which could well be the key to success later in life. When a mother relies on inducements and concessions to get her three-year-old to comply with her commands, she must be careful not to pander to the child's wild or expensive wishes and desires. It would be only a matter of time before the child start dictating to the mother. At that point his mother may not have the mettle to say no. Children, three years old, do not know enough about grooming to decide when a shower is necessary before going to the grocery store. The mother of an unkempt and shabby child in the mall, not the child himself, would be the recipient of disapproving and stern looks and murmured condemnation. On the contrary, every passerby would want to hobnob with the mother of the clean and smart kid. A mother should, therefore, be able to order, or if necessary, whisk, her toddler to the bathroom without quid pro quo.

Realizing that, Juliana told Christopher, "Daddy will buy you Power Rangers if you behave." It was a promise she knew would not be made good because of Stephen's growing disapproval of the action video tapes. But it would not be her responsibility if it remained unfulfilled. It was not the responsibility of the mother to atone for the father's lapses, she thought.

"I'm behave, Mummy," Christopher responded.

She grabbed him by the hand and, after correcting him, "I'm behaving, mummy," undressed and led him to the bathroom.

At that time in the morning, parking was hard to find around on Washington Avenue so Juliana and Christopher walked the long block. They walked at the latter's pace past the school and the playground. Everything and everybody along the way distracted Christopher who was unaware of his mother's loaded schedule for the day.

It was a bright spring day and human activity and traffic were understandably heavy on Park Place. After a particularly harsh winter in which record snowfall had descended on Brooklyn, all were delighted to emerge from hibernation. There was a group of men at the corner of Classon Avenue and Park Place fumbling with the open bonnet of a car. They interrupted their task to gape at a group of women moving in the opposite direction from Juliana and Christopher, most likely to the hospital. Christopher stopped to say, "Hi, Hi," to the men, waving at the same time. It was as if he understood and appreciated the difficult tasks of mechanics trying to get a lemon to move and to get upscale, psychedelic women interested in them at the same time. Juliana, impatient, whisked him away wondering about the commiseration.

Midway through the block, they came upon Mrs. Branston, who lived on the second floor. The last time Juliana had seen her she had been carrying a near-term pregnancy. That was in the laundry. They had discussed the pregnancy. Juliana had asked her if she was expecting twins as her belly was rather distended. She had said she did not want to know in advance. She preferred the surprise to the a priori knowledge because she couldn't do anything with the latter. Her stomach was much reduced in size even from the distance and Juliana knew she must have recently given birth. They stopped to exchange pleasantries.

"When did it happen?" Juliana asked.

"Last Sunday," answered Mrs. Branston.

"Did you have twins?"

"No."

"Oh my God! What did the baby weigh?"

"Almost ten pounds. He is at home with my mother."

"Congratulations. It's good that your mother has come to help you. Having carried him for nine months you need relief."

Not participating in the exchange was Christopher who was transfixed by what he was seeing to their left. There were two exuberant but unattended dogs lounging on the basketball court. It was still too early for the ball players to come in and the dogs owned the court. They were separated from the sidewalk by the wire mesh. While Juliana was congratulating Mrs. Branston, another dog had approached on the proximal side of the fence, held in a leash by her master. Immediately, all the dogs on either side of the fence started a barking match. They were prevented from pouncing on one another by the fence and the owner's tether.

Christopher watched the uncivil and impolite behavior with keen interest and amusement. The animosity and violence must have reminded him of the "Power Rangers" he had become accustomed to seeing in the video. He was trying to draw his mother's attention to the animalistic free-for-all. He tapped her side several times but she did not notice or respond until she and Branston disengaged. Then she paid attention to him.

"Mommy, three doggy shouting," said Christopher.

"Say 'three dogs barking.' Let's go our way. You must always leave barking dogs alone. Don't go near or they will bite you. When you see sleeping dogs, let them lie. Now let's go." As they moved on, even Juliana could not help reflecting on why the animals had showed one another so much vitriol. There was so much random and often senseless violence in Brooklyn among men, supposedly, the most tame of creatures. Intellectually less-endowed animals, she rationalized, must be obliged their fair share.

She applied a gentle tug on Christopher to overcome his inertia and his continuing captivation by the violent dogs. They approached Washington Avenue hand-in-hand, Christopher's right to Juliana's left. Every now and then, Christopher would break free his right hand to wave vigorously to puzzled passers-by. To Juliana, that was dangerous conviviality. With the ever-present danger of child kidnapping and other child-centered depravity, the mother of a kid who cozied up to complete strangers had a legitimate reason to be concerned.

Once inside Dravo, the neighborhood store, she grabbed a copy of the weekly catalog, placed Christopher on the shopping cart and proceeded to study the catalog over the next fifteen minutes or so. As the saying goes, time is money. Juliana thought that the quarter of an hour she spent studying the catalog was a good investment. There were some interesting sale items but not everything she wanted. She might have to visit the other stores on Washington Avenue for better bargains, depending on how much time and money she had left.

She knew Dravo like she did the creases on her palms which was to say she could make a good off-the-head diagram of the store. She did not depend on the banners high above the aisles for direction. Some item locations, however, did change, in which case she would get them by chance or then consult the banners. Her first port of call was the dairy section where she grabbed three containers of soy milk without consideration of price. Certain items were too important to be held hostage by monetary considerations. She made the rounds through the aisles throwing merchandise into the shopping cart. Some aisles were visited several times. Then she came to aisle 3A. On one side were different brands of peanut butter. Juliana closely examined the bottles for salt, calorie and cholesterol content, cost, expiratory dates, et cetera. She held each bottle in hand turning it around to read the information. Christopher was sitting on the cart close to the other side of the aisle where brand cereals were displayed. He was attracted to a packet of cereal with a large "Power Rangers" logo. Unbeknownst to his mother, he stood up to reach for and grab the packet of cereal. He laid his hand on the packet but lost his balance on the shopping cart.

He fell to the floor, striking his face. The commotion drew his mother's attention, who moved to catch him before he hit the floor. It was too late. In his fall, he pulled down almost all the racks of cereal. The store personnel also rushed to the scene just as his mother was pulling him from under the rubble of cereal boxes. The expression on Juliana's face was, understandably, anxious. She had seen the blood oozing from his mouth as he opened his mouth to cry.

"Call the ambulance," one of the store managers yelled out to his subordinates.

"What happened? Is he all right?"another store assistant asked.

"Can I have some ice please? Ice and gauze if you have. Thank you," Juliana replied. She did not have to explain what had happened to anyone. It was obvious that the little boy had fallen and gotten badly hurt.

Presently, some store employee brought Juliana ice cubes. She wrapped the ice blocks with a leaf from the catalog and placed it on Christopher's lower lip to control the bleeding. Christopher stopped crying.

"My mouth is bleeding Mommy," he complained.

"Because you fell and hit your mouth. You will be okay," she consoled.

"My mouth hurts, Mommy."

Christopher's bleeding had ceased after his mother pressed his lower lip with the ice block. The superficial cut on the lip was exposed. "Open your mouth," Juliana ordered him. He complied with the command. There was no other cut in his mouth. All that profuse bleeding seemed to have come from his lower lip. He had lost one lower front tooth with two or three of his upper teeth loosened but far from falling off immediately. Juliana continued to comfort him. She patted and massaged his back as if that was the injured part.

Mothers have the habit of stroking the back even when the injury and pain are elsewhere in or on the body. Certain parts of the body like the mouth, lips and face are not accessible or suitable for stroking. The face, especially the face of a child, is not only too uneven, it does not present enough surface area for rubbing. Luckily, mothers have discovered that by placebo or some other strange mechanism of action, stroking the back usually soothes facial pain. The store personnel were there with Juliana offering every assistance they could. She did not rub

Christopher's lips. It could have opened the cut even further. Without knowing what had happened, and if Christopher had not been bleeding, had the store officials seen Juliana rubbing her crying son's lips, they would have suspected that he must have eaten some cookie on the shelf and his mother was trying to conceal the evidence. As far-fetched and weird as it may sound, veteran shoppers like Juliana had seen it happen.

The ambulance had arrived outside the store, the two technicians rushing inside with their stretcher. The male had his hair braided and had most likely not washed it for the last several days. At the back and temples the rows were loose and in disarray. Three copper rings pierced his left ear, arranged in increasing circumferences from down up. Their diameters stretched out the space between the edge of the ear and the hair line. The lowermost ring was so precariously placed near the edge of his ear that a gentle tug would have torn his earlobe apart. He also had holes in his nose and right ear that were free of rings. He had probably, recently transferred all his rings to the left ear freeing his right ear and nose as a vogue avant-gardist.

His female partner was a young woman probably in her early twenties. It looked as if she was new to the profession. She walked behind her male partner as if she had not been hardened by experience or in deference to him. She looked athletic, in contrast to the man who could benefit from some trimming. She wore a flat beret burying her short, if any, hair underneath. It was green in color as was their starched, calico uniform. Her apparent sense of esthetics impressed Juliana as her beauty must have done the men. Though she spotted no earrings, her light lipstick and exuberant eyelashes were more than necessary embellishments for her natural beauty. For a moment, the store manager and his subordinates forgot about the patient and ogled her. She did not realize that her beauty had just stood in the way of, but may not have compromised, medical care.

Christopher was standing on his feet sniffling as children do when they have no energy or excuse to continue crying. Juliana continued to rub his back and offer words of encouragement and sympathy.

"Stop crying, Chris, everything is okay. You wanna go home?" she asked.

Christopher nodded.

"You wanna talk to Daddy on the phone?"

He nodded again.

"What happened to him, Ma'am?" asked the male ambulance technician.

"He fell on the floor and hit his lip. He will be all right. In fact he is fine now. Thank you for coming so fast, anyway. You would not need to take him to the hospital now. He will be just fine. He has a private doctor," Juliana explained.

"How did he fall?" queried the store manager.

"He is fine now. Don't worry. He is fine. Let me pay for my groceries and go."

"Did he trip on something or what, please? Was he walking when he fell?"

"As you could see, he fell and cut his lower lip. The bleeding has almost completely stopped and he is all right now. I'll take him to the doctor. Thanks, all of you, for your concern and prompt response. He will be all right. I'll pay and go. Incidentally, I had already picked up almost everything I wanted." Turning once again to the ambulance crew, Juliana thanked them for their prompt response. She had heard and read reports of delayed arrival of ambulance teams at the scenes of emergencies. It was reassuring that when she needed them, they were there in no time.

"What is his name please?" asked the technician.

"Christopher," answered Juliana.

"Christopher Latham," said Christopher.

"What is your name again?" asked the female technician.

"Christopher Latham, he said," Juliana repeated.

"It's all right, Chris. You are such a good boy. Do you go to school?" The female technician started to stroke his back while consoling him.

Christopher nodded again. "He goes to day care," said Juliana.

"American Day Care," Christopher filled in.

"That's right. American Day Care," said Juliana.

The female technician said, "Stop crying, Chris. I got to talk to your teacher. You are so great. I'm gonna bring you candy tomorrow."

"Power Rangers," said Christopher.

"Good! Tomorrow I'm gonna bring you Power Rangers," said the female technician. She waved to Christopher as she made that promise. Then she left the store the way she had come, walking behind her male counterpart. The store manager and his two male deputies sneaked a look at her as she made her way out. Then they turned to each other momentarily but did not say anything. That kind of eye contact spoke more than a million words. Usually when the women were gone from the scene, or as in this case the serious matter of the child's injury was resolved, the verbal analysis would take place. The men had noted the name of the female ambulance technician and the fact that she worked for Ever Ready Ambulance. Her male companion, as far as they were concerned, may never have existed. Men, generally, don't care about men.

Though Christopher had stopped crying and his bleeding had ceased, the store manager still wanted to know the exact and immediate circumstances that led the kid to fall and cut his lip. He had already asked Juliana twice without making any headway. All he had seen was a bleeding three-year-old being pulled from the rubble and his mother's anxious and worried facial expression. If the kid was knocked down by falling merchandise then the store was in for a big legal case. Perhaps, he theorized silently, the aisle manager arranging bags of rice on the other side of the shelf had suddenly jolted it launching the unidentified flying objects which knocked the kid down. That was the only scenario that made sense to him. He wanted to confirm his theory before calling his superiors in New Jersey.

"But Ma'am, how did he fall?" he asked Juliana for the third time.

Juliana thought that it was her fault. She had already enumerated, in her mind, what she had done wrong and steps that could have averted the fall. She should have borne in mind her son's history of hyperactivity. She should not have placed him up so high on the shopping cart. Having, placed him there, however, she should not have taken her eyes off him. She could have given him a toy to play with. With all that mea culpa on her mind, she was not going to answer the question the store manager had posed. She would deliberately evade the question rather than lie. The store was full of people browsing and buying and, most likely, hidden cameras. If she told a lie, the former, the latter or both might controvert her version.

"I have already said he fell on the floor and, as you can see, he nicked his lip. But he is all right now. It is not your fault, I mean, personally. I will take care of it. I thank you for your help. By the time I come back with him next week, he will have healed. I will take him to his doctor this afternoon. Don't worry about it. Let me just pay and go."

The store manager was not satisfied. He realized that he was making no headway with this woman. He would present the case with the woman's obfuscation to his bosses and if necessary their lawyer. Nobody would blame him for not having seen exactly what happened. He reassured himself. There were so many of these women with their children in the store that it would not be feasible to watch all of them for falling debris. In his three years in the store nothing like that had happened and he was sure management would absolve him from blame. He tried his best in calling the ambulance. It was the woman's choice not to take advantage of it. But the woman's decision to go to a private physician bothered him because InnerFaith Hospital, a much respected institution, was only two blocks away. He would have been more worried had he known that she was a nurse there. A private physician may not be an uninterested party. He or she may issue a report that is legally more damaging than a public physician, he thought.

At the counter, the store manager made two offers to Juliana as her bill was being tallied. First, would Juliana mind if he sent one of the store clerks to deliver the grocery? he asked. Without hesitation, she said she would not. Second, he pleaded with Juliana to leave her job or home phone number so that management could reach her for further assistance. To that, Juliana said she could not foresee the need for further assistance. She politely turned the request down. She was not prepared to have these people call her home every minute to find out how he was doing. That would be an unwelcome intrusion into her privacy. Most importantly, she did not think the injury was serious. The worst that could happen, she thought, was that he would lose some of his teeth. Given Christopher's age that, too, would not be a permanent loss. Nature would replace the dentition.

One of the first items the counter clerk checked in was the bunch of plantains. They were bulky and cheap in comparison with any other foodstuff. The demand for plantains was low and Juliana always selected the most ripe; the batch that the store would soon condemn and discard. Not only was it more delicious then, but also the price fell even further. One dollar could buy enough of them to feed her whole family. Since she started cooking them, Christopher and Stephen had come to like and expect them too.

The counter girl was apparently new. She did not know what plantains were called. She turned to the store manager and asked, "What are these, big bananas?"

"They are called plantains," said the manager.

"How are they eaten?" she asked.

"When I was in the military, we used to talk of MREs. I am sure you don't know what MRE stands for. It stands for meal, ready to eat. This is an ideal MRE. You can eat them uncooked especially when they are ripe like these. That is how I like them. You can boil and eat them alone or in combination with some other food. In the West Indies, where these come from, people like to fry them. They eat them with rice or black-eyed peas. Here in the store, we also have the flour. In Vietnam, we used to make pudding of the flour, eggs, and milk. Not only is the dish delicious but it is also nutritious. No U.S. soldier lost weight in Vietnam that ate it. It's also a West Indian delicacy. I have to take you to that West Indian restaurant down the block at Washington and Atlantic or if you want a choicer place, Nagisaki," proposed the manager.

"Where did you learn all these cuisines, Jose?" the girl behind the counter asked.

"From the Culinary Institute," said Jose.

"Which one? The famous one on Forty-Second Street in Manhattan?" she asked.

"No, the one in my grandmother's kitchen."

They all chortled at Jose's wit. The counter girl continued to check in Juliana's grocery.

"But we don't have to go to my grandmother's because she is no more. We can go to Nagisaki," said Jose.

"Where is that? I have never heard of that. Is that not in Japan where one of the atom bombs was dropped?" she asked.

"That is Nagasaki. There is a difference in pronunciation if you listen very carefully. I don't think they grow plantains in Nagasaki, Japan because their climate closely resembles ours. If you find any plantain growing there, it must be in an artificial biosphere for research purposes. You want to see the natural thing, I hope. Under ideal conditions, the plants can grow up to thirty feet or so. The stems are green in color, which enabled us to blend with them, in Vietnam, as a chameleon does with any environment. The broad leaves are attached to the trees by thick petioles. During rainfall, and the rainfalls in South East Asia could drench you in a minute, we used the leaves as umbrellas. The plantain trees and the camelia were my ideal battlefield vegetation in Cambodia and Vietnam.

"Plantains require high temperatures and heavy rainfall to grow. They cannot cope with the icy conditions that prevail here and in Japan. But you and I will talk. Let's finish with this very patient customer first."

"How are they grown?" the counter girl asked as she continued to check Juliana's grocery.

Computers made the counter girls' (there was no male among them) job easy. They would pick up the grocery from the rolling board, disarm the security tag and transfer it to the take-away bags without any responsibility for misrepresentation of prices. Juliana wondered what would have happened in the absence of computers. Her generation, she believed, had trouble adding two and two.

"It doesn't grow in this climate. If you want to see how they grow you may have to go to Vietnam. That is where I first saw them. Sometimes we used to survive on them in the jungle, until the air force located and resupplied us. Vietnam may be too far for you, though. It is not necessary to go that far to see how plantain is grown. There are land mines all over the place, to boot. I am ready to take you on a cruise to the West Indies where plantain planters plant the plantain plants in the plantain plantations. Like I said, let's finish with her first and we will talk."

Juliana looked at the fast-talking and cute-looking store manager. He seemed to enthrall the counter girl, though the latter did not immediately address his offer of more talks or a Carribean cruise. She was possibly still thinking of the precipitate offers or awaiting the details where the devil resided. Juliana knew that the smooth-talking store manager would not sponsor the young woman on a Carribean cruise just so that she would see what a plantain plant looked like. It was interesting to her how men utilized their assets, including the knowledge of a plantain tree, when making an advance.

The bill was more than all the cash she had at hand. She paid with her credit card. The trip back home from Dravo was similar to the one from home to the store except that they moved in the opposite direction, retracing their steps. They were accompanied by the aisle manager who was delegated by the store manager to deliver the grocery to the Lathams' home. Nearly everybody who shopped at Dravo lived nearby and the store personnel knew it. So when one of the store underlings was assigned to deliver groceries, they did not grumble. In fact, they relished it because of the tips they stood to receive.

There was a handful of young men out there on the basketball court. Despite the pain he was supposedly feeling in his mouth, Christopher was attracted to the players and waved effusively to them. The men who were sweating under the hood of the car near the corner of Classon and Park Place were still there, now joined by a fourth man, still working feverishly inside the open bonnet. When they came close enough, Christopher freed himself and tapped one of the men before his mother could restrain him. The man panicked with the thought that his pocket was being picked and took defensive action. He slapped the hand tapping him, turning at the same time. He heaved a sigh of relief as the little boy waved "Hi" before his mother pulled him away and apologized for the distraction.

The store assistant helped Juliana unload the grocery at the doorway. Juliana looked hard for a single dollar to give him and eventually found one. There were a couple of fives and tens but she did not think the young man's labor was worth that much. She knew that generally, most of the doctors' wives and nurses in the apartment block paid one or two dollars for such service. Anything above that could have sent the wrong message. The young man could have thought that her problem was not making money but spending it. Before long he might have planned a burglary if he had the proclivity.

Juliana's intention had been to call Stephen and tell him about Christopher's fall and injury. As soon as the store assistant left, she was reaching for the phone when it rang. She hoped Stephen was on the other end. He usually did not call early in the afternoon. But she hoped he was the one, anyway. At least, she would be reassured that he was functioning well. Since he started taking Somnazolam, she had been concerned about his job performance. To date, she had not heard any complaint or question from any of the other doctors' wives or tenants though gossip was rife especially in the basement laundry.

She picked up the receiver and was taken aback by who was on the other end of the line. "This is the office of Merchamb and Golsonbaum, Brooklyn's most aggressive trial lawyers," the caller announced. Juliana's heart skipped a beat. What had she—or Stephen—done to earn a call from those aggressive lawyers? She asked herself. She had never contacted a lawyer for any reason whatsoever. As far as she could remember, she had no unresolved appointments with the law. Nor did she believe that Stephen had come under the auspices of the legal system. She wanted to tell the caller she'd rung the wrong number.

"This is Mrs. Latham. How can I help you?" she asked.

"This is about your son's fall and injury in the grocery store. We are ready to help."

"The boy is all right now. Thank God. I am taking him to his doctor in just a few minutes for a routine checkup," said Juliana.

"We will represent you in the civil lawsuit and win the large cash awards you deserve for you. The best part of it is that it would cost you absolutely no money or time."

"We are not thinking of suing. It was not their fault he fell. I don't want to sue anybody. I just want to take care of him."

"May I just remind you that you are about to throw away a whole lot of money. The supermarket chain is a multi-billion-dollar business that has very little regards for the safety of customers. We understand the pain you and your whole family are feeling and we think Dravo should take responsibility. It will cost you absolutely nothing."

"No. Thank you for your concern. I got to go now."

"Well, if you ever change your mind remember we are here every minute of every hour, twenty-four hours a day for the three hundred and sixty-five days of the year. Give us a call and we will come to you."

She hung up and began to wonder how the lawyers got to know about the accident so fast. Immediately the phone rang again.

"May I speak with Dr. Latham please?" The caller begged with a sweet feminine voice.

"He is not here right now, may I take a message?" asked Juliana.

"I am calling from the office of Bovey and Hovey, New York's number one in personal injury litigation. It's about Christopher who was injured in Dravo."

"I have already decided I don't want to sue anyone for the accident."

"That is the natural disposition. Maybe you will change your mind when I give you these facts. Dravo has had multiple citations from the city department of consumer affairs and a number of other agencies. Last year they settled a case similar to your son's out of court for hmmm . . . I'm forbidden to reveal the terms. . . . They have so far failed to make court-specified structural changes on their shelves that could have prevented your son's injury. You have very strong ammo for the case. All you have to do is sign the papers and leave the rest to us. The next set of papers you will be asked to sign are your checks. Guaranteed."

"Thank you for your interest and concern. I still do not want to sue the store. It was not their fault. Right now I just want to take him to his doctor."

"Are you driving?"

"We are taking a cab," said Juliana.

"If you give us ten minutes, we will arrange transportation for you. One of our drivers should be there in about that time. Where do you want to be picked up?"

"That would not be necessary. Thank you, once again."

"Let me put it this way; in the next two and a half years, if you have any reason to change your mind, remember we are waiting to take the call and to win big bucks for you. After that time limit, you may have no right to sue."

"Thank you for everything."

Juliana thought hard about the medium by which the lawyers got wind of the accident. She was again interrupted by the phone. This time it was Stephen.

"J., I have been trying to call you in the last hour or so but the phone has been engaged continuously. What happened to Christopher? Two lawyers have just called me with offers to represent the family in suits against Dravo. What really happened there?"

"Christopher was sitting on the shopping cart. For one split second that I took my eyes off him, he stood up to grab a packet of cereal with a Power Rangers logo. He lost his balance and fell. He sustained a superficial laceration on his lower lip which bled for a little while. He

114

lost one lower front tooth. Two other upper front teeth are also shaky but they will probably hold."

"And why are all these lawyers calling me. Did you tell them you wanted to sue?" asked Stephen.

"No. Two firms have called here also. I don't even know who told them about it. I want to take Christopher to Dr. Alban's now. Geesh . . . it's getting late. Let me be going."

Juliana called Dr. Lucille Alban, Christopher's pediatrician. Dr. Alban was seeing her last patient. Though she had a tight schedule, she agreed to accommodate Christopher. Juliana liked her because she was always there when they needed her. She understood that children's illnesses usually did not come with prior warning and prior appointment was not always feasible. Her experience as a mother made her a better doctor. All her three children were successful adults. Now that she was single, her patients, the children were her obsession.

When Juliana arrived at the pediatrician's office, she met one woman in the waiting lounge. Dr. Alban was inside the examination room with another patient. Juliana thought she may have seen the woman before, for her face looked familiar. Possibly they had met in the same office during a previous visit. With children running helter skelter and mothers screaming to restrain them, it would have been impossible for Juliana and the other women to have given each other more than a fleeting look. The woman had two children with her. One about three years of age, was sitting on the carpet playing with his toy while his kin, not more than a few months old, rested uneasily on his mother's lap.

"Hi, how are you doing?" Juliana greeted her.

"I am all right. And you?" she responded.

"Fine. Have you been waiting for long?"

"No," she said flatly before adding, "I would not complain even if I had to. Dr. Alban is so good to me. I had no appointment for this visit. When I called about an hour ago, the receptionist told me she couldn't see me today. I insisted on talking to the doctor myself and she grudgingly transferred the call. I was surprised when Dr. Alban told me to come in, even though office hours had passed. Even if I had to wait for two hours I would not complain. Most other practices would have asked me to reschedule especially as the children are not really sick. They would have said 'This is no emergency. Come tomorrow.' Most of the doctors out there define an emergency differently from the way we parents know it. My children are fine but since I am traveling to the South tomorrow, I decided to bring them for a check up," explained the woman.

"Where in the South are you traveling to?" asked Juliana.

"Rankin County, Mississippi," she responded. "That is where my grandparents were originally from. Our great-grandmother died there yesterday at the age of one hundred and six. The whole family will be there."

"Oh my God! That is where my grandparents came from too. I still have family there. What is your name?"

"Lisa Owens, though our family name is McCorey. Most people in Pearl know the McCoreys. Our grandmother who passed away yesterday was the oldest person in Pearl."

"My grandparents came from Whitfield. In fact, my mother was born there. She came to New York in the early fifties. Her father, the Reverend Blaney, was well-known down there too. I have no doubt that our families down there know each other. When you get down there ask about the Blaneys. From what I understand, there was only one high school there in those days. They must have been in school at the same time."

It was unusual for Juliana to come across people from her roots. Both she and Lisa were very excited. For one thing, the population of that conurbation in the forties and fifties was undoubtedly low. Familiarity and, in many cases, consanguinity existed between the families. The two women felt like they were sisters. The atmosphere became even more animated when they discovered that they lived two blocks apart. They exchanged telephone numbers.

"What do you do?" asked Juliana.

Lisa replied, "I am a legal secretary. I work for a large firm of personal injury attorneys in the city."

"Oh my God! You are precisely the person I needed to meet. It is wonderful the way God arranges things. You must help now. The reason I am here is that my son fell in Dravo while I was shopping. No sooner did I reach home than the lawyers started calling. They all wanted to represent me in a lawsuit. I have been wondering how they got the information so fast."

"Did the ambulance take you to the hospital?"

"The ambulance came but I decided not to take him there because I wanted to bring him here. I knew that if I called Dr. Alban, she would see us no matter how many patients were waiting."

"Did the ambulance crew ask you for identification?" asked Lisa.

"There were two of them. A man and a young woman. The man begged me to sign a document so he could prove to his boss that he actually came to the scene of the accident. That was all."

"That was it then. The ambulance man gave your name to the law firms. We have them in my firm. No firm of trial lawyers can survive in this competitive environment without them. Each firm has a different name for them. We call them partners with a small 'p.' They get paid to reconnoiter crime and accident scenes for cases worth pursuing. There are all kinds of arrangements for their payments depending on their usefulness to the organization and their educational level.

"In my law firm, we have all kinds of professionals among our partners. Just think of the first people to arrive at crime or an accident scene and you are thinking of partners. The single most important question job applicants are asked in my firm is to list the first three categories of people to contact on behalf of crime or accident victims. Anyone who mentions family members first, fails. There was an MBA from Columbia the other day who flunked the oral test. The question is important because all the employees are engaged in the recruitment of partners. In your case, I am sure the ambulance driver was the partner. It would appear to me that he was a partner in more than one firm. You see, partners are not doing anything wrong, legally."

"Could it be the store manager? He was particularly interested in my identification and phone number."

"It is possible. It is possible. Well, that would make him a subversive. Money talks and you know many people would sell their parents for a few hundred dollars. For him to have been recruited as a partner, he must have a second job that places him in a strategic position. He could be an ambulance driver or a hospital employee. One of our most valuable partners is an X-ray technician. Nothing impresses a jury as a bone broken into pieces and displaced. I have no medical education but I can recognize a broken bone on X-ray. We also have doctors on our list though they report only directly to the lawyers.

"The one that would amaze you is the priest we have on the list. When I first discovered his existence, I came to the realization that money (she was pill-rolling her fingers for emphasis) not only talks but could corrupt even the most puritan. Then, I discovered that he was not really a priest. He was a fake. He roams the highways and mean streets offering, for the stricken, not only benediction for the life to come but also a lawyer's complimentary card, that of my boss, to help with the life here and now. He had been as good to my firm as his compensation has been to him. The good thing about his business is that when you see a priest, you don't suspect he may be a fake. If you do, the follow-up question would be why is he doing it? And without a motive, your suspicion becomes tenuous. No one, not even the cops, asks the clergy to prove their authenticity."

"Which law firm do you work for?"

Lisa realized she had already given away more company secrets than she should have. On the one hand she did not want to tell Juliana the name of the firm but the camaraderie was growing so intimately that she did not want to offend Juliana either. She was thinking of a way to parry the question and then change the topic with enough subtlety as to make the change unnoticeable. At that point, Dr. Alban came to her rescue. The latter opened the examination room door and projected her head out to assure Juliana and Lisa that she would soon be with them.

"Take your time. Don't worry about us. We are having fun here," the two women told her, almost in unison.

"You must tell me about it." She smiled as she disappeared back into the examination room, shutting the door.

Juliana looked in the direction of Christopher and Lisa's first son who were struggling for a Power Ranger toy. "Christopher, leave him alone with the toy. It is not your own. Leave him alone," she screamed. She moved to physically restrain Christopher as her order fell on Christopher's deaf ears. Pointing to Lisa's son who was fending off Christopher, Juliana asked what his name was.

"Johnson," said Lisa.

Juliana, gently shaking the hand of Lisa's other son, asked, "And him?"

"William."

"This is just like on my floor in the hospital. You know, I am the head nurse on the fourteenth floor of my hospital, InnerFaith Hospital. On any given day, we have so many Williams, Williamses, Williamsons; so many Johns and Johnsons that I sometimes wonder if it is due to the lack of other, equally beautiful names. It is very easy, except with proper care, to label one patient's blood with another's stamp. So far we have succeeded in preventing a major accident. It is very interesting how some names are very popular while many others don't appeal to parents. It appears to be so among most cultures. Not too long ago this common-name phenomenon reached a crisis point when we had five Korean patients at the same time. Four of them bore the same name—Kim. There was a lot of confusion among the staff. Luckily, three of the Kims were discharged within three days.

"I have always wondered about the origin and meaning of some of these names. When Christopher was to be named, my husband suggested Moses. I thought the name belonged to too distant a time. My husband was looking for a name that would convey a meaning compatible with the circumstances of his birth. I wanted a more contemporary name."

118

"What were the circumstances of his birth?"

Juliana turned to Christopher who was deeply absorbed in his play with Lisa's son Johnson. She was about to reveal a secret she and her husband were determined to keep to themselves and their close-knit friends. She had hardly known this stranger called Lisa but for some strange reason, she was already confiding in her. She had never talked so intimately with a stranger. Maybe Lisa was different from all other strangers she had met. They both could trace their origins to two adjacent hamlets in the cotton fields of Mississippi with a strong likelihood of consanguinity between them. They had just discovered that they were neighbors in addition. They shared equal admiration for Dr. Alban. During the time of their dialogue, they had seen more of themselves in each other. In a situation like that it was not surprising for them to enter the unguarded hour and begin to discuss their personal and professional lives in ways they would have otherwise considered unthinkable.

Juliana looked at Christopher again because she did not want him to hear what she was about to say. He was busy playing with Johnson. Children make, and break up with, friends so rapidly that parents must learn from them. Only a few minutes earlier Christopher and Johnson were at each other's throat over a Power Rangers toy. Now the Power Ranger was lying idle as they played with a toy truck, one propelling it to the other and back. Juliana was convinced Christopher was too distracted to hear anything she might say.

"He was abandoned at birth by his mother. A young woman found, and brought, him to my hospital. At that time I was working in the neonatal unit. He looked so innocent and cute that I fell in love with him. It was love at first sight. I easily prevailed upon my husband that we must take him home. My husband is a physician in the same hospital and it was not hard for us to scale the bureaucratic hurdles. It is our intention never to let him know. Later we discovered he was hyperactive. You couldn't take your eyes off him for one minute at home. Initially, we used to receive a lot of complaints from the day care about his hyperactivity. Recently, he has improved—especially after we bought him Power Ranger tapes—in the sense that his hyperactivity is more structured and predictable. I still bring him for routine checkup, anyway."

"Is your husband a gynecologist?"

"No. He is a gastroenterologist."

"I got that problem too, a lot of gas in my stomach."

Juliana, a restrained beam on her face, tried to dissect the unintended pun. "Incidentally," she explained, "most of his patients don't have gas problems. Gas itself is not a problem. It is just that what you feel as gas may portend a more serious diagnosis. Peptic ulcer disease, pancreas inflammation, gall stone disease and some other conditions can all present like gas. If it has been going on for some time, you should seek help. My husband treats patients with stomach ulcer, stomach cancer, bleeding and other diseases of the intestines. His practice involves, in the main, passing tubes through the mouth and rectum to look inside and treat them."

"My best friend is married to a doctor but, for the most part, she doesn't see him. I usually feel sorry for them," said Lisa.

"It is a problem, I can tell you. His typical week is like this: Monday to Friday, eight to five, he is in the hospital. Monday evening: Doctors' society meeting or tennis; Tuesday evening: his private office; Wednesday evening: moonlighting in the emergency department; Thursday evening: some professional meeting or dinner; Friday evening: update on the latest advances in medicine; Saturday morning: his private office; Saturday evening: moonlighting in the emergency department. Sunday morning: tennis. It is not always like that. Sometimes it is worse. In fairness to him, recently he has been spending more time with us because of the medication, I mean, soy milk he is taking. The soy milk is so heavy that it weighs him down as a sedative."

Juliana was embarrassed by the loose talk. She had recovered almost instantaneously to repair some of the damage. She was relieved the word Somnazolam did not flow out of her mouth. It was just one of those things. Some secrets are too hot to be concealed in one's mind. They have to be processed and released in such a way that they may not cause problems in the keeper's life. One good way is to reveal it cryptically to a stranger one might never encounter again.

"Do you have any other children?"

"My sister, we have tried everything. We have consulted all the world-famous Manhattan infertility experts, to no avail. All tests have come back normal. As you would imagine, it must be frustrating for my husband. A physician, he must heal himself. He feels very strongly about having his own biological child to perpetuate his pedigree."

"We had the same problem for the first five years of our marriage. I began to feel that he would look outside our home for better luck. I know what you have gone through because we also experienced it. Our inability to have children was driving my husband nuts and threatened our marriage. We had spent enormous time, energy and money and I was on the verge of despondency when we were given an unsolicited prescription by an acquaintance. It sounds incredulous but it works."

"What was it?" asked Juliana.

"You are a nurse and your husband is a doctor. Both of you know better than I do that it is not always the most expensive therapy that is most efficacious. Now the prescription is you and your husband have to do it on the floor, not in bed. That is how these two children came into the world. For the first five years that we did it in bed we came up empty-handed."

The examination room door opened again. The woman who had been inside with Dr. Alban exited with her tearful daughter. Dr. Alban again projected her head out of the room and after pleading with Juliana to exercise a little more patience, asked Lisa in. Lisa arose and gathered her children into the examination room. With William on her left shoulder, she turned back at the door toward Juliana. She supported William with her left hand and pointed her right hand and extended index finger at Juliana and emphasized for the last time, "Remember, on the floor," before disappearing into the examination room.

There was disbelief on Juliana's face. She was surprised not only by the bizarre and simplistic nature of the advice but even more by the conviction with which Lisa delivered it. There was no time or opportunity to draw out Lisa for the details or proof of her panacea for her infertility. It appeared to have come from some primitive or ancient culture. It was, in reality, a powerful anecdote which no one could vitiate.

It wasn't long before Dr. Alban was ready to see Juliana and Christopher.

"Sorry you had to wait so long," said Dr. Alban.

"You don't have to be so apologetic. I should be the one to apologize for keeping you so long past your closing time," said Juliana.

"So what happened to Christopher?"

Juliana explained what happened at Dravo while the doctor examined Christopher. The latter was playful and in high spirits. There was a small, non-bleeding cut on his lower lip and one missing lower incisor tooth. The rest of the examination was unremarkable.

"Christopher, you are going to be all right. The cut on your lips will heal in a few days." Turning to Juliana, she added, "Children have a remarkable healing potential. You parents know that even better than we do. Given his age, the lost tooth will re-grow too. He is not in pain now because of the Tylenol you have already given him at home. If he complains of pain at home, give him one or two more doses of Tylenol. As for his hyperactivity—you did say on the phone the other day that it has improved . . . "

"That's correct."

"In retrospect, you and your husband were correct to have refused treatment for the condition. I myself think there are still questions of diagnosis and of efficacy and safety to be addressed before large scale treatment with currently available drugs could be adopted. I think he is coming alone fine."

Juliana thanked Dr. Alban for the visit. They bade each other a nice day. She got Christopher fully dressed and left.

Back home she beeped Stephen to brief him on what had been going on. He did not answer which meant he must have been doing some procedure. She turned her attention to other household chores with the intention of beeping him again some time later.

Life Under the Influence

Stephen was chatting with the nurses while preparations were being made for the next case when his beeper rang again. Ms. Hayes, Nosborrow, Ranoche and Juliette Painter were all present in the lounge. The room had to be cleaned and perfumed for the next case. The instruments had to be sterilized and readied. He looked at the beeper and realized his wife was paging him. He picked up the phone and called back. Juliana informed him that they had come back from the pediatrician's office and everything was fine. He shot back that he would see her later. He dismissed her quickly because he wanted to rejoin the ongoing conversation about the state lottery.

"I think the $125 million is too big a sum to be won by one person. They should split the money and make it possible for at least two players to win," Nosborrow was saying.

"Reduce the stakes and you reduce participation. I would like to win the $125 million. But I don't think I can win. The geographic odds are stacked against me. In the last six months it seems only Westchester county residents have won. If you want to win the $125 million, you may have to move to Westchester County," said Ranoche.

"Somebody in the Bronx and another in Queens won the last draw and split the fifty million. The wheel of fortune, it seems, is moving near. Don't be surprised if the winner of the next draw is from Brooklyn," said Ms. Painter.

In the last ten minutes or so, Stephen had yawned four times. He felt tired and weak but was able to function. He did not complain to any of the nurses because he did not want them to start making fun of him. It was, after all Friday, his busiest day, on which he was expected to be tired. Part of his lethargy, he reasoned, resulted from not having worked out in the last two weeks. When he yawned for the fifth time, however, he felt some embarrassment. The fact that the yawn was contagious, affecting all four nurses in quick succession only partially helped to restore his composure. But it did prevent the nurses from ridiculing him for his incessant yawning and general appearance.

"Dr. Latham is something wrong? You look kind of dull today. You have, in the last ten minutes, yawned about six or seven times," noted Ms. Nosborrow.

"Interestingly nobody knows why we yawn. Thank God it is Friday. I will be able to sleep well tonight since I am off this weekend. I just hope my son will permit me to. Tomorrow morning I will be able to go to Prospect Park to shake off this listlessness," said Stephen.

"Are you sure it is not hunger? We got snacks here. We don't want our dear doctor to collapse here," said Ms. Hayes.

Stephen, smiling, said, "Thank you Ms. Hayes, the Compassionate. I feel full."

"I know what it is that makes him yawn so much," said Ms. Ranoche. "It is not hunger because he ate not long ago. It is tiredness resulting from having worked too hard, though not in the hospital. It is not his son who doesn't let him sleep. He is just too shy to say who doesn't let him sleep. I know because last night I was under his bed, counting."

All burst out laughing with the exception of Juliette Painter. Her take on the situation was entirely different. She was Stephen's neighbor and secret admirer. Several discreet observations had led her to believe that Stephen's wife Juliana was giving him a raw deal. She had watched as he almost never answered his pages when she was at the other end. When he did answer, she had also noticed, there was lack of depth and breath in the conversations. Now she was convinced that her nagging was responsible for his inadequate sleep. Not lost on Ms. Painter also was the fact that Dr. Latham, an anti-smoking crusader of some sort, was living with a chain-smoking wife. The matter was too emotional for him to talk about and the fullness of his heart, Ms. Painter reasoned, must be affecting his countenance.

Presently, the room and the next patient were ready for the procedure. The junior doctors had seen to all necessary preparations for the procedure. They had obtained the informed consent. In doing so they were surprised by not only the number of questions the patient had asked them but also by how much he appeared to know about the procedure. He was the kind of patient that intimidated interns. He had told the junior doctors that he had just turned fifty and had decided to comply with the little known government recommendation that all men and women aged fifty or older should be screened for colon cancer. To the amazement of the interns and residents, he had also said that though the recommendation called for screening with flexible sigmoidoscopy, he was opting for colonoscopy which he was sure had a higher diagnostic yield. He had done his homework, he assured them, and did not need any lecture on the benefits and risks of the procedure. But he refused to divulge the source of his knowledge or what he did for a living. He would only admit that he had never even applied to a medical school or received any education in a related field. They were convinced he had either dropped out of medical school or had been stripped of his license by the authorities for some violation.

Stephen walked into the room with Ms. Painter and Nosborrow and found Mr. Seb Bruwa on the table. They shook hands as they exchanged pleasantries.

"You were able to make it. That is very good," said Stephen.

"My health comes first. I promised you I would make it even at the expense of other commitments," Bruwa explained.

Stephen turned away from the dignified patient to tell his staff about him. "Mr. Bruwa," he began, "is a man of extremely high IQ. When I saw him in the emergency room some weeks ago, he was on the verge of turning fifty. I was impressed by his body of knowledge. I wished I knew half as much. We discussed screening for colon cancer among other things. As soon as he turned fifty, he called me back to say he was ready to go.

"If any of you had the opportunity to participate in the dialogue, you would have concluded I was talking to a professional colleague, not a man who had never received any medical education whatsoever. There is a lot he knows that people in our profession don't. He knows, for example, that cancer of the colon is the second deadliest cancer after lung cancer and for the most part it is preventable. Believe it or not, he also knows that a woman older than seventy-five is by far more likely to die of colon, than of breast, cancer.

"When he called me, he insisted on having colonoscopy rather than the recommended sigmoidoscopy. When I asked him why, he said it was the wave of the future. Like most sages in history, he lives ahead of his time. Although he had never undergone this test, he is fully aware of the risks and benefits of, as well as the alternatives to, the procedure.

"He owes his gratitude to the U.S. Army, which discovered his high aptitude and commendable attitude. He was given wide latitude while on the force because of the discovery. You know the motto, 'Be all you can be'. One of the options he chose to exercise was early retirement. I have no doubt that he will live long. Having said all these, I must say I am disappointed in him for two reasons. He should have studied medicine. He would have been a great asset to the profession. Secondly, he should have produced at least one offspring so as to pass the intelligence on. I think it would be a great tragedy for society if his great traits are interred with him in the final analysis."

Mr. Bruwa, who had been brimming with visible exhilaration as Stephen sang his plaudits, interjected. "That was what they kept telling me in the army. The army had, and still has, a special interest in eugenics. That should not surprise anyone here. Believe me, my seeds have been planted far and wide and I have already seen the flowers. I cannot say more without creating a stir here. I am ready for the colonoscopy. Let's go," he concluded causing quite a stir all the same.

"So are we, Mr. Bruwa. Give him fifty and two, Jack," said Stephen.

Jack, one of the junior doctors working with Stephen, slowly gave Mr. Bruwa injections of the sedative medications Demerol and Somnazolam while explaining to the patient that he might feel some burning sensation at the site of the injection. "I am more concerned about amnesia and depression of my respiration. I am not worried in the least about the burning sensation," Mr. Bruwa responded. All the nurses and doctors were wondering what kind of a patient he was. Without any formal medical education how could he have known about the specific toxicity of these drugs? They wondered.

In a few minutes Mr. Bruwa was sedated but fully conscious. The lights were dimmed to enhance the solemnity and formality of the occasion. All chattering came to an end. The procedure was started with the tube introduced into the patient's rectum. As it was slowly and carefully advanced, with all eyes glued to the television monitors, the patient ran commentary and asked questions underscoring his deep knowledge of human anatomy.

"Is that polyp in the sigmoid?" he asked Stephen. Five minutes later he said, "That must be the transverse colon; the folds are triangular." When the tube reached the end of the large intestine, he heaved a sigh of relief. "Finally, the cecum. Look at the opening of the appendix and the ileo-cecal valve." By now, all members of the team, as they would tell one another later, had become convinced that the patient was dubiously concealing his medical background. When it comes to protecting professional turf, medical personnel probably have no rival. None of the nurses and doctors attending Mr. Bruwa could be easily convinced that some interloper could master their jargon so thoroughly. Stephen's strong affirmation that Mr. Bruwa had no formal medical education only helped to deepen the enigma.

"As you can see Mr. Bruwa, there was one polyp in the rectum. The rest of the test is normal," said Stephen.

"I see that and am happy. Thank God. I am ready for the polypectomy. I know you are going to inspect carefully on your way out so as not to miss any lesion. Then you will snare the polyp?" asked Bruwa.

"That's right," said Stephen as he carefully withdrew the tube.

Silence fell once again upon the room except for the buzzing of the machines, a sound the team had heard so much that it had become a part of their lives. They had become oblivious of it. Stephen gradually pulled back the instrument taking time to inspect the entire wall of the colon. He knew he was dealing with a patient who knew nearly as much as himself. Even a temporary lapse in focus and attention could result in the patient himself discovering a lesion Stephen could have missed. That would be rather embarrassing.

"There it is," Mr. Bruwa said pointing to the monitor as Stephen stumbled once again on the polyp. Stephen also saw it almost at the same time and he was not happy that Mr. Bruwa had pointed it out first. He wrapped the wire loop and ran electric current around the stalk, cutting it off. The patient was gratified that he had not felt any pain.

"Thank you, Dr. Latham for preventing me from developing colon cancer. I don't have to worry about it for ten years, do I?"

"I would say three. We'll see you in three years," said Stephen as she pulled the tube out of the patient's rectum.

"Though the American Cancer Society recommends that I repeat this test every three to five years, I am ready to do it more frequently. This is such a deadly, yet preventable, cancer that no one should suffer and die of, or with it," said Bruwa.

Suddenly, the overhead phone operator announced that there was a code in the recovery room down the hall from the endoscopy unit. The recovery room was used by endoscopy and surgical patients as a halfway house after their procedures. Most patients reunited with their loved ones there to recount how terrible or terrific the procedure had been. Anytime a patient was in distress there, Stephen would send one of his assistants to go and see because there was a chance the patient was one of his. Immediately following the overhead announcement, the recovery room nurse called the endoscopy unit to summon any available doctors. They were already on their way. Though the endoscopy nurses were not expected to go, they went all the same.

What attracted them was, in part, theater. Whenever a code three-three was called in the hospital, it meant a patient was about to die. Usually the immediate cause was a heart attack. Certain steps were taken by the hospital community when a code was called. At least one elevator would be commandeered to ferry people and supplies to and from the scene. Any employee not participating in the code, despite his position in the hospital's administrative or academic echelons, would be barred from boarding the elevator for the duration of the code. The telephone operators would cease receiving, handling or reconnecting nonessential calls. In the laboratories, blood and other tests, for all patients but the victim of the code, would be suspended. It was as if the hospital community was mobilizing for war.

At the bedside itself, the most senior physician (not in terms of age but professionally) would self-appoint himself or herself commander-in-chief. In the rare instance that the most senior physician lacked self-assurance, some insurgent colleague would assume command and let the former retreat from the vicinity without fuss. The code leader would select one of the male physicians to "check the pulse" and if there was none, as was more often the case, to "start CPR." The selected doctors would then deliver rhythmic and powerful thrusts to the sternum in an attempt to flog the heart back into life. The action would be supplemented with the injection of powerful medications to stimulate the heart. The power of the code leader, the eclat with which he carries out the task, the frenzy at the bedside and the partial but controlled shut-down of the hospital are all elements of the code theater. It is so captivating that it always stops visitors and unconcerned, uninvited hospital workers cold in their tracks. But it is not the drama that impels physicians to the site of the code.

There are other important elements at play which must be mentioned. While everyone knows how and why society deals out the death penalty, no one knows how natural death selects its victims. But once death picks its target, the hapless soul usually suffers with one or more symptoms including fever, pain, shortness of breath, and altered mental status to name just a few. The misery usually goes on for a variable period of time before the patient's demise. In almost all cases of hospital deaths, the deceased is innocent of any crime that would be punishable by death under the law. This suffering, misery, and pain before the final exit of the innocent is another important attractant to the scene of the code. But again, it is not an important driving force for the physicians.

Physicians advance to the scene of the beleaguered under the influence of copious, natural adrenaline, because they consider themselves, rather deservedly, the most competitive species in town. In all phases of their professional lives, from the entrance examination into, and survival in, medical school, they depend heavily on their competitive instincts. Ask them to come forth with ideas on how best to diagnose, prevent or treat a certain disease condition and you have controversy in your hands. The ideas would be so powerful and ambitious and they'd be delivered with such messianic conviction that the toughest job in the world would be to select the winner. It is this competitive instinct that largely whips physicians to the code scene. If their opponent is death itself and if the latter wins more than nine times out of ten, "So what?" they would ask.

Stephen was left in the endoscopy unit with Mr. Bruwa, who was sitting in the wheelchair. While dictating his report, they engaged in a dialogue. Stephen, too, had been impressed by Mr. Bruwa's medical knowledge; knowledge he thought could put some physicians to shame. He remembered also what Mr. Bruwa had told him in confidence in the emergency room weeks ago. Stephen knew a lot about most of his patients, especially how they earned their money. Not that he had qualms about receiving tainted money as long as it was not dripping with infectious blood. But he would like to know how this patient before him was making it. The big problem was that when it came to talking about himself, Mr. Bruwa spoke in tidbits and with obfuscation.

"Mr. Bruwa, how have you been since we met in the emergency department? What have you been doing with yourself? When you said your seeds have been planted far and wide and the flowers had already bloomed what did you mean? Where and how did you plant those seeds?"

Bruwa, with a smile, said, "In many places, I would say. You have asked me too many questions at the same time. Even for a man with a high IQ, which I am happy to be endowed with, answering all those questions without asking for a reminder is an impossible mental task. But I know why you ask. You are a very smart doctor. That is why I came back to you. What you have done to me is like when you have carnal knowledge of a woman. She loses all inhibitions and begins to tell you her most intimate secrets. Seriously you went into me further than any man could with a woman. You know me internally more than any other man or woman in the world does. Any reason I may have for hiding my external profile from you has become untenable.

"I am going to tell you everything you need to know about me with the understanding that it would be held in the kind of confidence that is consistent with a consummated physician-patient relationship. This is for your ears only and I mean it in the strictest sense. Since I am not about to tell you anything that may pose a threat to the physical well-being of a third party, I expect you to be the sole custodian of the information ad infinitum. I will tell you who I am, what I did for Uncle Sam and what my reward was and why the information is to be kept secret. I don't want you to think you have been treating a ghost."

At that point, the nurses and junior doctors returned from the recovery room in a stampede. The fact that they came back so fast suggested one of three scenarios to Stephen. The first was a mock code.

In that case some internal or external inspector might have wanted to see how fast the code team would respond. If that was the case the hospital must have performed excellently.

The second scenario was a slow code. Officially, there was nothing like a slow code and the term was never to be found in a patient's record. However, some patients were so hopelessly sick and debilitated that all the interns and doctors decided that trying to save them would be not only futile but also unwise. The families of such patients were often considered difficult. That is, they insisted that all and every deliberate effort be made to keep their relative alive. Usually if the heart of such a patient stopped beating, the doctors would make timid and brief attempts at resuscitation. All participants would hear the whisper as soon as they arrived on the scene, "Slow code, slow code." Slow code was usually applied to elderly, terminally-ill patients with cancer all over the body. Increasingly, it was being applied to patients with terminal AIDS who were completely wasted to the bone and in coma for a long time. It was a good thing that the state did not decree the minimum duration of a code. It was left entirely to the whim and caprice of the code leader. Stephen always thought families of such patients who thought they had the final say were engaging in self-delusion.

Finally it was possible that some frightened nurse just out of training school had panicked because a patient was not responding to her stimuli. Stephen remembered those hectic days when he used to take in-house calls. He remembered the first day a false code was called for a sleeping patient when he was an intern at Union Hospital. That was the young nurse's first day on the floor. With their hearts palpitating, they had made it to the bedside. The patient had leapt out of bed when the first doctor tried to position him for resuscitation.

He and Mr. Bruwa looked at the endoscopy nurses and assistant doctors with amazement. They were all panting heavily, an indication that they had not been working out. Then, Jack spoke.

"It was a mistake. It was a false code," he said between labored breaths. "One visitor came into the recovery room to see his grandfather who was awakening from anesthesia after surgery. They are recent immigrants from Botopar. Apparently in their culture, young men have to prostrate and lie still before their grandparents. Neither the patient nor his visiting son spoke English. When the boy collapsed before his father, Ms. Luke thought he had fainted and called the code. By the time we got there, the boy and his grandfather were engaged in a deep conversation. I don't think they knew what had happened."

"All is well that ends well," said Stephen.

"So, Dr. Latham, as I was saying. I have been keeping a low profile, doing the same things I have been doing, you know and just having a good time. When I see you in your office, we'll talk more," concluded Mr. Bruwa.

Stephen understood Mr. Bruwa's bunkum. The re-entry of the doctors and nurses changed the group dynamics and precluded the revelations. He feared that Mr. Bruwa may have cracked under the influence of Somnazolam. If that was the case, the opportunity was lost for the next several years. He discharged him to the recovery room with instructions on when he could leave the hospital.

He was done for the day, finally. He just had to inform his wife of the soiree he and Dr. Kurman had planned for the evening so that his tea or coffee would be ready when he got home. He thanked all the nurses and bade them a happy weekend. As for him, he told them, he would be in Prospect Park early the next morning. Listening attentively among them, was Juliette Painter.

Stephen arrived home that evening not long after Juliana and Christopher had returned from the doctor's. Though he felt tired, he still planned to go to the evening's important occasion, a reception for the president of the American College of Physicians. Such meetings were planned ostensibly for pleasure. In reality, they were business meetings in which physicians renewed old ties and made new ones. The main benefit for subspecialists like Stephen was that colleagues they had not seen for years would start referring patients to them again. Some of such patients would come to like Stephen so much that they would jilt their primary physicians.

Juliana was in the kitchen when he walked in. There were bags of groceries between her and the open refrigerator, indicating that she was putting them away. Stephen tiptoed to a few feet from where she was bending over the grocery, her head partially immersed in the fridge. Among other things, she wanted to assure that the Somnazolam was well dissolved in the soy milk. Matters relating to the Somnazolam experiment always commanded her complete attention. For a moment, Stephen stood there looking over her arched back thinking of the most dramatic way to announce his arrival and presence. He started to say, "Guess who has come to dinner," just as she stood up to ease the spasm on her lower back. She was so startled on seeing him that she let in a gasp. Did Stephen see her mixing the Somnazolam and the soy milk? She pondered. The answer would depend on what he said first.

"Relax, I just walked in."

"I did not hear the door slam as usual. You must have a magic touch," said Juliana.

"I have to go to a reception for the ACP president. I see you are in the kitchen. I hope you have not prepared dinner. There is going to be a lot of food there. I just need a cup of coffee to hold me in the interim," said Stephen.

"First of all, Christopher and I are just coming back from Dr. Alban's. I thought you would ask, 'How was your day?' "

"Well that was the first thing I said when I walked in but I got no response. I figured I should place my itinerary on the table first and discuss the day's events when I am well seated."

Christopher emerged from the bathroom to mob his father and to display his missing tooth and lower lip cut. "Look, Daddy, my teeth came out," he said pointing to the newly created gap in his dentition.

"Say, 'My tooth came out.' " Stephen stuck out his right index finger, as he corrected and cuddled his son, to emphasize the singularity of the lost tooth.

"My tooth came out," said Christopher.

Stephen went into the room to change his clothes with his mind fixated on the evening's reception. He expected to meet his cardiologist friend Dr. Ramsey there. The latter had a lucrative practice in Queens but many of his patients lived in Brooklyn. They had discussed mutual referrals whereby Dr. Ramsey would exclusively see all his patients in need of cardiac evaluation and Stephen would be the sole gastroenterology consultant for Dr. Ramsey. Since Dr. Ingor also wanted a piece of the action from Dr. Ramsey, Stephen must go early to the meeting. He had to have an audience with Dr. Ramsey before the latter started drinking for he had a tendency to over indulge.

Fully dressed, Stephen came to the living room for a wrap-up of the day's happenings and for his cup of coffee. There was a thick ball of cigarette smoke in the living room. He did not like it. He would not complain because he did not want to spoil his outing. He held his breath for as long as he could.

He descended into the armchair before the TV, took the remote control in his left hand as Juliana brought him the cup of coffee.

"It's lukewarm. I don't want you to go to party with scalded lips. Your colleagues may conclude I gave you a violent and scalding kiss," said Juliana.

Stephen, savoring his coffee, said: "That would be a kiss of death. I know you would never do that to me. I married you because you are the one person who would never hurt me, J. It looks as if you make my coffee with a thermostat. This is very good coffee. Where did you buy it from?"

"At Dravo, before Christopher fell and injured himself. The store personnel were very concerned. They thought we were going to sue. But it wasn't their fault. What really surprised me was the speed with which the lawyers got wind of the accident. When I got to Dr. Alban's, there was a legal secretary who told me of partners with a small 'p'. Ever heard of partners with a small 'p'?"

The remote control device fell from Stephen's hand as he dozed off. He apparently did not hear some of what Juliana was telling him. He was now nodding his head about once a minute. Juliana suggested to him to go to bed and cancel the outing. At Juliana's urging, he stood up, went to the bedroom and climbed into bed. That was most unusual of him. The fact that he did not insist on going to the reception even in his drowsy state was consistent with a new and worrisome personality trait that Juliana had recognized in her husband. He had become too suggestible for her comfort. His ironic comment that she would never hurt him also disconcerted her. Overall, however, she was satisfied that he stayed home one more night, away from the Borbles and the Oscars.

Stephen would sleep for the next six hours.

The Quiet Neighbor's Watch

Juliette Painter had lived in apartment 4-N, actually a studio, since she graduated from nursing school and assumed work eleven years earlier. All the N apartments were reserved by the hospital administration for nurses. The "N" was entirely coincidental. It was not abbreviation for "Nurses." The adjacent M apartments were set aside for Doctors. The N studios on the four lowest floors were reserved for young nurses just out of training schools. For the most part, the spacious studios satisfied the housing needs of the nurses because their household wares could fit in a carpetbag. With time, they would marry, make money and children. Their needs would outgrow the studio and they moved out making way for younger nurses. The whole transition, on the average, took about four years to complete.

That was the norm in some of the N and other apartments in the staff housing of InnerFaith Hospital. The cycle, however, stalled in some of the N apartments like Juliette Painter's. When she moved into studio N eleven years earlier, she was full of optimism that in about a few years, she would move out with her husband. She had already begun to fantasize about the size, location and the cost of the house the couple would buy. In conversations at work with other nurses, she was gathering information about neighborhoods, housing-market trends and the minutiae of house hunting. One thing she had known was that in house hunting you had to begin early and never buy in haste. There would be nothing wrong, she had been told, with shopping for a year to guarantee satisfaction.

Several years after settlement in the studio, she was forced to reappraise those fantasies. Her affair with her college and nursing school sweetheart was at a standstill. Mike Bartley was a good chiropractor and masseur and would probably have made a good husband. But he was fifteen years older than she was. Her mother was bitterly opposed to it while her friends made her the butt of guarded jokes. It was not too long before she became convinced that the voices of her friends and family were the voices of wisdom. Then she began to see things as they never were with regard to Mike. The fact that he could not cook became a prominent negative. Since she, herself, could not cook, she thought her husband should be a culinary expert. Expertise in cooking Chinese food, which she was fond of, would have been a big plus.

With his negatives so high in her mind she had made it clear to him, her friends and family that the relationship had no future. She stopped picking up or returning his calls and withdrew completely from him. Her close friend and nursing school classmate Angela Jones gave her all the necessary encouragement during that difficult period. Juliette felt some guilt, though, because Mike had been a great financial help when she was in the nursing school. She wished there was a way to compensate him or to convince him that she was not an ingrate. But Mike would not take material compensation.

Mike had read the handwriting on the wall. For several months they did not hear from, or about, each other. Then, she learnt that Angela Jones and Mike Bartley were planning marriage. The espousal date was already fixed. When she confirmed the news, she cursed, "Absolutely incredulous back stabbing!" She remembered the male student who used to exclaim "O God, protect me from my friends and I will take care of my enemies," in the nursing school. There was an ironic truism in the exclamation after all. She would confront Angela and hopefully apologize to Mike for her foolishness and behavior. Mike the magnanimous would probably give her absolution, she thought.

She entered a period of dating doldrums for the next several years. She had always thought of improving her career prospects. As her family plans were temporarily on hold, she enrolled in a part-time master's program in nursing at Medgar Evers College. While there, she had started planning for her future again. No serious-minded young woman could stop planning for the future until the future arrived. Marriage considerations could never be low in the scheme of things for a woman in her late twenties. She had met a few men and begun dating again but they all turned out to be clowns.

She vowed never to befriend any single woman for the rest of her life even after marriage. She did not want any more Angela Joneses in her life. But every normal person needs friends to confide in.

Among all the coursemates she met at Medgar Evers, she had admired Selina Johnson, who was a nurse at Brookdale. Selina's husband Seward Johnson, also a nurse by training, was one of their professors at Medger Evers. Juliette and Selina had become so close that they were thought to have blood relationship. There must have been some reluctance between them for whenever they were together they were asked, "Who is the older?" Juliana increasingly began to see the semblance between the two friends. She would juxtapose their photographs and scrutinize them for anatomical nuances. The eyelashes were similar in length and orientation because they bought them from the same vendor. The hairstyles were quite approximate because Selina had dropped her hair dresser and started patronizing Juliette's. They were about equal in thinness and busts. At the end of the examination, she would come to the conclusion that there were enough grounds—artificial ones—to call them sisters.

Close to the end of the program, tragedy struck. Selina and Juliette were going to dinner across Bedford Avenue after the lecture one evening. Traffic was moving lazily on Bedford. The two women were waiting for a break in the procession to cross the street. Behind and beside them were some other pedestrians, most likely Medgar Evers students. Out of nowhere, suddenly, a jeep careened off the road and ran smack into the party. Most were fortunate enough to dash out of harm's way. Selina was not so lucky. The wayward vehicle pinned her against a fire hydrant for at least ten minutes before instant volunteers freed her. The ambulance arrived with the police about ten minutes later and took the unresponsive Selina to InnerFaith hospital. She died later that night.

Selina's death at the hands of an alcoholic driver was a big loss for the two closest people in her life—Juliette and Seward. Juliette had many friends in her life but none was as compatible with, or as close to her as Selina was. When she asked in her elegy to her, "What shall I do without you as life will never again be the same for me?" she actually meant it. She had bandied such words before in the hospital when people had obliged her little favors. For the first time ever she realized how she had been making light very heavy words. For the rest of her life, she would probably just say, "Thank you very much for . . . I sincerely appreciate it."

With the grief period behind them life had gradually returned to near normalcy for both Juliette and Seward. She completed her masters in nursing in the remaining few weeks. She continued to keep in contact with Seward. They went out to dinner on several occasions. The physical distance between them was like that between siblings who had been mourning a beloved one for the last two weeks—feet apart. Then one week before Juliette was to complete the master's program, they went out to dinner again. Over a bowl of fillet salmon and rice with shrimps, Seward said to Juliette, "I know life will never be the same again for me. No woman could fill the void created by Selina's departure. But I intend to remarry as soon as I can. I have already started looking around. Where you come in, I think, is to help me look around also. Any woman who withstands your close scrutiny must be a good material for me."

Juliette greatly admired Seward Johnson. He was more than six feet tall and slim with a flat abdomen. His boyish looks belied his thirty-nine years. For him to have become a professor at that young age underscored his intelligence. Those were qualities no young woman could quarrel with. But Seward had more. He was an excellent cook himself and he was proud of the fact that dinner was almost always ready before his deceased wife returned home. Though both of them worked, he usually got home first. He would be, to most women, a dream come true.

As she slept over Seward's parting words, Juliette Painter was deeply immersed in fantasies and imagination. Could she present herself to Seward and still maintain her self-respect? How could a woman who had absolutely no romantic relationship with a man walk up to him and say, "Marry me?" And if the man said, "No," where would she hide her face? How would she handle the shame? If on the other hand he said, "Fine," and his ex-wife was the woman's closest friend what would society say? That she had not been a sincere friend. That even when she was alive, her friend was sleeping with her husband or at least had the fantasies. That she was happy her friend died. Some may even go further—that she had prevented her friend from jumping out of danger. Or worse still, that she pushed her friend in front of an onrushing jeep so as to inherit her husband. That would be the worst form of covetousness. She would be guilty of fatal attraction leading to murder.

If there had been a way to determine Selina's wishes, they would have been Juliette's deciding factor. It was likely that she would have wanted Juliette, her best friend, to take over her office. Juliette also was not sure of Seward's motive in giving her the assignment. If he was interested in her, as she was in him, why did he not say so? After all he was a man, the aggressive species ordained to strike the first blow in fights as well as in love. Was Seward also undergoing the same soul-searching that she herself was embroiled in? The thought that a lifetime opportunity was slipping through her hands made her tremble. Finally, she had decided that in the interest of social decorum she would not make any move yet. Even if she was going to make the gesture, it should not come so fast.

It was about that time that Juliette Painter was redeployed to the endoscopy unit from the neonatal unit. Many nurses had applied for the position because of the kinder job description. Only one vacancy existed and the selection procedure became rather controversial.

Charges and counter charges began to fly. Matters were further complicated when rival nurses' unions sought to exert influence in favor of one or another candidate. The short-listed staff nurses had been invited to an interview. In fairness to all, they had been given a surprise written examination. Juliette had come out far ahead of everyone else and she was given the job.

The nurses in the endoscopy unit worked in pairs. Juliette was linked up with Salomy Hicks, a homely young woman of her age. They got along fine. It was her responsibility to orientate Juliette about the unit having worked in there for three years. Within a few days of Juliette's arrival they were talking not only about the job but also about their personal lives. Salomy had given Juliette the impression that she and her man were talking marriage. Juliette told her one morning over donuts, when they had no procedure, of the assignment Seward had given her.

That was the last time Salomy discussed a personal matter with Juliette. Salomy had enrolled in the Medger Evers master's program but had dropped out, due to personal problems, before Juliette joined. She remembered that all the women in the class wished Prof. Seward Johnson had been single. That afternoon as soon as she got home, she had looked up Seward's phone number in the "White Pages." She had called him.

"Juliette Painter asked me to give you a call. She and I work together in the endoscopy unit," Salomy had told Seward Johnson.

That was the origin of the Seward-Salomy romance. While it blossomed, Juliette had no knowledge of it. The first time she heard of it, six weeks after Selina's death, Salomy and Seward were planning their wedding. Seward had called to thank Juliette for the referral and to inform her that preparations for the wedding had reached an advanced stage. Juliette was beside herself when Seward had added that he regretted that Juliette had not been available. Cold perspiration had broken out over her forehead that chilly night.

That was almost five years ago. Juliette had never fully recovered.

But shortly after that imbroglio, Dr. Stephen Latham appeared on the scene. The acting head of the endoscopy unit arrived after a long wait. That day, the nurses saw a heartthrob. When he revealed that he had been assigned apartment 4-M in the staff housing, next to Juliette, the latter hoped he was single. She would do whatever was necessary to get him, if not at work, across their balconies.

Her hopes were dashed later that day when she learnt he was moving in with his wife.

138

The Lathams moved in next to her. His wife was made the acting head nurse on the fourteenth floor. Hardly had they settled in than rumors started spreading about the martial difficulties the Lathams were having. First and most important was that they had been grappling with infertility. Rumors had it that they had made many attempts to produce a test-tube baby, to no avail. Those close to them said that the problem was with the wife whose tubes had become blocked, apparently, after repeated attacks of sexually transmitted diseases in the years before she had met Dr. Latham. There were also rumors that Dr. Latham was displeased with his wife's chain-smoking.

Perhaps these rumors spread because Mrs. Latham did not get along well with her subordinates. She was known to pour contumely on the nurses aides. On one occasion, she was reported to have told a cleaner that she lacked a thinking faculty and that it was not her (Mrs. Latham's) fault. Juliette had also heard rumors that Mrs. Latham had wide mood swings especially after her long visits to the bathroom. The mood changes were thought to be drug-related. When some vials of Demerol and Somnazolam were stolen from the controlled drug cabinet, she was a prime suspect but nobody had the temerity to say so. There were other ways for the unscrupulous to obtain narcotics without stealing them from the console. If she had been at fault the first time, then she must have become smarter. The easier way for her to have stolen Demerol, or other controlled drugs, would have been for her to pocket a patient's prescribed dose, after giving the patient a placebo instead. That was how the nurses at Brookville Hospital were caught.

Juliette could not independently confirm any of those rumors.

What she did know was that Dr. Latham had been trying to get his wife to quit smoking. Actually, even that statement was considered guesswork. Juliette had observed her smoking on their terrace. Although Dr. Latham was very reticent when it came to talking about his wife's smoking, one of the few pieces of his mind he did allow on one occasion was his aversion to the habit. Though he had spoken in general terms, it did not require a genius to deduce that it must have been a sticking point in his household.

Juliette sympathized with Dr. Latham even though the latter did not complain. He reminded her of Seward Johnson, her professor at Medgar Evers college. There were uncanny physical similarities between them. They were both equally handsome, tall and thin. They had similar wrinkles on their faces. Even their eyebrows looked similar in thickness and contour. She often wondered if they knew each other.

She would have asked Dr. Latham about Seward if not that she wanted to forget about the latter and keep her options open with the former.

Juliette was becoming convinced that Mrs. Latham did not deserve him. The best way to have established that without doubt would have been to befriend Mrs. Latham and gain her confidence and secrets. But Juliette had written off women. Every time she befriended a woman she ended up losing. All her friends were now men. Even though most of the men coming her way were jokers looking for instant gratification, there were a few good ones. It was ironic that she would not deal with women, including Mrs. Latham who was her professional colleague and neighbor.

In the years since they had become neighbors, Juliette had entered the Lathams' apartment twice. Both occasions were during the birthday parties for Christopher. Most of the nurses and other staff of the endoscopy unit had been present as had been other tenants. She had used the occasions to make crucial observations. The Lathams had their bedroom adjacent to her studio with their family bed wedged against the wall they shared with Juliette. During both birthday celebrations, there had been more guests than had been expected and the crowds had overflowed into the bedroom. During Christopher's first anniversary Juliette had gone into the bedroom ostensibly to caress the celebrant. Since there were guests already sitting in the Latham's family bed she joined them, causing the bed to creak.

As evidence mounted that the Lathams were not getting along, Juliette began to make close observations both at work and at home. The first evidence she gathered was that every time Stephen stepped out of his apartment, his wife would slam the door behind him. Juliette imagined her cursing, "Good Riddance," as she slammed the door. The Lathams always left their back door open to increase circulation. They would have left the front door ajar also but the mechanics of it were that no matter how widely it was opened it would slam shut. The wider it was open the louder the sound it would produce. On occasion, a strong tail-wind from the back door assisted the closure of the front door. What Juliette heard was only the slam. She did not know the mechanisms producing it.

Juliette left her doors—front and back—open all the time she was at home. She lived in a corner studio and the doctor who was supposed to be living opposite her spent nearly all his free time in his Long Island country home. Crime was not a problem in the building. In all the years she had lived there, she could remember two break-ins. In one, a mammoth-sized piano was stolen and many people thought it was a hoax or an insurance scam. In the other, a loaf of bread was reported missing. So Juliette could afford to keep her door open without fear of crime. By so doing she could monitor her neighbor's ingress and egress.

Another crucial observation Juliette made was that she never heard the neighbors' bed rasp at night on the other side of the wall. She knew the bed to be so shaky that any violent movement at night would generate sounds that would be transmitted across the common wall. Her bed on the other side of the wall was also wedged against the wall. She had converted it to a listening post. In the beginning, she would lie in bed and press her better ear, the left, hard against the wall. All she heard on the Lathams' side of the wall was dead, ominous silence.

To increase the sensitivity of her listening device, she once burrowed several holes in the wall just below where she thought the Lathams' mattress level was. The holes were not through and through. Rather, a very thin membrane separated Juliette's studio from the Lathams' apartment.

It was supposed to pick up sound in the Lathams' bedroom and vibrate like the mechanism in the human ear. And Juliette was supposed to pick up the vibrations with her receiver. She would plug her receiver into one hole after another and listen in the dead silence of her studio for life on the other side. Never did she pick up any vibration.

Unbeknownst to Juliette, the Lathams were sleeping on the floor. When they were moving into apartment four M, the family bed did not survive the rough and tumble of moving. Not only did it sag in the center, but it made so much grating noise at night that it was becoming an embarrassment. In arranging their bedrooms, Stephen and Juliana had wedged the bed against the wall they shared with Juliette to curtail the wild agitation. But they realized that the bed knocked on the wall rhythmically. Juliana had convinced her husband that they should be sleeping on the floor.

"Some neighbors are crazy," she had told Stephen. "If this bed continues to knock on this wall giving the woman on the other side sleepless nights, the cops may come calling in the heat of the night."

Stephen had agreed, knowing fully well that the Brooklyn cops loved investigating such sleazy cases involving middle-class people. There was little chance of a cop being shot and their friends in the media would have loved the leaks. Sleeping on the floor was also therapeutic for Stephen's mild lumbago. They had been sleeping on the floor ever since.

Juliette Painter had concluded that her neighbors, Juliana and Stephen, were hardly on talking terms in there because of the continuous silence she was hearing. Her theory was that Stephen came home each day to find his apartment one huge smoke-filled chamber in which he could hardly breathe. He would then retire to one corner until it would be time to go to work the next day. She thought Stephen had given up on trying to change his wife's smoking habit and was probably looking for a way out. If her theory was right, she thought, she (Juliette) must be poised to strike. Experience had taught her that the woman died that kept quiet and a low profile in the face of opportunity.

She recalled that earlier in the day at work, Stephen had shown signs of severe fatigue. He had seemed to be yawning every minute. Though the other nurses made jokes about his lack of drive, she thought Stephen deserved sympathy, not ridicule. There were other changes in his personality that had surfaced. Earlier on at work that day, when Dr. Latham was going downstairs, she had asked him to bring the nurses something to munch on. He had come back with doughnuts and soda. In all the years they had been working together, he had always brushed aside such entreaties. That was further evidence to Juliette that Dr. Latham may be ready to deal.

Dr. Latham's apparent readiness to respond to feelers was in stark contrast to his previously impervious persona. Lying in her listening post with thick earmuffs plucked into one of the burrows in the wall, she reflected on the overtures she had made to him in the past. She remembered the night he had rescued her from Roosevelt Field, Long Island. She had promised to give up absolutely anything or part of her in appreciation. She remembered her most brazen move on him, the day she cornered him in the Endoscopy Unit in scrubs with the hair on the top part of his chest exposed. She had tugged on the hair and pronounced them, "bare assets." But he didn't get it or was not yet ready to deal.

It may have been a question of timing, Juliette thought. For everything under heaven, there is time, including a time to give up on your wife who is uncompromising in her smoking or unable to bring forth offspring, Juliette fantasized. And the time, she concluded, had come.

She was in the dreamworld when she heard a slight commotion on her neighbors' terrace. She took off her earmuffs and went to investigate.

The time was eleven at night. Stephen had awakened from his prime-time slumber about half an hour earlier. He had missed the evening's reception for the American College of Physicians president. Juliana was lying outside on the terrace enjoying the clement spring night weather. Christopher was out there with her. In the living room, Stephen took up the remote control and scanned the stations for an interesting news or current affairs program. He found none, not surprisingly, as most stations were showing oldies. He joined his family on the dimly lit balcony, lying beside Juliana.

"Too bad I overslept and couldn't attend the reception. My business is set back somewhat. But I wonder what really happened. Why did I fall asleep so fast and slept for so long?" asked Stephen.

"I think your health comes first. Sometimes you need to slow down. The money will come. In fact we are doing very well compared with your colleagues," said Juliana.

"Did anybody call while I was asleep?"

"Dr. Kurman. He called to find out when you were departing for the party. I told him that you were too tired and you were already in bed. You know, he understands that you have busy Fridays."

Christopher went into the living room and fetched his pillow and pillowcase and brought them to his parents. He had already tried and failed to insert the pillow inside its shrunken case. He handed the two items to his parents and lay down in between them. "Daddy, put it inside for me," he pleaded.

Stephen's attempts to put the pillow inside its case were unsuccessful. Just up from sleep and under the residual influence of Somnazolam, he still could not coordinate his fine movements. Secondly, the terrace was not well lit, and finally, his recumbent position was awkward. He asked Juliana for assistance.

"Hold the pillow case for me," he said. Still, the shrunken pillow case was too tight to be over come by his gentle pressure.

"Don't force it," said Juliana. "It is too tight. It will not go in."

"Let us try," said Stephen.

"I said no. I should know when it is too tight. Don't force it, I said."

That was the argument that had brought Juliette to her balcony on the other side of the partitioning. She listened again as Juliana reiterated to her husband, "Don't force it. I should know when it will not go in." There were two close slits in the partitioning. Juliette peeped through one and then the other. She saw the widely separated pair of legs. Though Christopher was lying quietly between his parents, his legs were too short to be seen down there. Juliette Painter had expected to see a bundle of closely wrapped four legs. She was convinced that the positions of the legs, as she had seen them, were not confused by a parallax snap.

"That's it," Juliette concluded as she walked back to her bed, "she is denying him sex. The moody woman must be in one of her sore ebbs," Juliette concluded about her neighbor Juliana Latham.

The main problem with remote listening or sensing, especially when the technology employed is primitive, is that everything the listener hears, from dead silence to full sentences, is amenable to warped analysis and interpretation. But Juliette Painter was satisfied with what she had heard. She had been listening for weeks but tonight she had an earful. If, in addition to all her shortcomings, Juliana Latham was denying her husband sex, she reasoned, the marriage must be irredeemably doomed.

Juliette would no longer wait in the wings. She would present herself to him rather obtrusively. For once in her life, she had to be ahead of the game. She was thirty-five years old and by most observers the most beautiful woman in InnerFaith Hospital. Her beauty was so exquisite, it repelled men. She was already counting the assets she would bring into the relationship: fecundity, submissiveness to his sexual desires and wealth. She was worth more than anybody in InnerFaith knew; her late mother had been given a large cash award in a court case.

Juliette remembered that Stephen would be jogging in Prospect Park the next day. He had told them so at work. She would pursue him to the park in her first move tomorrow. She must bathe and retire immediately. As she stood before the mirror in the bathroom, she beat on her chest above the towel wrapped around her torso and vowed:

Beauty so exquisite, it must go for the kill.
From this locus to the public park,
I will prowl and charm him with my sex appeal
Till between us two is lit a spark
That'd, in short order, his forced celibacy heal.

Running with Juliette Painter

The next day Stephen was awake at six, absolutely determined to make it to Prospect Park. While still recumbent, his mind was already tracing his route to the park. He would hit Classon Avenue and ascend the incline to Eastern Parkway. Then he would veer right past the Brooklyn Museum to Grand Army Plaza where he was sure traffic and the vegetable market would slow his pace. Finally, he would enter the park and reach the track and take on all comers. One of his greatest strengths, he mused, was that even if he took several weeks' break from the track, he could still debut strong.

While he dressed up for the jog he longed for the days when he used to run at least three times per week until his pulse slowed down to forty times per minute. In those days he carried no excess fat and his stomach was adherent to his back. Those days were gone forever. Family, work and age were catching up with him. Once he hit the track, however, he vowed he would continue from where he had stopped several weeks ago and go round the three-mile track at least three times.

Juliana was still soundly asleep when he was set to step out. Her sleep must have been interrupted by Christopher. She would have wanted his warm body in bed that morning. She did not like to be in bed alone at dawn. But he would have to go. He decided against disturbing her. It would be better for him to leave a note for her, he thought. That still left open the possibility that he would have a lot of explaining to do upon his return. She would complain about his having left Christopher bare in that chilly dawn and of not having closed Christopher's window. She would also express her disappointment that he had not bought the newspaper even though she rarely read it. All would be red herring, but he would understand.

The weather was exactly what the weatherman had forecast the previous night. The sky was overcast with light clouds. The mercury was high and good to savor. The weatherman had forecast northwest winds at ten miles per hour. Stephen pondered the necessity and accuracy of forecasting wind vectors. Winds have their own minds and answer to no one. When their mood is good, they move as gentle breeze ferrying away the body's heat by convection and leaving joggers with understandable elation. That was what every track star desired. With winds, head or tail, runners lose. Tail winds help and hurry runners along, giving them a false sense of speed. Any records broken or set are bound to be disregarded. Head winds tend to hamper and hinder joggers producing a false sense of speed all the same. Occasionally winds become mad and, with bunkers from nowhere, move with deadly force, shaking if not leveling everything in their path. All, including brave runners, have to find bunkers. It would be better for runners if strong, unfair and restless winds just stood still.

He was still grateful to his favorite weathermen and woman, Sam Champion, Bill Evans and Veronica Johnson. Though their craft was not an exact science, they exuded so much confidence especially when forecasting warm weather that you would think it was. Whenever they said the weather was going to be good, it almost always was. Stephen could understand the pain they felt when delivering the bad news—the arrival of bone-chilling, nose-numbing winter winds from Canada. It was the kind of pain he felt when telling patients about unfavorable prognoses. He was happy that they did not have to endure such trauma the previous night. The weather that morning, true to prediction, was gorgeous.

Stephen walked out into the breezy calm and in no time, was at the corner of Sterling Place and Classon Avenue. One side of Sterling Place, to Stephen's left, had been closed to traffic for years making it a dead-end street. No one, it seemed, liked a dead-end-street. Neighborhood residents turned it into a free parking lot, a rare class of real estate in Brooklyn. No traffic was flowing on Sterling, across Classon and Stephen did not have to wait. He just ignored the traffic light which ordered him, "Don't Walk." That was the moving violation that Brooklynites liked to commit because there was no threat of being summonsed.

Whenever he came to that intersection, he wondered why it was taking so long to complete work on the subway bridge that caused the closure. Once again, he thought of calling the office of State Assemblyman Al Vann. The permanent closure of that subway bridge had caused the neighborhood serious traffic problems. He usually remembered Al Vann when he came to the intersection or was stuck in traffic on Franklin Avenue and could not make a right turn. He moved on, however. With the bridge out of his sight, Al Vann also disappeared from his mind.

He ran up the natural treadmill called Classon Avenue toward Eastern Parkway. His spirit was willing, his joints weak and crepitant. The upward slope to Eastern Parkway was the first hurdle in his path and possibly the most difficult part of his jogging routine. He had come to develop a healthy respect for that patch of the street. Those walking leisurely and consorting with their lovers were unlikely to feel the same way. He was grateful that the gradient was not more acute.

The parking garage attendant was standing sentry at his post, near the corner of Lincoln and Classon. He also worked as a security officer and driver at the hospital and he had a certain level of familiarity with Stephen. At that time of the day and week, the average Brooklynite was in bed but he was standing out there alone. He must have been enjoying the weather. But Stephen had seen him out there in hostile weather as well. Once, when he and Stephen were riding in the hospital bus to one of the satellite clinics, he told Stephen of his recent encounter with some neighborhood hoodlums. It had happened at one in the morning several nights previously. Two, presumably armed, young men were approaching him provocatively. As he dashed inside the garage for his life, he had related to Stephen, he could hear one of them yelling to the other "run, run, he is going for a knife." Neighborhood hoodlums are not rocket scientists or physicians. They almost always misinterpret their victims' moves. Unfortunately, their countermeasures, far from desirable, often leave deadly consequences.

Yet he stood there morning after morning, having made peace with his lot. He held his cigarette between his pursed lips, two streams of smoke issuing astride it. Perhaps, he did not inhale for there was no smoke blowing out of his nostrils. With his left index and middle fingers, he took away the cigarette from his mouth in order to exchange greetings with Stephen and to shake off the detritus. He was stoutly built with firm and powerful pectoralis muscles.

"How are you doing, doc?"

"Good, and you?" Stephen replied in the best of Brooklyn tradition as he ran past.

At the corner of Eastern Parkway and Classon Avenue Stephen saw that traffic was, for a Saturday morning, heavy and, as usual, fast on Eastern Parkway. His first rule of jogging was "never stop until you are ready to stop." Jogging for him was not like walking, which he could pick up after a brief or long interlude. Jogging in place to maintain his momentum, while waiting for the green light, he surveyed the imposing buildings around him. The St. Francis De Sale School for the Deaf was in front and to his far left. He had never seen the students or teachers come and go even though he had driven and run past the compound so many times. He wondered if the teachers were also deaf. He thought about deaf language and communication; how they handled neology and bunkum.

Brooklyn residents were streetwise and Stephen was no exception. That meant they did not stand at street corners as statues. They watched their backs even while looking forward. Danger could be lurking nearby or approaching fast. They turned back and surveyed their environments like a scanning radar system. Within the one minute or so he was at that corner, Stephen had turned back twice. The second time he did, he could not believe who was closing in on him. He was in no danger, for he was being tailed by his nurse and next-door neighbor, Juliette Painter. He knew that she worked out in the gymnasium. Her physical features were compatible with long distance running. Stephen was surprised to see her so early in the morning. Though the light had changed to the impolite command "Walk," he did not cross the Parkway. He jogged in place until she caught up with him. They exchanged banters while still jogging in place.

"How are you doing, Ms. Painter? You are up and running so early! You are going to live long," he said to her.

"With you by my side, I will surely go a long way. I heard and saw you leaving home and I thought I should come and watch your back so that you don't get hurt."

"Good to see you. Come'on, let's cross the Parkway. We've got the light and the right."

They crossed the parkway to the other side and came closer to the School for the Deaf and Prospect Heights High School behind it. Disturbance of the quiet from motorists, construction work and revelers were constant features of life on Eastern Parkway. The Department of Education probably and properly took the decision to insulate the studious students of Prospect Heights High from the cacophony with the deaf students. It was a no-lose decision. On one side Prospect Heights High abutted on Classon Avenue. The traffic flowing into or across Eastern Parkway from Classon was tightly controlled in volume, speed and noise. Across Classon Avenue, Prospect Heights High faced a serene and languid park in which a rich vegetation was coming back to life in the early spring weather. The vegetation looked poised to absorb noise emanating from the heavy traffic on Washington Avenue. All these mufflers had been placed around the school to create a conducive learning environment, an absolutely important determinant of students' performance. There was no reason in Stephen's mind for Prospect Heights students not to excel.

Stephen and Juliette turned right on the far side of Eastern Parkway and began to make their way to Prospect Park. No one could traverse that stretch of Eastern Parkway without paying homage to the Brooklyn Museum. Undoubtedly the most massive and imposing edifice on the parkway, it attracted visitors from far and wide. Juliette had been watching the Washington Avenue side of the huge building right from the moment they crossed over Eastern Parkway. With the corner of his eye Stephen noticed that she was running slowly and losing balance because of the attention she was paying to the museum. Then, in short syllables compatible with her steps, she explained her fascination.

"I have been inside that museum several times, one of the most respected in the entire world. They must have more than a million collections and I think it is a rich community resource. But I have never paid attention to the external beauty of the building. I know they have some alto-relievos in front but I have never seen the names on that wall. Have you ever been inside?" she asked.

Stephen had also joined her in gazing at the names and high-reliefs on the museum wall facing Washington Avenue. He, too, could not remember having seen the names before. Part of the explanation was that during most of his jogging, that wall was covered by vegetation. Even now, as they gazed on the wall, they were at the mercy of the exuberant giant sequoia trees. The branches fluttered gracefully in the morning breeze frequently opening windows to the wall through which the names could be read. Stephen branched into the park to take a better look at the names on the wall and what message he could read from the list. Both of them continued to jog in place to keep their momentum. They both spoke in brief syllables and sentences.

Once he entered the park, the monument honoring Dr. Ronald McNair caught his attention first. He carefully read the epitaph as Juliette also looked on.

As he began to shake his head, Juliette asked him, "What's the matter?"

"The *Challenger* accident should never have happened. This is what happens when opportunistic politicians in Washington intervene for their personal gains. The *Challenger* was not fit to fly that day. President Reagan was going to make a major campaign speech about his achievement in space and his aides made sure it was airborne. It doesn't take a rocket scientist to know that a faulty spacecraft should be grounded. Unfortunately, rocket scientists lack the capacity to resist political pressure. For that reason the rocket scientists deserve some blame and you will not hear me say again, 'It doesn't take a rocket scientist to do this or that.' "

"I still remember the fireball. May he and the other victims rest in peace."

They turned their attention to the Washington Avenue side of the museum.

"I see the name Nebuchadnezzar, the king of Babylon. He was a despot with a troubled mind. He had frequent nightmares which he challenged his learned subjects to interpret. Those who failed to offer a satisfactory explanation were summarily executed. He cast some of his Israeli captives into blazing furnaces over religious differences and used still some others as lion fodder. His wickedness was so extreme that heaven was in a hurry to bestow upon him his just dessert. He was turned into an animal and cast into the wild. Such punishment heaven has not dispensed to any human ever since. He can only be in the museum as a bouncer."

"I think he repented after his ordeal among the animals. He was restored to his throne and ruled with remorse and humility. It must have been in recognition of his second epoch that he was appointed an usher rather than a bouncer in the museum. As you can see, he is in the company of Cyrus the Great, the Persian emperor and military strategist who believed that a commander must be ready to endure more than the men he commands. I bet you would be hard pressed to find such exemplary leaders today. Cyrus is a good usher," said Juliette.

"That must be Cyrus, the satrap. He was a man of unrestrained ambition who organized thousands of mercenaries in a futile power struggle against his brother Artaxerxes. He paid for the insurrection with his life. A man like that could only be a bouncer, not an usher."

They were still jogging effortlessly in place as they spoke. The fact that they were not out of breath was a testimony to their fitness. It was also because they were able to synchronize their dialogue with their steps making one maneuver a part of the other.

Stephen led the way out of the park toward the front of the museum with Juliette immediately behind and to his right. She was still looking at the wall for a glimpse through the tree branches. "Well, Dr. Latham, if the two men were too violent to be ushers," she asked him, "surely, the next name to Cyrus' must be an usher. Manu is a Hindu god. He or she must be pious enough to be an usher."

"Everyone else on that panel was a solid citizen. A god would feel too uneasy in this company unless he or she is also fiendish. I am sure that is not Manu the Hindu figure. That must be an abbreviated form

150

of Manuel the Portuguese emperor who reigned at the zenith of the empire. He squandered the empire's wealth on his marriages to three Spanish princesses, one after the other. The biggest blemish on his reign, however, were the pogroms against Jews and Mudejares. Every man on that panel has such a horrible record that would displease even the most reactionary politician today. Even nature has no use for them. The authorities had planted a copse here but nature turned it into a forest of tall trees. That was nature's way of pulling a curtain over these men and their malevolent lives. I still suggest to you that these men are bouncers."

By now they were directly in front of the museum and gazing at the busts high up on the wall. They had their backs to the parkway where the traffic roared and squelched to a halt in front of the red light. Motorists, waiting anxiously for the green light to continue their journeys, turned to the upward-looking joggers with the corners of their eyes for a cursory look. Underneath, angry, weary but reliable trains cried and screeched to deserved stops at the Eastern Parkway station. Juliette and Stephen continued to jog in lockstep while arguing about the message, significance and function of the men whose alto-relievos they were looking at.

"Up there is a man fit to be an usher. He's David the son of Jesse. His epic confrontation with, and eventual slaying of, the monstrous Philistine Goliath will forever remain a source of succor for all those against whom great odds are stacked. From the most humble beginnings, he rose to become the king of Israel. Israel was in need of security from its hostile neighbors, as it does now, and he provided it. The state of Israel will never know a more powerful king," said Juliette.

"It is true that he was a very powerful monarch. Don't forget that he was also a sexual deviant who spent most of his time on his rooftop observing naked, bathing women. He perfected the act of voyeurism. In no time he identified and zoomed in on the elegant wife of one of his bravest subjects, Uriah the Hittite. While the latter was still fighting for David's kingdom, David put his wife in the family way. His most offensive act was his letter to his general to send Uriah to the most fierce flank of battle so that Uriah might be slain. Indeed, Uriah was slain and we should look at it as murder in some degree, first, second or tenth. It is still murder, a felony.

"Of all of them up there, there is no happier man than David because he has been placed in a vantage point to see some Bed-Sty or Crown Heights woman in the bathroom. From this angle, as you can see, he has strained himself so much that he has ripped his zizith from his ephod. If he was not so far and high up there, I would have liked to tell him, 'quit straining your neck, David. There are no outhouses in Brooklyn,' " said Stephen.

"I see you don't think King David is fit to be an usher. Saint Peter, who is also up there clearly must be. He certainly recognized the Lord when all other disciples were not so sure. He alone came to the defense of the Lord during the Passion, severing off the ear of one of the attackers. For his reward, he was used as the foundation of the Christian church. He went on to provide able leadership to the early Christians."

"Don't forget that he was also a man of little faith and a man in need of spiritual support. He almost sank when he attempted to walk on water but Jesus came to his rescue. It is true that at the initial stages of the Passion and Crucifixion, he severed a soldier's ear with his sword which Jesus re-anastomosed theurgically rather than surgically. When confronted at the height of his Master's suffering, he lapsed into opportunistic denial. Remember what he told the maid, 'Woman, I know him not.' Before the cock crowed, he denied his Master not once, not twice but three times. You have to decide whether what I have just outlined is the resume of an usher or a bouncer.

"I also think that as building material his hagiographic remains, like yours and mine, turned out to be mud and magma rather than marble, materials unfit even for scaffolding. A house erected on those materials is like one divided against itself. It cannot stand except with incredible architectural ingenuity and painstaking, time-consuming masonry. That is why it took nine hundred years to complete his Saint Peter's Basilica in Rome."

"If you condemn even Saint Peter as unfit to be an usher then you must consider Saint Paul. He was the most prolific Christian letter writer. No one else contributed more to the Christian bible or to the spread of the Faith in the early days," insisted Juliette.

"He was also the most potent anti-Christian crusader, putting many adherents to death in a very violent no-holds-barred wave of repression and driving others underground until he saw the light on his way to Damascus. Most hate mongers don't end up seeing the light and for that reason, he deserves our commendation and appreciation. Then he went on to write all those epistles. If I could lay my hands on the original scrolls he is clutching against his chest, there are two passages I would like to erase," said Stephen.

"And which are those?" she asked.

"I would go into the fifth chapter of his first epistle to Saint Timothy and rewrite that verse twenty-three in which he advised Timothy to 'drink no more water but wine' for his stomach pain and other infirmities. It is a verse I have heard too many alcoholics and mental derelicts quote. You know as I do that alcohol has no empiric or definitive therapeutic role in the management of abdominal pain. It is one of the commonest causes of abdominal pain in our society today. That prescription remains as possibly the most discredited, yet durable, example of medical quackery in the literature.

"The second passage that ought to be erased is the second chapter of the same epistle to Saint Timothy, verses eleven and twelve. He said there that 'It is shameful for women to speak in the Church. If they have questions let them ask their husbands at home.' There are several problems here. While he must have been cautioning against noise rather than preaching, the passage has been interpreted by mainstream Christendom and society at large to keep women back. I don't think there will be a female pope, ever. If women couldn't speak in the church, it is hard to imagine where else they could. The church should be the ultimate-level playing field.

"Another problem with the passage is that millions of women are unable, or have chosen not, to marry. It is not clear to whom they should turn to for their questions. Even in traditional households, while the husband is often the miser, the wife is far more commonly the wiser. She nurtures not only the offspring but also her man, restraining the latter from unhealthy behavior like smoking, alcoholism and drug abuse. If such women were to take questions to their spouses at home, they might just sit back and enjoy their husbands' buffoonery. While it would be hard for a woman to choose Saint Paul as an usher, it is his earlier anti-Christian murderous repression that stains his resume. That was when he was called Saul of Tarsus. I hope he rose to that pedestal with one caveat: a complete repudiation of his first coming."

Stephen and Juliette continued their stationary jogging with their attention fixed firmly up there on the wall. The traffic on Eastern Parkway flowed smoothly as dictated by the lights making their programcd green-yellow-red-green cycles. Some workers, including some cops, passed Juliette and Stephen into the museum. It appeared neither party noticed the other. The joggers moved a few yards toward the public library and were now facing another set of busts on the wall, that of Greek philosophers. Juliette continued to insist that they were looking at ushers for the museum while Stephen only saw bouncers.

"Dr. Latham, look at Solon's name up there. He did not harm anyone. Don't you think he had the resume of an usher?"

"There is no doubt that Solon was a great archon. In one stroke he abolished slavery in ancient Athens, moving with more force than William Wilberforce. He deserved the eponym 'Great Emancipator' more than did Abe Lincoln, because his edicts were clear. Lincoln's

Emancipation Declaration was, after all, cryptic and ambiguous. Solon was also an unusual democrat who shared power according to wealth, not birth. But when his policies brought upheaval and controversy to Athens, he abdicated and began to subvert his city-state from exile. Imagine what could have happened to us if Lincoln had absconded during the siege of Washington, D.C. Like they say, if you cannot stand the heat, don't go into the kitchen. Now I ask you, Do you want Solon the subversive and turncoat as your usher?" asked Stephen.

"If only I could see how he looked like, it might help me decide. I wonder why he was denied his high-relief," said Juliette.

"Everything that happens in the world is a sign of the times. Legislation setting aside this land for the museum was passed in 1888. This was the period of Redemption for the anti-emancipation forces. Abolitionists and emancipators, like scalawags, were in retreat everywhere. Frederick Douglass sought the republican presidential nomination that year and got only one vote—his own—an unenviable record that will stand for ever. Solon could not have been given his relief in that environment."

"I would have Sophocles, the theatrical innovator, costumer, one of the greatest playwrights of all time and a scenic actor as an usher. Wouldn't you?" Juliette asked.

"That suggests that you have a predilection for senseless homicide, suicide, wanton touching of, and disrespect for, women; the violence of sexual passion, and attempted rape. Do you?"

"You have just delved into the domain of gangster rappers and heavy metalists. You are not talking about Sophocles, a playwright who has firmly held his place of critical esteem for more than two and a half millennia."

"I am talking about the author of *The Women of Trachis* in which all these lyrics are sung. Together with his compatriots Aeschylus, who shares the panel with him, and Euripides, they set the Dionysia and popular drama on a tragic course. For several reasons, Sophocles did more harm. He expanded the ensemble, introducing a third actor and a larger chorus. He lived to be a nonagenarian at a time when a forty-year-old man was an old man. He occupied various public offices. Those who suffer from organic hyperbole call him the Great Innovator and Tragedian. You, the iconoclast, have just called him a gangster rapper. I don't think that is the type of an entertainer you want as an usher," Stephen said.

"Socrates is also on this panel. Few philosophers have influenced Western thought more than he has. He was a wise man who taught that rational people will consciously choose good and shun harm. In recognizing that women were equally talented as men he was living ahead of his time. He had no tolerance for specious arguments. He believed in proofs and in the truth. These are positions you would agree with. You have to agree that he would make a good usher."

"He was, no doubt, a wise man whose main objective in life was a simple wish to get along well with everybody. He married his wife Xanthippe not because he loved her so much. Her fabled temper was described as hot, short and bad. He married her, he said, because if he could cope with her, he could cope with everybody else. A marriage should not be an experiment. Rather, it should be a source of merriment. No man should endure such a woman as Xanthippe.

"When Socrates' experiment failed, he started drinking heavily. The fairy tale that he could sip as much ouzo and oenomel as he wanted without ever getting drunk is a simple exaggeration at best. Taken in an adequate amount, wine would make any man drunk though the manifestation may run the whole spectrum from catatonia to coprolalia. When he declared ex-cathedra and ipse-dixit during the dinner party, in the house of Agathon the Elegant, that his flat nose was superior to a long one, he must have been inebriated. A wise philosopher who desired proof for every position or theory could only talk like that under the influence. It would appear that he went to the Hades for a nose job, for his nose in this statue is long.

"Alcohol affected Socrates behavior in other ways. He became a barefooted, peripatetic and pathetic vagabond dressed in tatters. Here they have clad him in more chiton than he ever owned in his seventy years. Under the influence of alcohol, Socrates roamed the streets of Athens denouncing the Sophists. In so doing, he stepped on very powerful and big toes. As the saying goes, those who live in glass houses, and I might add, those with skeletons in their consoles, should not throw stones. Socrates was indicted on several counts of corrupting the youths of Athens. He was found guilty by the Ecclesia and sentenced to death by chemical ingestion. The question is, could this ex-con be a good usher for the youths of Brooklyn?" Stephen asked.

"I think most pundits would return a 'no' to that question. On the other hand even the curator of the museum would agree that Herodotus of Halicarnasus who is also on this panel would make a perfect usher and guide. He was the father of history. For his wide and distant travels and his experience with peoples and places, I would also call him the father of geography. The world is a museum and no one knew the world more than did Herodotus. He is easily an ideal usher," said Juliette.

"I think you have to take accounts of his travels with a pinch of salt. The civilized world in his time was no larger than Asia Minor and the Mediterranean Basin with Greece and Athens, in particular, at the epicenter. At the periphery were uncivilized, primitive and savage tribes. Explorations in those territories would have been virtually impossible. There were no reliable means of transport, food preservation or insecticides to control the Mediterranean fruit fly. Equestrianism had not been adequately developed. There were no materials of enough tensile strength to make a durable halter. The stirrup's invention was at least a millennium away. Horseback riding was so unreliable in those days that when Athens was mobilizing for the battle of Marathon, against the forces of Darius the Persian king, they dispatched the legendary marathoner Pheidippides to ask Sparta for help. Neither was sea-travel easy. The Meltemi and other etesian winds were very hostile to cruise ships as seafarers, from Saint Paul to Carl Petersen, would tell you. The winds were more than a match for the galleys and triremes.

"My friend Dr. Kim believes that the strongest evident that Herodotus undertook the trips was his treatise on ancient Libyan women. In summary, he wrote, the more lovers ancient Libyan women had the more honor they earned. He did not have to go ashore to find that out. He could have heard that from wind-battered, macho Libyan fishermen in the gulf of Sidra. Or he could have heard it from the thousands of Greek hoplites returning from foreign expeditions. I think Herodotus destroyed his credibility as an authentic explorer when he said that he did not know, and had not met any man who knew, if Europe was bounded on the west by a body of water. Finally, you have to be wary of the man who likes to be called the father of history when there was history even before he was born. You have to wonder what else he would want to misappropriate," suggested Stephen.

More museum staffers passed Juliette and Stephen as they made their way to work inside. Stephen was impressed with Juliette's stamina and dexterity. She was able to run in place, in lockstep with Stephen while carrying on a purposeful conversation. They paid no attention to the traffic or pedestrians. But no one else paid attention to the talking joggers gazing at the wall of the museum. Juliette was equally impressed by Stephen's forceful defense of his positions. Though she did not necessarily agree with all his positions, in the interest of her seduction mission, she had to offer concession, not confrontation. But she would try to score at least one victory.

"I concede that round again though I still believe these men were selected as ushers not as bouncers. Consider Thucydides. He was one of the most unbiased war correspondents of all time even when writing about his enemies. He did not report every rumor he heard like Herodotus did. Would you view him as a bouncer? He doesn't look threatening, after all."

"Thucydides was the most trusted military commander of his Athens. Yet when the town of Amphipolis was besieged and the responsibility to defend it fell on him, he failed rather miserably. That is why, I think, the architects, 'McKim, Mead & White' made him look like a woman here. For his punishment, Thucydides was banished into exile. His selection here is a disservice to General Lafayette, the revolutionary hero who in 1825 laid the anlagen for the building of the Brooklyn Apprentices' Library, the precursor of the museum. Now I ask you, in which capacity an AWOL marine would fit better, as a psychedelic usher or as an intimidating bouncer?" asked Stephen.

They moved a few yards yet again toward the public library to a position that afforded them a tangential view of the library side of the museum. Up on the wall and at the same height as the other high-reliefs were the busts of Virgil and Cicero. Juliette looked at the two men's names for a moment, turned to Stephen and smiled. They were still jogging in lockstep, the only way they could have kept it going for so long. They continued their argument.

"Virgil was a farmer's son, a real country boy who rose by dint of hard work to the prominent position as the greatest Latin poet. What is wrong with a poet being an usher, Stephen?" asked Juliette.

"Virgil represented what is most wrong in politics, nepotism. Because of his contacts with, and connections to, influential imperial ministers, he abandoned farming and did not have to worry about his personal finances. He then devoted himself entirely to literature. That, in and of itself, was not necessarily bad. He established himself as a great poet when he wrote about the beauty of the Italian scenery. His works on the beauty and pleasure of real country life also added to his stature. What detracted from it was his last work, *The Aeneid,* in which he reveals his fascination with violence. He was so ashamed of his writing in *The Aeneid* that he did not want it to survive him. When he contracted a fatal febrile condition on a visit to Greece, he ordered it destroyed. Only the emperor's decree saved it for posterity. After his death, anti-Christian pagans looked up to him with religious veneration with his writings as their Bible in the early days of Christianity. Could you as a Christian nominate this paganic demigod, who eschewed so much violence in his works, for usher?"

"You've won that one too. But his compatriot, who stands next to him, Cicero the Roman consul, was the most eloquent orator in the

Senate. He was elected aedile at the youngest age allowed by law, soon after he learnt to put on his toga virilis. He became quaestor at the age of thirty-one. His stature was so great that he was given the eponym 'Father of his country' while others hailed him 'Imperator.' One of the greatest lawyers ever, he has humbled himself here as an usher."

"His fibrebrand speeches and acerbic tongue carried the Roman Senate, and the plebians outside, too far. He was the most unscrupulous lawyer, politician and orator that the Roman empire knew. None of his political opponents could survive the juggernaut of his castigation on the floor of the Senate. Since he was overfond of wine and frequently drunk, it is hard to say whether some or all of his irrational behavior was alcohol-related. When he was broke, he divorced his wife of thirty years, not because of her violent temper, but because he had met a younger woman with a lot of cash. He was probably under the influence. When, as a praetor, he sat on that curule chair and sentenced a Roman citizen to death without trial, much to the embarrassment of his lictors and fasces, he was probably drunk again. That error led to his discovery as a phony, his expulsion from Rome and the burning of his house to the ground. He sneaked back through the back door to continue his intrigue and deadly power play but was put to death by Emperor Mark Anthony's decree. The world's most celebrated defense attorney did not stand to defend himself. He attempted fleeing by sea but was caught and executed at the rostra. Former U.S. Senator Joseph McCarthy was his understudy. Clearly, he had the profile of a perfect bouncer."

"You have to ignore the facts and approach it with common sense, Stephen. They have at least two million objects there in that landmark, organized into seven curatorial departments, two research libraries and an archive. There is also a canteen in which the food is very good. They are already improving existing conditions and looking into the next century. Think about it. Nobody will invest so much in an institution only to scare away customers with a cordon of mean-looking, no-nonsense bouncers. You've got to go in there and feed your eyes and brain."

"The only way you're gonna convince me these guys are ushers and not bouncers is if you tell me they were selected by a television talk-show host. Then I will go in there by gatecrashing, if necessary, through the side of Herodotus. He looks exhausted after one of those his short forays into Europe."

"Your points are well taken, though. They could have done a better job of selecting their ushers. If they desired a figure that would be acceptable to most Americans, one who had made more contribution

158

than anyone else to the collection, collation and preservation of species, they could have chosen Noah. His Ark was the world's first act of museum building. There are also two Greeks who should have been selected but I don't see them. Aristotle, one of the greatest thinkers of ancient Greece did not only establish the first serious library, he also established a museum in the Lyceum in Athens. Alexander the Great, who conquered the then known world of Africa, Asia and Europe commanded his generals to collect items for his former teacher Aristotle's museum. Finally, I think they should have honored the first Christian martyr and his pile of stones, Saint Stephen. Why do you think they didn't do that, Dr. Stephen?"

Stephen turned toward Grand Army Plaza and Juliette followed by his side. In response to her question, he started to sing. She recovered from her initial amazement to join in singing the old Baptist doxology:

When the Saints are called up yonder,
When the Saints are called up yonder,
When the Saints are called up yonder,
When the Saints are called up yonder,
I'll be there.

This rendition highlighted certain facts for Stephen. He became painfully aware that he had not been to church since his grandmother passed away several years ago. As a result, he had almost forgotten his lyrics. He was not sure if the correct wording should not have been: "When the roll is called up yonder . . . "

He turned right, then left to assure that no one was listening and watching. Not that he thought there was anything necessarily wrong with singing in public. It all depended on his tone, the lyrics and what else was going on around him. Early morning shoppers going to the vegetable market at Grand Army Plaza hearing that familiar tune might even join in. On the other hand if he raised his voice too high, especially in the presence of a disinterested crowd, it might suggest that he needed psychiatric evaluation.

As they made their way toward the public library, the rendition was disrupting his jogging rhythm. He was learning the hard way that running is not just a set of coarse swinging movements of the limbs. The mind, the mouth and even memory participate significantly, albeit inconspicuously. Thus, the introduction of some other endeavor like singing, which requires fine movements, might overwhelm those faculties and bring a runner to a standstill. Only with the necessary talent and adequate conditioning can an athlete achieve and sustain the satisfactory synchronization. Juliette had stopped singing, apparently because she had never tried it before.

Sensing her difficulty, Stephen also stopped singing. He knew as well as anyone else that when running with a partner, he had to do everything to keep their rhythm stable. He turned back one more time to look at the museum wall but they were too far gone and he could not see it. He turned briefly to look at Juliette and resumed their talk in short syllables. "Come'on, let's get away from here, away from the blasphemy and iconoclasm." She smiled but did not say anything.

In front of the library, the light stayed green and the pair of runners could not immediately cross into Prospect Park, past the vegetable market. Stephen and Juliette said nothing to each other as they waited anxiously for the traffic to come to a stop. Grand Army Plaza was the magnificent labyrinth where all of Brooklyn met. They were at the edge of Flatbush Avenue facing the nearly empty vegetable market with their backs to the library. To Stephen's left, Flatbush coursed lazily to the beaches of Far Rockaway where Stephen had met Juliana. His mind went back to that date but it would have been inappropriate to mention it. In front and to Juliana's right was the giant monument to the Defenders of the Union which was erected in the Civil War era. The defenders were in obvious need of defense from excoriating weather conditions. Funds had recently been set aside for that. Now that he was standing so close to the monument, Stephen could understand why the huge appropriation was necessary. Flatbush formed the perimeter around it before drawing a beeline to Manhattan. Eastern Parkway and many other feeder streets had a common source in Grand Army Plaza. Traffic flowed into and out of them as Stephen and Juliette waited. The business district of Park Slope and the leisure forest of Prospect Park lay on opposite sides of the Plaza. The subway trains roared underneath. Finally, traffic came to a full stop and the runners dashed to the park, side by side.

On the track, joggers of little endurance were walking and, perhaps, returning home. He looked at his watch as he always did. It was 6:30 A.M. They could turn right and go down the long descent in which case they would face the sharp ascent toward the end of the three-mile track. Or, they could turn left and then end up with a long exhausting hill to completely circle the track.

Not knowing which of the Hobson's choices she would like, Stephen turned to Juliette and asked, "In which direction would you like us to run?"

"As you like it, Dr. Latham," she replied. Then she added, "I am here for you."

He turned right, to his well-studied route, and she followed. As they began to pick up pace, with trepidation, his muscles and bones creaked in protest. He had been through this before, he told himself. He liked to run in the same direction as most of the other runners because overtaking them gave him instant gratification.

On several occasions he had run into trouble, literally, with this disdainful attitude. He would try to pass a young man by but the latter, in a clear display of manly ego and hormones would not concede defeat. Both Stephen and the young man would accelerate until one, usually the latter but on rare occasions Stephen, would relax with exhaustion. On this day there would be no such melodrama as he had a guest-runner.

They were running at her pace, or so Stephen thought. Halfway round the track, he felt exhausted while she was going strong. It was as if she possessed the energy and stamina to leave him behind if she so desired. Only humility and deference to her boss appeared to be preventing her from making the attempt. He would be more energized after the first lap, as in the past, he comforted himself. They were not conversing, for the most part. Only occasionally would Stephen ask her, "How are you doing?"

She would reply "I'm fine" and he knew she was right.

There were a few familiar faces from the hospital in the park. Paper-thin, Ms. Anderson, of the general supplies department at InnerFaith was running opposite them. She never seemed to recognize anyone, even in the hospital. They did not exchange glances or greetings. Most likely, Juliette did not even know Ms. Anderson worked in the hospital. He did because they had served in the same committee.

There was a sixty-year-old man standing at one of the exits to Flatbush Avenue with a prominent surgical scar on his sternum where his chest must have been split into two at surgery. Stephen had no doubt that the man must have undergone heart-bypass surgery. To most people in the park the scar must have been inconsequential. Stephen had acquired the third eye with training and was seeing things beyond the obvious. The value of the trained eye, he told himself, was beyond description. The man was breathing fast, exhausted from perhaps running a few hundred yards as prescribed. Just before Stephen and Julie ran past him, Stephen looked down, quickly inspecting the man's bare legs to see if a vein had been removed to patch his heart arteries. The classic scar was there. Stephen wished him good luck.

A trio of obese middle-aged women reminded Stephen of his patients who would swear passionately of how little food they consumed but still had trouble losing weight. For as long as Stephen had been jogging in Prospect Park the trio had been walking there. They took their time, strutting with the grace of sumo wrestlers in the direction opposite Stephen's. They probably swore to their physicians that they exercised rigorously. Their enormous widths occupied a lot of space on the track forcing Stephen and Juliette to veer apart, forming an ellipse around the heavy weights.

They had gone halfway through the track when Stephen asked Juliette a question. "You off today?" he asked.

"Beeper call," she responded.

She slapped her side pocket to emphasize the fact that she had her beeper in her pocket.

"I am on call too. Let's hope they don't call us," said Stephen.

"Would've gone to the club. Like the treadmill. Can count calories there. But, it's lonely there. Saw you leaving the block."

They spoke in short syllables and mostly incomplete sentences. Even for veterans, this is the most practical form of communication in this situation. Attention to syntax and grammar is irrelevant here. They were running close to, and almost touching, each other. Most other runners probably mistook them for a couple. Stephen responded to her preamble. "Once again, I am happy you came to keep me company," he uttered, reflexly stooping to avoid the overhanging foliage even though his vertex fell well short of it.

Just beyond that point, walking opposite them in white trunks and an inscription-free white T-shirt, was the highest-placed public official Stephen had ever seen in the park, Congressman Charles Schumer. It appeared his mind was away at Washington where his pet, the ban on certain types of assault weapons, was under renewed Republican threat. Stephen had seen congressmen and even the president jogging on TV but he could never be sure if it was the real thing or it was just made for TV. Mr. Schumer was jogging without cameras, so it was real. Some people look different on TV than they do in real life but Charles Schumer, whom Stephen had never seen live, was the same. If Stephen had not been running with a guest, he would gone up to, and shaken hands with, Mr. Schumer. So much money (some of which was described as soft) grease the palms of congressmen that Stephen wondered the firmness of their grip. Though Mr. Schumer was one of the cleanest members of the House, and may not have been the best gauge, he still could have provided a clue, if only because he was the only congressman Stephen had ever met.

They came upon the most open area of the track. There were a few players on the tennis courts on the other side of Caton Avenue and ragtag soccer players beyond, on the parade grounds. The course was beginning, the slow upward slope. This part of the track always took its toll on even the most agile runners. For the elderly it was, in the true sense of the phrase, an uphill task. To the left of Stephen and Juliette were a lanky, elderly man and an energetic young woman. The latter was walking leisurely, the former running very hard but still having a hard time keeping up with her. The man was saying something apparently important to her and, in doing so, contributing to his own breathlessness. During the brief moment they were aligned side by side, Stephen could hear the man say something about "fun." Stephen surmised the man was probably discussing mutual funds. He looked like he might be a mutual fund manager.

When they came back to their starting point, Stephen looked at his watch again. They had completed the first lap in thirty minutes, just three minutes short of Stephen's personal best time. Juliette, Stephen was convinced, could have threatened or in fact broken that record if she had to. He knew he had his work cut out for him. He would have to increase his routine. They completed the second lap in exactly the same time. Usually, he stopped there. He did not like to go for the third lap. But because Juliette looked so strong, Stephen led her into the third and final lap. He knew that would be the limit of his endurance. He would have to call it off at the end of the third round even if she wanted more. A ten-mile race for a busy physician who had not seen the track in weeks was a respectable showing, he thought.

By the end of the third lap he was feeling claudication in his calves. He knew he would probably not have achieved the feat if Juliette had not run behind, and later beside, him. It is often said behind every successful man there is a woman. Conventional folly has defined that woman as the spouse. Token competition from, and the desire to impress, a woman often impels a man to success and that woman is seldom the spouse. By the time she becomes the spouse there is little else to prove. Dr. Stephen Latham was glad Juliette Painter had nursed him to set a new record for himself. Now he was done.

Just beyond the Grand Army Plaza exit, there was a decrepit wooden bench on Julie's right side. It was an invitation to sit down and relax or recoup. After expending the last modicum of energy climbing the hill, Stephen thought, the bench could not have been more appropriately situated, at the top of the hill. He knew his partner, too, was tired and would be relieved to be invited to sit down. Without saying a word, he turned toward the bench. Julie followed. A long period of silence and labored breathing followed as they sat facing the track and the baseball field beyond.

Several joggers, some of whom Stephen had left behind, filed past. Some other interesting figures also followed in the parade. There was a young man clutching a half-empty or half-full bottle of diet Pepsi in his right hand, a walkman on his left with his chest bare. He was walking gently in the runners' lane. Stephen had seen him on previous occasions before. He never ran and he never left the track unless the bottle of soda was empty.

"You've got a lot of energy, Ms. Painter. How come I have never seen you here before?" Stephen broke the silence.

"I go to the Brooklyn racquet club, you know. It's like being in the closet. For you to come out, you have to have somebody out there. Somebody you can depend on. This is a tough place for a woman to come to, by herself. You know what I mean."

Stephen nodded in agreement even though he was not sure she was referring to the sour grapes of an aging single woman or the threats that female runners face in the park.

"First, I heard your door close. Then I saw you down there on the street with those boyish legs. Then I dressed up and followed you. You have been running for a long time. You've got more stamina than anyone I know. I wonder why you have only one baby," she said. They both giggled.

They were interrupted by a band of cyclists passing on the track. They were closely packed and moving at very high speed. They probably belonged to the same club. Despite their number and speed, they avoided collision with one another. For a moment they stole the show from everyone else in the park. Stephen marveled at their coordination and flamboyant attire.

"This is one of the best sports," he said matter-of-factly to Juliette, referring to the cyclists. "You can burn real calories and you use all muscle groups. It's like swimming. The only reason I don't have a bike is because I don't like the way they meander around cars. It's like David and Goliath."

"Dr. Latham, I have been having some discomfort around here," Julie said while making circular movements with her outstretched right index finger around the area between her navel and her lower rib margin. "Sometimes it moves up my chest, especially after I eat. I am sure it is not acid reflux disease," she added, indicating her state of denial, which is legendary among nurses and doctors. "I have tried Prilosec on and off but it gives me a headache. Dr. Richards ordered all kinds of tests during my last physical. I think every test came back

164

normal. I got copies and I'll let you see them. When will you be in the office?"

Juliette had actually come to the park to establish rapport with Stephen. She had come to the conclusion that his marriage was on the rocks and that he would be most vulnerable to seduction and suggestion at this time. Last night, she had discovered that his obnoxious wife was, in addition to her other shortcomings, denying him sex. She knew that there was no other time a man could be more vulnerable. She had pondered over what complaint to bring to him. She decided against a symptom that might lead to the diagnosis of a condition with negative social stigmata or one that would lead to referral to another physician. She settled on heartburn though what bothered her was her heart's burning desire for him.

Stephen lectured her, "There is no reason why you should not have endoscopy if you have this pain. Denial and empiric treatment are not good for you, because you do so much for patients with less severe complaints. During the conference I attended last week, it was revealed that three gastroenterologists were unable to attend because they had advanced cancer of the stomach. They had been ignoring the symptoms for too long." "You remind me of them."

"I might eventually need to have the test but for now, I would like you to review the test results I've got. Will you be in your office in the afternoon tomorrow?" Juliette asked.

"Hmmmm, tomorrow is Sunday. I will be there from two to three, cleaning up."

"In that case I'm just gonna pop in with the results. I'm gonna be on call, in the hospital from eight to eight. I will want you to give me a good physical, whole body examination," Juliette said, stroking her body from head to groin as if that was where her body ended. "How was El Paso?" She asked about the medical conference Stephen attended the previous week in El Paso.

"It was terrific, well attended by experts from all over the world. I wish you were there. The lectures, the five-kilometer race, which I would have won had I not lost my way, the food, which was everywhere. It was real fun. I gained five pounds which I must now lose in three weeks. The tours were said to be good but I didn't participate in them. I crossed the border to Mexico and I bought this T-shirt there," he said pointing to "Mexico" inscribed on his T-shirt.

"There were so many people crossing the border that El Paso in Spanish must mean 'to pass.' At least that was my impression while crossing the border," Stephen said.

"How did you communicate with the Mexicans?" Julie asked, perhaps just to contribute to the discussion.

Stephen grinned. "It was a comedy of tongues. There was a Haitian guy in the group who spoke Spanish well. He had gone to Medical School in Mexico. Wherever we stopped, he would begin to speak Spanish, fluent Spanish. Just about the same time the Mexican guy would reply in perfect English, better English than you would hear in downtown Brooklyn. Without saying anything, we would all turn to each other and smile. The scene repeated itself several times. I think it was really entertaining."

More entertaining was his experience at the topless bar. But those lurid details were not for the ears of a professional female colleague he was meeting in the park for the first time. The information men give out is filtered based on the degree of familiarity, gender and ulterior motive. He had gone to the topless (actually, topless and bottomless) bar with the other three members of the group. No sooner had they sat down than they were mobbed by an equal number of fresh girls. As the girls were about to sit on their laps, he had waved his outstretched hands before the girls, a motion which in the somber environment of the strip club meant an explicit no.

They had spent about five hours in Mexico, four of them in the strip club. The dollar was the favored currency in the night club as it was elsewhere in the city. While in the strip club in Ciudad Juarez it had become clear to Stephen and his entourage that despite the celebrated freedom of expression Americans enjoyed, the state still determined the extent to which strippers could expose themselves. By contrast, the Mexicans had deregulated the industry to the extent that not only were teenagers not barred, but the girls exposed themselves completely, leaving nothing to be imagined. No wonder, Stephen thought, there were so many American teenagers in the nightclub.

The band of nimble cyclists was passing again. For a moment all conversations stopped as everybody looked up to admire them. Their uniform was colorful. The handful of riders in mufti at the tail end of the parade were probably outsiders. They displayed impressive familiarity with their craft. Many were riding with their hands off the bars. Since their course was sloping downwards, there was no need to pedal and some of them seized the opportunity to place their legs in various positions, depending on their deftness. Stephen remembered some terrible injuries he had seen in the emergency room among cyclists and began to worry about the possibility something going wrong with this group. One point of consolation was the fact that they all wore crash helmets, perhaps in compliance with their professional code of conduct.

"When did you leave for El Paso?" Julie asked.

"On Sunday the twelfth," Stephen replied, indicating with his facial expression that he would like to know why she asked.

"Ms. Hayes was complaining on the following Monday that the unit had been left in a bad shape. Did you have any procedure before your departure? You know how Ms. Hayes likes to complain." The last statement was intended to assure Stephen that if he had been responsible for the mess, she, Julie, would not join Ms. Hayes in blaming him. She was almost certain that Stephen had worked that day because he had been the one on call.

"I had been called by the intern on call that Sunday night that there was a thirty-nine-year-old man passing blood in stool and in shock. When I got to the emergency room, guess who the patient was?" Without waiting for Julie to answer, Stephen answered the question. "Charles Felder."

"Charles Felder again?" Julie exclaimed in exasperation.

Charles Felder was well known to the endoscopy unit of InnerFaith hospital. In fact, his notoriety had spread beyond the endoscopy unit and most of the young doctors had come to recognize him as a great malingerer. His Medicaid abuse was so flagrant that New York Medicaid restricted him to InnerFaith Hospital for proper surveillance. Previously, he used to go from InnerFaith, to Brookdale, to Kings County and Brooklyn hospitals obtaining prescriptions for the most expensive medications which he sold to unscrupulous pharmacists at give-away prices. He knew exactly what to tell overworked interns to obtain a specific diagnosis and the right prescription.

Six months previously, when he heard on the news that the injection for treating heart attacks was more than two thousand dollars per unit dose, he pulled off a great scam in order to be able to obtain prescriptions for it. He presented to the emergency room complaining of "severe, continuous pressure-type chest pain made worse by the slightest effort," to put in his own words. Because he also gave a history of heavy cigarette smoking and high blood pressure, his condition was taken seriously. When all the preliminary test results were normal, he agreed to have a tiny tube passed from his groin to his heart to take a picture of his heart vessels. He was told that he had not suffered a heart attack when that test turned out to be normal. "I know I got a heart attack and I need a prescription for T-A-P." He was referring to TPA, the expensive treatment for select cases of heart attacks. The next day a doctor who moonlighted at Brookdale Hospital said at rounds that Mr. Felder had presented similarly at the latter hospital a month previously and had been given the same diagnosis and prognosis.

Now that the state had restricted his insurance coverage to InnerFaith Hospital he had to devise ingenious scams to outwit suspecting doctors. There was a lucrative underground trade in the drug Zantac used for the treatment of stomach ulcers. The intravenous drug-abusing community widely held the myth that it could potentiate a high. Pharmacists were making a killing buying it at five cents a tablet from the likes of Mr. Felder and selling it to legitimate users for one dollar more. Mr. Felder came to the hospital complaining of severe stomach pain above his navel and vomiting blood.

He had known from all his previous encounters with the medical profession that doctors might dismiss a complaint of stomach pain as hysterical. Bleeding from any part of the body was always taken as seriously by the doctors as by the patients. Tell a drowsy intern on call that you had been suffering with stomach pain for the last year he might just dose off. To wake him up don't shake him, but tell him that you saw a tinge of blood in your urine or feces yesterday. The first time Mr. Felder complained of vomiting blood he was whisked to the endoscopy room. A compete examination revealed no disease and he was again dismissed as a fake. Still, he aggressively demanded a prescription for Zantac. That was three weeks ago and Julie was there. So when Stephen mentioned Charles Felder, Julie understood.

"What did Felder complain of this time?" Julie asked.

"He complained of severe stomach pain, dizziness and red blood in the stool. When the poor intern examined him, his blood pressure was very low and there was blood in his stool. Naturally, the intern had to call me. Since my flight was two hours away, I did not want to pass the buck to Dr. Robinson."

"You know if he was in your position, he would never have gone in," Julie interjected. She was referring to Dr. Wayne Robinson, who had a reputation for passing the buck especially if the patient did not have good insurance coverage.

"So we went into his stomach and it was absolutely clean," Stephen continued.

"We did colonoscopy for him as you would expect. There was a tinge of blood in his rectum which could not be explained by any disease process. Interestingly, there were several shells of slow-release Procardia. He had taken an overdose of Procardia to lower his blood pressure and had given himself an enema of tap water tinged with animal blood. When we placed all the inconsistencies and the possibility of death from Procardia overdose before him, he admitted to his scam. I had only thirty minutes to catch my flight and I only caught it because it was delayed for twenty minutes."

On the track, the young man with the bottle of Pepsi cola passed leisurely. There was little soda left in the bottle which meant he would soon leave the track. Behind him was a group of four Asian teen-age roller skaters. The two boys and one of the girls were very experienced in the sport. They were all paying attention to the other girl whose gait was unsteady and hands were flailing in air. Stephen could also tell from the generous padding over her knuckles that she was an amateur. It looked like an initiation for her. Perhaps she was one of the boys' new found love in which case the affair could be strengthened by a common obsession. Presently, she began to thrash and spin violently in air. Within a few seconds, she fell to the ground on her buttocks. The natural padding of that part of her body assured soft landing. The rest of her team broke out in laughter while helping her to her feet.

Stephen looked at his watch. It was almost ten o'clock. He had appointments to keep.

"Ms. Painter, I am running late to a professional meeting." They both stood up and began to walk home through the Grand Army Plaza exit. They talked about a few hospital issues until they reached Washington Avenue, in front of the museum. Julie thought it would be unwise for both of them to return to the staff quarters side by side.

"Dr. Latham, I have to collect something from my niece on Washington and St. John's," she feigned. They turned to face each other for the pleasantries. Then she added, "I'll see you tomorrow at work. Don't forget I'll be coming for a *complete* physical." As she spoke those last words, she gave him the kind of disarming look and smile that spoke more than a thousand words. Retracing his steps home along Classon Avenue, Stephen reappraised the whole encounter, including all the suggestive utterances she had made. Whatever her intentions, Stephen vowed to keep their relationship strictly professional.

Later that afternoon, Stephen was paged to the hospital to see a young alcoholic who had come into the emergency with the complaint of vomiting blood. The emergency room physician in conjunction with Stephen had determined that the patient needed endoscopy.

Stephen arrived at the emergency department at about three that afternoon to find the miserable young man, Anthony Sowell, lying with blood mixed with stomach contents in the bowl.

"I am Dr. Latham. I am a gastroenterologist and I take care of patients who are vomiting blood. How much do you drink?"

"Every day, about six pints of Vodka," answered Mr. Sowell.

"When did you start vomiting?"

"Last night after drinking for most of yesterday. Initially I vomited clear fluid. Later it became bloody. What could be the cause, please?"

"Were you retching too?" asked Stephen.

"A lot."

"Most likely you tore the lining of your esophagus or food pipe. It is necessary for us to look inside your stomach."

"How do you do that?" asked Mr. Sowell.

"I'll take you upstairs, give you intravenous medication to make you drunk. You know what it means to be drunk. I will pass a long tube through your mouth into your stomach. You will see everything. The advantage is that we will identify the source of bleeding and if there is active bleeding I may be able to stop it. Are there risks involved? Yes, there are. I could tear your stomach but that is most unlikely. You could bleed as a result of the procedure, again that is most unlikely."

Mr. Sowell gave his consent for the procedure and was taken up to the endoscopy unit where the nurse, Juliette Painter, was getting the equipment ready. As soon as the patient entered the room, he developed cold feet. "What happens if I don't undergo this test, Doc?" he asked Stephen.

"Probably you will still be okay. If your bleeding is due to a tear in your lower food pipe as I strongly suspect, most likely you will be just fine. If it is due to something else, I cannot say unless I look inside. There is an 80 percent chance of the bleeding stopping whether I do anything or not."

"I'll skip the test. I had it three months ago. They found a tear in my food pipe. Then the doctor told me he shouldn't have done the test. He told me to stop drinking, also. I'll take my chances. I refuse the test. Thank you, Doc. Thank you, Nurse."

Stephen had no choice but to comply with the patient's wishes. That was the typical behavior of some veteran patients. They usually thought they knew too much. Sometime their gut feelings were right. Stephen was relieved also because after the marathon that morning, he needed to rest that afternoon. Juliette was also happy because she would not have to stay back and take care of the soiled instruments.

Transporters were summoned to wheel the patient out as nurse and doctor finished their short notes. When patients refused procedures, they did the doctors and nurses a lot of favor. They, or their survivors if they exsanguinated, could not turn around and sue for negligent care. The doctors did not have to complete large volumes of notes detailing the most minute aspect of their intervention. They could just complete their notes in one sentence, "The patient refused the test."

Stephen finished first and bade Juliette a nice weekend. He went into his office to take care of some correspondence. Stephen had hardly sat down when he heard a tap on the door. It was Juliette. That was here first time ever in his office, which was located directly opposite the endoscopy unit. Being that it was a Saturday afternoon, the hallway, usually a beehive of activity was completely deserted. On any typical weekday, she couldn't have summoned enough courage to cross the aisle into his office. If she did at all, she would have egressed as fast as one escaping an inferno. The tongues of the other women on the floor may be more lethal than an inferno. But secrecy and loneliness embolden even the fainthearted.

"I am sorry for this intrusion, Dr. Latham. I just thought this may be the best time to come see you. Are you too busy to see me now?"

Stephen felt railroaded. He was not prepared for this. "No, no . . . no. Come in," he said.

"These are the lab results we talked about today."

She removed two sheets of paper from the envelope, opened them and placed them before Stephen who was separated from her by the desk. The tests had been done as part of her application to the U.S. Army Nurses' Corps. The main reason she wanted Stephen to see them was to prove to him that she had been tested twice in the last six months for HIV, Gonorrhea, Syphilis, Hepatitis B and C and a myriad of other sexually transmittable diseases. All the tests on both occasions had come back negative, without even a trace of past exposure. She was a clean woman and proud of it though it would have been imprudent and audacious for her to have told him so. In the days when sexually transmitted diseases, especially AIDS, and the fear associated with them were so pervasive, the few good men needed assurance that they were getting an unblemished prize, she thought.

Stephen perused the reports, line by line with a pen. The latest was only a week old. He was impressed and Juliette saw as he nodded and the wrinkles on his face smoothened out.

"This is excellent, really excellent. All together, you had seventy-six tests and all came back negative. I can tell you, I have not seen a healthier woman or man in all my years of practice. All I can say is whatever it is that you are doing or not doing is good for you. Keep it up."

"Not doing."

"Good for you. Keep it up."

"The other thing we talked about in the park, my eye, remember? I have seen the ophthalmologist down there. He couldn't find anything wrong. I still occasionally have visual field defects. Could you examine them for me, please?"

"I do have an ophthalmoscope somewhere here but I have not used it for ages. Let me see if it is in one of these drawers."

He rummaged through his drawers and found the diagnostic set in the fourth drawer he opened. The set had not been opened for at least five years. Despite, or rather because of that it was in excellent condition. When he was in medical school that was the most expensive appliance he had to buy. To date he treasured it among his relics. He had doubts in his ability to recognize pathology in the eye, especially if the lesion eluded the eye specialist. But he was a stubborn guy who almost never shied away from challenges.

He took out the ophthalmoscope. It was free of dust despite having laid in limbo for all those years. He stood up from his seat and explained that the optimal condition for examining the eyes was a darkened room. He asked if Juliette had any objections to his switching off the light. "No, not at all. Let's do it," she replied. Stephen switched the light off and pitch darkness descended upon the room immediately. He groped his way to where she was sitting a few feet away. Standing before her, he shone the ophthalmoscope light on the opposite wall and gave her the instructions. "Look straight there please," he instructed her as he flickered the ophthalmoscope light on the wall. Then he stooped in the dark to look into her eyes. Proper examination of the eye with the ophthalmoscope demands that the physician's eye be no more than one or two inches away from the patient's in a dark room. No other aspect of physical examination brings the physician's face so close the patient's. When the physician and the patient do not coordinate their head movements properly, an accident can happen as it did on this occasion.

As Stephen stood in the dark to examine Juliette's eyes, he misjudged her position and their mouths touched. On the other hand it looked as if she was blessed with the gift of scotopia. Before Stephen could realize it, her tongue was out like that of a cobra exploring the inner recesses of his mouth. She rose immediately to the occasion and wrapped her hands around him. Stephen heard her murmur, "Let's do it Steve, please don't say no." Gently, Stephen lowered the instrument onto the desk. Even during a moment of unaccustomed ecstasy, delicate and expensive equipment must be handled with care. Then, in reciprocation, he wrapped his hands around her. The assembly stood still for a while, then it slithered choreographically to the heavily carpeted floor where he pinned her for a good time.

That was the birth of Dr. Latham's parallel life. He led the double life for the next several weeks and would make changes in his schedule and practice to accommodate both lives. He started carrying two beepers. The hospital beeper was not sophisticated enough to carry messages. With the extra beeper, Juliette would live instant messages for him. She could be sitting with Stephen and other nurses at, say, breakfast when she would leave the message for him on his beeper. "Call me at 1100 stat. Love, J," the typical message would say. That was one of the phone numbers in the side rooms of the endoscopy unit. Stephen would slip into his office for the important exchange of kisses over the phone. On other occasions, she would leave not so urgent messages on the answering machine in his office replete with kisses and all that.

They would continue their prearranged rendezvous in his office at odd hours when the floor was as silent as a graveyard. As Stephen descended deeper into her bosom, she would become more and more emboldened. She would miss her next period, and that would be her most potent leverage over him. Then she would come up with the idea of skipping town. The elopement would coincide with her call up for army duty. Stephen, who was still living under the influence of Somnazolam, would go along.

Dinner with the Family

Stephen returned to his apartment at about eight that evening to find Juliana with a guest—one of the other doctors' wife. Stephen did not know all the doctors' wives. He only knew the familiar faces. The two women must have been engaged in a comic conversation, for when Stephen opened the door they were laughing heartily. It must have had to do with women's issues, the kind of talk housewives don't want their men to hear. Stephen should not have asked what the matter was. But he did ask, impulsively, anyway.

That was the only thing he could say before holding his breath. The two women had been smoking and a thick cloud of smoke hung over their living quarters. He could not protest the cloud because that could have upset their guest. He intended to do so once she was gone. In the meantime he held his breath, a familiarly futile maneuver because sooner, rather than later, he had to gasp.

Juliana obviously did not want him to know the subject of discussion, at least, in the presence of her guest. Instead of answering the question, she changed the subject. "You've been gone for long. Did you have a lot of work to do?" she asked.

"It was just a mess," Stephen responded. "You won't believe what I had to do in the last five hours." The statement's hidden truism illustrated to Stephen how often he had misinterpreted other people's generic statements.

"Poor you. Steve, this is Mrs. Reza," said Juliana.

The brief introduction sufficed because Stephen knew the only Reza in the building, a quiet and withdrawn microbiologist. He had never met his wife and child. Juliana had met and befriended her in the laundry. The next day at work, he would have to tell Dr. Reza that he had met his wife the previous day. That would assure Dr. Reza that his wife was in the building, with Stephen's wife, as she may have told him. Some husbands had bad nerves and were in constant need of corroboration, from independent, unsolicited sources, of their wives' whereabouts and activities. Dr. Reza appeared to fit the profile.

When Mrs. Reza was gone, Juliana told Stephen the joke that had caused them that delirious laughter when he walked in. She and Mrs.

Reza had been talking about Mrs. Granakty, Dr. Granakty's wife. She had arrived from Botopar, her husband's native country, two weeks earlier. Though she spoke some English, in contra-distinction to most Botoparese, she appeared to have been lost in America. On her first full day in America, she was so excited by the phone that she picked it up. Within a few seconds, she had heard an instruction, "If you want to make a call, hang up then dial again." The message was repeated three times. She was looking for a spot on the ceiling from, and a thread with which to hang up the phone when her husband walked in.

The next day she had gone to the bank armed with her ATM card that her husband had given her. She went with her friend Mrs. Reza. Mrs. Granakty had forgotten the instruction that her husband had given her about the ATM machine. When the machine said, now tell me your personal code, she started whispering to the machine, "Moniya Granakty, Granakty," until the machine posted another message "sorry I have not heard from you. For your protection, you are being disconnected. It will be a pleasure to serve you next time." Then she had put in the card again. This time she actually shouted so that the machine would "hear" from her. That was what had drawn Mrs. Reza's attention to the flustered Mrs. Granakty two machines away. Mrs. Reza then helped her with her banking. Mrs. Reza said if there had been more than two other people at the bank it would have been very embarrassing, an expansive and still chuckling Juliana told her husband.

"I am hungry. Is there anything to bite here?" asked Stephen.

"Sure, we've been cooking all day. You know we shopped yesterday. We got your favorite West Indian fried plantain, macaroni and cheese, white rice and salmon stew and black-eyed peas. I also made salad with hot mustard dressing. If you don't like the spectrum, I can make you a peanut butter sandwich. Make your choice or choices," said Juliana.

"Oh boy! I am so hungry and greedy that I feel like having a little of everything."

"What happened to you that made you so hungry?"

"You know I ran thirty miles this morning. Then when I went to the hospital this afternoon I nearly worked myself to death," said Stephen.

"I keep telling you, you got to slow down sometimes, workaholic. Hang in there for the next ten minutes and dinner will be ready."

Christopher was running up and down. One minute he was messing with the VCR, the next he was plucking the leaves off the flower.

"Don't do that, Christopher. Leave that alone." Stephen found himself issuing restraining orders.

Juliana, from the kitchen said, "Now you see what we go through when you are not here with us. Put on his 'Power Ranger.' "

"Come here, Christopher. Come tell me what you have learned in school. What is the name of your school?" asked Stephen.

"Mrs. Andy," replied Christopher.

"Mrs. Andy is your teacher, Christopher. You don't know the name of your school?"

Christopher nodded.

"Christopher, tell me, what is one plus one?"

"One cookie, Daddy?" asked Christopher.

"Yes, one cookie plus one cookie. What is it?"

Christopher tried to add up the imaginary cookies using his index fingers. After examining his extended fingers for one minute, supinating and pronating his hands as if the maneuvers would change the sum, he came up with an answer. "One, Daddy."

"One cookie?" asked Stephen.

Christopher nodded.

"What happened to the other cookie?"

"I ate it."

Juliana screamed from the kitchen, "Food is ready, guys."

"Christopher, what did I tell you about cookies?" asked Stephen.

"Junk food," said Christopher.

"Yes. It is junk food and you should not eat it. If you eat it, what did I say will happen?"

"That you will lose all your teeth and become a baby again."

"Thank you. Now come'on, let's go eat good food."

Juliana had put everything on the table. Stephen helped himself to his favorite entree of West Indian plantains, rice and salmon stew. He dished out black-eyed peas and salmon stew for Christopher. The salmon stew was apparently too spicy for Christopher. "Too hot, Daddy," Christopher complained. Stephen tasted it and he, too, could just barely tolerate it.

"Put it in the fridge Daddy," said Christopher.

"No, the fridge will not make it better. Let me give you chicken stew," said Stephen.

As he dished the chicken stew for Christopher, he turned to Juliana. Concerning the salmon stew, he said, "You blew that one, J."

"I know. It was just a momentary lapse in focus. Christopher was active. He was jumping from one chair to another," explained Juliana.

176

"Well, everything else tastes just about right. That is 95 percent for you. Better than anything I ever scored in school exams."

"Look, Daddy, this water is dirty." Christopher tilted his cup of water to show the dirt in it. He had inadvertently poured a spoonful of black-eyed peas and the chicken soup into his cup of water.

"You got to pay more attention to what you are doing. You can't be playing and eating at the same time. The water is dirty. Don't drink it," said Stephen.

"The water is dirty, Daddy. You go to wash it?"

"You got to pour it away in the sink. You cannot wash it."

"Why not, Daddy? Yesterday when my shirt is dirty, Mommy wash it," said Christopher.

"Yesterday when my shirt was dirty Mommy washed it. That is what you should say."

Christopher started to repeat after his father. "Yesterday . . . "

"You have food in your mouth. Don't talk. Finish that chicken," said Stephen.

"I don't want anymore," said Christopher.

"Okay, drink your water let me go and give you a bath," said Juliana.

Stephen finished his main course and had some salad with mustard dressing for snack. While Juliana gave Christopher a bath, he made himself a cup of coffee to help push down any solid food particles that may have stuck to his esophagus. He shook the container of soy milk vigorously for proper mixing. He had not been drinking milk during the week so he was going to make up for it this Saturday night. He filled the cup three-quarters with the milk, much more than Juliana usually added to his cup of coffee.

Juliana came out of the bathroom with Christopher and found Stephen sipping his cup of coffee at the dining table. Although the cup was only half full, or half empty, Juliana could see that it was so diluted that the milk must have been way out of proportion to the coffee.

"Do you now drink your milk without coffee?" she asked.

"You know I have not been drinking milk during the week because it is too heavy. It make me lazy and sleepy. Just to make up for it I added much more milk than usual," said Stephen.

Christopher, who was already dressed for bed made a request of his father. "Daddy, can you go to Key Food and buy me chicken?"

"Let's go to bed Christopher. It's time for bed," said Juliana.

"What minute it is now, Mommy?"

"It's ten-thirty. Let's go."

She whisked him away to his bedroom. Christopher had had a day full of activities. He was a tired kid. He fell asleep pronto.

Juliana was clearing the dining table when Stephen emerged from their bedroom, casually dressed to drive out to Key Food to buy Christopher fried chicken. She couldn't believe her ears when Stephen told her where he was headed. She knew he had just ingested a large dose of Somnazolam and would soon fall asleep. Driving would be extremely risky under the influence. But it was the suggestibility that bothered her more than anything else. "You can't go out now," she protested. "Key Food Supermarket is closed by now and Christopher is already asleep. Forget it, Steve. Do it tomorrow."

Stephen went back into the bedroom. Juliana would find out five minutes later that he had not even changed into his night clothes when he dozed off. "This Somnazolam is something else," she murmured inaudibly as she joined him in bed. He was deeply asleep. She couldn't wake him up to change into his night clothes. She stood up and went to the medicine cabinet and retrieved the Somnazolam literature. She took it to the bathroom, locked the door and read it all over again. She paid particular attention to the section on untoward effects. The manufacturers did warn that there were no studies on, and the Food and Drug Administration had not licensed, the long-term use of Somnazolam and the behavioral changes that might take place could not be predicted.

For more than thirty minutes, she weighed the risks and benefits of stopping the treatment. With stoppage, all the personality and behavioral changes could possibly be reversed. She wondered if these changes were actually related to the drug. "What if they were due to lack of rest?" she asked rhetorically. After all, he was working too hard. She was satisfied that the experiment had achieved its objective of keeping him at home and away from the prying eyes of desperate Brooklyn women. Mel and Elsie Borble as well as Merry Oscar crossed her mind again. "Who knows what could have happened in lieu of the drug?" she asked herself again.

After thoroughly weighing and reweighing her options, she resolved that what was needed was not total abandonment of the intervention but a better management of the dosage schedules. What happened tonight, was an isolated instance of Somnazolam overdosage. If it became a pattern, then she would consider stopping the experiment. She, not he, would be the one to make his coffee henceforth and she would ensure that he got only homeopathic doses.

Nobody ever relinquishes power without regret or resistance especially when that power is discreet and can be used to control the behavior and movement of others without being held accountable for its abuses and excesses. When under attack, or undesirable results are produced, it is usually more expedient for power to make token concessions rather surrender all together. Mrs. Juliana Latham had an explicit wake-up call to desist from further intervention in her single-patient trial. Yet, even in the face of incontrovertible evidence that she was turning her husband into a zombie, she engaged in pursuit of alternative theories and adopted only insufficient changes. She was not willing to let go of her power over him. She rejoined him in bed for the uneventful night.

A Night of Dreams

Over the next several weeks, Mrs. Juliana Latham continued to feed her husband homeopathic portions of Somnazolam increasing it only on special occasions when she absolutely wanted him at home or, on other occasions, by accident. There was no other egregious display of Somnazolam effect on his mood or behavior. Juliana was happy with her management of the experiment.

Then one Friday night after an exhausting stint at work Stephen came home just to change, relax with a cup of coffee and then proceed to a meeting of Brooklyn gastroenterologists at the Evergreen. When he walked in Juliana was in the bathroom. She had been trying to reach Stephen at work since she came back at about three-fifteen in the afternoon. She wanted to tell Stephen not to plan any outing for the evening. Her dentist had called that the crown she had been waiting for had arrived. She had checked her schedule for the next week vis-a-vis the dentist's. The most convenient date and time for her to go to the dentist was that evening. Being Friday, Stephen had instruments in his hands and was unable to respond to his pages. When he called back later, just minutes before he left the hospital, there had been no response.

With Juliana in the bathroom, he fixed himself a cup of coffee. Stephen decided to ingest all the soy milk in the container, including the debris because there wasn't enough to leave behind. When Juliana came out of the bathroom and found Stephen sipping his coffee, the first thing she did was to look in the fridge. He had drunk all the Somnazolam-rich milk. She knew the prognosis.

With the towel over her trunk, she asked Stephen, "I hope you are not going anywhere. I must go to the dentist now. I have been waiting for the crown. She called before I left work that it has arrived. There is no better time for me to go see her than now. I was thinking you would stay with Christopher,' she said, as she entered their bedroom to dress up. Stephen followed her there. The conversation continued as she dressed up.

"I must attend the Brooklyn Gastroenterologists' Association (BGA) meeting. I am running for President and the elections are today, a few hours from now."

"How come you never told me you were running for an elective office?"

"It is my fault. I have run a sloppy campaign. I am an outsider. But it was only today I agreed to present myself as a candidate for the presidency."

"Let's do it this way, Steve. My dentist is only a five-minute drive away. She is waiting for me as we speak. My original plan was for Christopher to stay with you. I will take him so that you can rest. You look so tired. Something must be wrong. I'll be back in less than one hour and since your party is in the Evergreen, you will be able to make it on time. I'll call you as soon as I get there," said Juliana.

By the time she had completed the last sentence, she was on her way out the door. She knew that Stephen would fall asleep in minutes and would not be able to answer the call. With so much Somnazolam in his system, he was a time bomb waiting to implode. Juliana and Christopher left Stephen alone at home.

Juliana came back after about one hour and found Stephen slumped in the chair. She awakened and led him to the bedroom. There, she helped her hapless husband change into his night clothes. There was no doubt in her mind that Stephen would not remember how he changed into his pajamas. After taking care of the household chores, including putting Christopher to bed, she too went to join him.

She was stunned to hear Stephen talking aloud and clearly in the dark. She called out, "Steve, Steve," as she turned on the light. He did not respond but continued to talk. Juliana shook him vigorously, calling "Steve, Steve." Stephen still did not respond. She realized at that point that this was real. Stephen was not the type to dissemble or pull off a prank like that on a night he should have been running for office. He continued to talk even though he was not arousable.

Juliana had heard of somniloquists before but in fairy tales. She was excited and afraid at the same time. Afraid because she had little doubt in her mind that the development was Somnazolam-related. Not knowing what to do, she lay beside him to listen. Perhaps he was saying something of importance. "Blessed serendipity. This may be my husband unplugged," she remarked audibly.

"Hello, Mister, this is my son Christopher," Stephen was saying. "He and I are trying to determine if this is my right or left hand. Could you tell us if this is my right or left hand? . . . Let's go, Christopher. That man doesn't know anything. He is just bigger than you for nothing. We asked him if this is my right or left hand, a simple alternate-choice question. He flunked it. He said 'ridiculous.' Now, you know that

I don't have a ridiculous hand. My hand is either left or right, certainly not ridiculous. Let's go find a wise man to solve the dilemma for us."

Even Juliana could not help laughing at that utterly ridiculous question. How could a grown-up man walk up to another and ask him such a question unless he was a moron? She too would have dismissed Stephen with one word, 'ridiculous.' But, she reasoned, you could not read too much into dreams.

"When it is time for you to have lunch," he continued in his deep sleep. "You have to insist on it, Ms. Nosborrow. Don't let us drive you crazy. Believe me if you collapse here the work will still go on. I am going on sympathy-hunger strike. I will forego my lunch today as a result."

Juliana knew Ms. Nosborrow, the endoscopy unit nurse, well. She and the other nurses in the unit worked hard and even missed their lunch frequently but not without making their displeasure well known. Nobody liked to be deprived of his or her lunch even when, as in the case of the weight-obsessed Ms. Nosborrow, it consisted of a lean doughnut, an apple, and a diet soda. Juliana, who was the head-nurse on the fourteenth floor, also occasionally missed her lunch when they had emergencies. She wondered when her husband would forego his lunch for her sake.

"This is Dr. Latham. Somebody paged me from there," Stephen started to say again pausing frequently for his dream interlocutor's comments or replies to his questions:

Yes, chief, What can I do for you?
What is the patient's name?
Hold it, let me write it down, Chief.
Angela Batesman. How old is he? I mean how old is she?
When did the bone get stuck in her esophagus?
Is there anything on x-ray?
She does not need emergency endoscopy. Bone always lights up on x-ray.
If you don't see it, it is not there. It's not a needle in a haystack. It cannot hide.
All she needs right now is a piece of advice to leave the bones for the dogs. It will cost her nothing. Ideally I should bill her but she is, I think, a nice old lady. Old enough to be my grandmother. I am not averse to working pro bono.
Send her to the GI clinic on Friday. I will be happy to see her.
Okay, Chief?

Stephen fell silent again but not for long. Juliana shook him gently but he was still not responsive.

Hello. This is Dr. Latham. I am sorry I was on another call. Where is the patient right now? When did he come to the emergency? Listen, when you are presenting a case you start by telling me the name and age of the patient. Let's go back to the beginning. This is a . . . twenty-six-year-old man . . . Name! Name! Name! . . . I am writing. Slow down a bit. Gu-ti-er-rez. Is it Ramon Gutierrez?

Is he that youthful-looking, smooth-talking guy with tattoos on both arms?

Okay. Read the tattoo. Does it say "Love, Miranda?"

What does he want this time? (Pause.)

He is not sick. He doesn't have pancreatitis. Don't give him any narcotics. (Pause.)

That should be his last dose. Don't give him anymore. He is not sick.

He goes from one emergency department to another complaining of severe abdominal pain with the sole aim of receiving some narcotic injections. He denies alcohol ingestion; he had no gall stones. He has had ERCP, abdominal sonogram, secretin stimulation, plain abdominal x-ray, endoscopic ultra sound. You name it; he's had it not just here but also in Kings County, Brookdale and Methodist. All tests have been negative.

If you call Dr. Graham at Brookdale now, he will tell you the patient was there last week. (Pause.)

Absolutely no narcotics and discharge him home.

Juliana tried once more to awaken Stephen to no avail. Stephen had never been in such deep slumber before. If he had not been talking so coherently and breathing at ease, she would have been tempted to move decisively to awaken him. He resumed talking again and she, listening.

"Chief, you should have been at the lounge today. Drs. Ferray and Goland were at each other. Some of us just settled down to watch the action. It was really wild. I have never seen a thing like it, live. Ferray said Goland had been spreading rumors that he—Ferray—had decided never to prescribe Prozac again because the drug company representative wouldn't sleep with him." Stephen was giggling after a long pause.

"You know how visibly shaken Ferray was when he came to Sutherland's birthday party. Both Goland and his buddy Sutherland knew that not only did Ferray badly desire that Rep but also that Ferray would have done anything to get her. The moment they saw Ferray at the door, they made the Rep sit on Sutherland's lap. That was what Ferray saw upon entry into the hall. I think they could have done it with more panache." Stephen paused again apparently listening to his interlocutor.

"I don't think he is, though you could be right. If you are right, he must be bisexual then. You know he has a resort home in West Palm Beach, Florida. Lizzy and that her friend with low-cut spent the long weekend there with him and Dr. Goland." He paused again before adding, "I can't tell you who was with whom. You know the kind of morals Goland and Sutherland have. It could have been a round-robin weekend."

He fell silent again. Juliana knew Dr. Sutherland the endocrinologist but none of the other people in that love rectangle Stephen had just described. She would have thought that Sutherland, who was in his late sixties, was too old for that kind of behavior. With these men, she lamented, you could never be sure. She jiggled Stephen again but he resumed the somniloquy rather than awakening.

"Chief, how is your Chief doing? . . . He is leaving? It must be a bluff to get some more money. Let us call that . . . malingering (chortle). Your Chief has got to be careful. You know how much he is making. He has no better place to go. You know he tried it last year and got something for it. They may cut him loose this time. . . . This is a new administration." He paused for a minute or so.

"Your Chief should be happy he passed his Boards. Look at the real-life drama unfolding in dermatology department. Dr. Seewater passed his Boards. They crowned him Chief and gave him more money. Dr. Brenner didn't and never will pass. You can't eat your cake and have it. The guy is too much into his private practice. He will never pass. Yet, he still wants to be Chief of the department. You know Dr. Seewater put up a sign on his door which read, 'Dr. Seewater, Chief of Service." Brenner went and pulled it down. Somebody should tell him this thing is not by force or Mike Tyson and Hulk Hogan would be better candidates."

Juliana was wandering why Stephen had never discussed the power-play and intrigue with her. After all, she knew Drs. Seewater and Brenner and their wives well. She would have to ask some of the other nurses and doctors at work next week. Stephen was speaking so coherently that it was almost inconceivable that he was not describing real-life situations. She was still excited and longing for more.

"Chief, were you on call yesterday? How was it? Did you work with Dr. Washington? (Long pause and chortling) I am sorry for the women who sleep with him. . . . Last week Renee placed a message on his beeper. The message said, 'Smile, I am waiting.'

"You don't know Renee? You don't know that girl with long hair in bonuses department? Not only did he show the message to me but he also showed it to Tasha. You know, the women know each other. . . . Yesterday there was absolute pandemonium on the thirteenth floor. Renee and Tasha wanted to kill each other all because of him. . . . They have both been suspended indefinitely. Luckily for Tasha, she is in the army nurses' corp. I know she is leaving for Arizona next Saturday because one of my nurses is in the contingent too."

He changed his position from prone to the left lateral facing Juliana now. Juliana could see in the dim night that his eyes were closed. She jostled him once more but he just kept on talking, only pausing long enough for the other party or parties to contribute.

"It's because of the way he talks. You know how he talks big. . . . The first day Dr. Kurman worked with him, he kept talking about his Volvo and rising stocks in AT & T, GE, IBM; how they had appreciated and how he was on to something even bigger without specifying it. He boasted about his homes in Vermont and in the Poconos and his type of women. He let it be known that he preferred women with big busts. The very next week, from what Kurman told me, one of the women who had heard him underwent breast implant surgery to make herself more competitive. It is the kind of talk that blows the women's minds. . . . You know the woman I am talking about . . . " He whispered a name inaudibly.

"Kurman was, like, how did this guy make it so big? One day Kurman and I went with him to obtain an article from his Volvo. Believe it or not, this guy has a 1970 Volvo. The chassis is not worth one hundred dollars. I am not kidding, 1970. It is dented on both sides and the paint is flaking off." He was giggling freely.

He paused again and continued his deep sleep. Juliana knew Drs. Kurman and Washington. Stephen had whispered the name of the woman into his interlocutor's ear. Perhaps she would have recognized her too. Then he started talking again.

"Oh! I've got a page. Excuse me, Chief."

One full minute passed before he responded to his page. "Hi, J, I was with some friends. It took me so long to reach the office. You know how I hate to keep my only true love waiting (He kissed on the phone and then paused.) You've got nothing to worry about. The message will be very clear, in simple language. It will be very clear. You have my word that the message will be clear. You will have the chance to revise the main message and the appendices before she sees them." There was a brief pause and then he kissed again.

Juliana wondered what message that could be and to whom it was intended. Of all the dreams Stephen had been dreaming, she noted, that was the first time he was talking to her. He could hardly finish a sentence before transmitting a kiss across the line. In real life, their conversations were devoid of such surplus emotions. Dreams had a way of stripping away human inhibitions, she thought.

Stephen started talking to another Chief. "Chief, I have a message or messages for you. I saw 'S' in the clinic yesterday. The clinic was light and she came in to talk about you. (Pause.) I keep telling you that even if you hide your exploits or spoils from me, the women themselves will keep coming with the confessions." He paused and started laughing. "Relax. I'll tell you what she said. Are you in a hurry?" There was another long pause.

"She started from your lower extremities. She asked me where you bought your shoes from. Obviously, I did not know. She said your shoes are so romantic. That was the first time I heard something like that.

"She said she liked men with long legs and stout gaits like yours. As for your hands, she said the first day you placed them on her neck she almost passed out. At that point I was wondering (giggling) what would prompt a cultured and soft-spoken man like you to place a choke hold on an angel. But, then, she added that she had never felt such rapture. She went on to describe Malley's bedroom in Suffolk in relation to the encounter. That was her way of hinting at her what I first thought was a one-night stand with you." He paused again to giggle.

"She was effusive about her relationship, affair or whatever you want to call it, with you. She contrasted you with her on-again, off-again boyfriend Tim. You are very straightforward and predictable with her, she said, unlike Tim who is very slick. She said she had fixed Tim very well. When she traveled to D.C. with her high school sweetheart, she had asked Tim to pick her up at the railway station though she had arranged to come back by flight into La Guardia Airport.

"With you, she said things are different. You tell her everything you do. Then she dropped a bombshell. She said there were three women you slept with within the hospital that she strongly disapproved of—Mary Briansons, Gege and Florence of incentives department. When she listed all these three women I had never suspected have anything to do with you, I thought to myself, 'Boy, my chief gets around.' She said Mary had no sense of public decorum while Gege was too old for you. As for Florence, she said her tastes were too high for her short stature. She added that you must have had trouble finding that 'pigmy' (an epithet I hate to use) in your wall-to-wall bed. Chief, I didn't even know you had a wall-to-wall bed (giggling).

"Then she asked me if I thought you and the women were in the same class. You could discern her disdain for the three women as well as the envy and agenda in the tendentious question. Now let me put it to you, Are you in the same class with those women? And if you are, is the class academic, socioeconomic or sexual?" He was giggling again, unrestrainedly.

"I thought she was done at that point but I was mistaken. She started complaining about what the South American woman did to you; how you are too good to be treated like that. I wanted to tell her that you have actually married the South American and she is studying in North Carolina. But when she said you were not yet prepared to marry and she was happy with the way you jilted the South American, I desisted. She started saying in a somber voice, "But it's too late for him and me; it is too late for us.' I had no choice but to rekindle her hope. I told her it was probably not. Then I discovered she had been running circles around her main desire when she implored me to put in a word for her. Now the word I wish to put in for her is in the form of a question. Is it too late for you to retire?" He paused to listen to the answer.

Juliana lay still beside her dream-disinhibited husband who was revealing his hidden profile. This was a man who went to work early each morning and came back late completely exhausted at night. Did he really have time to engage in all that intimate talk or was this just the meaningless ramblings of sleeping human brain? Either way, it appeared to Juliana that they faced a long night. Every time he started talking, she would listen quietly.

"Believe me every plan is on track, J." He started to say again. Juliana had no illusions that he was talking to her. She listened attentively for evidence that he was discussing a real life situation. "The plane tickets are ready," he continued, "and you have already taken care of the accommodations. The way I see it, the desert is waiting anxiously for us. Like I said before, the message will be clear. Every question will be preempted and answered and every bone of contention will be broken in advance. To boot, you will vet the draft. (He paused and a long kiss followed.) Hmmm. I understand why you are so excited, J. I think your feelings are surpassed only by my fantasies. I see ahead of us opportunities, boundless as the desert that will surround us.

(There was another long pause and a kiss across the line.) I'll see you tomorrow."

Some of the conversation made sense to Juliana. She had to leave for a nurses' conference in Philadelphia the next Friday. She had discussed her travel plan with him days earlier. There were inconsistencies, however. She would be traveling by train so the reference to plane tickets was a nonsequitur as were the references to desert and message. It was impossible to read too much into dreams, Juliana thought. She was also intrigued by the glut of kisses and emotion because they contrasted with her usually curt and hurried conversations with her husband.

After several minutes Stephen, who was still deeply asleep and unarousable, resumed his conversations. "Ch—ief, I saw 'S' and her friend on the second floor a short while ago. (Pause.) Chief, you know I have retired. You can have them both. 'S' asked me if I had seen you since she came to the clinic. I said I had not. Chief, I hate to be telling all these lies for your sake. Why don't you tell her and all the others that you are married and your wife is doing her doctoral work in North Carolina? (Pause and a giggle.)

"But Chief, I am really afraid for you. You are unnecessarily exposing yourself to AIDS. Last week, Mildred came from Detroit. You didn't use it. The day after she left, Joanna came from Philadelphia. You did not use anything. (Pause.) But how do you know she is a clean girl. You have been to Phillie. Right from the thirtieth Street Station, you see men with long faces; men in pursuit of happiness. (Pause.) Chief, I am surprised that you are still arguing like that."

Juliana was wondering who among his friends Stephen was talking to. She thought she knew most of his friends. There were more than two hundred doctors in the hospital and it was likely he was talking about one she did not know. Generally, Stephen never even mentioned the sexual escapades of his friends to her. She did not know any of his friends who fit the resume Stephen had excerpted: a physician whose wife was studying in North Carolina. That was the problem with dreams. She could almost never ignore them. Yet, she was always at a loss as to what to do with them.

Stephen continued his dream-talk. "I think the time has come, Chief, for women to sit back and take a second look at men, with their arms folded around their busts and their heads turned slightly to one side. If they have already done so, a third look would be in order. The old definition of 'Mr.—or, in your case—Dr. Right,' which you are a paragon of, must be reevaluated. You are a tall, handsome hunk with a sugar-coated tongue and lips and, most important, it must be that you are able to get the job done. You have a six-or-more-figure income per annum. (Pause.) All right, even if it's a five-figure salary, you still have other qualities. You have your thousand-dollar designer suits, your Rolex watch and your Vermont country home. It doesn't matter that your Mercedes Benz is leased. That is the car they see you with. I am not suggesting, Chief, that you surrender those accouterments. They are your spoils for not having followed the allure of petty cash and dropped out of school. But, Chief, the time has come to do away with these criteria for defining 'Mr.' or 'Dr. Right.' I think women must now formulate a new set of criteria that places at the top, the man's risk of transmitting AIDS. If these women apply the new definition of Mr. Right to you, you will surely come away with failing grades. You will not be as busy as you have been lately.

"As the head of the AIDS clinic who dispenses condoms three times a week, you can do better, Chief. Please practice some of what you preach. Somebody like you should never leave home without it. It should be your American Express card. It would be very unfortunate if the Physician Director of an AIDS clinic spreads and then dies of AIDS all because of sexual indiscretion. Physician, heal thyself," he said giggling.

Juliana was impressed with Stephen's counseling of his friend. The conversation was so well structured that it could not have been nonsense. She would have to investigate in the hospital and find out that doctor on the suicide mission. She was satisfied that Stephen took the AIDS scare as seriously as the dream suggested. Finally, the deposition was leading somewhere, she thought. The problem was that all the doctors were chiefs. Even the most junior doctors, the interns, were chiefs without subjects. It was a universal title that conferred anonymity. It would be virtually impossible for Juliana to identity all the chiefs mentioned by the chief lying beside her. She shook Stephen hard again. But he responded by resuming his somniloquy.

"The matter is still being handled by the hospital security. If I am not fully satisfied, I am filing a report with the police and then a lawsuit. I cannot tolerate such a flagrant attack."

Juliana was still very attentive. She had never been told of an attack. Again, she did not want to read too much into it.

Stephen slept for the next ten minutes. During that time, Juliana kept wondering how little she had known him. Most likely that was the case, she thought, with the other housewives in the building. If anyone had ever asked her, "How well do you know your husband?" Her quick answer would have been "very well" or "completely." Tonight, she realized she would have flunked the test.

"This is Dr. Latham. I was paged," Stephen said without any sign he was about to wake up. "Yes, Chief, how many cases do you have to discuss with me? . . . All right. The first one. Hold on. Let me get my pen and paper. Yes . . . Mildred Santiago, forty-years old, abdominal pain." He paused. "She has already been seen by Dr. who? . . . Do me a favor. Would you? Tell Dr. Rousam to back off. Even before he went to medical school, I had been seeing this patient. What's going on here? There used to be what we called professional courtesy. These kids don't know anything about it and it's getting worse. Also tell Ms. Santiago that I am sending one of my residents to come and see her immediately. As soon as I finish the procedures I am doing I will come and see her. But tell Dr. Rousam to back off."

Juliana was deeply concerned by the harshness of the message. She knew Dr. Rousam, who had just finished his residency and joined the physician staff. Dr. Rousam was apparently trying to build his practice and in so doing was obviously stepping into hostile territory. She had heard physicians complaining of other physicians stealing their patients especially when referred for second opinion. Some doctors guarded their turfs with the tenacity, though without the arsenal, that would match that of Brooklyn's crack-cocaine dealers. She remembered the sixty-five-year-old quadriplegic who was admitted to her floor the previous week. During the first two days of her admission, her Attending Physician of record was changed three times before the administration stepped in to resolve the dispute. The patient had solid, overlapping medical insurance coverages. First, one physician had adopted the patient in the emergency department. Then the second one had come to the floor to change the patient to his service. The next day, the third physician, Dr. Rousam had come to the floor to make the final change.

The changes and the final resolution of the dispute occurred in such a genteel manner that only the most observant doctors and nurses had noticed what was going on. But turf wars, whether fought by street vendors of illicit merchandise or between nations in a desert storm, are always dangerous free-for-alls without rules or referees. The risk of escalation almost never recedes unless one antagonist-party has been whacked. There was so much harshness and intensity in Stephen's warning shots at the upstart Dr. Rousam that even Juliana trembled. She hoped the hapless intern would repackage the message for Dr. Rousam by taking the sharp edges off. If he was smart enough to be a doctor, she thought, he should not lack the common sense and tact to do so.

"Who's the second patient?" Stephen asked the intern. He was still deeply asleep. Then he paused, apparently, for the answer.

"Oh, Glenice Stephens," he echoed. "I have been seeing her for the last three years. What are her complaints today? . . . She has been scheduled for what procedure? . . . Tell Dr. Tesh to leave her alone. She should not do it. I have already scheduled the patient for next week. Tell her so. She should not do it. I have been seeing the patient for three years. Why can't they talk to the guy who has been treating the patient for courtesy and continuity of care? Do me a favor please. Tell her not to touch her and tell Glenice I'll see her in my office tomorrow. Okay, Chief."

Juliana made another ill-fated attempt to awaken him. She was again reminded of how much energy and time her husband had to spend fending off poachers. The message to Dr. Tesh was less confrontational. It still surprised her because she knew Stephen and Dr. Tesh to have worked together in many hospital projects. It appeared that when it came to procedures and billing every man or woman was unto himself or herself.

"What is the patient's name?" Stephen asked whoever was presenting the cases to him. "I don't know him. Tell me about him. I am writing. John Selton . . . fifty-six years old . . . a gradual onset of difficulty swallowing for two months . . . has lost . . . ten pounds. Has a significant cigarette-smoking and alcohol-abuse history. Okay, admit him to my service. Tentative diagnosis if cancer of the esophagus. I'll see him after the procedures. If I am unable to see and schedule him for the procedure, you must baby-sit him until I can do so. You must make sure no one else does the procedure." There followed a five-minute pause.

"Hi J, sorry I couldn't answer the page earlier. You know how urgently I like to answer the pages. You are fully packed and ready to go, I hope. We'll go over the message Friday night and then off to the desert. Love you, bye."

One full hour elapsed before he uttered the next word. In the meantime he twirled in bed from one position to another as if something was making him uneasy. Juliana could not sleep, either. She was still reflecting on what she had done to her husband. After reducing the dosage of Somnazolam to homeopathic portions, she had thought all would be fine. It was now obvious that that may have been a mistake. What would happen the next weekend when she would be traveling with Christopher to Philadelphia for the nurses' conference? she asked herself. How would his staff react at work if he dozed off and started spilling their most intimate secrets, including the fact that she had finally convinced him that to increase their fertility, they should do it on the floor?

Suddenly, Stephen started singing, "What have you done for me lately . . . " He was not a gifted musician and Juliana doubted he could have rendered even the first stanza of any hit album. Out of guilty conscience and fear, she pulled Stephen up to the sitting position.

"Steve, Steve, you must wake up now. This is getting out of hand. I can't take it anymore. Stop it, please," she harangued. Stephen stopped singing, opened his eyes but slumped back into bed. He did not wake up till about nine in the morning.

Juliana stood up and went into the medicine cabinet. She took the Somnazolam literature to the bathroom, sat on the toilet-seat cover and sobbed uncontrollably. Before rejoining Stephen in bed, she vowed to terminate the trial. She would have to dispose of the stock of Somnazolam in a way that would not arouse suspicion, perhaps after her trip to Philadelphia. Even after she returned to bed beside her husband she continued to sniffle as if that was a lullaby for him. Finally, she too lapsed into a deep slumber till well into the morning.

The Luncheon Breakout Session

The next Friday morning, Juliana was up very early. She was going to a nurses' conference in Philadelphia. She had spent the whole of the previous evening preparing for the three-day conference. The first program of the meet was to start at eight that morning at the Philadelphia Marriot. She had originally planned to go the day before but out of concern about what might happen to Stephen had postponed her departure till the morning of the conference.

After that frightful night when Stephen mystified, entertained and finally scared her with his somniloquy, she decided to place him on close observation. Stephen had awakened in satisfactory condition apparently oblivious of the night's high drama. He had conducted himself well but still suffered from lingering suggestibility. It was such that he was often doing his son Christopher's bidding when he was expected to just say no. Juliana was worried about his performance at work.

That Friday morning after Juliana and Christopher were fully dressed and ready to go, Christopher decided he wanted to wear his Power Rangers slippers. To Juliana's amazement, Stephen went into Christopher's room and fetched them.

Stephen drove Juliana and Christopher to the Franklin Avenue subway station where they caught one of the early morning trains to Penn Station in Manhattan. Even as she kissed him before alighting from the car, she was more concerned with what could happen to her husband than with the perils of riding one of those dawn trains. Deserted coaches, night marauders and exhausted train engineers were not yet on her mind. Christopher turned back and waved to his father who reciprocated with a smile to remember before her mother pulled him gently away. The time was five-thirty.

Stephen drove back home to catch up on his sleep to prepare himself fully for another mammoth Friday. He set the alarm clock to awaken him after thirty minutes. The early interruption had left him feeling clumsy. The next thirty-minute aliquot of sleep was necessary to complete the integer. Even if he woke up late, he might still make it to his post on time because he did not have to worry about Christopher or Juliana's plans.

The day was hectic as usual. After all, it was Friday. He started by seeing his new inpatients with his residents. Then he did his procedures and by twelve midday, he was ready to go to lunch. He did not usually eat in the hospital cafeteria because of the long lines and waiting time. His nurses had assured him that day that the hospital administration was feting the employees and extra hands would be available to serve the food.

The administration was showing its appreciation for the employees' cooperation during the state inspection about two weeks earlier. That was the second inspection in six months. Six months earlier, the state inspection had gone very badly for InnerFaith Hospital. Before the inspection team had arrived, the administration had embarked on a massive re-education and indoctrination campaign.

The administration had clues that the state would zero in on fire safety and the vision of the hospital. The employees were expected to know what to do in case of a fire alarm or actual outbreak. In cases of the former, all employees were expected to arise and go to the nearest fire alarm station where a code was posted for deciphering the tintinnabulation.

In the event of an actual fire outbreak all employees were expected to know what to do. The answer was summarized in a mnemonic: "RACE." It had been said in no uncertain words that the license of the InnerFaith hospital to operate depended on all staff members knowing what to do if fire broke out. To ensure that everyone knew what the mnemonic stood for, administration officials, especially those from the fire and safety department, had fanned out to educate the staff on the meaning of each of the letters.

The "R" stood for "rescue the patients," not for "run" from or "ransack" the place as criminally inclined witnesses were wont to do in a fire situation. The "A," all had been told, stood for "Alarm" by calling the operators to make the announcement and not for "abscond" from the vicinity. The "C" stood for "Confine" the fire though many employees would have behaved as if it meant for "Create confusion" or "Cry." Although personnel were expected to take care not to be caught in the blaze, the letter "E" did not denote "Escape" but "Extinguish the inferno" and "Evacuate the patients."

Equally important for all employees to memorize and to reproduce to the state inspection team was the vision of the hospital. They were expected to know that InnerFaith hospital was "committed to providing cheap but efficacious service to Brooklyn and it environs, referring patients to other centers if they so desired and to providing Brooklyn and its environs with caring and diligent doctors and nurses." The vision statement was so long and difficult to remember that Stephen feared at least one staff member would not be able to quote it verbatim to the inspectors.

In the run-up to the state inspection six months ago the indoctrination and reeducation campaign had reached a feverish pitch. Everywhere one went in the hospital, there were groups discussing the response to a fire outbreak and the hospital's vision. In some cases when Stephen passed some introspective and lonely workers by, he could hear their soliloquy. There was no doubt in Stephen's mind that they were trying to grapple with "RACE." It would have been hard to find an employee who did not know what "RACE" meant or one who did not know the hospital's vision in part or wholly.

Finally, the inspectors had arrived. During the full week they had spent in the hospital everything worked excellently, with clockwork precision. As providence would have it, even common accidents like burst plumbing, too much or lack of heat did not occur. Considering that the inspection had taken place during a period when the weather was particularly fickle, it was a remarkable achievement and the kudos belonged to the engineering department.

Whoever had hinted the administration of the inspectors' area of interest appeared to have been wrong. The endoscopy unit had been the last department to be inspected. Stephen and his staff had heard that every department had performed marvelously and they were not ready to let the hospital down. When the team arrived to inspect the unit, Stephen and his staff had been waiting in ambush with "RACE" and "vision" but they would not be given the opportunity to regurgitate the prepared answers.

The inspection team consisted of two men and one woman. They had been introduced by the hospital's chief operating officer. They had asked no question about fire or vision. The male inspectors had spent most of the ten-minute tour ogling Ms. Juliette Painter. Stephen was satisfied with the decoy. All the questions had been asked by the female inspector.

"On the average, how many procedures do you perform here per day?" asked the inspector.

"About ten," answered Stephen.

"How many of those patients died during, or because of the, procedure?"

"None."

"My mother died of cancer of the colon. How many colon cancers do you see here?"

"We have a major colon cancer screening program for all our patients fifty years or older. Even though we are in a high-risk area of the country, we have cut the number of new cases to record low levels," replied Stephen.

"Keep up the good work. You are doing very well and I applaud you. Thank you and have a good day," said the inspector.

The inspection had ended on that good note as it had in all the other departments. Experience indicated that when the state inspectors praised you on the spot, you had done well. When they were not satisfied with what they had seen, the inspectors usually showed little emotion. They would retreat into the seclusion of their hotels to list their citations, the impending release of which would keep hospital administrators scratching their heads. In the inspection six months ago the state officials had behaved as if they had been sent to sing the hospital's praises. Hospital chiefs were very buoyant and they had shown it in the extravagance of the luncheon organized for the inspectors on the last day. Contrary to hospital tradition, even wine was on the menu.

The luncheon had taken place in the nurse's reception hall. Everybody who was anybody in the administration had been present. State aid to the hospital and many other problems facing health-care delivery in Brooklyn and the state in general were discussed in the convivial atmosphere. There had been no doubt in all the revelers' minds that the final state report on InnerFaith Hospital would be a public relations coup.

Then, the female inspector had sneaked out to the bathroom. While she was out, she had whispered something into the ear of a security officer. Shortly after that, there had been a fire alarm. Of all the officials wining in the auditorium, only the fire chief, Edmund Escheveo, had gone out to investigate. The nearest fire alarm box and the code for the alarm bells were just outside the hall. The number and sequence of bells indicated that the fire was in the nurses' reception hall where the luncheon was taking place. The fire chief knew it was a false alarm. Though the inspection had been officially concluded, Mr. Escheveo had been disappointed that his bosses had not gone out to investigate the alarm. He also knew better not to show his disapproval then or thereafter. Even when he was displeased and disappointed with his bosses, he followed his survival instincts in Brooklyn's tough labor market and just smiled.

At the end of the luncheon, the inspection team was leaving the hospital finally when they came upon Mrs. Lula Mae Thinker. Mrs. Thinker was eighty years old and had worked in InnerFaith Hospital for the last fifty years, longer than anyone else. She had worked as a nurses' aide, transporter, and, finally in the last twenty years, ward clerk. She had been at the hospital when even some of the senior physicians were born.

Her longevity was becoming a burden rather than an asset to the hospital. She was coming under increasing pressure to retire. The administration and the Union were joined in an unusual alliance against her. The administration was looking at the bottom line. Mrs. Thinker had more benefits than any other employee. It would have cost much less to employ a part-time ward clerk in her stead. The Union had to pay her medical insurance which was exorbitant because of her age and multiple ailments. Union officials feared that if she suffered a catastrophic illness, it might deplete their insurance outlay.

Mrs. Thinker had been resisting the attempts to oust her. She lived alone and was afraid that retirement would hasten her death. She intended to work until she dropped, if necessary, as ward clerk emerita, an offer both the administration and the Union had rejected. Mrs. Thinker had become convinced that there was a campaign of calumny and smear being waged against her. She believed the forces arrayed against her were spreading rumors that she had Alzheimer's disease. Her greatest disappointment was that even Dr. Ryan of the employee clinic had been recruited into the conspiracy.

Her first day back at work after a two-week vacation had coincided with the last day of the state inspection. She had missed most of the re-education on fire-fighting and vision-seeing. During her lunch break she had gone to see Dr. Ryan to complain of occasional insomnia of recent onset. Instead of Dr. Ryan concentrating on that problem he kept asking her if she had hallucinations and all kinds of silly questions. The most ridiculous was when Dr. Ryan asked her what she would do first if she went into a room and found the faucet open and the room flooded. Did Dr. Ryan also believe the rumors that she had dementia? She had asked herself. She had respectfully answered the question and left the clinic. She was on her way back to the sixteenth floor when the state inspection team came upon her.

Upon entering the hospital from the street, the security desk was straight ahead about six feet from the floor. To the left of the door was a glass shop. The door to the glass shop was in line with the main door. On the glass shop door was a "Test your vision" sign just above a Snellen chart. Further to the left of the glass shop but projecting beyond it was the gift shop. Between the security desk and the gift shop, a red banner hung from the ceiling. By standing below or behind the red banner, an employee could test his or her vision. There was a statement on the wall which said, "If you can read this, your vision is twenty-twenty," with an arrow pointing to a portion of the Snellen chart.

Mrs. Lula Mae Thinker was standing there just behind the red banner when the state inspection team drew close to her. She had just determined that her vision was twenty-twenty. The female inspector lifted her ID off her left breast, examined it for Mrs. Thinker's name as if she was long-sighted and then she said, "Ms. Thinker, I have some short and simple questions for you." Standing several feet away and looking attentively on was the president and chief executive officer of the hospital, Amos Soween. Behind him was the whole administrative hierarchy.

Mrs. Thinker had immediately concluded that her nemeses had finally caught up with her. Never before in her fifty years in InnerFaith Hospital had she seen the president and chief executive officer himself (there had never been a woman in that position) descend so low as to participate in a witch-hunt. The administration had tried everything to force her out but she had successfully resisted their machinations. Now, she had asked herself, what aces did they have up their sleeves? What kind of ridiculous questions were they going to ask her and, if she did not know the answer, would it be the last straw? And why were all the big shots so interested in witnessing what might be her gaffe?

Whatever their intentions were, she was going to answer them as respectfully as she had responded to the ridiculous questions Dr. Ryan had asked her in the employees' clinic. If her answer led to a guffaw that would be their problem, not hers, especially if they asked her a question about computers. When she started working in InnerFaith, there were no computers anywhere in the world and she was not ashamed that she did not know anything about them. If they became more particular and asked her about windows, the only windows she knew anything about were the large ones on her floor. In her fifty years in the hospital, she could count off her fingers how many deranged patients had plunged to their deaths out of those windows.

Mrs. Thinker had mistaken the female state inspector for an administration official. She had heard on the floor that an inspection of the whole hospital was ending that day. Since her floor had already been inspected, she did not anticipate meeting the team. Nobody had told her anything about "RACE" or "vision." She just thought she had come face to face with the conspiracy against her.

Mrs. Thinker had responded to the young woman, "Yes ma'am, go ahead and ask me the questions."

"For how many years have you worked here?"

"Fifty."

"Wow! Congratulations! Then you must know the hospital in and out."

"I guess so," said Mrs. Thinker.

"Mrs. Thinker, what is the vision of the hospital?" asked the inspector.

Mrs. Thinker had not heard the full question because her hearing was deteriorating. She had, however, heard the key word, "vision." She thought the young woman was asking her what her vision was. She was proud to announce that she had a normal vision. "Twenty-twenty, ma'am," she had responded.

"Very good. The second question is what would you do if a fire broke out on your floor or place of work in this hospital?"

Mrs. Thinker's fears were confirmed. What a ridiculous question to ask anyone, she had thought. Did they expect her to say she would jump into the fire and be consumed or through the large windows on her floor? That would just tickle them to delirious laughter. They would get rid of her by concluding that she had suicidal ideation, she reasoned.

"I would not jump into the fire or stand there to be consumed. Though my legs are not very quick, I would run from the fire," Mrs. Thinker had answered the inspector.

"Very good. Thank you, Mrs. Thinker. It is a pleasure talking to you. Keep the good job up. I have no other question for you."

It was obvious to Mrs. Thinker that her answers displeased the powers that were watching. They had expected her to fumble. She had been satisfied that she had not given the team any excuse for the boisterous laughter they might have expected.

That was how the state inspection of the hospital had ended six months earlier. There had been few illusions that the state conclusions would be glossy. The report had arrived two weeks later and it had been clear, brief and devastating to the hospital. The state had concluded that employees at InnerFaith Hospital, the whole order from the chief executive to ward clerks, were not prepared to respond to a fire outbreak. A blaze at the hospital, the report had added, would be absolutely disastrous to the staff and patients. The hospital had been given two months to make amends or face mandatory closure.

Most employees had held the elderly Mrs. Thinker responsible for the woeful performance. The administration officials who had also blown their chance did nothing to put the facts straight. Only deep insiders got the full picture. The vilified and scapegoated Mrs. Thinker developed high blood pressure and couldn't continue. The glass shop was ordered to remove the Snellen chart ostensibly because it was distracting employees from their work. Heads also rolled in the administrative echelons.

With thousands of jobs and careers on the line, it was back to square one with the catch words, "RACE" and "vision." By the time of the repeat two-day inspection, nearly all employees had mastered the meaning of "RACE" and the "vision." Those whose brains were too atrophied to cram the new material were given the two days off. As with the first inspection, every employee chipped in to make the physical and functional environment attractive. The inspection went well and the state report gave InnerFaith a new lease on life.

It was to show their appreciation for the employees' contributions to the successful inspection that hospital administration officials decided to fete the staff that Friday. Stephen's nurses encouraged him to go early. For as long as any employee, including Ms. Hayes, who had worked in InnerFaith for close to thirty years, could remember that was the first time the hospital administration was throwing such a bash. Until he got down to the cafeteria and saw the celebration, Stephen had not really believed everything he had heard about the threat of closure. He, too, had memorized "RACE" and "vision" in order not to become an embarrassment to his unit rather than to impress some state official.

Although he had heeded his nurses' advice and gone down to the cafeteria as early as he could, there had already formed a long line. Free food, not rare in the hospital, was always a powerful attractant. It also had a potentially corrupting influence on those who came under its spell. Stephen had seen strict vegetarians and other food faddists change their eating habits extemporaneously. He had also seen some of his colleagues on strict weight-losing diets eat in advance as if they had reservoirs when everything on the menu was absolutely free.

Though the lines were long, they were moving rather fast because of the number and caliber of the people serving the food. The president and chief executive officer, Amos Soween himself, was serving the lentil soup. Stephen had never seen him in the cafeteria. In fact very rarely did anyone see him in the hospital. It looked as if he had never ventured out of his office once he settled in. His presence and humility at the luncheon was likely to endear him to his hospital community.

The chief operating officer, David Treven, had donned an apron and with a long butcher's knife was operating on the beef as if his title was based on that skill. Beside him was the chief of the surgery department, John Cranxon, doling out the fried chicken. Stephen wondered why the latter had not switched stations with Mr. Treven. The chief of nursing, Brenda Alderton was on the other end making the coffee for those who cared for it. There was enough variety to satisfy all tastes and enough administration officials to dish it out.

Stephen saw Dr. Kurman at the far corner close to loud speakers, which were blaring deafening disco music. After filling his bowl with morsels of almost everything on the table, Stephen joined Dr. Kurman on his table. Both of them positioned themselves to face the food counter. From their positions, they could see every employee, especially the women. Stephen knew that Dr. Kurman would ask him about Sylvia Turner, who had asked Stephen to "put in a word for her" with his good friend Dr. Kurman. Since Dr. Kurman was a good dilettante, they would be able to discuss the latest fashions as the young women paraded themselves. Kurman must have chosen the spot because their voices and laughter were likely to be drowned by the loud music.

"Chief, what's up? This is a big party," said Stephen.

"Every important functionary is here today. I have never been served by such an august team. They are all very happy, as, indeed, all of us should be, that the state did not close the hospital down. I just hope in this indulgence all employees would be kind to their guts. If they aren't, you may not be able to handle the avalanche into your gastroenterology clinic," said Dr. Kurman over the music.

"If I can't cope, your 'S' will help me. She had been coming to my clinic regularly now. I think you should make your intentions and marital status known to her. If you would permit me, I could break the bad news to her," Stephen told him.

"That girl is looking for money. I am on the run, Chief."

"But why not tell her so, if necessary, with tongue in cheek?"

"Chief, you don't do a thing like that. All she needs is money and I think Dr. Baez is already given her enough. She has also been with Dr. Thielber and you know nobody has more money in this place than he does. I don't want to see her again or say anything. My best option is to keep running. You never know what will happen. Chief, who is in front of the chief of surgery?" asked Dr. Kurman.

Dr. Marcel Kim arrived with his plate full. Stephen could sense from Kurman's change in tone and subject that it was necessary to switch to another topic. Although Dr. Kim was as close to Stephen as he was to Kurman, not all group secrets were held in common trust. The secrets and gossip were held in concentric circles among the three of them and a fourth member of the in-group, Emmet Godswill, who was not yet present. Kim was not privy to the Kurman-Sylvia Turner affair and Kurman wanted to protect her privacy.

Stephen and Kurman almost did not notice that Dr. Kim had sat down next to them as they focussed on the young woman being served food up front. Kim also sat facing the long food counter. The young woman was wearing a blue and white shirt with epaulets and a brown skirt. She also had on purple jelly sandals to complete the attire. Stephen had never seen her before. Kim also joined in evaluating the young woman. The music was loud but enjoyable to the initiated. The men turned to one another and asked almost simultaneously, "Who is that?"

In the meantime Dr. Godswill joined them at the table with his food. It was exceptional for the whole clique to gather at the same time in the same place. Everybody turned to Kurman for an answer to the young woman's identity. He seemed to have insider knowledge of the female employees. If he had no idea, nobody else would.

"She is the new audiologist. Her name is Doris Weston. She is available for the best bidder. She had a four-year-old child from her first and only marriage. Who wants to have the first crack at her? She will only go out with you on a date if you don't mind her son tagging along. Finally, she sleeps in the same bed with her son, a practice she has vowed to maintain until she says, "I do," to some man. Her telephone extension is one-zero-seven-eight," Dr. Kurman informed them.

"How did you know all the facts, Chief?" asked Stephen.

"Chief, this is incredible. When did you meet her to gather all this information? Where is her office?" Dr. Kim asked.

"In the sub-basement between housekeeping and engineering," said Dr. Kurman.

"Kurman's hands are full as are Kim's. Emmet, since you are so active and presentable, why don't you try first. You should only go there with a noble intention to marry. I keep reminding you gentlemen that the threat of AIDS is real. The last person I should be telling that to is Kurman, who heads an AIDS clinic," advised Stephen.

"Oh my God! Who, for God's sake, is standing behind Dr. Sutherland?" Dr. Kim asked.

Dr. Kim was attracted by the new arrival on the food line. She was a tall, slim, young woman most likely in her early twenties with a red, side-tab pantsuit. The matching red jacket had a notched collar, button front, shoulder pads and back darts for a flattering fit. As the lady in red passed through the food line, Stephen and his coterie followed her all the way with their eyes. She was drawing attention from men and women on other tables, though for different reasons. "Who is the lady in red?" Dr. Kim again asked.

Dr. Kurman relented. "She is the new MRI technician. She was hired only two weeks ago. The waist of the pantsuit is elastic and the size ten white satin stretch bra she had underneath that jacket is rather expensive. That gives you an idea of her tastes."

"Chi—ef, this is not fair. How did you know so much about this young woman. This is really unfair. When did you get underneath her jacket?" asked Dr. Godswill.

"I have not said you should not go there. I am only giving you inside information. By the way, her name is Sherry Priested and she lives on West Twenty-fifth Street. I can tell you her unlisted phone number if you like. This is real inside information that could be useful to you someday," said Dr. Kurman.

It was not clear that all the detailed descriptions given by Kurman were correct. That he boasted often was well known to his friends. What was not clear was whether, and how much of, what he was saying was braggadocio. One clear and probably intended consequence was that none of the other predators would go near the two psychedelic women. Kurman's knowledge of the most intimate secrets of the young women in the hospital gave him real power over the clique. The statement that "knowledge is power," was, with Kurman correct. Whenever Kim and Godswill saw a new and lovely face they turned to Kurman for a quick profile.

At the food counter there appeared a gazelle, a six-foot slim young woman with long hair. She was wearing a blue, button-trimmed long dress with gathered, elastic back and a back zipper. She had a gold-rimmed pair of glasses. As she made her way though the food counter, the four men turned to each other.

Then Stephen asked, "Who's that?"

Everybody turned toward Kurman, who was savoring his soup and beaming. He cleared his throat as his friends listened eagerly. "She is the secretary in the audiovisual department. Her waist is twenty-four inches and she has a permanent scar on the anterior aspect of her proximal right thigh due to the skin she had donated for her burnt brother," he said.

"Kurman, is that knowledge based on first-hand knowledge or hazardous guess work?" Stephen asked.

"How could you guess anything like that?" retorted Dr. Kurman.

"Is that based on professional, clinical observation or what, Kurman?" asked Dr. Kim.

"That would be a violation of my professional code of conduct and relationship with her. I have never seen her in a professional capacity?"

"It must be based on carnal knowledge, then," Dr. Kim supposed aloud.

Kurman smiled broadly. He may have wanted to add something but was prevented from doing so as Dr. Godswill's assistant, Dr. Charlene Brentford, approached their table. She had just assumed duty at InnerFaith the previous week and had not yet met and made friends in the hospital community. After being served her food, she had surveyed the tables and seen her boss Dr. Godswill and had decided to join him so as to discuss a problem. In the cafeteria, people sat according to familiarity, friendship, and fraternity. It was not uncommon for some tables to be overcrowded with guests while some other tables were occupied by only one guest each. That was never due to antisocial behavior on the part the lonely workers or rejection by others. The lunch hour was usually the only time to empty the mind of pent-up preoccupations. Most of the staff was too busy with their chores to even call friends or engage in a tete-a-tete with coworkers. When they arrived in the cafeteria, they sought out those who had something in common with them.

After being served her food, Dr. Brentford had surveyed the crowd. The only familiar face was her boss'. As she drew close to the table, the men were becoming uncomfortable. They were turning on their chairs as if someone had suddenly wetted them. Godswill whispered that she was his new assistant. The men realized that was the end of their freewheeling appraisal of the women being served food up front. Many of the young women had never eaten in the cafeteria before even though the food was first-rate quality. On this free-lunch day, they had emerged from their offices in the basement and sub-basement.

"Hi Charlene, sit down," Godswill motioned to the opposite side of the table. She was sitting on one side, facing all the four men as if she was attending a job interview. The men had crowded to the side with their backs to the wall so they would have a full view of the stars and beauties parading up front. Godswill directed Dr. Charlene Brentford to sit so that she would not see what was going on. During the time she would sit there many other young women the Stephen's group had never seen would make their way through the lunch counter. In reaction, the men would pinch or pad themselves or step lightly on one another's toes under the table. Out of respect for, or embarrassment as a result of, Dr. Brentford they kept all their reactions covert and muted.

"Charlene, these are some of my friends I have been praying to God to protect me from so that I can face my enemies," Godswill said. Pointing to each of his friends in turn he introduced them "Dr. Kim the nephrologist, Dr. Latham the gastroenterologist and the last, but by no means the least, Dr. Kurman, the AIDS specialist." Turning to Charlene he said to his friends, "Charlene comes to us from King County Hospital eager to face the challenge ahead of her. If any of you requires her services, you know how to reach her in my office."

Charlene was glum as she attacked her food from the edges. Godswill had employed her in part because she possessed a cheerful personality. She could electrify an audience with her snow-white smile. On this occasion, she was obviously disturbed. It was nothing that happened at work, though, because she had just come in having spent the morning at a peripheral clinic.

Godswill hoped all was well with her two children. To be sure, he asked her "Charlene is everything all right?"

"I am all right. It is just the ticket I got on my first day here. I made a left turn onto Classon Avenue from Eastern Parkway when the light was a green arrow indicating that one could not make a turn there. The wicked cop was standing right by the street corner. He immediately jumped in front of my car and asked me to pull up. Tomorrow I will have to go and defend it in court. I am afraid I will be found liable," Charlene said.

"Do you have a lawyer?" asked Kim.

"No. I can't afford or stand one."

"The fine is seventy-five dollars," said Kurman.

"That is not the point," said Stephen. "The insurance companies will use that as an excuse to milk you dry. A Brooklyn driver with at least one moving violation is a gold mine for them. Over the next four years, that summons will cost her at least five thousand dollars. It may even affect her credit rating."

"Many other drivers turned there and were stopped by that officer. I think he was standing in ambush. He must have summonsed at least fifty drivers. The city bus driver also made that turn but was allowed to go scot-free," said Charlene.

"You have to fight it. You just can't surrender like that. Go to court and tell them with so many people turning there, it was unfair of the government to summons them. So many people could not be wrong at the same time, especially as the city driver was let go," said Dr. Godswill.

"First of all, guys, the fact that others committed a crime is not an excuse for the next person to do the same. Two or more wrongs do not make a right. It is well known that the state can commit a crime and get away with it. How many police cars have been involved in collisions? Have you heard that the drivers were even tested for alcohol at the scene? That is a losing defense strategy," said Stephen.

The music was still blaring, forcing everybody to raise his or her voice. The lunch counter was still busy with familiar and unfamiliar faces. It was as if all the two-thousand-odd employees of InnerFaith had come to lunch at the same time. The high officials were still there serving the junior staff in a voluntary reversal of roles. Even as they put together a defense for the distraught Dr. Brentford, the men did not fail to notice the parade of elegance taking place up front. Not that there were no men in the line. For practical purposes, Stephen and his friends just did not notice them.

"Charlene, think hard. I am sure there must have been some authorized vehicle behind you like a fire truck, an ambulance or even another police car racing to the scene of a reported heist. I am sure you made that turn to make way for the authorized vehicle and no one can fault you for that. If you really think hard and go back in time you will remember that there had been at least one. They're not rare on Eastern Parkway," said Stephen.

"Hmmmm. Unfortunately, I don't think there was one at that particular point in time," Charlene remembered.

"What an impeccable defendant have we here? You got to think harder, Saint Charlene," said Dr. Godswill.

"Was there any injury or damage to property as a result of your turning there, Charlene?" asked Dr. Kim.

"No."

"That means the judge will look favorably upon your case," said Dr. Kurman.

"That would depend in part on whether the judge is a man or a woman. Women tend to be tougher on women and men on men. Even if the judge is a man, Charlene will still need a reasonable defense or excuse. If, for instance, the officer is a big fool, one who does not know south from north or southeast from northwest, there may be reasonable doubt in her favor. Unfortunately for Charlene, there are almost no big fools in the police force," Dr. Godswill pointed out.

"But how could she establish that the cop would be an unreliable witness?" asked Dr. Kim.

"Charlene, you've got to cancel your day in court tomorrow. They will reschedule the case. Still you will go to the court and evaluate the officer and the judge. If you are lucky, the judge could be a man with a soft spot for women and the officer, a big fool! You could also gather some other useful information. For instance, you could discover that all the women summonsed had long hair. If you can prove such bias with powerful statistical data, you may smile out of court," offered Stephen.

"That will not make it. But why not go and tell the judge that you had a critical patient to see. With such a defense, I will gladly volunteer my services as amicus curiae," said Dr. Kurwan.

"That is a hackneyed defense strategy that has earned many a professional guilty verdicts. Since she had not told the officer so, the judge will dismiss it as afterthought. She should have shown the officer her beeper, the name and location of the patient and the nature of the illness," Stephen said.

"Why not go to court and tell a flat-out, bold-faced lie that the traffic light was not working at the time? Traffic lights also need and, indeed often, take a break," said Dr. Godswill.

"The judge will turn to the officer and ask, 'Did any other motorist report such a problem to your department?' The officer will confidently say no one else did. Once you establish your disrepute as a perjurer, the prosecution will just roll over you to a conviction. I have an infallible, ironclad defense. I have been to one of those courts before. I think you have all raised sustainable points of law. I think you are all in the wrong profession. You should have gone to law school. This is what you should do, Charlene, and it's straight from the book *Moving Violations for Dummies*. Cancel your appointment for tomorrow. Go to court and gather materials for your defense. When your next appointment draws near postpone it again and again until you reach the limit. By the time you go to court, the officer will have retired and gone to Florida. Schedule your court appointment for the height of winter. No officer will fly from Florida to New York to testify on a case involving an innocuous turn by a lovely young woman.

"Arm yourself with a diagram of the intersection complete with arrows and all kinds of icons. Make it a busy diagram with fanciful writing. On that day, make sure your case is the last. The elderly judge will be exhausted by the time your case is called. When you hand him the diagram, he will take a cursory look at it. He will not understand a thing in it and will make it "exhibit one" and put it away for good. You will tell the drained judge that you were driving in your neighborhood and you knew all the lights and turns well. You did not intend to turn there but you thought that the officer who was standing by the street corner was conducting traffic. Since the officer will have retired, I can assure you, you will walk out of that court absolutely scot-free. Can anyone of you poke holes in this defense strategy?" asked Stephen.

They were all silent as they turned to each other. The crowd was now thinning out. The chief executive and all his stout assistants were still humbly serving the employees, even the gluttonous ones going for their second or third rations as if they were eating in arrears. Next to Stephen's clique, the music kept playing on while the d.j. danced away. Stephen received a page on his other beeper. He knew Juliette Painter wanted to talk to him, urgently. He told his friends, "Guys, I've got to answer my page. There is something so hot none of you could even imagine it. Expect my special call tomorrow or the day after unless a chinook or some other mischievous whirlwind whips me to the Arizona desert and you guys don't see me again," he said with a jovial smile. He walked away while his friends were making light of his latest prank.

The Elopement

Juliana Latham was beside herself at the nurses' conference in Philadelphia. Her husband was constantly on her mind. During some of the sessions, she had hardly heard anything the speakers were saying. She was worrying if Stephen had dozed off at work and resumed his somniloquy and what kinds of commands he was executing for his nurses, due to his suggestibility. She had tried to call him several times at work during the few coffee breaks she was allowed. The operators had been impatient with her and she had not succeeded in reaching him. At the end of her long day she retired to her hotel room and placed a call to him. Stephen had just finished changing his clothes when the call came.

"Hi Steve, how was your day today?" Juliana asked.

"All right, I guess. After seeing you and Christopher off, I came back to take the balance of my sleep. My Friday was full and festive. We had a big party. The administration decided to show their appreciation to the staff over the success of the last state inspection. The feast was unimaginably big. Too bad you missed it. Most of your colleagues were there," Stephen informed her.

"So presumably you will not need my cooking for the weekend."

"Possibly, even beyond. I have had enough, you know to last a very long time. How is Christopher?"

"He is fine. Many of my other colleagues also brought their kids. I think they must have had a good time. He is already asleep."

"Tell him I love him," said Stephen.

"You sound rather tired. Go and sleep and take care of yourself until we come. Love you."

"Love you too and good night," said Stephen.

Almost immediately, Stephen received another page from Juliette Painter who was on call at the hospital. They had planned a rendezvous in his office. After listening to the evening news, he put his clothes back on and headed back to meet his date in their hideout, his office. The endoscopy unit with the surrounding offices was a typically quiet neighborhood, like a cemetery. The atmosphere was particularly conducive to the meeting between Juliette and Stephen. They had realized that the fire in their affair was such that it could no longer be kept under wraps. They were meeting, frankly, to discuss their joint response to Juliana.

For weeks they had been planning the trajectories and stations of their lives. Everything had been in pieces and fragments. But after meeting for about three hours, Stephen and Juliette Painter agreed on the most tangible details of where they would go from there the next day. Actually, Juliette had meticulously planned everything. She was pleasantly surprised that Stephen had not raised any objections. Stephen went home and, for almost the first time in weeks, slept naturally and adequately.

That Saturday morning, Juliana was up early in her Philadelphia hotel room. Her series of lectures was to begin at seven that morning. She placed a quick call to her still sleeping husband as she was still concerned about his state of mind. "Hi, Steve, I thought I should give you a quick call before I rush out to my program. What are your plans for today?"

"Everything is parked. I am on schedule with the plans. I will be ready for the flight at one this afternoon. We will leave home at about eleven thirty. As we said yesterday, the desert patiently awaits our arrival," Stephen said.

Juliana did not understand what her husband was saying. It did not make sense. She surmised that he was probably still dreaming. She would call him during her lunch break at twelve. While taking Christopher to the day care for the children of the conference attendees, it was intriguing that Stephen's dreams seemed to focus on deserts. There was no logical reason for the obsession. For as long as she had known him, he had not been to or even discussed his interest in deserts or physical geography.

During her midday lunch break, she darted to her room and placed another call to him. There was no answer. Not even the answering machine responded. For the fifteen minutes she was in the room, she redialed the number repeatedly as if the lack of response was due to her having called a wrong number. She let the phone ring continuously while she munched on her muffin and washed it down with untouchably-cold diet soda. At the end of the quarter-hour, she gave up. "That free bird," she cursed, "wait until I return to cage you again." She returned to her program.

Three hours later, she returned once again to her room and placed yet another call to Stephen. Again, there was no response. She went back to her program for the balance of the day. She hardly heard anything the speakers were saying for her mind was far away in Brooklyn, New York. When she left him, the previous day, Stephen's mind appeared to have been intact except when he had gone into the bedroom and fetched Christopher's 'Power Rangers' slippers. It was possible, she feared, that the Somnazolam effects had recrudesced perhaps in a new and grotesque presentation. She was happy when the moderator announced the end of the day's activities and the fact that the next day would be truncated for some reason.

Again she scuttled to her room, her mind far out-pacing her and her heart pounding. She placed one last desperate call to her home in Brooklyn. No one picked it up. She called Dr. Emmet Godswill who lived on the fourteenth floor. Dr. Godswill had no information on Stephen's whereabouts. Juliana was even more unsettled when Dr. Godswill told her Stephen's joke the previous day that a wind might whip him away to the Arizona desert. She would have to be pushed to the wall before airing dirty linen in public. So she refrained from discussing her concerns with Dr. Godswill. Instead she called the hospital operator to beep him for her.

The situation, for Juliana, became even more warped when the operator told her that Dr. Latham had turned in his beeper the previous day. In InnerFaith Hospital, that usually meant resignation. Juliana's worst fear had come true. There was no reason, she could recall, that would make her husband resign and turn in his beeper unless the influence of Somnazolam had suddenly taken an overwhelming turn.

If Stephen had resigned his appointment with the hospital, where did he go? Juliana began to ponder the imponderables. Suicide, abscondence from home, lying at home in coma and worse, were some of the ugly scenarios that made the sudden flight though Juliana's mind. The operator had no further information about Dr. Latham. It was like calling a phone number and hearing, "The number you have called is no longer in service. No other information is available." It is a sobering and disarming message when you must absolutely reach the party that is supposed to be at the other end.

Juliana made the impromptu and proper decision to forego the remainder of her course and return immediately to Brooklyn. She rushed to the conference day care and signed out Christopher. They checked out of the hotel so hurriedly that the concierge smelled a rat. But he did not ask questions. It was not his business and irate guests checking out was all too familiar to him. All he managed to say was, "I hope you enjoyed your stay. Please come back."

The return journey by train no New York was on time from departure to arrival. In contradistinction to her previous travels, she did not allow herself even a minute of sleep. Neither was she able to read any of the materials she had in her bag. She was still pondering her husband's fate. Nothing that she could think of was reassuring. For once, she came to the summation that the Somnazolam intervention, especially continuing it in the face of early signs of trouble, had been a huge mistake.

When the train pulled up at Penn Station in New York, she made another frantic call to her home, hoping to detect evidence of life out there. The phone rang until the recorded message said, "The party you have called is not responding."

"I don't need you to tell me that," she returned as she slammed the receiver to join the local train to Brooklyn.

She hailed a cab at the Franklin Avenue station in Brooklyn. Under normal circumstances she and Christopher would have walked home defying the men's hisses, cat calls and the diminishing threat of assault and robbery. But Juliana couldn't wait to get home. She was now clinically agitated, though she would not let Christopher or passersby know it. How could Stephen resign when he had such a lucrative practice with everything going for them? If something horrible had not happened to him, what were his plans? Why would he not give her any inkling about such a momentous decision? She continued to ask herself these questions until she found herself smack in front of her apartment door.

She knocked on the door but elicited no response from inside. As she inserted the key into the hole with trepidation, her heart was now racing palpably and rapidly. The first, and perhaps only thing she saw when the door opened made her heart skip a beat. It was a cynosure no one could fail to see upon entry into the apartment. Several feet away from the door was a white envelope lying on the carpet. On top of the envelope, was their long serrated kitchen knife stained from the handle to the blade with what appeared to be caked blood.

"Oh my God! Jesus of Nazareth! Steve, why would you do this to yourself?" Juliana screamed in this time of extreme emotional distress. She believed that her husband had committed suicide.

She skirted the gruesome package to survey the rest of the apartment as her heart pounded away. She did not want to read the suicide note before finding his body. If that was true, his decomposing body must be in there. It did not take a criminologist to note the absence of a stench, or signs of a violent struggle. Juliana with Christopher, who did not know what was going on, searched the rooms, compartments and niches one by one but there was no life in there. Her husband, dead or alive, was nowhere to be found either.

Then she discovered that one, two and three of his boxes were missing. Some but not all of his clothes as well as other personal effects had also vanished. Notably, his credit and bank cards were missing as was his driver's license. Her thought processes were now changing. "This must be an abduction," she thought. "Why Stephen?" she asked as she continued to reconnoiter the apartment. Brooklyn was no paradise. It had its fair share of crime. On the other hand, it was no opulent and ostentatious resort and abductions were as alien as ice hockey.

She regained her composure and approached the package to find out what the faceless kidnappers' ransom was. She picked up the knife and examined carefully. The red stain did not smell or feel like blood. Juliana had extensive first hand knowledge of blood stains in the hospital. She dropped the knife down, opened the envelope and brought out its contents. They consisted of one handwritten note on a legal-size paper and three smaller packages. They were labeled, "DIVORCE PAPERS," "CUSTODY" and "ASSETS" respectively. The handwriting was not Stephen's. Attached to the handwritten note wa a photograph of Stephen and their neighbor Juliette Painter conjoined mouth to mouth.

Juliana dropped the envelope on the sofa and sat down to read the handwritten note. It read:

FROM: STEPHEN LATHAM, MD
TO: JULIANA LATHAM

Dear Juliana,

This is a clear message for you. I don't intend to mince words or dissemble. It has taken me a very long time and considerable introspection to reach the decision, formulate and execute my plans. I have left, never to return.

For years, you and I have been trying to procreate. After spending considerable resources, time, and energy, it is obvious that we are never going to have a biologic offspring of ours. You know how strongly I feel obligated to continue my pedigree. I have known for sometime that you had not come completely clean with me on this subject. No husband should have to gather information about his wife's past medical history through the circuitous route I was forced to take. Your permanent inability to conceive was bad enough but it was your lack of candor that hurt the most. Suffice it to say, however, that neither of these facts played the decisive role in my decision to walk.

Far more important was your complete disregard for or, perhaps, active contravention of my sumptuary advice. For years I tried to make you quit smoking, to no avail. Your chain-smoking left a thick cloud of suffocating chemicals in our living quarters, which made it impossible for me to breathe. Increasingly, I used to come into our home and hold my breath until I would collapse in bed without knowing what hit me. I am not ready to hold my breath indefinitely. The man who lives with permanent apnea is, by definition, dead.

The periods of apnea were beginning to take their toll on my physical and mental status as well as my job performance. Colleagues and co-workers who used to commend me for being so spry and energetic now commiserated with me for being dry and lethargic.

Probably the last straw was when I declared my candidacy for the presidency of the Brooklyn Gastroenterologists' Association. On the day of the election, the stench of cigarette smoke was so pungent that I must have held my breath for at least five minutes before slumping in bed. My failure to attend the meeting that evening or call to explain my absence has left a permanent gorge on my reputation among my peers.

I have decided to leave so as to live. Now you may enjoy your smoking without worrying about my choking.

I am walking into the warm and everlasting bosom of somebody you know extremely well, Juliette Painter, whose handwriting you are reading now. We are off to the Arizona desert where the future and opportunities before us are as boundless as the expanse of unexplored, treasure-rich land. We already have a great expectation that should come to fruition in about nine months.

This decision is not conditional but final. Please don't try to track us down as we will be evasive, elusive and incommunicado. We've got three appendices and three self-addressed, stamped envelopes enclosed within this package. Please find in one, the divorce papers. Kindly sign them in duplicate and return my copy in the envelop. Find in the second package how I have split our assets. You keep our Long Island home and the three hundred thousand dollars, nearly all our cash savings. Finally, find in the third appendix, transfer of Christopher's custody to you.

Please note that Juliette and I have moved on. Nothing is contingent upon your approval and/or consent. As a result, it would be in your interest to sign these forms and return our copies to the post office box indicated on the envelope. I have made these concessions so that you might take proper care of Christopher, whom I love very well.

Good luck and bye forever.

The note was signed by both Stephen and his new sweetheart, Juliette Painter. What hurt Juliana most were her neighbor's signature and photograph. Although they had lived adjacent to each other for years, they had not interacted much. Juliana had never seen a woman with such a desire to spar and win. She wondered why her husband (or ex-husband) did not pay her his last respect by not allowing that leech Juliette Painter to sign the note.

Her mind swung to Somnazolam, the substance that very early on had revealed its diabolical potential to ruin the future of a rising star like Stephen. She felt sorry for him, for not having considered stopping the intervention when he initially showed evidence of suggestibility. She felt like crying for her beloved husband but even crocodile tears refused to flow.

She remembered the dreams when Stephen was talking about the desert and being ready to go. It did not make sense then. Not that it totally made sense now but she blamed herself for not considering her neighbor's shared initial when Stephen was talking to "J" in the dream. Her neighbor Juliette was the target of her bitterness and her determination to fight back.

She picked up the photograph. Holding it aloft, she vowed in two limericks:

She plotted and eloped with Steve, making him my ex
In spite of the grim message of the dream lusoria
Because the scheme was not suspected with any index.
But this leech will pay dearly for my dysphoria
With chronic fantod, fights and fatigue from my hex

In the final analysis, Juliana must surely flip the con
By buzzing his ears with an exotic and exhorting sound
Whose true meaning and origin are not in the lexicon
Until he listens, heeds and promptly turns back to town,
The voice of my fawning, cunning and beckoning leprechaun

Juliana paced up and down while Christopher stared in confoundment. She went to the medicine cabinet. All the packages of Somnazolam were still there arranged in one box as she had left them. She snatched the box very violently as if she was contending with someone else. She was babbling and still confused not knowing where to go from there. She walked to the garbage container and capsized the Somnazolam vials in there.